JOURNEY OF STRANGERS
Elizabeth Zelvin

OUTSIDER BOOKS
New York

OUTSIDER BOOKS
Copyright © 2015 Elizabeth Zelvin
All rights reserved.
ISBN-13: 978-0692591499
ISBN-10: 0692591494

For Brian, always

By Elizabeth Zelvin

Historical
Journey of Strangers
Voyage of Strangers
"The Green Cross"
Kingdom of Strangers (forthcoming)

Mystery
Death Will Get You Sober (Dead Sober)
Death Will Help You Leave Him (Dead Wrong)
Death Will Extend Your Vacation (Dead in the Hamptons)
Death Will Save Your Life (Dead Guru)
Death Will Pay Your Debts (Dead Broke)
"Death Will Clean Your Closet"
"Death Will Tie Your Kangaroo Down"
"Death Will Trim Your Tree"
Death Will Tank Your Fish & Other Stories
Death Will Fire Your Therapist & Other Stories
"The Man in the Dick Tracy Hat"

Urban Fantasy/Mystery
Shifting Is for the Goyim (e-novella)
"A Shifting Plan"

Acknowledgments

Heartfelt thanks to Rabbi Ilene Schneider for her invariably prompt and useful response to my many questions about Judaism and Hebrew. Thanks, too, to Professor Avigdor Levy of Brandeis University, who took the time to answer my emails, suggested helpful source materials, and personally looked up the names of the numerous Sephardic congregations in 1490s Istanbul, which I needed to rule out before I could make one up; and to my dear friend Nadia Merdassi, whom I relied on for such fine points as how to say "Grandpa" in Tunisian Arabic. Finally, love and gratitude to my husband Brian, whose voracious reading and tenacious recall of history saved me from some glaring errors and omissions. He supports my writing in many ways, from paying the rent to tiptoeing quietly away when I'm in the grip of the muse. He has my permission to say, "I told you so," on the subject of my belated discovery of the joys of research. I take full responsibility for all errors of fact or plausibility, either inadvertent or because they suited my story.

Cast of Characters

known to history
Joanna, a Jewish girl
Simon, her brother
Shmuel and Benjamin (Benji), her half-brothers
Riva, her stepmother
Ezra, her father
Diego, a Jewish sailor, formerly with Columbus* on the second voyage to the Indies
Rachel, his sister, also returning from the Indies
Hutia (later Ümīt), a Taino survivor of the Spanish conquest
Fernando, a sailor
Doña Elena Mendoza y Davila, Diego's and Rachel's mother
Captain (later Governor) Alvaro de Caminha*, *donatario* of São Tomé
Doña Marina Mendes y Torres, a Spanish *converso*, Diego's and Rachel's aunt
Ernesto, Doña Marina's major domo
Javier, a soldier, formerly Doña Marina's footman
Belmiro, a *degradado*, formerly a Lisbon pimp
Imaculada, a *degradada*, formerly a Lisbon prostitute
Felicidade, a *degradada*, Imaculada's crony
Mateus, a *degradado*, Belmiro's crony
Hernan and Esteban, Doña Marina's men at arms
Natan, a Jewish boy abducted with Joanna
Señor Ortega, Doña Marina's man of business
Duarte, a Portuguese soldier
Captain Velez, captain of the *Santa Cecilia*
Celeste and Isbel, two young passengers on *Cecilia*
Doña Julieta, their chaperone
Amir, a Moorish corsair in service to the Ottoman navy, formerly a slave in Seville

Frei Jerónimo, a priest bound for São Tomé
Signore Andrea Boccanegra, a Genoese banker
Beppo, his apprentice

Pero Alvares de Caminha*, Captain Caminha's cousin
Giuseppe Adorno, a Genoese banker
Signora Boccanegra, Signore Boccanegra's wife
Niccolo Pesaro, a Venetian Jew, a trader and sutler to armies
Three hungry unpaid soldiers, bent on robbery or worse
Yenenga, a Mossi *feiticeira*, a slave in São Tomé
Aldo Bianchini, a Jew of Ancona
Signora Bianchini, his wife
Their children
Rabbi Gershon, a rabbi of Ancona
Moshe Nahman, a Jew bereft of his children
A Jewish trader in textiles from Salonica, staying at a caravanserai in Istanbul
A Jewish boy of Istanbul who knows the way to the Seville congregation
Elvira and Susanna, Diego's and Rachel's sisters
Akiva Davila, Elvira's husband, a rabbi
Efraín Mendoza, Diego's and Rachel's father
Malka, the Mendozas' neighbor, a woman who has lost her children
Hasan, a son of Prince Cem* and the hostage of Sultan Bayezid II*
Kira Chana, a Jewish purveyor to the Sultan's harem
Solomon, her son
The Kizlar Agha, chief eunuch to the harem
Bülbül Hatun*, Nigar Hatun*, and Ayşe Hatun*, mothers of the Sultan's grown sons
Adile, Gülizar, Nesrin, Seyhan, Melike, Ulviye, and Hanöm, junior ladies of the harem
Gülbahar Hatun* and Ferahşad Hatun*, senior ladies of the harem
Mustafa, a swordmaker
Dīrenç and Doruk, Balkan eunuchs to the harem
Saláh, a Tunisian sailor, Amir's cousin
Babune, N'goran, Fafale, Kwaku, Mawuwo, and Nunke, men of the Baule and Ewe peoples, escaped slaves
Brou, a woman of the Baule people, an escaped slave
Musa, a Turkish oarsman
Kemal, a Turkish sailor
Five Tunisian muggers
Amir's Tunisian grandfather

Miguel, a Portuguese Jewish fisherman and a former galley slave
Mishambo, Nkonde, and Shanda, men of the Mbunda people, shipwrecked escaped slaves
Ekuwa, Aminata, Lumusi, and Kamina, women of the Ewe and Wolof peoples, escaped slaves
Maria (formerly Mira) and Cristiano, New Christians of São Tomé
Miriam, his wife, Akiva's mother
Nahum, a printer, Susanna's betrothed and later husband
Avram, Malka's husband, the Mendozas' neighbor
Akiva's brothers, of the Seville *minyan*
Two printers, Nahum's friends, of the Seville *minyan*

PART ONE

The Isle of Crocodiles

Chapter One: Joanna

In the commotion on the Lisbon docks, Joanna stood like a statue. Simon's hand, sticky from the handful of dates that had made their hasty breakfast, clung to hers. She felt no fear, although all around her, women were screaming and children bawling as the king's soldiers wrenched them apart. Her anger filled her to bursting.

A mother, on her knees, hugged a soldier's legs, pleading, "Take me instead! I will be your slave, I will do anything!" She seized his sash and clung to it.

"Take your hands off me, woman," the soldier said. "It is the king's will."

The sash ripped, and the woman fell to the ground, where she lay pounding her fists against the sodden boards of the dock, moaning, "No! No! No!"

A child of four or five kicked at a soldier's booted shin, his chubby face mottled with rage.

"I won't go with you! I won't!"

The soldier backhanded him across the face. The blow sent the child sprawling. The soldier picked him up by the scruff of the neck and tossed him at a passing priest.

"Here's another for you." He dusted an invisible speck from his collar. "The king wants them saved for Christ. Were I a less pious man, I would wonder why he bothers."

A young woman who sold oranges in the market, her eyes streaming with tears, clutched a girl who could not have been more than two to her breast. As Joanna watched, she leaped into the sea with a wail of despair.

A line of soldiers shoulder to shoulder extended their pikes to form a moving barrier as they advanced, pushing back a mob of shrieking parents. A gray-bearded rabbi pushed aside the pike at his chest, intoning curses in Hebrew until he was seized, shackled, and marched away.

They were picking the little ones, who soon would not remember that they had ever been Jewish. Surely at twelve she was safe, too big to interest them. But Simon was only eight. He was tall for his age, a beanpole of a boy and growing fast. Please, Ha'shem, she prayed, let them overlook Simon.

Her father, his second wife Riva, and her two small half-brothers stood not far away, a pretty little family group with their arms around each other. As she watched, her breast beginning to swell with the familiar resentment, a soldier pressed his pike against her father's chest, pushing him and Riva back.

"Here! We'll take these two. Come along, no dallying! We'll make good little Christians of you in no time."

"No! No!" Riva shrieked.

Shmuel and Benjamin began to cry.

"Not my babies! No! Ezra, do something!"

That was so like Riva. She had been demanding that others do something, while she enjoyed the drama of her own emotions, since the day Father had brought her home, two years after Mother died.

Father made a feeble attempt to pluck at Riva's sleeve as she flew at the soldier, pounding on his chest in its impervious corselet. The soldier let go his grip on Benjamin to box her ear with a careless fist. She fell to the ground, sobbing, as another soldier scooped Benji up, grabbed Shmuel in an iron grip, and hustled both boys away to where the black-clad priests droned over their baptismal basins.

Father, ineffectual as always, was too shocked to think of helping Riva up. Exasperated, Joanna strode over to her stepmother and took her by the arm. Riva looked up at her, cheeks smudged with tears, her black hair, usually so smug and tidy, hanging in lank strings around her face.

"You! Joanna! Do something! Someone must look after them. Here! Soldier! Take these two."

She shoved Joanna toward the nearest soldier herding several boys and girls away from their frantic parents. Simon, still clinging to her, was borne along in her wake as the soldier pushed her into the midst of the pack of miserable children. They were forced toward the frowning priests, formidable in their black robes as they seized each child by the arm, gabbled hasty words in what must be Latin, and roughly pushed their heads into the water.

When Joanna's turn came, she held herself rigid, glaring at the priest who gripped her arm. She would not let them think that she consented to this mockery. A few drops of water could not destroy the might of Adonai. She wished the Lord had chosen to show himself in Lisbon this day. An earthquake or a burning bush would have been welcome and not beyond His powers. She shut her ears to the priests' mumbled prayers, the frantic pleas of parents, and the howls of terrified and bewildered children.

"Sh'ma Yisroel, Adonai Eloheinu . . . " Back in Granada, when they had still been permitted to worship in the synagogue on Shabbat, she had loved the way the cantor and the congregation sang the prayers. If she had been a boy, she could have studied Torah. She would have liked that. Even Father had admitted that she was quicker at study than Simon or their older cousins.

"The Lord is my shepherd . . . " She had known King David's psalm by heart since she was three. "Though I walk through the valley of the shadow of death, I will fear no evil, for Thou art with me . . . "

They could call her a Christian and bind her in slavery, but her soul was her own. She refused to let them break her. She would fear no evil, and she would never forget.

Chapter Two: Diego

We came ashore at Cadiz, wretched, hungry, and eager to see the last of our shipmates, whose casual cruelty to the Taino captives had made the voyage from Hispaniola a harrowing one. Two hundred of the five hundred who had been forced aboard the ships in Isabela succumbed to disease, starvation, and sheer misery during the crossing. The Spaniards tossed them overboard without ceremony like so much refuse. My sister Rachel spent much of the voyage at the lee rail, vomiting as if she could expel the horror of what was happening. The sailors believed her prone to seasickness. They had not seen the ship's boy Rafael clambering up the ratlines, brown and grinning, on *Mariagalante* two years earlier. Our friend Hutia, safe only because all believed him our slave, never left her side. Even more helpless than we to avert his people's fate, he looked as if he would never smile again.

My friend Fernando, the only man aboard of whom we had a good opinion, sympathized with our distress without truly sharing it. Eager to lift our spirits, he taught both Rachel and Hutia to play at cards, which took some skill. Since merely throwing a pair of dice did not, he tutored them in cheating as well.

"Do not wrinkle your nose at me, Diego," Rachel said. "We will be obliged to live by our wits until we can rejoin Papa and Mama in Italy, and we must be prepared to use any tool that comes to hand."

The sailors would not wager with a woman or a slave, so it fell to me to game with them. I had resolved to take no booty from the Indies. But

Rachel, persuasive as ever, argued that impoverishing myself was no virtue.

"Any wealth you sacrifice serves only to enrich our shipmates," she pointed out. "Do you think they will spend it worthily? In alms to the poor, perhaps?"

Since the men late of Admiral Columbus's company talked of nothing but drinking Cadiz dry as soon as we landed and swiving the ladies of the dockside brothels till they could neither stand nor catch their breath, I could not make much of a defense.

"Where did you learn to argue so, my sister? I swear you would make a lawyer!"

"It comes of listening while you and Papa studied Talmud," Rachel said. "For do not the learned rabbis disagree on every point? It is all simply a matter of interpretation."

"Give over, brother," Hutia said in Taino. "You cannot win when Rachel stands her ground. What is a lawyer?"

With grim determination, I set about relieving the Spanish sailors and soldiers of the gold that had cost so many Taino lives. As a result, we disembarked considerably richer than we had been when our caravel left the Indies.

"We need horses," Rachel said. "Or mules. Hutia, do you think you could sit a horse? And had I better be a lady or a boy? Doña Marina will surely have news of Papa and Mama and the girls by now. We must travel to Barcelona to see her as soon as possible. And we do not want any trouble on the way."

"What is a mule?" Hutia asked. "If it is less dangerous than a horse, I am willing to try it."

"Less terrifying, but more stubborn," I said.

"I wish I had my own mule, Rosa, back," Rachel said. "She had the sweetest temper."

"Only when you went the way she wished," I said. "We must find lodging for the night. Tomorrow we will purchase mounts. I shall ride a horse and carry my sword in full view. You two will be my servants. Rachel, you had better don your boy's garb. We are still a long way from Firenze, and the lands we must cross may not be at peace."

I knew Cadiz well, thanks to the months I had spent two years before, in 1493, assisting in the preparation of Admiral Columbus's fleet for the second voyage of discovery. Having found modest lodgings well away from the docks and dined gratefully on fresh bread and meat that harbored no living creatures, I made my way back toward the harbor, taverns frequented by sailors being the most likely source of news. I left Rachel and Hutia behind, despite my sister's indignant protests. I could best gather information by listening unobtrusively.

"I do not wish to attract attention," I said. "Our recent shipmates would be amazed to see a youth in breeches who so resembles the lady with whom they shared the crossing of the Ocean Sea. Hutia, tell her she must stay within. She will not listen to me."

"I always listen to you, Diego," Rachel said, "even when I do not do as you say."

"Rachel, enough," Hutia said. It was comical to see how quickly she turned demure, eyes lowered like the biddable girl she had never been. "We will have a pleasant evening together."

Her face came alight with mischief.

"So we shall. My brother has been too close a chaperone in our cramped quarters on the ship."

"I thought Hutia would come with me," I said.

"I will stay with Rachel," Hutia said.

"We are no longer on shipboard, Diego," Rachel said. "Did you come to think that Hutia was truly your slave?"

I checked the protest on my lips, since it would only incite her to continue teasing me. If they fell to kissing the minute my back was turned, I could not help it. I trusted Hutia not to let matters go any further.

"Give the landlord some coin and bespeak a tub of hot water," I said. "You'll feel the better for a bath."

I was in sore need of one myself, after weeks at sea, but it must wait. As I had expected, the biggest news of the hour in the taverns was the return of Admiral Columbus's caravels with their cargo of exotic slaves and tales of the earthly paradise we had conquered. The bustling port, however, drew ships from every Christian city on the coast and gossip from all around the Mediterranean. By the time I had downed more tankards of ale than I cared to, I had heard that the French had invaded Italy, that the Turk cast covetous eyes on Europe, and that the Italian city-states formed and broke alliances so often that it was difficult to know which side they were on at any given moment.

None of this news had reached Hispaniola, the few ships that had arrived being more interested in the Spaniards' future in the new world than the politics and conflicts of the old. Spain itself was currently at peace. But such was the tangle of alliances among Europe's princes that war could strike anywhere at any time. Italy was in turmoil, and Papa, Mama, and the girls, whom we had imagined safe and happy in Firenze, might be anywhere. All of Jewish history taught that no matter where or when trouble struck, Christian folk found comfort in blaming the Jews. Our adventure in the Indies was over, but new dangers lay before us.

The First Letter

Firenze, December 1492
Dearest Rachel,

We have finally reached Firenze, after a journey made longer by the difficulties of finding fodder for the beasts of so large a caravan and of crossing the mountains at the onset of winter. However, we considered ourselves lucky to be part of such a large and well guarded company. You may have heard that Lorenzo de Medici, who had long made Firenze safe for the Jews, died earlier this year. But the Jewish families in the city have made us welcome, and we must hope that Lorenzo's son Piero will prove as able a protector of our people. We are comfortably installed in a pleasant little house. The city is peaceful for the moment, although a self-styled prophet named Savonarola, whose followers are called the Wailers, causes much excitement by preaching that trouble is coming from the north. So far, he directs his zeal toward reforming the Church rather than persecuting the Jews. It is a great relief to be able to go to synagogue and observe Shabbat openly. We all shed tears of joy when we fastened our *mezuzah* to the door. Papa, Elvira, and Susanna are well. We pray constantly for your happiness and safety and for our dear Diego's as well. May Adonai watch over you! Remember the words of King David: "He that keepeth Israel neither slumbers nor sleeps." It is too soon to hope for word of Admiral Columbus's great venture. But we must never doubt that Diego will return. When he does, he will contrive a way to restore you to us. We miss you so much, darling Rachel!

All my love, Mama

Chapter Three: Joanna

The soldiers chivvied a sea of weeping children, too many for Joanna to count, toward the farthest dock. They seemed barely human in half-armor that clanked and glinted, their faces grim under their helms. Their long pikes formed a cage, constantly pressing against the children at the edges of the crowd into a space so cramped that Joanna lost sight of Shmuel and Benji, although she still held Simon tightly by the hand. The lamentations of the bereft parents faded in the distance until Joanna could hear only the children's sobbing, the slap of ropes against masts, and water lapping against the wooden dock. Some of the older children clutched the smaller ones in their arms.

"Joanna." Simon tugged at her hand. "I can't breathe."

Joanna crouched and hugged him fiercely. Simon never whined. He was such a gentle and obedient little boy. How would she manage to keep him safe? At least she and Simon, unlike most of the children, were not crying out for their mother. Since Mother died, Joanna had been Simon's comfort and protection. If only they could stay together, they would be all right. Where would they be taken? How would they live? Surely some grownups must be charged with looking after them. Some of the two-year-olds were still in diapers, and many had soiled themselves. The close air stank of excrement.

"Hush, sweetheart," she said.

"I'm scared."

"I know, my darling. It will be all right." Her voice trembled.

"Where are they taking us? Will we ever see Father and Riva again?"

"I don't know, my love." She drew back, still clutching his hands, so she could look into his eyes. "Simon, we must not let them part us. You must hold on tight to me, no matter what. Do you understand?"

"Yes, Joanna. I'm not so very scared when you hold my hand."

A shot rang out close by. Joanna jumped. Some of the children screamed. A gentleman in a brocaded cloak, the bejeweled hilt of the sword at his side glinting, stood on a crate that elevated him above the crowd of frightened children and their guards. Ranks of soldiers were arrayed to either side of him. Their captain held a smoking arquebus pointed at the sky.

"Quiet, all of you!" the captain barked.

Soldiers all around the perimeter of the crowd repeated his words, banging their pikes on the dock for emphasis or cuffing those nearest to them about the head.

"Hear me well!" the finely dressed gentleman cried. "I'll say this only once. I am Captain Alvaro de Caminha, by the grace of God and King João your newly appointed governor and master. You will be quiet and obey orders, whether given by me or any of my soldiers or the seamen on these ships. If you do not, you will be flogged, hanged, or shot without hesitation."

A shocked gasp rose from Joanna's throat in unison with those all about her. They would flog and hang children?

Simon tugged at her hand, pulling her down so he could whisper in her ear.

"Are we going on the ships? Who are those people at the far end of the dock? Will they come with us?"

"Shh, you must not speak," she said.

Looking over a mass of children's heads, she noticed for the first time a new group of men and women, meanly dressed and surrounded by soldiers armed with pikes and swords.

"Strike their chains," Captain de Caminha commanded.

The newcomers had indeed been chained. They stamped their feet and rubbed at their wrists and necks as the soldiers went among them. The chains clanked as the soldiers kicked them into piles at the side of the dock.

"Silence!" Caminha roared. "You will not be bound during the voyage, but you will work—and work hard, not like the dishonest, lazy scum you have been until now. Never forget, for I will not, that you are *degradados*. You can remain degraded and despised for the rest of your lives, or you can leave your shameful past as criminals behind. The choice is yours. This is your chance for a fresh start, and I strongly advise you to take it. The most industrious among you will prosper. The lazy and rebellious will die. Mark this well. You will be settlers of a wild land, but one that can be tamed. Riches—in sugar and slaves—are to be had, if you but labor and conform to my laws, for I have the king's authority to rule absolutely the land to which we sail."

Degradados! They would be thrown together with murderers and thieves! So much contempt did the King of Portugal have for the Jews. And the women must be prostitutes. Joanna had only a vague idea what prostitutes did, but she believed it had something to do with nightly thumpings of the bed and laughter—the only occasions on which she ever heard her father laugh—from their chamber, from which Riva would emerge the next morning, preening like a pigeon.

Caminha was still speaking.

"The King wishes to populate this new land with families. Men and women who are already coupled, whether in wedlock or not, tell the soldiers or the priests who will pass among you. Those who are sinners will confess and be joined in marriage. The king desires Christian families, and I will see to it that all do his will. If you do not choose a mate, one will be chosen for you. We will have no men burning or women idle on my ships. Nor need you wait to start those families until we reach our destination."

At this, some of the adults sniggered. With growls and menacing looks, the soldiers quieted them.

"Yes, you will breed," Caminha said, "and populate His Majesty's colony with stout workers. You will also be given these children to keep as your own. They are Christians, newly baptized and ready to serve Our Savior, the king, and me. Our priests will instruct them. You will feed and house them and teach them industry and obedience. Their duty is to you, and in return, I hold each couple responsible for one or more of them. Once your marriage is confirmed and children assigned to you, I advise you to catch what rest you can, for we board the ships at dawn. Any who attempt to escape, man, woman, or child, will be made an example. On pain of death, you sail for your new home on tomorrow morning's tide."

Chapter Four: Diego

𝕿𝖍𝖊 𝖏𝖔𝖚𝖗𝖓𝖊𝖞 𝖙𝖔 𝕭𝖆𝖗𝖈𝖊𝖑𝖔𝖓𝖆 was tedious rather than perilous. Doña Marina welcomed us. We did not tax her tolerance by presenting Rachel in breeches or Hutia as her suitor. He had grown adept at looking humble while not permitting anyone to remove him from Rachel's side.

As we had hoped, our aunt had finally received letters from our parents, though the news they contained was stale.

"It is only to be expected," Doña Marina said. "Even the most competent courier may be delayed by mishap, foul weather, or the misfortune of meeting bandits or roving soldiers."

"Soldiers?" Rachel's tone was apprehensive.

I saw Hutia's lips tighten.

"We saw soldiers behaving very badly in Hispaniola," I said, "despoiling native villages and killing even women and children."

"I am not speaking of a few ill-disciplined men attacking savages," Aunt Marina said.

On the pretext of putting my arm around Rachel, I pinched her arm to warn her against voicing her indignation at this description of the Taino. Beneath her skirts, she kicked my ankle hard.

"War spreads through Europe," Aunt Marina said, "as none know better than my Italian bankers. Their news is more reliable than most."

"We have heard that King Charles of France invaded Italy last year," I said.

"He marched into Firenze with ten thousand men," Doña Marina said. "Piero de Medici welcomed him for fear that the city would be sacked if he did not."

"It was Lorenzo de Medici whose protection Papa counted on. But he is dead."

"His son is a weakling," Doña Marina said. "They call him Piero the Unfortunate. Once the French had entered the city, he fled. The people declared Firenze a republic. Ridiculous!"

"Then what has become of Papa and Mama?" Rachel's lip trembled, though as a rule she was as brave as a lion. Having had the adventure she craved, she longed for home more deeply than she admitted.

"If they had stayed in Firenze," Doña Marina said, "I believe I would have heard by now. They could be anywhere. Wars cost more than monarchs are willing to pay, and it is said that companies of soldiers roam the countryside, hungry and unpaid except for what they can wrest from the peasants and townsmen in their path."

"Wherever they are," I said, "we must find them, no matter how dangerous the road."

"You must not go alone," she said. "You must seek a well guarded merchant caravan or a reliable vessel bound for Genoa."

Rachel emitted an unladylike snort. She had accompanied the fleet to the Indies in 1493 only because the captain of the last "reliable vessel" I had found for her had been a villain who intended to rob, assault, and sell her into slavery.

"Are there not pirates on the Middle Sea?" I asked. As a sailor who had traversed the Ocean Sea with the Admiral, I had as much courage as any. But that great unknown expanse was empty, while we might encounter a host of enemies on the Mediterranean.

"Turkish corsairs and pirates from the Maghreb seek Christian slaves for the Sultan's harem and his navy's galleys."

I could read the sparkle in Rachel's eye. I pinched her arm again to prevent her from reminding our aunt, sincere *converso* that she was, that we were not Christians.

"If your ship travels in convoy and stays close to the coast," Doña Marina said, "you may travel safely enough to Marseille and thence to Genoa. I will give you letters to my bankers there. Or you may take the land route, although it is said that desperate soldiers swarm over the land like locusts."

Bidding my aunt goodnight, we retired to our chambers, where we could talk freely.

"Let us go by sea!" Rachel burst out the moment the door closed behind the servant who had shown us in. "We need not waste our gold on passage. We can sign on as hands. Rafael longs to be under sail again."

"Don't be absurd, Rachel. If we sign on, we will have no freedom of movement. And what of Hutia? An able seaman does not need a servant."

"I can learn to be a sailor if I must," Hutia said. "Rachel, listen to Diego for a moment. Let us think calmly about what is best to do."

"How can you be so bent on adventure, Rachel?" I snapped. "I am worried sick about Papa and Mama and the girls."

"So am I!" Rachel retorted, her cheeks flushed pink with indignation. "That is why I would prefer occupation. You are not a girl. You don't understand what torture it is to do nothing but sit and wait!"

At that moment, a commotion arose at Aunt Marina's gate. We had been lolling on the great tented bed in Rachel's chamber, which faced the street, although well protected by a veritable thicket of wrought-iron grillwork, as was the fashion. Evidently, in spite of the vaunted modesty of Spanish ladies, their guardians expected them to seek adventure, if not physically prevented, by clambering out the window and down the nearest tree, or worse, letting a suitor in. Of one accord, we rose and rushed to the window. Peering out, we saw the men at arms on guard arguing with a ragged beggar who, unlike most, did not cringe and slink away but waved his arms as he expostulated with them. To our amazement, one of the men at arms suddenly embraced the beggar, lifting him off his feet while the other guard wheeled and ran into the house, shouting for Ernesto, Doña Marina's elderly major domo.

"Diego, I believe those are *our* men at arms!" Rachel cried. "Hernan! Esteban! They crossed Spain with us, Hutia, and took very good care of us. Indeed, it was not their fault when I ran away in Cordoba and the gypsies had to rescue me. As for the ragged boy, he looks familiar too. If I could but see his face—"

"I'll go and see," I said. "Hutia, you had better return to my chamber, lest the servants find you here alone with Rachel. We do not wish Aunt Marina to demand that I dismiss you from our service."

Hutia stepped back to a correct three feet from Rachel, who still pressed her body against the window as if she would squeeze through the grillwork if she could. He bowed stiffly. It was astonishing how in a few short hours in the house he had learned to imitate Ernesto's dignified manner.

"I am merely responding to my lady's summons," he said. "She wishes to know what transpires below."

I could not help chuckling.

"You are getting as bad as Rachel! I will go and find out what's afoot."

To my surprise, Doña Marina herself stood in the tiled front hall, regarding the shabby newcomer with a remarkably benign expression. All eyes turned toward me as I entered the hall.

"Sir!" The men at arms, who were indeed our old companions, sprang to attention.

"Sir!" To my surprise, the newcomer straightened up and offered me a soldierly salute. His grimy face, youthful under a tangled scruff of beard, was alight with pleasure.

"Do you not remember my former footman, Javier?" Doña Marina said. "He is home from the wars and will have news that we must hear. But first, he must be bathed and fed. See to it, Esteban, and find him clothing fit for a member of a civilized household. Hernan, you may return to duty. And Javier, if you wish to re-enter my service, you had better shave that beard before I lay eyes on you again. It is riddled with lice!"

Javier fell to his knees.

"My lady! I thank you! I wish for nothing better, and may the Blessed Virgin reward your graciousness."

"Never mind that, boy," Doña Marina said. "Your duty is to get well and strong."

Her sharp eyes had discerned his bone-deep exhaustion and the welts and scars on his body that might be wounds or rat bites.

"Aunt, may I ask my sister to join us? She will wish to hear Javier's news as well."

Two years before, Rachel had wound this particular footman around her little finger, persuading him to help her run away from this house when I had refused to take her with me to the Indies. He would be cock-a-hoop to hear she had actually succeeded in making the voyage. I had no hope whatever that she would refrain from pouring out the story.

"Do as you wish," my aunt said, her tone tart but a smile tugging at the corners of her mouth. "I am no longer mistress of my own home when you children come to stay."

As she swept out of the room, Javier scrambled to his feet.

"Sir! I am glad to see you safely home. Did you make your fortune in the Indies? Is my lady Raquel with you?"

I had better remind Rachel that even among these trusted servants, she must remain Raquel, as she had been before, first in Barcelona, then among Doña Marina's Christian friends in Seville, and also during our last months in Hispaniola, when she could no longer pass for a boy.

The Second Letter

Firenze, April 1493

Dearest Rachel,

Our first Passover in Firenze! Thanks to Ha'shem, we are all in good health and had kin at our Seder table. Our cousins, the Davilas, arrived here a month before us and have been very kind in helping us get settled. Papa, my cousin Chaim, and his eldest, young Akiva, who is studying to be a rabbi, shared the reading of the Haggadah. Papa insisted on telling the story of our liberation from slavery in Egypt in Castilian as well as Hebrew, to the delight of the little Davilas. Chaim and his wife Miriam have three children who would otherwise have been whining and complaining they were bored and hungry, as you and Diego used to do and Elvira and Susanna before you. Miriam is expecting another in the summer. She never tires of saying how this baby brings good fortune, since it will be her first not born in the shadow of the Inquisition.

In your convent in Barcelona, you could not keep Pesach. I hope you remembered the story of how God spared us and Moses led us safely out of Egypt. Know that you and Diego were in our hearts as we sat around the Seder table and will be so until we hold you in our arms again, *im yirtzeh Ha'shem*. Do the nuns allow you to see the night sky? There was a blood moon on the night of the first Seder. Papa's friends among the Moorish scholars of Granada claimed that such upheavals in the heavens are natural phenomena that can be studied and even predicted. When we opened the door for Elijah, we all went out to watch the red shadow gradually steal over the familiar moon until the night was suffused with a baleful darkness. Many others on our street had come out to see, both Jews and Christians.

Most saw the eclipse as a portent. The monk Savonarola declares it yet another sign that a conqueror is coming from the north to sweep away corruption in the Church. Ha'shem knows it is corrupt, with a Pope who keeps mistresses and elevates his children to high office. I am sure the nuns never speak of that, but only of his Aragonese birth and his friendship with King Ferdinand. But we have had enough of conquerors too! Indeed, we celebrate Passover as a yearly reminder that in every age, oppressors have tried to destroy us. Perhaps the rabbis will add a chapter to the Haggadah telling of our own Exodus, this cruel banishment from a land that we called home for a thousand years. But as Papa says, we must not let our anger become lasting bitterness. As always, we Jews survive. *Im yirtzeh Ha'shem*, with God's help, we will make this new land our home.

All my love, Mama

Chapter Five: Joanna

The gray fog shrouding the docks was beginning to lift when Joanna stumbled after Belmiro and Imaculada, her new "parents," toward the ships. They had been given dry bread and a meager measure of sour wine the night before and bidden to lie down and sleep where they stood on the rough planks, with the sea below them slapping at the thick posts and stinking of seaweed and rotten fish. Shmuel and Benji, *baruch Ha'shem*, had been given to a crony of Imaculada, a woman named Felicidade, who did not bother to chide them when they hurried to Joanna with glad cries. The boys had huddled all around her like kittens in a basket, their sobs and whimpers fading into sleep. So she had been warmer than she might have been. But the night air was damp, and her linen dress was soaked. She shivered, wishing she had her thick wool cloak. But it had been left at home, neither her parents nor any of the neighbors dreaming for what reason the King had summoned all the Jewish families to the harbor. It was a small cruelty on top of the greater cruelties that none of the children had so much as a poppet or a keepsake to remind them of their mothers.

Six sailing ships lay at anchor not far offshore, two towering carracks and four graceful caravels that danced upon the waves and tugged at their moorings as if impatient to be off. The boarding was well organized. Soldiers sorted out each group of *degradados* and children and directed them to one boat or another, herding them as if their pikes were shepherds' crooks. Sailors loaded them onto boats and ferried them out to the waiting ships. Their rough voices, shouting orders to this group or that, held no malice, but Joanna could detect no pity in their eyes.

"Hey, soldier!" Imaculada called out to one burly fellow as they reached the front of the line. "That's a stout pair of arms you've got on you. What else have you got that might be to my liking?"

The soldier laughed.

"Too bad we didn't meet a week ago," he said. "It would have been my pleasure to show you."

"And mine to keep you up all night," she said with a lascivious wink, "and leave you so sore that you would have been abed this morning, not reporting for duty."

Belmiro stepped up behind her, placing a possessive, hamlike hand on her shoulder.

"How about a coin, soldier?" he wheedled. "My lady doesn't give her smiles for free."

The soldier laughed again. He took Imaculada by the arm and pushed Belmiro toward the waiting boats.

"And how has pandering profited you, you rogue? You're lucky to be transported and not hanged. You'll have little use for coin where you're going and less luck selling your lady's favors. Have you not been told there'll be black African slaves for all of that? Are all of these brats yours?"

"These two are those they dumped on me," Imaculada said carelessly. "The smaller two are my friend's. Are we bound for Africa, then?" She tugged at Joanna's hair as the most convenient way to move the children along. Simon clung to Joanna's hand and the two little ones to the back of her dress.

"They didn't tell you?" the soldier said. "We're bound for São Tomé. It's an island off the Guinea Coast. The king's navigators discovered it years ago, but the colony's not been much use to him till now. Captain Caminha will whip it into shape. Come on, girl, you too," he added as Felicidade sauntered up to him. Her man, Mateus, followed her, a wiry little fellow whose small, red-rimmed eyes never rested, but darted to and fro as if constantly on guard against danger or seeking advantage.

As Joanna helped the children to clamber aboard, Felicidade asked the soldier, "Do you sail with us, then? If so, my friend Imaculada and I might yet offer you a ride you'll never forget." She tossed her head, then licked her finger and ran it slowly over his jawline.

Mateus appeared to be no more offended than Belmiro by this offer. The soldier glanced briefly at him as if wondering if he too would demand coin, but he did not.

"When the slaves arrive from the barracoons of Elmina on the mainland, we'll be needed to make sure they behave. There'll be a thriving trade in no time. Some will work the plantations, but the rest will be sold off to fill the king's coffers, and we won't lose by it. Why, some say they'll even pay our wages in slaves. I'll stay a year or two and make my fortune. You lot had better say your farewells to Lisbon, because they'll never let you set foot in Portugal again. But look on the bright side. In five or ten years, you may not want to. You may be rich plantation owners and fine ladies by then." As he turned away, signaling to sailors on shore to loose the ropes and the steersman to give the rowers their stroke, he added, "There are worse fates than transportation."

Joanna had listened to this whole exchange with burning resentment. At the same time, she wanted to hear all she could about the unknown land ahead of them. Africa was hot, was it not? Perhaps she would not miss her woolen cloak. She must keep her wits about her if she wanted to keep Simon, Shmuel, and Benji safe. What a fool she had been to think Riva the worst mother in the world. She could count on no help from Imaculada in making her way. At best, she prayed the woman would remain indifferent to the children with whom she had been so unwillingly saddled. If they only left her alone, she could manage. She knew she could! As for her gentle, weak father, she regretted every impatient or critical thought she had ever had of him. She had been given one of Adonai's great blessings, a father who loved her, and she had been too stupid to be grateful. He must be in agony now, with all four of his children lost. She closed her eyes.

"Please, Adonai," she prayed, "comfort him, I don't know how, but somehow. Let him remember me with love."

Her eyes flew open as she felt a jolt. The boat had reached the ship. Its side loomed above her, high as a castle wall. Above it, she could see the very top of the biggest mast with a kind of bucket, big enough to hold several men, swaying near its tip. The sailors aboard the boat threw stout ropes up and over the side. Sailors on the deck above, visible only because they were leaning over the rail, tossed more ropes down. Was that swaying, knotted web a ladder? Could she possibly climb up it? She had no choice. Could the children manage? Benji was not yet five. She'd better make a game of it.

"Come on, boys. Let's pretend the ship is the apple tree in our garden. Remember how we used to play the apple tree was a ship? And now we're sailing for real."

What about children who were too small to climb? Would they hoist them up somehow or throw them into the sea? She must teach the boys self-reliance. Every skill they could learn would better their chance of survival.

"Simon, you go first. Hold tight. That's right, put your hands above the knots so they cannot slip. Now one foot on the rope that goes across, like a step or a low branch on the apple tree. Go on. Pull with your hands, and bring up the other foot. That's my brave boy! Benji, you go next. Here, I'll lift you onto the first rung."

She helped Shmuel onto the ladder behind Benji, boosting him with her hand under his bottom. She grasped the ladder, her hands closing on it just below Shmuel's. She leaned forward so he could feel the heat of her body.

"Go on, boys," she urged, making her voice sound cheerful and confident. "I'm right behind you."

By the time they all reached the deck, the fog had lifted completely. The light, crisscrossed by shafts of shadow from sails and rigging, dazzled as it bounced off the water. It would be a beautiful day.

Joanna hardly had time to look around before Imaculada said, "Come along! And keep those brats moving. No telling what them soldiers will do if they get underfoot."

The *degradados* and the children were ushered through a low, dark doorway and down a narrow wooden ladder. Tall Belmiro cracked his head on the lintel.

"Mind the hatch," a sailor said, a well calculated second too late. Cheerful and half naked, with a ring glinting in his ear, he grinned and winked at Joanna.

Imaculada peered into the gloom.

"What is this?" she demanded. "You're putting us in the hold? Are we cattle, to be stowed away in the dark? And are those *pigs* I see?"

Joanna ducked under her arm to look. A couple of hanging lanterns cast a dim light on the area near the ladder. Straw was strewn on the planks. A water barrel stood in one corner with a battered tin cup perched atop it. At the far end of the chamber, fenced off by a lattice of planks, forty or more pigs milled about, snuffling loudly as they jostled one another for space. The farmyard smells of straw and fresh manure fought the sea scents of salt air and fish for dominance.

Imaculada stood at the foot of the ladder with arms akimbo.

"If we're to be lords and ladies on the island, we deserve better!"

The sailors above ignored her. Felicidade, descending the ladder behind Joanna, nudged Imaculada forward.

"Don't be a fool, woman," Felicidade said. "We'll

have plenty of room. Why, my new gentleman friend from last night—"

"Already?" Imaculada uttered a harsh crack of laughter. "You are a quick worker! A soldier?"

Felicidade grinned, displaying a stained and incomplete set of rotting teeth.

"I said a gentleman, did I not? One of Captain Caminha's household. He had a room over a chandler's shop."

"And a fine feather bed?" Imaculada said, hovering between envy and sarcasm.

"A straw mattress with only three other gentlemen to share it and no more than a handful of fleas. He told me much. On the smaller ships, the Lisbon folk must bed down on a plank or coil of rope on deck. We're better off down here, and we can still come and go as we please. Why, he told me they'll load ten times our number of African slaves, once they catch them, in this same space. We're neither bound nor crowded, so stop complaining!"

Sniffing, Imaculada turned away. After inspecting the entire hold, she chose a corner as far as possible from the pigs. At her command, Joanna and the children set about collecting heaps of straw and forming them into rough beds. Belmiro and Mateus went back on deck to watch Lisbon harbor recede in the distance as the ship departed. The two women busied themselves in arranging their possessions, for unlike the Jewish children, each *degradado* had been allowed to bring a small bundle on the journey. Felicidade produced a horn comb, evidently a great treasure, and she and Imaculada took turns combing out each other's hair. This process included picking out a quantity of prison lice, with many insults and much bawdy banter.

"You could tell the girl to do it," Felicidade said. "I can lend my comb, though I'll box her ears if she damages it."

"Let her be," Imaculada said. "I'll have a use for her soon enough."

Toward evening, Imaculada cornered Joanna.

They had eaten a meal of gruel and ship's biscuit with water from the barrel, and the boys had gone to investigate the pigs.

"Well!" the *degradada* said.

"Senhora," Joanna responded warily.

Imaculada snorted.

"Good enough!" she said. "At least you don't expect to call me *Mamãe*."

"No, Senhora."

"Do you bleed yet?" Imaculada asked abruptly.

"Yes, Senhora."

"How long? When did your courses start?"

"A year ago, Senhora." Joanna's bowed head and respectfully lowered eyes concealed such a blaze of rage that she would not have been surprised if Imaculada had burst into flame. But the woman noticed nothing. She could ask intrusive questions, interrogate Joanna like the Inquisition itself, but she would never know her thoughts. Never!

"Let's see what kind of tits you've got on you."

Joanna shrank away as Imaculada seized the neck of her gown and tugged it down, exposing the gentle swell of her breasts. The woman grunted with satisfaction.

"You'll do." She turned away, no longer interested for the moment.

Joanna, shaking with fury, pulled her gown back up to cover her breasts.

"Go fetch those boys and order them to bed," Imaculada said without turning. "You too. I'm going to douse the lantern. It's asking for a fire to leave it on all night, a wooden ship with all this straw and God knows what stowed elsewhere, wine and olive oil and the like, no doubt. And before you think to whine about the lodging, it's bigger than a prison cell in Lisbon, I'll tell you that. And I doubt the rats are hungrier than prison rats."

"Rats?" Joanna's throat was dry, her voice a gasp.

"Aye, every ship has rats. Are you stupid, not to know that? Hear me well, my girl. You'd better make the best of your condition, because it could be worse." She turned and smiled at Joanna, her eyes glittering with malice. "Indeed, I can guarantee it will get worse."

Chapter Six: Diego

As soon as Doña Marina had retired for the night, Rachel, Hutia, and I trooped down to the kitchen, where we found Javier sitting on the scarred oak table—a liberty my aunt's formidable cook would have allowed no other—devouring bread, cheese, and paper-thin slices of cured ham while he regaled his audience, every soul in the place except my aunt herself, with a more embellished tale of his adventures. He leaped off the table and offered Rachel and me a hasty bow.

"Don't be silly, Javier!" Rachel said. "Go on with your story."

Javier swallowed the lump of food that bulged in his gullet with an audible gulp.

"Yes, my lady. You know that the French king assembled an army of 25,000 men and built a navy as well, the better to press his claim to the throne of Naples. We did not reach France until autumn, when we learned King Charles had already crossed the Alps. By then they had with them several thousands of Swiss mercenaries, terrible men as big as giants who train for war their whole lives and will fight for whoever pays them. We set out after them. Winter comes early in the mountain passes, and I was lucky to fare better than most in that treacherous terrain, thanks to my boyhood in the Pyrenees, which of course we had already crossed."

"Get on with it, lad," Esteban said. "You are not slogging through the Alps but telling a story. Did you catch up with them? Did they give battle?"

"The battle came later," Javier said. "We almost caught up with them in Genoa, for the Genoese gave

28

them safe passage. But we did not. In mid-October the French and their Milanese allies sacked Mordano, a fortress near Bologna."

"I thought Milan was our own ally," Hernan said.

"It is now," Rachel said. "Doña Marina heard it at Court. She said the Milanese themselves are hard put to it to know which side they are on."

The servants laughed at this.

"It is no matter for jest," Javier said, with the most solemn visage I had ever seen him wear. "Do you fools not know what a sack is?"

The youngest scullery maid shook her head.

"Do not tutor me in warfare, boy," Esteban said. "When soldiers besiege a town and win, they must have booty. Everyone knows that."

"Have you ever seen a sack?" Javier challenged him. "Have you even gone to war?"

"Both Esteban and Hernan there came to my lady's service fresh off the farm," the cook said.

"I had training in arms!" Esteban said. "So did we both. If you wish to challenge me, I will gladly cross swords with you, once you've had a chance to fatten up and get your strength back."

Javier shook his head.

"A sack is not a feat of arms," he said. "It haunts me that if we had moved faster, we might have arrived in time to relieve the siege and prevent the sack. Once they had breached the walls, they fired and destroyed the fortress and put every surviving man, woman, and child to the sword."

"They killed children?" the cook asked. "What kind of monsters would do that?"

"Such monsters as your countrymen, my friend," Hutia said in Taino. "It happened in Quisqueya." He and Rachel exchanged a speaking glance.

"Tell me, Javier," I said, "what did you hear of Firenze?"

"The people there opened the gates to King Charles," he said, "and cast flowers in his path."

"Doña Marina told us," I said, "that the Medici had to flee. Did that not cause turmoil in the city? Did the

Florentines take advantage of the unrest to loot and fight among themselves?"

"Oh, no," Javier said. "The people welcomed the soldiers, and there was no unrest at all. The only disturbance was a few attacks on Jews."

The Third Letter

Firenze, July 1493

Dearest children,

At last! At long last we have news of you both, thanks to your Aunt Marina's connection with the Medici bankers. We shed tears of joy to know that Diego has returned safely from his perilous voyage on the Ocean Sea. But the news from Spain is troubling. Can they not be content with having banished us? Must they continue to hunt us down? It appears they are suspicious even of those who did as they wished and embraced the Christian faith. We fear especially for Rachel. By the time this letter arrives in Barcelona, if indeed it does, I pray that Diego and my good-sister between you will have found a way to restore our precious girl to us. We all long to see you too, Diego, but we understand you must remain with the Admiral while his star is high and his favor protects you.

Speaking of stars that rise and yet may fall, Papa bids me send a message to Doña Marina, advising her to withdraw any funds she may have with the Medici bank and place them elsewhere. More and more of the Florentines declare that Piero de Medici is a tyrant, too fond of art and luxury to attend to the true wellbeing of the city. Some even call for government by some sort of council of prominent citizens, not least among them the monk Savonarola, whose popularity grows daily. They say he is not intolerant of the Jews, is even considered "soft" on the Jews by those who rail most loudly against us. According to Papa, all this means is that he has a sincere and benevolent desire for our conversion!

Your sister Elvira is spending much time with young Akiva Davila, and we—Akiva's parents and Papa and I—are beginning to talk about the possibility of a betrothal. Your sister Susanna is wild for a wedding. She also longs for her turn to be the Mendozas' marriageable daughter! She thinks herself and Elvira both far too old to be single still. As you know, Papa and I believe that a mature young woman who has had time to think and look around, as well as develop household skills, will make a more contented wife than a girl pushed into marriage while still in the throes of puberty. I speak frankly, Rachel, my darling, for I wish you to be well prepared to deal with both the joys and the adversity that life will undoubtedly send you. I married your father for love and have never regretted it, and I vowed that all my daughters would have a say in whom they wed. Fortunately, Papa, who is the best and kindest man in the world as well as one of the wisest, is at one with me on this point. Diego, dear boy, I say nothing to you of marriage, but Papa and I hope you will not spend your whole life as a wanderer. When the time comes, there are many lovely Jewish girls in our community who, besides their maidenly virtues, have perhaps more hardihood and courage, a wider breadth of understanding, than they would have had they never been forced to leave Spain.

As for young Akiva, who as I wrote you before is studying to be a rabbi, it is a respected calling, of course, the most respected of all. But a rabbi is dependent on the goodwill and prosperity of his congregation and community. And if the community fails to prosper, or worse, is dispersed—as we were from Spain, and before that from England and France, not to mention our slavery in Egypt and the Babylonian captivity—how then will a young rabbi earn his bread and feed a family? All of this, as you can imagine, is the subject of reasoned discussion among the young couple's parents and hot debate when Papa and I are at home alone with the girls.

Papa *would* let all of you follow along when Diego studied Talmud (which as far as I can tell is all about arguing), so we must expect you to have strong opinions and be bold about expressing them—especially, as Elvira points out, when it involves your own futures.

Pray for us, my darlings, as we do for you, and may we all be together before another year is past.

All my love, Mama

Chapter Seven: Joanna

𝕿he first two weeks aboard the carrack were a period of unremitting seasickness for everyone around Joanna. For her, the time passed in a blur of squealing pigs, howling children, the stench of vomit and feces, and the moans and curses of the *degradados*, with intermittent infusions of brine. The sailors periodically upended barrels of seawater and tossed their contents down the hatch in a swooshing flood that doused the inhabitants of the hold and made a soup of straw, pig filth, and the contents of slop buckets. Joanna and a boy of eleven named Natan, the eldest Jewish child on the ship apart from Joanna, were among the few who did not get seasick. They spent wearisome hours swabbing the hold in a permanent crepuscule that robbed night and day of meaning. The sailors tossed down ship's biscuit at irregular intervals and allowed the prisoners one small barrel of brackish water at a time. There was never enough water. Joanna was thirsty all the time. She took a grim satisfaction in seeing the *degradados*, especially Imaculada, brought low, though she punctiliously wiped the woman's sweating brow and washed away the aftermath of each round of puking. Seasickness could not last forever, and this dockside whore—a word Riva would have boxed her ear for using—would have absolute power over her for the foreseeable future.

She and Natan talked little at first, for he was Lisbon born, rather than a refugee from Spain like her family. Besides, he had the attitude of Jewish men toward women that she tried hard to nip in the bud in Simon: contempt so unquestioned that boys like Natan did not perceive it as an attitude at all. Women were not fit to study Torah, unclean even to touch at a certain time of the month, creatures so inferior that in daily prayer, each man thanked Ha'shem for not making him a woman. But he was still a fellow Jew.

One day, the sailors left the hatch open. With no more than an exchange of glances, Joanna and Natan crept up the ladder onto the deck. The day was gray, the air salt and misty, but Joanna raised her face to drink it in. A perfumed garden could not have enchanted her senses any better. The two children, fearful of detection, stayed close together. Heavy swells made the ship pitch with every wave, and the sailors on deck were fully occupied in keeping it on course. As they crouched behind a giant coil of thick cable, it began to rain. They would be drenched if they made a dash for the hold. Besides, having tasted momentary freedom, Joanna had no desire to bring this adventure to a close.

A bulky canvas tarpaulin covered an unidentifiable mound of equipment a short distance away. In one bound, Joanna reached its shelter and slithered under the edge. A minute later, Natan followed her, sliding in beside her. They knelt shoulder to shoulder, panting more from excitement than the exertion of the dash across the deck. She felt his warm breath on her ear.

"What if they close the hatch cover?" he whispered.

"We wait till no one is looking, then we open it." The scorn in Joanna's voice raised it above a whisper.

Natan shushed her. The rain drummed on the tarpaulin above their heads. Their nest within the canvas folds smelt warm and tarry. The sailors' shouts to each other as they worked sounded impossibly distant.

"Do you think we'll be missed?"

"Don't you know all Jews look alike to them?" Her lip curled.

"My new father calls me Jug Ears," Natan said. "He's pulled me around by them enough. I think he'll know me again."

Joanna snorted. Natan did have big ears that stuck out from his head like the handles of a jug.

"Do you call him Father, then?"

"Of course not! He's only a *degradado*. I plan to better myself when we get to São Tomé. I won't be a child forever, and I won't be counted among the dregs for long."

"How do you plan to accomplish that, Jewish boy?"

"That's just it," he said. "I'm not a Jewish boy any more. It's as a Christian that I will seize my opportunity. I'll seek favor with Caminha and his men. In ten years I could be a *fazendeiro* with acres of sugar cane and slaves at my beck and call."

"Fool!" Joanna said. "You are a slave yourself. Have you not noticed?"

"You're the fool," he retorted. "The Africans they plan to buy and sell will be the slaves. It is only just that we should be the masters. We are white, after all."

"Not to these Portuguese," Joanna said. "I lived in Granada, where the Moors ruled justly and with respect for the Jews until King Ferdinand conquered them. There were many scholars and wise men among the Moors. King Ferdinand did not see us as black and white, but threw us all out even-handedly."

"Leave the hatch open," a deep voice said close at hand, "while the rain lasts. It costs us nothing to give them the benefit of fresh water."

Natan clapped a hand over Joanna's mouth. Neither of them had heard anyone approach above the drumming of the rain. The sailors went barefoot on deck. Besides, the ship, the wind, and the water were never silent. Joanna chided herself for not thinking sooner to collect what rain she could. A bit of tarred canvas would hold it. Now she would have to wait until the sailors moved away.

"There's deaders down there, sir," another voice said.

"It had better not be ship fever," the first voice said. "*Degradados* or the brats?"

"Nay, the jailbirds are but landlubbers. They'll get their sea legs soon enough. The little 'uns, though, some might have lacked for water. Who knows if anyone down there bothered to see to it? And others likely puked and choked on it. What shall we do with 'em, sir?"

"They're only taking up space down there," the officer said. "And the bodies will rot the faster when we reach the tropics. We don't need 'em as ballast, with all we're carrying for the new colony. Get a crew and throw them overboard. Then roust out some of those lazy pimps and pickpockets and make them give the hold a good swabbing. Make sure the men bestir themselves. Stand over them with an arquebus if you must. Even if there's no taint of ship fever, it can't hurt to be sure."

Chapter Eight: Diego

We lingered in Barcelona, hoping daily that word of our family's whereabouts would reach us. As news of the ravages of war in Italy trickled in, we became ever more concerned for their safety and fearful about our chances of being reunited with them. The few letters we had received had been two years on the road. Even the most reliable courier to whom they entrusted a message might be diverted, robbed, or dead long before crossing the Pyrenees or reaching a Spanish port. For once, Rachel did not declare I worried too much.

To make the most of our time, as the days lengthened into summer, we took to daily weapons practice at a farm outside the city that Doña Marina owned. Rachel's travels had begun there back in 1493. A fallow field that wind and birds had sown with coarse, springy grasses and wildflowers offered us space and privacy to improve our skill at arms and play the occasional impromptu game of *batey*. Rachel, ever the optimist, had secreted a *batu* in her baggage when we left Hispaniola. The men at arms, who often joined us, soon grew adept at bouncing the resilient sphere off their shoulders, heads, and knees. Javier, whose wounds still limited his duties, might excel once he was able to run. None of us would ever surpass Hutia, who had been a *batey* champion in Quisqueya. Meanwhile, I crossed swords with Hernan and Esteban daily. Javier, who had become a passable swordsman, offered the perspective of one who had been forced to kill his opponent in order to save his own life.

In that sunny meadow, it was hard to remember

that our lives would be in frequent danger whether we traveled by land or sea. But so it was. Rachel took to wearing a loose gown and tunic to conceal the shirt and breeches underneath. She insisted on lessons in swordsmanship, dismissing as irrelevant the men's initial discomfort at seeing a lady's legs exposed. Some of her gold from the Indies went to purchase a light sword made to her measure with a fine blade of Toledo steel. Hutia's people had been so unfamiliar with edged weapons when they first encountered the Spaniards that many had taken severe cuts when they grasped them by the blade. He was still too ill at ease with swords to carry one, though at Rachel's insistence, he learned the basic moves of fencing.

"You must be able to defend yourself," she said. "What if you manage to stun an opponent, let us say, a French soldier encountered by chance, with a rock or cudgel, and then two of his companions come at you with swords? Will you stand there helpless, waiting to be killed? Or will you seize the sword your first enemy has let fall and give a good account of yourself?"

When it came to throwing knives, it was another matter.

"You could almost match the gypsies!" Esteban said, when after a few days' practice Hutia had demonstrated his skill by hitting a mark on a distant tree five times in a row.

"Gypsies—these are the Roma of whom you have spoken?" Hutia asked Rachel.

"Yes, and it is no surprise that you can throw a knife with the best of them," Rachel said, "though those we met near Cordoba had much skill. Among the Taino, Esteban, the smallest children hunt for the pot, bringing down birds and small animals, some no bigger than a rat, with stones. And you have not yet seen him bend a bow. If you will show me the coin in your purse, I will stake whatever odds you like on Hutia to best you at archery."

"I will take your wager," Hernan said. "Do you not

remember that Esteban bested the gypsies with his bow?"

Rachel's eyes gleamed.

"Show me your money, then," she said.

"Rachel," Hutia protested, "I have never used a Spanish soldier's bow."

"And you need not do so now," Rachel said. "I have a surprise for you." She unwrapped a bulky package of coarse cloth to reveal a bow much like those the Taino used. "The arrowheads are steel, but as you can see, they are fletched with feathers I brought from Quisqueya."

The Spaniards crowded close, hefting the bow and exclaiming over the beautifully fletched arrows, their brilliant red color a reminder of the paradise we had found, now vanishing under Spanish conquest and settlement.

"Rachel, these are beautiful. I thank you." Hutia's eyes filled with tears. "I will think of my home in Quisqueya every day I carry them, and when I come to use them, may they find the hearts of your enemies."

"The Taino make their arrowheads of fishbone," I told the men, hoping to divert their attention from the way Rachel and Hutia were looking at each other. "Their virtue for killing lies not only in their sharpness, but also in the Taino habit of dipping the tips in poison."

"Do not forget that I too am an archer," Rachel said. "Taino women live more freely than their European sisters in many respects."

"You had better let Esteban guide your practice, Rachel," I said, cutting off whatever Rachel might have said next, probably an artless revelation of the Taino habit of going, as the Admiral always put it, "naked as their mothers bore them."

"Gladly," Rachel said. "There is always room for improvement. And Hernan, I have ridden mules, but I am no horsewoman. Perhaps you can help me there, and Hutia as well."

"I will be content to ride a mule," Hutia said. "It

seems to me that horses can discern that I have but recently made their acquaintance. They do not think I have a right to give them orders."

"It is only a matter of training," Hernan said.

"What say you, Javier?" Rachel asked. "You are the one with experience of war."

"I was a foot soldier," Javier said grudgingly. "I had neither horse nor mule, except once when I captured the mount of a fallen French soldier. But soon enough, my captain took it away for the use of someone of higher rank. Still, you must have a horse, my lady. If you are pursued by a troop of mounted soldiers, a mule will serve you ill, whether you wish to stand and fight or run away. And there's nothing like a horse to keep a crowd of angry villagers at bay."

At this, Hutia looked grave, Rachel shuddered, and I sighed, all of us thinking once more of Quisqueya.

At Javier's suggestion, I worked at fighting from horseback with staff or cudgel, using stout branches of varying lengths, as well as with my sword. At first, Rachel and I found it comical to hear how seriously the erstwhile footman took his new role as our armsmaster. But we soon grew used to it.

What we could not do was persuade Javier to be as helpful to Hutia as he was to me and Rachel, his resentment no less palpable for being unstated. At first I thought he envied the three of us our ability to spend each day together in perfect accord, each of us taking the others' teasing in good part and finding cause for laughter even though we took our practice and the dangers we would soon encounter seriously. But once I started paying attention, I noticed that he gazed at Rachel with longing. He simmered when Rachel smiled at Hutia or found an excuse to touch him on the arm and glared whenever Hutia kissed her hand, a courtesy he had adopted the first time he had seen it done. Javier grew even more jealous when Hutia put his arms around Rachel to show her some trick of bending her bow. He found ways to distract Rachel's attention or belittle Hutia's skill without seeming to.

"They say the Turk can shoot a volley of arrows from horseback at full gallop," he said one day when Rachel was particularly cock-a-hoop about her archery, having split a series of wands pinned to a tree trunk at the far end of the field.

"Who is the Turk?" Hutia asked.

"They are a heathen people," Hernan said, "who wish to conquer the world."

"Heathen are folk who are not Christian," Rachel explained. "The Turks' God is called Allah and his prophet Muhammad."

I knew Hutia would demand a more detailed theology lesson later, but all three of us knew better than to dwell on such a subject in the company of Christians.

"We will not meet any Turks in France or Italy," I said, "though it is said that they trade with Venice."

"If you travel by sea," Esteban said, "you might, for it is said their corsairs infest the Mediterranean."

By now, the men at arms, of course, were privy to our mission to find our parents. If they guessed the reason our family had left Spain, they were tactful enough to ask no questions. Europe was currently so unsettled, its politics so dire, that not only Jews but any folk outside a fortress might find themselves homeless and in danger.

"The Turks are not the only pirates," Javier said. "Some say the Knights of Rhodes, who still consider themselves crusaders, will attack any rich shipping to fill their coffers against the day they go forth to retake the Holy Land."

"Nor is Portugal a friend to Spain these days," I said, for this was a subject on which Doña Marina and I had talked.

While Spain sought new wealth across the Ocean Sea, Portuguese navigators had also been seeking a trade route to the Indies, not by sailing west as Admiral Columbus had, but by exploring the coast of Africa, sailing ever farther south in the hope of finding a way around it to the east. So far, the chief riches they had found consisted of African slaves, who were proving more robust in enduring the European climate than the Taino the Admiral had taken captive.

"Whether we go by land or sea," Rachel said, "we will undoubtedly face dangers. Yet we must go, and I say the sooner the better. Summer will not last forever."

"I wish it would," Javier muttered.

One day, Javier invited Hutia to accompany him on an expedition to shoot birds in a wood at some distance from the farm, saying the local fletcher needed feathers for the substantial number of arrows we had ordered. I said nothing but followed them at a distance. I did not think Javier intended serious harm to Hutia, but I could not rid myself of unease. When I came upon them, Hutia had tripped in a rabbit hole and lay sprawled on the bumpy ground, thick with an uneven cover of grass and wildflowers dry enough to smell like fresh hay. His bow and arrows lay out of reach of his hand, and he had reached out to Javier to help him rise. He was laughing. Javier stood looking down at him, making no move to assist him. He held his right arm behind his back, his fist clenched around a sizable rock.

I put my arm around him in a comradely fashion, effectively immobilizing him, while I extended my other arm, pulling Hutia up. With an exclamation of thanks, Hutia bent and began retrieving his scattered arrows. Javier had dropped the rock the moment I touched him. His face and neck burned bright red with shame as much as anger. I drew him away so Hutia could not hear.

"Whatever you were thinking of doing," I murmured, "think no more of it. It will solve nothing and can only cause you harm."

"It is not fair!" Javier burst out. "If she can marry a savage, why not a soldier?"

"My friend," I said, "you cannot imagine the sacrifices he has made for love of her. Nor is it certain that my father will bestow her hand on him, even provided we find my family without any of us getting killed."

I was tempted to say more. Would you deny your Lord Jesus Christ to win her? Would you submit yourself to circumcision? For Hutia was determined to embrace Judaism, knowing that my parents were unlikely to consent to the marriage on any other condition. But it would be folly to reveal as much to Javier. A spiteful word to the Inquisition would part Rachel and Hutia forever. Jealousy had turned Javier from a simple, loyal youth to a man whose rashness meant we could not trust him.

Later, when I could speak to Hutia alone, I advised him to watch his back.

To Rachel, I said only, "We must leave soon."

"That is what I said," Rachel said. "We have only to find a ship. Or will it be a caravan?"

"Whichever offers itself first," I said, "since both land and sea seem to hold their share of perils. Either must be headed in the right direction: toward Firenze, but not in the direct path of a French or indeed any other army."

Having crossed the Ocean Sea, I found it hard to view the Mediterranean with apprehension as far as natural dangers went. But as I roamed the Barcelona docks, seeking information as well as possible passage, I found that the sea captains and sailors I met had great respect for the Middle Sea, especially in the fall or winter.

"The Turk," one old salt told me, "he'll keep a-goin' through November. So make sure you pick a ship with cannon mounted on it to give 'em the greeting they deserve, and them damned pirates out of Rhodes too, that'll board a Christian ship and plunder the cargo same as any heathen. But come All Saints Day, you'll find me snug at me own fireside, feet up on the hearth and a flagon in me hand."

As for the overland route, not many merchants wanted to plunge into the heart of a continent at war.

"Ye'll find many folk, whole villages and towns, that fear sack or have survived it," a weathered muleteer who had crossed France many times told me, "running away from Italy with this latest madness going on, but few willing to travel toward it, not a-purpose."

"Is it possible to cross the Alps by accident?" I asked, signaling the tavern keeper to bring my informant more wine.

"Nay, but if an army in search of food and livestock accosts your caravan, no matter how well guarded, you'll flee in whatever direction leads away from it. Don't count on finding a well guarded caravan, neither. Most of the fellows who love a fight joined up last year on one side or t'other. They'll live to regret it, so they will."

Much of our time at Doña Marina's was devoted to the study of languages. We all knew the importance of being able to communicate, no matter where we went. Indeed, Papa had taught us that wherever our home, Jews were ever citizens of the world. He had made sure we knew a serviceable amount of German, French, and Italian as well as Latin and Byzantine Greek. Our skills, however, had grown rusty, and all the European languages save Spanish were new to Hutia. In the afternoons, when it was too hot for weapons practice and the servants drowsed, we would sit in the cool, tiled courtyard and pretend we were travelers already, met at some wayside inn, and challenge each other to maintain a suitable conversation in all these languages.

Occasionally, Doña Marina, who was well versed in these tongues as well, would sacrifice her siesta to join us, putting us all on our mettle. She soon realized that Hutia was quicker at languages even than Rachel. This increased her respect for him and allowed them to talk more easily and relax in each other's company. More often, she summoned her man of business, Señor Ortega, to tutor us. Since he had to look after Doña Marina's interests all over Europe, not only was he fluent, but he also had practical suggestions about the journey.

"You might consider learning Turkish as well," he said one day, as we sat sipping wine after a lively lesson. "Even if Venice keeps the Ottomans confined to the Balkans, encroaching no further on Europe, their empire is ever more important to European trade. It is a useful skill. I am not fluent myself, but I can send you a young man from Edirne, the city the Byzantines called Adrianople, who can teach you the basics and help you with pronunciation."

"We are most likely to need to speak Turkish," I said, "if we are boarded by corsairs."

"We must hope it does not come to that," Señor Ortega said. It would have comforted me more if he had assured us this was unlikely to happen. On the other hand, if he had, we might have been less inclined to trust his judgment about everything else he told us.

The more we delayed, the more difficult it might be to catch up with the family, even if we knew where they had gone. I did not want to think of the dangers, not only to Papa and Mama, but also to my sisters Elvira and Susanna, young women dependent on others to protect them. I doubted any other Jewish girl in Europe, or any Christian girl either, could match Rachel's ability to defend herself or her skills to survive in any imaginable circumstances.

Summer was waning, with crops ripening in the fields, pigs and chickens growing fat, and the leaves of even the lushest trees heavy with dust, before I found the opportunity I sought.

I burst into the shaded courtyard behind Doña Marina's house, where my aunt and Rachel, dressed demurely in a gown for once, sat plying their needles. Hutia sat at Rachel's feet, disentangling the colored skeins of yarn she was using in her embroidery. A new footman, very young and nervous, was pouring wine with fruit floating in it from a pitcher that had been left to cool in the well, a refreshing drink on such a hot and airless day.

"I have found us a ship!" I said.

The Fourth Letter

September 1493

Dearest children,

We have had no further word of you and no way to know whether our letters reach you, though we miss no opportunity to send one on its way. Last time Papa inquired, the gentleman he spoke with, an agent of the Medici, was not only discreet but remarkably distant. Papa concludes that your Aunt Marina has removed her affairs from Medici hands as he suggested. So that letter, at least, must have arrived at its destination. Papa says his sister is wise enough not to invest her wealth in one place but spread it about so that whatever happens, a portion of it, at least, will always be safe. And you may be sure he has taken a leaf from the same book with regard to our girls' dowries and whatever else we could salvage from the wreck of our fortunes in Spain. But these Italian states especially are so quarrelsome that it is hard to know where we, much less our money, will be safe.

You will rejoice to hear that Elvira and Akiva Davila are betrothed! The Davilas are fine people, and we like them very much. Indeed, I grew up with my cousin Chaim, Akiva's papa, and I know he and Miriam already love Elvira like a daughter. Family is more important than ever in these troubled times. We and the elder Davilas spend much time discussing the latest news and rumors so we can make a wise decision about what to do if it should become necessary to leave Firenze. There! I have said it! We hoped this beautiful city with its love for art and learning would be our permanent home. But to be Jewish in these times is always to have one bag packed and one foot out the door.

It is said that King Ferrante of Naples is most hospitable to the Jews. He is said to value the artisans among us, especially the dyers and weavers, and has even stated publicly that we must be protected. The Davilas have been urging us to consider moving to Naples while Italy is relatively calm and safe travel possible. But King Ferrante's reputation is not uniformly good, in spite of his kindness to the Jews. Rumor has it that he not only imprisons and executes his enemies, but has them embalmed and clothed as they were in life, so he may display them to his guests in a sort of museum. Papa does not believe this tale, but who could possibly invent such a thing?

We have heard that King Ferdinand and Queen Isabella have commissioned Admiral Columbus to mount another expedition to the Indies. Diego, if you accompany him, you must contrive a way to send us word before you go. Above all, let us know your dispositions for Rachel! We ask Adonai to keep you both safe, my darlings, and bring you home to us.

All my love, Mama

Chapter Nine: Joanna

Joanna stayed on the alert for another opportunity to sneak up on deck unobserved, but Imaculada, finally recovering from her seasickness along with the other *degradados*, kept a sharp eye on her. Cranky and demanding, she would not allow Joanna even to empty the slop bucket over the rail without supervision. Joanna took a free breath only when Imaculada and Felicidade had a fancy to take the air, as they called it. This consisted of promenading up and down the deck with skirts hiked up and bosoms well in evidence, exchanging provocative glances and bawdy quips with any man they encountered, whether soldier, sailor, or gentleman of Captain Caminha's entourage.

Joanna still slept poorly on straw thinly spread over heaving planks, with the patter of rats' feet and the desolate wails and whimpers of the younger children as lullabies. Once recovered from the nausea of sea travel, all of them were subject to gnawing hunger as well as aches and fevers, runny noses, and in some cases the welts and bruises of beatings by the *degradados*. Through slit eyes, she would watch Imaculada slip out at night past the snoring Belmiro and climb the ladder to the creaking hatch. If she held her head at a certain angle, Joanna could see a bit of starlight or the warmer light of a lantern falling on Imaculada's upturned face or on the hand that helped her up and then slowly lowered the hatch cover. She would wake again to hear Imaculada return, hours later, a faint jingle about her person revealing that she had recently added coins to her purse.

The children were allowed on deck for brief periods of religious instruction, since the priests charged with educating them to be good Christians flatly refused to descend into the stinking hold. Lessons consisted of many repetitions of something called the Credo and something else called the Pater Noster, both in Latin, which Joanna recognized as prayers only because they ended with Amen.

"But what does it *mean*?" Joanna ground out through her teeth at some point during every lesson. This usually earned her a slap on the cheek or a clout on the ear, though once, an exasperated priest swung his heavy crucifix at her head, laying open her cheek with a sharp corner of the silver cross.

To her surprise, Imaculada made much of this mishap. She insisted on sewing up the split cheek, having unraveled an old shawl for thread and acquired a precious steel needle by barter of an unspecified nature.

"You'll never be a beauty," she said, while Joanna bit down on a rag so that she would not scream and squeezed Simon's hand tight enough to make him wiggle and moan in protest. "But you can be pleasing to the eye, and so I'll keep you. A badly scarred face is in neither of our interests. If they take you in disgust, it will be a poor return indeed on my investment."

Joanna listened to this speech with dread. Simon was too young to confide in, and Natan, when she mentioned her fears, dismissed them.

"You must do whatever they tell you to," Natan said. "If we strive always to please them, eventually we will gain their trust. By that, and by showing ourselves good Christians, we will prosper. Then, once we are grown, we can become people of means in this new land. You are lucky that your Christian mother cares for your appearance. She is no doubt thinking ahead to the time when you may be given in marriage."

"You do not understand!" Joanna said. "You are a boy." And a pompous fool, she added silently. "Have you not realized they plan to breed us with the African slaves to create a populous colony? They may call it marriage, as they call the *degradados* our parents and ourselves Christians, but it is no such thing."

One night, instead of slipping out as usual, Imaculada made her way over to where Joanna lay, feigning sleep. Imaculada stooped and shook her shoulder.

"Girl! Get up! I know you're not asleep, so stop pretending. Don't you want to come out on the deck? The air is cooler there, and I've a mind to share it."

Joanna's eyes flew open. Slowly, she sat up.

"Why are you being kind?" she asked warily.

"Aren't you my adopted daughter?" Imaculada twisted her face into a simulacrum of sweetness. "We could be companions, you and I. I need not treat you as a child any more. Are you not pleased? Girls always want to grow up to be women as fast as possible. Come."

She drew Joanna up and linked arms with her, chattering gaily though in hushed tones about the beauty of the night and how she had always wanted a sister. Her grip was too tight for Joanna to pull away. When they reached the ladder, Imaculada pushed Joanna ahead of her, putting an intrusive hand beneath her rump to force her to climb. Joanna's heart pounded, and her breath came in short gasps. Imaculada followed so close behind that she felt smothered, as if the woman were an enveloping feather bed. At the top of the ladder, Joanna stopped. Imaculada reached past her and knocked on the underside of the hatch cover in a complicated pattern. She braced Joanna with her other arm, so she could neither fall nor get away, not even by flinging herself off the ladder.

The hatch creaked open, and a bearded face peered down.

"Have you got my prize?" the man demanded eagerly. "I won it fair and square, and so Belmiro knows."

Imaculada gave a lazy, seductive laugh at odds with the brisk shove she gave Joanna, sending her stumbling onto the deck. Imaculada held out a hand for the man to help her onto the deck like a court lady.

"I warned Belmiro not to play at dice with you," she said. "But if our little arrangement works out as I hope, I'll say nothing to him of how you won."

"What are you talking about?"

"Come now, soldier, let us understand each other. I am a keen observer of human nature, and I have played at dice since earliest childhood."

Joanna, staring at the ground and trying not to think, cast a quick glance upward. The man was indeed a soldier, not wearing a steel helmet or a leather corselet, but shod in boots and with a short sword at his waist that looked as if it had been blooded in battle.

Imaculada grasped Joanna firmly by the forearm and pulled her toward the soldier, more as if inviting him to arrest her than to present them to each other.

"Here is your prize," she said. "And you have a small gift for me, do you not?"

Grinning, the soldier tossed a coin to Imaculada, who caught it deftly.

"Joanna, this is Duarte," Imaculada said calmly. "He has won you for the night, and you will be a biddable young woman and do whatever he tells you to. I will have none of your lip or whining, and you will speak of this to no one. If you disobey me on any count, I will know."

"You said she was a frisky one," Duarte said, eyeing the trembling Joanna with some skepticism.

"She does not know your ways yet," Imaculada said. "But she will learn. And remember why you had to risk so much to gain this night's particular prize. Now I will be gone, for I have business of my own to attend to. Return her in good condition, soldier, and before first light, or you will get no more of her."

Joanna's pulse pounded in her ears. She felt near

to fainting. A sensation of terror invaded her trembling legs, her arms, and the mysterious region between her thighs.

"Come along then, girl," Duarte said, not unkindly. "I know a quiet corner where none will disturb us. Let's get that ugly gown off you and have a look."

There was no escape. The moon was new, so the night was too dark for her to see him well, or he her. He led her to an even darker corner of the deck, beneath a tented triangle of canvas to shade them from stray lantern light. It seemed that his idea of having a look consisted of stripping off her gown, mercifully not ripping it, and running his fingers up and down her whole body both inside and outside her shift. As he touched her in places that until now only she had owned, she twitched, writhed, and shivered, bewildered by the variety of sensations that she could not name or understand. It was as if her own body betrayed her.

Why do I not fight? she asked herself, twisting her face away as he nuzzled her neck. If I were not a coward, I would do something. I would scream or bite him. It would be no use, but maybe I would not feel such shame. Adonai, I beg you, be with me even in this terrible shame.

He lowered his body onto hers and began to rock, his thick thighs pushing her legs apart. A finger poked abruptly into her, then smeared a sticky wetness across her belly. The man laughed softly.

"Ready, are you? Be a good girl, now. Ahh, that's the way."

Pain pierced a part of her body so utterly unfamiliar to her that she could not imagine how he had reached it. His weight pinning her down, he slammed himself against her several times, then gave a grunt of satisfaction and rolled off her. She lay stunned, staring up at the canvas that blotted out the sky.

I cannot look the stars themselves in the eye, she thought. I would kill him if I could, and that woman too, but I cannot. I have no pride left. I am consumed with shame. I am broken.

"The wench didn't lie about you being a maid," he said. "No tears? That's a good girl. See? It wasn't so bad." He reached between her legs to stroke briefly another unfamiliar place. This time, she did not feel pain, but a momentary sweetness that somehow outraged her more than all that had gone before.

He cupped Joanna's head in his hand, and she thought perhaps now he would draw her forward and kiss her. Instead, he pushed her head down onto his lap. She flinched away from the sticky feel of his flesh against her cheek.

"Now, here's a thing you may not know about a man," he said in a conversational tone. "Even the best of us is not always ready to go again at once. But there's a way a sweet lass like you can make him ready. Once that's done, I promise you will like it better the second time."

Chapter Ten: Diego

"Here is a letter of introduction," Doña Marina said, "to the governors of the Banco di San Giorgio in Genoa. King Ferdinand and Queen Isabella have accounts there."

"So does Admiral Columbus," I said, stowing my aunt's letter carefully in the oiled pouch that already held our letters of exchange. "He recommended his bank to me when we parted in Hispaniola, assuring me it had the highest reputation."

"It does," she said. "Its influence is political as well as economic. The Republic of Genoa handed over the governing of Corsica to the bank some forty years ago, and they made a better fist of it, by all accounts, than that quarrelsome pack of fools themselves."

My aunt had decided views on republican government. I kept an open mind, having no great opinion of absolute monarchs either. Besides the letters that would make funds available to us in Italy, I bore a quantity of gold concealed about my person, as did Hutia and Rachel. We also carried purses of silver coins of varying purity that might be taken out in marketplace or tavern without arousing deadly greed. We had exchanged our gold from Hispaniola for Florentine florins and Venetian ducats through Aunt Marina's most trusted banker in Barcelona, a sincere *converso* of unassailable reputation like my aunt herself. It was he who had told me privately that the Genoese bank employed Jewish agents in the lands around the Black Sea, where Ottoman influence was strong. He deemed this information would increase my faith in San

Giorgio's trustworthiness, and it did.

On the other hand, Genoa's stability, like Firenze's, depended on the precarious balance of power in Italy as a whole. For that reason, we had deposited some of our funds in Barcelona, counting on letters of credit to release equivalent sums for use in various cities on our travels.

"It seems odd to be leaving money in Spain," Rachel said, "when so much of the country's wealth was confiscated from Jewish families."

"We must be practical," I said. "Who knows what may befall us once we leave Barcelona? If all else fails, we can count on Aunt Marina to watch over our interests here."

"It will be hard to say goodbye to Aunt Marina," Rachel said. "I remember well how frightened of her I was when we first met, she seemed so stern and stiff. But she has proven a true friend."

"She has indeed," I said.

"I am still frightened of her." Hutia grinned.

Doña Marina had greeted with reserve our introduction of an Indian savage into her home, even one well clothed and speaking excellent Castilian. But her courtesy to him had never faltered. And lately, I had come upon them together in the garden, Hutia grooming her favorite lapdog as he told her about Taino methods of farming and the beauty of Quisqueya's forest and mountains.

"We will never return," Rachel said, "will we, Diego? This is truly our farewell to Aunt Marina and to Spain."

"We must not complain, Rachel," I said. "We are not departing destitute and in fear with the Inquisition breathing down our necks."

"I know," Rachel said. "We are lucky indeed. And I do love an adventure!"

Although my view of adventures was more sober than Rachel's, I could not forbear to feel a lightening of the heart when we stood on the docks at first light, ready to board the *Santa Cecilia*. A sprightly caravel out of Valencia, bound first for Marseille and then for Genoa, she tugged at her moorings as if eager to be off. Along with passengers, she carried a cargo of oranges and olives.

"You will see more galleys than sailing ships in Mediterranean waters," Captain Velez told me when he learned that I had sailed with Admiral Columbus. "But give me a caravel any day. My *Cecilia* is a ship for true sailors like you and me."

I too had a fondness for caravels, having returned to Spain in the plucky little *Niña* in 1493 and shipped on *Mariagalante* later the same year. Captain Velez welcomed us aboard, offering Rachel his own cabin. She would share it with two young sisters and their chaperone, who were traveling to join family in Avignon.

"So you will begin the journey as a young lady," I told Rachel.

"With my breeches underneath," Rachel retorted, "the better to fight or swim should we meet any mishap. And I will not promise to like the two young ladies or obey their chaperone!"

Captain Velez was particularly proud of the caravel's ordnance: a bronze bombard, set amidships, from which stone balls could be fired.

"*Cecilia* has not much cargo space," Captain Velez told me, "but she would carry more goods were it not for this beauty. She is heavy, but I would not sail the Mediterranean without her. We have a store of crossbows and arquebuses as well and seamen who know how to use them. I will show you and your man where they are kept."

I thanked him, though in my private opinion, the weighty bombard was as likely to send *Cecilia* to the bottom, should she be disabled in a storm, as to save us from a seaborne enemy.

Of the passengers, only Doña Julieta proved prone to seasickness. Her charges were a lively pair, half French and half Spanish. The elder, Celeste, was twelve. The younger sister, Isbel, was a mischievous eight-year-old, as full of pranks as a monkey. Rachel found herself playing chaperone to the extent of running after them to make sure they did not get swept overboard or fall from the rigging in their attempts to investigate the fighting top.

"It is a fitting punishment," I told her, "for all the worry you caused me when you sneaked onto *Mariagalante*."

"Nonsense," Rachel said. "I will teach them to climb the rigging properly. Then they will not fall and can go wherever they like. Had I the means, I would teach them to swim as well. Then they would be prepared and safe, no matter what happens."

Before Rachel could carry out this program of tutelage, Doña Julieta gained her sea legs and emerged from the cabin to resume a sterner chaperonage of the girls. Captain Velez remained friendly, as interested in my tales of navigating the Ocean Sea and the isle-studded waters of the Indies as was I in learning all I could about sailing the Mediterranean. Adrift with respect to my unknown future, I deemed that such knowledge might prove useful later on. According to Captain Velez, the great sea teemed with traffic: carracks, caravels, and galleys of varying size, along with innumerable smaller boats. The Ottomans, the Venetians, and the French all had substantial fleets. Ordnance like *Cecilia*'s bombard as well as handguns were becoming ever more popular, not only in warfare, but in dealing with the raids of corsairs, who sought constantly to board and capture any vessel caught out alone. Captain Velez seemed confident that no ill would befall us, since we sailed reasonably close inshore in a season of fair weather.

Of even greater interest to us, Captain Velez could give us more recent news of conditions on the continent than had reached Aunt Marina in Barcelona.

"The French king did not stay long in Firenze," the captain said, "though they say the Florentines fell over themselves to offer him treasures to decorate his new palace at Amboise. A spineless lot, the Florentines, though they managed to kick out the

Medici tyrant. Charles took Naples without a siege. The old king abdicated when he heard the French army was approaching, and his son is but a young pup who fled without putting up a fight. But the French may be hard put to keep what they have taken, now that this new league has formed against them."

"What league is this?" I asked.

"They call it the League of Venice," he said, "or the Holy League, though to my mind there's not much holy about any of 'em. The Pope's a part of it, and so are the king and queen of Spain and all their kin. Why even the Duke of Milan's joined up, though he invited the French king to Italy in the first place. Naples, too, as young Ferrandino hopes to regain his throne. They won't keep from quarreling long, but perhaps they'll stick together long enough to kick Charles out of Italy. That's the point of it, though they *say* their purpose is to prevent the Turk from advancing any further into Europe. Right scared of that, they all are, especially Venice, since the Ottoman's trade is a threat to theirs, though they're happy enough to be bedfellows with the heathen on and off, when it suits their purpose."

"What of Genoa?" I asked.

"They've managed to stay out of it," he said. "Charles's armies passed it by. You'll be safe enough, and I'll do good trade there before I head back to Valencia. Of course, there's no saying what the French will do once they decide to turn around and go home."

This reassurance made me worry less, at least about the next leg of our journey. But we had reckoned without the winds. An unseasonable storm blew up overnight, sweeping us far off course. None of us got any sleep that night.

"The god of storms on this sea must be a cousin to Juracán!" Hutia shouted as we battled the raging winds to help the seamen lower the sails.

By morning, the storm had blown itself out but left us with a cracked mainmast and with no sight of land in any direction. As the captain considered our bearings and the sailors began to work on the damaged mast, a shout from aloft made all of us rush to the rail, where through the hazy air we saw three galleys bearing down on us. They were a terrifying and beautiful sight. The ships were long and slender, built low to the water with a shallow draft and a slim, questing spar projecting from the bow. The banks of oars sliced the water in perfect unison as the vessels sped toward us. The hulls were painted a rich blue-green that reminded me of the waters around Hispaniola. Each galley had a single mast and flew a fluttering pennon that displayed the crescent and star of the Ottoman Empire.

Caught with our sails down, we could not outrun them. The sailors leaped for their arquebuses and crossbows, and a team evidently trained for the purpose clustered around the bombard, which unfortunately pointed away from the rapidly approaching vessels. The captain stopped them with a word.

"Nay, lads," he said. "They have janissaries aboard. We're so outnumbered that putting up a fight would but lead to all our deaths."

"What are janissaries?" Rachel asked. Her voice quivered slightly, though her fists were clenched and her chin well up.

"They're the Sultan's own soldiers. They capture them young from their own Christian territories, turn them Muslim, and train them up to fanatic loyalty to the Sultan. We cannot beat them, and if we try, they will show no mercy. I am sorry."

"What will they do with us?" Doña Julieta quavered. She clutched Celeste's and Isbel's hands in hers, though whether for their comfort or her own, it would have been difficult to say.

"Slaves to row their galleys, most like," a sailor said, "or workmen to build their fine mosques in Istanbul."

"And the women?" Doña Julieta looked near to fainting.

No one answered her. Hutia took her by the arm to help her stand. Rachel patted the little girls on the back and stood by them, one hand resting lightly on Isbel's shoulder. I had not felt so helpless since the day I saw Spaniards cut down my Taino friends. We watched in silence as the lead galley drew alongside and threw out grappling hooks.

The party that leaped from their vessel onto ours consisted, by the look of them, of sailors rather than the terrible janissaries, though some of these covered the boarding party with wicked-looking recurved bows of a kind I had not seen before. They were barefoot and bare-chested, muscles gleaming on their brown skin. They wore white turbans and full trousers that did not impede their movement. Most carried long knives, but a couple, boarding more slowly than the rest, kept their arquebuses trained on us.

The man who seemed to be their leader was young, slim, and dark. His white teeth flashed in a grin of exultation as he caught sight of the girls, now huddled against Doña Julieta's skirts with their soft blonde hair rippling enticingly about their heads. Reaching out, he pried the girls loose and bore them, shrieking, to the rail. Ottoman sailors lifted them over it and handed them off to others on the galley. The young leader turned back to us and grasped Rachel by the arm. Rachel stiffened and met his eyes with a snarl of pure defiance. The corsair's eyes widened. His grip on Rachel's arm loosened as he fell back a step, looking astonished.

"Raquel?"

"Amir!" she cried.

I would not have recognized him, but Rachel was right. It was the Moorish lad she had insisted we rescue from slavery when we left the Espinosas' house in Seville.

The Fifth Letter

February 1494

Dearest children,

I write to you as an act of faith, although I know that Rachel may already be on her way to us and Diego in the Indies, far beyond the reach of letters. The news is uncertain at best. King Ferdinand of Naples, he they called Ferrante, has died, and his son Alfonso is now the King of Naples. As always, we must ask ourselves whether this is good for the Jews. The father regarded us as assets to his kingdom. The son is an unknown quantity. There is also a rumor that Charles of France is assembling an army in Toulon to invade Italy and claim the Neapolitan throne. They say that Duke Sforza of Milan encourages him to do so, since young King Alfonso has designs on Milan. These Italians are worse than a Beit Din, a roomful of rabbis squabbling over a passage of Talmud! Worse, they are playing with human lives, not merely theological interpretations.

We are thinking seriously about leaving Firenze. But we have yet to settle on a destination that will guarantee us safety, either on the road or when we arrive. Since Toulon is a port city, Charles will have a navy as well as an army at his command. That means he will be able to beseige such Italian ports as Genoa, Naples, and Venice by sea as well as by land if he so wishes, although for now, it seems that Genoa stays neutral and Venice allies itself with France, apparently because Charles claims any such mission would be merely a necessary prelude to crusade against the Turks. The Ottoman Empire is the greatest rival Venice has in trade, naval power, and desire to conquer fresh territory, so one can understand why. Firenze at least lies inland, so it cannot be attacked by sea. But the thought of armies at the gates of the city is a terrifying one. I do not mean to frighten you, my darlings. But you must cross these troubled lands if we are ever to be reunited. It is essential for you to be as well informed as possible in planning your journey.

Elvira and Akiva are a quite a pair of lovebirds, so happy to be together planning their married life down to the number of sons and daughters they will have that it is a pleasure to behold them. As if children can be made to order! Of course, they cannot marry now, with everything so unsettled. We must husband our resources and prepare to meet an unknown future as a community. Elvira takes the disappointment well. She says they will be all the happier when we have found some peaceful land where she can make her nest. I am glad she has the optimism to believe that such a place exists.

Susanna has been sneaking out at night. She does not know that Papa and I know. We suspect she is seeing an Italian boy. Papa says she has been taught good principles and will not go too far unless we arouse her defiance by trying to stop her. Besides, considering the likelihood of an Italian war in the near future, the situation will resolve itself without our interference. I should not admit this to you, my children, but I take a secret joy in her adventure. Young girls should have some romance in their lives! Looking back at how we lived in Seville, never dreaming that we should have to leave, I remember only sunshine and a sense of security that Jewish children of today will never fathom. I was never happier than in that precious time when Papa came courting. He was not my only suitor, you know! But he was the one for me, and I wish for all of you the joy of such a match. May Adonai bless and keep you, my darlings.

All my love, Mama

Chapter Eleven: Joanna

"Credo in Deum Patrem omnipotentem," Frei Jerónimo said, his steely eyes under tufted brows boring into those of each cross-legged child in turn as he paced back and forth along the deck in front of them. "Repeat after me."

"Credo in Deum Patrem omnipotentem," the children chorused in quavering voices.

"Creatorem caeli et terrae," Frei Jerónimo said. He looked angry, as if God's creation of heaven and earth affronted him personally.

"Creatorem caeli et terrae," the children repeated.

Even the youngest, some of whom had gone dumb with the shock of their change in circumstances, were forbidden to shirk the daily hour of religious instruction. Since it was the only hour each day that they were permitted out of the hold, most went willingly. They had already learned that they would be whipped if they failed to participate in the chant, made a mistake when called on to recite alone, cried, or soiled themselves. The smallest, children of three and four who could not always prevent the last of these, had to remain after the lesson to scrub the deck, bare bottoms tingling under the lash, while Frei Jerónimo harangued them on the terrors of Hell. Since he delivered these sermons in Portuguese, never explaining the Latin of the catechism, the children took his vision of Hell to be an apt description of Christianity and of the horrors that awaited them at the end of the voyage.

Joanna, whose blood boiled at the idea of professing belief in something she could not understand, had pieced together the meaning of the

Credo and the Paternoster with some grudging help from Natan, who suspected her of poaching on his territory in currying favor with the priests as well as the gentlemen in Captain Caminha's train. Joanna had no intention of currying favor with the priests, and she already knew the gentlemen all too well. Imaculada had lost no time in selling her services to those who could pay better than the soldiers. Some were cruel, deriving their pleasure from pinching, slapping, or choking her as they pumped their way to release. Others used her with indifference, walking away afterward without a word as they would have wiped their hands on a piece of cloth and then tossed it aside after a greasy meal.

Since she could not appear to lack compliance with the catechism, Joanna joined in fervently on the passages with which she took no issue. She still believed in God the Father Almighty, Creator of heaven and earth, outraged and disappointed though she was by His negligence toward his Chosen People of late. When it came to *"et in Iesum Christum, Filium Eius unicum, Dominum nostrum,"* she bowed her head as if in reverence, so that Frei Jerónimo could not observe her refusal even to move her lips. By the time they got to *"remissionem peccatorum, carnis resurrectionem, vitam aeternam,"* her mind would be racing with all the retorts she could never utter aloud. They believed in the forgiveness of sins, did they? Did they really think their Jesus would let them into Heaven no matter how many defenseless children they stole, raped, and enslaved? A fine God that would be!

Each morning, a tidying of the hold preceded the catechism. This consisted mainly of disposing of the bodies of any children who had died during the night. There were some to be rolled out and tossed overboard every morning. While the dreaded ship fever did not erupt, dehydration and malnutrition took their toll. So did beatings by the *degradados*, who had no better way of expressing their frustration with the rigors of the voyage and the

65

uncertainty of their lot, since fighting with knives among themselves was forbidden. This would not have stopped them, except that such fights as broke out were swiftly punished with the lash and confiscation of the knives. The threat of loss of a hand on the second offense persuaded the *degradados* to seek safer forms of relief. Their simmering resentment did not abate as time went on. Joanna took to visiting the pigs to avoid the long, boastful conversations of Belmiro, Mateus, and their mates, reminiscing about their clever thievery as if they had been princes of the Lisbon streets rather than culled by Caminha from the city's prisons.

Belmiro did not abuse her himself, not because he was supposed to be her father, but because he would have had to face Imaculada's wrath had he done so. However, he took to staking her in the endless games of dice that the *degradados* played among themselves and in card games with the soldiers, equally bored. The sailors had not much time for games of chance, between their duties and sleep, and tended to hold themselves aloof from the rest. They were not sentenced to life on São Tomé but would see Lisbon again before the year was out.

Mateus was a sly and effective cheater at both cards and dice. The others regarded this with amusement and admiration. So he often won Joanna, not bothering to take her up on deck when Belmiro shook her out of sleep and handed her over, the wiry little man slithering out of his breeches and onto her in full sight of his companions, to their lewd amusement.

Mateus's behavior not only caused her misery but also earned her Felicidade's enmity. Felicidade was a pouter, insinuating rather than commanding when she wished to get her way. A woman who would always reserve her spite for a weaker target, she left pig manure in Joanna's bedding, called attention to her whenever she spied Joanna seizing a moment of peace to compose herself, and set the little boys under her control, Shmuel and Benji, humiliating tasks whenever Joanna was at hand to see her do it.

Joanna's resentment of her half-brothers as the cause of her captivity had died the moment they clung to her, crying, on the dock. She lived in fear that they would die, either before the voyage was out or once they reached the island, which the sailors who had seen it described as consisting of a single volcanic mountain, impenetrable forests, and pestilential swamps. She had less fear for Simon, who was old enough to serve Belmiro as a page and messenger and whom Belmiro treated with a careless kindness. He had never had a servant before, and it pleased him to order the boy about. Simon did not know that the messages he sometimes carried concerned the selling of his sister's body. Joanna thought that she would die of shame if he found out. She did nothing to challenge his liking for Belmiro. For the moment, it guaranteed his safety and continued life.

To endure the nightly assaults on her body, Joanna learned to retreat within her mind and transport herself far away, as if the indignities committed were happening to someone else. Most often, she would draw on childhood memories of walking with her mother in the gardens of the Alhambra. She did not know how it had come about that her mother had been welcomed in the palace of the Moorish Sultan, but she remembered women's laughter, crystalline like the fountains that plashed and sparkled everywhere amid a profusion of colors and scents. She remembered laughing herself, chasing and being chased by children of her own age, dressed in white, down colonnades of slender columns ending in delicate stone tracery. In time, the memories became so vivid that she could summon them at will and become that little girl, actually forgetting for minutes at a time where she was and what was being done to her.

It did not occur to her that she might become pregnant until Imaculada pressed on her the remedy she used herself. Her stepmother Riva's response to

Joanna's first bleeding had been to slap her cheek and say grimly, "You are a woman now."

"I'll not bear on anyone's command," Imaculada said, "and you, with your narrow hips, might easily die. Do as I say, and if you're lucky, you will not conceive."

Natan, older than Simon and, Joanna reluctantly acknowledged, quick and clever, knew what was happening to Joanna but did not have the imagination to sympathize or comprehend the horror of it.

"Why can you not make the most of the situation?" he asked her one day as they talked in the hold while she mended a shawl of Imaculada's and he polished a pair of one of the gentlemen's shoe buckles. "You should do as I do. I believe I will achieve more and grow richer as a sugar king, a *fazendeiro*, than I could ever have if I had stayed to inherit my father's shop in Lisbon. Captain Caminha is the King's chosen *donatario*: he will be the Governor of the island when we arrive, with absolute authority over all. I strive to please him even now, and I believe he knows me by sight. Soon I will make sure he knows my name and considers how I can be of use to him. He has no sons. They say he will make his cousin, Pero Alvares de Caminha, his heir. You have a connection with Dom Pero, do you not? You would be foolish not to use it."

"One would think you were sailing on a different ship than I," Joanna said, "bound for a different island. Ambition makes you stupid. You cannot control your destiny. You are a slave. We are slaves!"

"We are not slaves," Natan said. "The black Africans will be our slaves, and we will be their masters."

"I am here against my will," Joanna said. "My body belongs to any man who wishes to use it, and it is not even I who sell it, but my masters. When we arrive in São Tomé, I will be forced to labor without pay. I will never be permitted to leave the island except by death. What, fool, is your definition of a slave, if I am not a slave?"

"It is different for a woman," Natan said. He glanced sharply around the room, lowered his voice, and leaned toward her. "*Baruch atah Adonai Eloheinu melech ha'olam, shelo asani isha.*"

Joanna regarded him with contempt as her mind raced with blistering responses, rejecting one after another as unlikely to pierce his complacency.

"If you still thank God daily for not making you a woman," she said finally, "you had better not let your friends Captain Caminha and Frei Jerónimo catch you doing it. And while you're at it, don't forget the rest of that *b'rucha*. The Talmud also bids you thank Adonai for not making you a gentile or a slave."

Not waiting for his reaction, she rose and stalked across the hold to contemplate the pigs, whose honest adherence to their true nature she much preferred to Natan's hypocrisy.

Chapter Twelve: Diego

"Are you a pirate?" Rachel asked.

"Not exactly," Amir said. "Not at all, in fact, though that does not mean we are not bound to take Christian vessels when we come upon them."

He bade his crew step back a pace while we conversed. I could not help hoping that this meeting had improved our fortunes, although Captain Velez and Doña Julieta still waited anxiously to learn their fate. Amir's men busied themselves with relieving *Cecilia's* crew of their weapons and chaining them together for transfer to the galleys. I kept one eye on them and noticed that some of the oarsmen had left their benches to help organize the prisoners and consider the problem of the cracked mast. I concluded they must be free men, not slaves as Christendom believed the Sultan's rowers to be.

"Surely you must let us go!" Rachel said. "I do not plead for myself alone, nor even just for Diego and my betrothed, but kind Captain Velez—the little girls—the poor sailors, who have done nothing to harm you!"

"Raquel," Amir said, "I owe you my freedom, indeed, my life. But I am not the commander here. I will plead with him for the two who rescued me, as honor demands."

"And my betrothed?" Rachel put her arm protectively around Hutia. "Can you not say he helped you too?"

"It would go against my faith to lie to my commander." Amir cast a curious glance as Hutia. "But I will do it, rather than cause you pain."

"Hutia is no enemy of the Turk," Rachel said. "He

is from—"

"Do not tell me!" Amir said. "I would prefer to commit no further lies. For the others, alas, I can do nothing. And this ship is our prize. Although you may be granted your freedom, you will have to come with us."

"Where are you going?" Rachel asked.

"I may not tell you my mission," he said. "But a prize crew will take the caravel to Istanbul, the prisoners with her."

"What will happen to the girls?" she said. "They are only children!"

"The Sultan takes a fifth part of all ventures on land or sea. These two, being maidens, may be sent to Istanbul for his own harem."

"Amir! How can you?" Rachel cried. "You have been a slave yourself!"

"It is not a bad life, Raquel," Amir said. "They will be given every luxury."

"Every luxury but freedom!" Rachel said.

"Does any woman have freedom, even in Christian lands?" he said. "No one will touch them, not even the Sultan until they are older."

"For pity's sake, Amir," I said, "can you not hold them for ransom? Their father is a rich French knight of Avignon. Surely there must be a way."

"I will do what I can," Amir said, "though I may need all my credit with my commander to save the three of you."

"And the chaperone?" Rachel pleaded. "Poor Doña Julieta."

"Oh, very well," he said. "For your sake, Raquel, I will try. We'll take her along in any case to tend the children. The crew won't want them underfoot on the voyage back to Istanbul. That will save her from getting thrown overboard, since she'll not have much value as a slave. Perhaps her master will ransom her along with his daughters."

"And the captain?" I asked, though I knew the answer could not be a welcome one.

Amir shook his head.

"Bound for slavery, I fear. In fact, you may advise him that there might be a way out, if he will take it. Sultan Bayezid is building up his navy. He has need of experienced sailors, especially those who know the coasts of Europe. If he is offered a choice between Islam and slavery, he would do well to embrace Islam."

"If he turns Muslim to save his skin, will they not distrust him afterward?" I asked, thinking of the *conversos* and the Inquisition.

"Not at all," Amir said. "It is not our way. Once a man accepts the Faith, Allah's hand is on him. And who are we to distrust one whom Allah trusts? At any rate, no Muslim may be made a slave."

"I will tell him," I said, "now, if I may."

Amir said a few words to his men in Turkish. Señor Ortega had been right. Rachel, Hutia, and I would do well to learn that language as soon as possible.

"I will talk to my commander," he said. "These sailors will guard you. I have told them to treat you with respect, as you are my guests, not my prisoners. They will escort you to speak with the Spanish captain now."

"I thank you, Amir," I said. "I am deeply grateful."

"So am I," Rachel said, "truly, Amir. But will you not tell us of yourself? Where did you go after leaving us?"

"I went first to Tunis," Amir said, "where my grandfather lives. But for me, Tunisia is not home. Granada is lost, and the Ottoman star is rising. So I made my way to Istanbul. But I must not delay getting my commander's permission to release you into my custody."

"And speak to him about ransoming the girls," Rachel reminded him.

"One more thing," he said. "If I cannot dissuade my commander from making you strip, it may go harder for you. He has fought against Christians, whom he calls uncircumcised dogs."

"It will not trouble me," I said, "because I am

circumcised. I am a Jew, and so is Rachel, whom you call Raquel."

Amir's eyes widened.

"I did not know," he said, "but so much the better. We have many Jews in Istanbul. Sultan Bayezid welcomes them, believing the Spanish king a fool to throw away so many gifted scholars, merchants, physicians, and artisans. You might do worse than to settle there, if, as I surmise, you are seeking a home."

"We must find our family," I said, "before making any decisions about the future. They were in Firenze, but we doubt they are still there."

"Perhaps you would like to come with me," Amir said. "To Jews, I may reveal our mission. We are bound for the Iberian coast, where some Jewish fugitives are still in hiding, waiting to be rescued. Sultan Bayezid is in earnest in wishing to acquire them for his empire."

Rachel's eyes lit up. After all that had happened, she still could not resist an adventure. I sent a quelling glance her way. Hutia, reading her as well as I, pressed his palm into her shoulder as if to suppress her enthusiasm physically.

"We cannot," I said. "We must continue on our quest to find our parents. Besides, are not all the Jews long gone from Spain? It has been three years!"

"Perhaps," Rachel said, "some of the *conversos* have been so ill treated by the Inquisition that they have thought better of their decision to turn Christian. The Christians are not like your Muslims, Amir. No matter how sincerely a Jew may convert, he is still a Jew to them."

"Many of the Spanish Jews," Amir said, "fled only as far as Portugal. Now some of them are seeking a way to leave Iberia altogether. That is my job: to issue my Sultan's invitation and carry them to Istanbul."

"Are they not required to turn Muslim?" Rachel asked.

"Not at all," Amir said. "Under Ottoman rule, those who are not of Islam live in their own communities, conducting their own affairs in peace. They pay taxes, of course. But to us, the Empire's Christians and Jews, like Muslims, are People of the Book, and that must be respected."

"Having once left Spain," I said, "a land that did not want us and still seeks to kill us, we have no wish to return, even on a mission of rescue."

"Very well," Amir said. "I will request permission to put you ashore under cover of night. We are not as far as you may think from France, and our oarsmen are swift. By the way, your companion, Raquel's betrothed—is he circumcised too?"

"It would be better to avoid an inspection," I said. "But we can swear on any oath you like that he is not a Christian."

The Sixth Letter

Firenze, April 1494

My dearest children,

I write this greeting with a heavy heart, knowing it unlikely that either of you will ever see this letter. But as I pray that Adonai still spares you, I must send what news I can give. We leave Firenze with no clear idea of where we will come to rest. We think of you constantly. I am thankful your Papa is not like Abraham. He would never agree to sacrifice his child as the patriarch Isaac did, not even at God's direct command and to secure His blessing for generations! Papa laughs at me when I say this. He says that I cannot expect God to think like mere men and women and that to understand Torah we must sometimes think of the stories in it as parables rather than literal fact. He has little enough to laugh at these days.

Diego's letter of last September, telling us that Admiral Columbus's fleet was off at last for the Indies and Rachel sailing on the *Strega* to Livorno, did not reach us until three weeks ago. Crumpled and stained with dirt and water and what looked like blood, it had passed through many hands. Although its content was so worrisome, nonetheless, I was glad to get it. Needless to say, Papa went at once to Livorno to seek what news of the *Strega* he could get. The *Strega* has made port there two or three times since last fall, but not a single man whom Papa questioned, including sailors who had shipped on her, had seen or heard tell of a lady passenger then or at any other time. Those who knew Captain Olivero personally laughed at the very thought. It seems he is not a man to inspire confidence. Perhaps Diego realized this after sending off the letter and did not put Rachel on the *Strega* after all. But if that is what happened, where is Rachel? Oh, my darlings, I fear you are forever lost to us. Diego may remain in the Indies, for I gather this second voyage of Admiral Columbus is one of settlement as well as exploration. Papa counsels me not to speak my worst imaginings of what may have befallen Rachel, for they serve no purpose but to make me distraught, which distresses Papa and the girls and exacerbates their fear and sadness. They will need all their courage for our own journey.

We have had no further word from Doña Marina. Were Italy not so unsettled, Papa would go to Genoa, where she may have sent later news of you. The bankers there will certainly know more than we do about events throughout Europe that might have affected your plans. But we have been strongly advised not to venture north. Charles's armies are not expected to march out until fall, but already the roads are filled with folk fleeing, as we will. All fear the possibility of being besieged, or worse, having their homes invaded should a siege succeed. Already, Firenze is crammed with terrified Neapolitans and Romans, while Florentines stream out of Firenze in all directions, believing Milan or Venice may be safer. There were once many Jews in Sicily, but Ferdinand and Isabella rule that land, and they were all expelled in 1492, as we were. It is said that some converted, but most sought refuge in Naples. So those poor souls, like us, find themselves on the road a second time.

We taught you children always to seek blessings in adversity. I remind myself of that advice as I see refugee families struggling to transport not only themselves but as many possessions as they can carry. The richest have wagons piled with furniture and household goods, plate and paintings, linens and tapestries. Susanna, who is fascinated by the constant passing parade and often seems to forget that we will be among them soon enough, swears she has seen two sundials and a marble fountain. Fools! They would do better to fill their wagons with food. The French will not carry sufficient provisions for their troops across the Alps. They will have to live off the land and can only devastate it. The blessing in this is that it gives a sort of timetable for the invasion, as Charles would be ill advised to come before the harvest. If he does, there will be famine this winter for invaders and invaded alike, besides the grim prospects for besieged cities.

Lest you think me miraculously become a military strategist, little else is talked of throughout Firenze. Papa and Cousin Chaim and young Akiva, whom I suppose I must start considering a man since he will soon be a rabbi and Elvira's husband, analyze every bit of gossip and speculation in calculating our chances of success in reaching safety. Chaim, who is a skilled carpenter, is building us two wagons, with Akiva as his apprentice. It is a measure of our fears that Akiva does not complain about this use of time that he might otherwise spend studying Torah! We have two sturdy mules, and the men have been taking turns at guarding their shed each night. One reason for us to leave now, rather than wait till summer, is to reduce the chances of their being stolen or taken from us by force. We will carry feed for the mules in the wagons as well as food for ourselves and the bare necessities. Having said goodbye to my most cherished family possessions in Seville, I am not too attached to the contents of our house in Firenze, though I am sad to think of the pleasure and hope with which the girls and I chose every cup and curtain. I take only our *mezuzah*, which I would nail to the doorway of hell, should such a place exist and fortune take me there.

Believe me, my darlings, if I thought there were still a chance of either of you seeking us in Firenze, wild horses could not make me leave! Ha'shem guard you, wherever you are. And if by some miracle one of you reads this letter, do not seek us in

Christendom. The Christians will never let us rest nor cease to blame us for every ill that befalls them. We will try to make our way to Ottoman lands. Cartography is considered an art here in Italy, and Papa and Chaim have scoured the city for maps showing the route we must travel, as well as talking to merchants, drovers, and caravan guards: in short, to anyone who might help us. We believe we will be safer on the east coast, in Ancona or perhaps Bari, until we can leave Italy altogether. Of course, we will not admit we are Jews while we are on the road. We have still to persuade Akiva to bow to expediency so far as to cut his *payot* and hang a cross around his neck. He is so proud of his status as a budding rabbi! But if Papa and Chaim cannot persuade him, his mother will. Miriam does not mince words, and she must get it through his thick head that pride must bow to matters of life and death. I am trying to get Elvira to understand that the reason Papa and I almost always agree is that his intelligent, sensible opinions are truly in accord with mine, not because a wife should defer to her husband as invariably the wiser!

Once we reach the coast, Ha'shem be our guide, we will cross the Adriatic Sea to Albania, which is ruled by the Sultan, as are the lands beyond it, Macedonia and Bulgaria. Should we get so far, we will seek out any Jews in those places and form our own opinion of how they fare. Our dream is to find a Jewish community in which we can openly live as exactly who we are. It is hard to believe that we will find one even in Istanbul, where this Sultan Bayezid who is said to respect the skills of Jews resides. But we must try!

I will leave this letter with the Medici bankers and send a copy by a trustworthy courier to Marina's bank in Genoa, as the second most likely place for you to look for it. Both Genoa and Firenze might be in French hands in a few months, but surely Charles needs bankers as much as ever Ferdinand and Isabella did. If the cities are not sacked, even if the banking families are ousted, with luck, papers in their care will not be destroyed. May the blessings of Ha'shem be with you always, my darlings. You are ever in my heart and Papa's too, whatever may befall you.

All my love, Mama

Chapter Thirteen: Joanna

As the weeks wore on, three things kept Joanna from despair. One was the knowledge that Simon and the little ones needed her. It was her duty to keep them alive. She never doubted that their lives were worth preserving. Much as she despised Natan, perhaps he had the right of it in believing that a door of opportunity might crack open for a hardworking and sufficiently quick-witted Jewish slave, if he were a boy. Another was her growing ability to absent herself completely from the proceedings when Imaculada sold her body or Belmiro gambled it away. Her mind learned to wander the gardens of the Alhambra at these times in a freedom made sweeter by her mother's presence. The price she paid for these reunions was the aching sense of loss when she came back to herself.

Besides these saving graces, she realized after a while that, the price of her body having been settled before the transaction itself, and the men having no further interest in her once they had spent themselves, no one bothered to look for her or summon her back to the hold for some time afterward. This left her free to creep forward to a spot well before the foremast. Huddled with her arms around her knees and a scrap of sailcloth wrapped around her to shield her from a casual glance, she sat for hours watching the ship's prow cleave the sea, content to feel spray stinging her face and taste salt upon her lips. At these times, contrary to her periods of dissociation with the men, she felt more fully present than she had since her mother's death. Both future and memory fell away, leaving her in a timeless, unselfconscious moment of serenity.

No one on board told the children how long the voyage would last or spoke of their fate on the island. Joanna could measure the passing of the days and weeks only by the phases of the moon, which ripened like a great cheese every month, then waned and vanished into darkness, showing a sliver of pale fingernail before it began to round out into a golden ball again. She knew the air was getting warmer, and so were the waters of Ocean. It rained seldom. This meant fresh water was scarce, but Joanna, who felt herself less a prisoner when she could see unbounded sky, was meanly glad that not only the captives but their oppressors too went thirsty.

In the meantime, she cherished every wonder that she saw. Sometimes it was a school of flying fish: hundreds of long, slim forms, in color a dark blue gray shading into silver, that leaped from the water to sail through the air on frilled wings like a bird's. They might glide half the length of the ship, then land on the surface of the water and skid along it, raising a wake of spray like a flock of ducks before they soared into the air again.

Occasionally, the whole school lifted itself high enough to land upon the deck, where all at liberty to do so would leap upon them with knives and clubs at the ready, desperate for fresh food. Joanna could manage to beat or stamp three or four fish into submission and stow them among the rags that remained of her one dress without drawing attention to herself. The first time, it took her several hours to find a tool for scaling them, a sharp shell that she secreted away for further use. Then she had to persuade the boys to eat the fish raw, as she had no means of cooking them. They needed nourishment, having grown wan and lethargic with little activity and even less food. She thought of keeping none for herself. But if she starved to death, the boys would have no protector. Besides, Simon, quick to guess her intent, forestalled her by pointing out that in order to persuade the little ones to eat raw fish, she must show them she did so herself.

Even more marvelous than the flying fish were the families of sleek gray dolphins. They too could lift themselves from the water, but rather than leaping blindly to their own destruction, they leaped and dove in unison at a safe distance from the ship, smiling as if they knew exactly what they were doing. Once, she spied a whale, a vast creature that struck awe into her heart as it rolled lazily from one gray side to the other, waving a black and white fin like a flattened pillar in salute. The leviathan swam alongside the ship for several miles, prudently twisting and diving to avoid the sailors' spears, but close enough that Joanna could hear it breathe and see how it blew a spout of water from a hole on top of its head like an animated fountain. Finally, with a derisive flip of its fin at the frustrated sailors, it arched its back in a dive straight downward, its broad tail rising from the surface like a giant's fan, and plummeted toward the depths, to be seen no more.

Her only other refuge was rage. Most of the time, it burned within her whether she was tossing to and fro on the now filthy straw waiting for the brief release of sleep, shoveling pig muck, gulping down the prisoners' scant daily supply of water, or singing lullabies to Shmuel and Benjamin. Her mind seethed with plans for escape. On the ship, she could do nothing. She must be patient. She might have to wait until the boys were bigger and stronger. She would not leave them behind! On an island, surely there would be places to hide, perhaps even a way to reach the mainland. If sugar grew there, so must fruits and other foods. The island must have concealing forests like those she could see when the ship passed close to the shore. Perhaps one of the black slaves everyone talked about would help her. Surely they must long for freedom as she did.

One night, when the moon was new and the dark

sky flooded with stars, she saw a school of luminescent fish, glowing pale green and ghostly in the inky depths. The circumstances were not auspicious: the soldier Duarte had bent her over the rail and was doing his business at her back, while remarking in a conversational tone that they had entered the Gulf of Guinea and would reach the island soon.

"There's no saying what's to become of you once we get there, girl," he said, "but you've made the voyage less tedious, and that's a fact." He pushed himself upright and slapped her on the rump. "You won't get easy work like this, I wager. They'll set you to laboring in the cane fields, and you'll miss your time aboard the ship."

Fuming, Joanna ground her teeth, determined not to turn or answer. I will remember only the beauty of the fish like a school of green lanterns, she thought. I will regret only that I did not kill you the first time you forced yourself on me. Not only this great ape but every one of them, soldier or sailor, gentleman or *degradado*, She would kill in a heartbeat without a second of remorse. Perhaps she could swim to the mainland. Such fish as these might light her way to freedom. An island was surrounded by water. It might even have rivers. I will survive, she thought. I will gather skills and weapons. I will bide my time.

Three days later, they arrived off São Tomé. After the usual splashing disposal of the dead, the children in the hold were herded up onto the deck, roped together so they could be easily controlled. Of more than four hundred children who had been crammed into the carrack's hold, less than one hundred remained. The caravels, of shallower draft, sailed closer to the shore. The second carrack appeared over the horizon as they peered at an island that seemed devoid of human life. There was nothing to see but a rim of beach, not scalloped into bays but smoothly rounded like the edge of a plate, backed by a tangle of impenetrable dark green forest. The land rose to a single peak far in the distance, with odd-looking formations, more like upthrust fingers than mountains, popping up through the canopy of trees. After an interminable wait, as the day grew hotter and more humid, sailors from the other ships rowed the captains and other important folk to Captain Caminha's flagship to consult with him.

Frei Jerónimo summoned the children to spend the time "usefully," as he declared, in repeating the catechism. Joanna sat well back, hoping to escape notice. The priests, ship's captains, and commanders of the soldiers conferring with Caminha passed to and fro behind her, so close that if she had dared stretch out an arm or leg, she could have tripped one of them. Ears peeled to gather what information she could, she caught tantalizing snatches. The *degradados*, Belmiro and Imaculada included, hung about the edges like spectators at a parade, subdued for once. Joanna suspected that they too were fearful about their future.

The interminable catechism ended at last. When the great ones had gone back to their own ships, the whole fleet raised anchor. The ships sailed eastward along São Tomé's northern coast, with the island on their right. The children were sent below but given more than their usual portion of stale water and weevily biscuit. However miserable life on shore might be, there would at least be fresh food.

"They spoke of a settlement called Ponta Figa," Joanna told Simon. "That is our destination."

"Fig Point!" Simon exclaimed. "Will we have figs to eat?"

"I would not count on it," she said. "But even the great ones do not know what we will find. There has been little news from the island in Lisbon for the past year or two. At least there will be plenty of water, as many rivers flow from the interior."

"How fare the children on the other ships?" Simon asked.

"I heard nothing of them," Joanna said.

"I did." Natan, overhearing this as he passed by,

squatted down beside them. Having ingratiated himself with Frei Jerónimo by serving as his acolyte, he was wearing a far better garment than the children's rags, a thick black woolen robe too big for him that swirled around his wrists and ankles and was clearly hot enough to make him red-faced and sweaty. "Of the two thousand who boarded with us, less than half remain. They expect the island fevers to kill off many more. There will be other dangers too. They speak of giant man-eating lizards, crocodiles, that live in the swamp, as well as snakes and vermin."

"You will be safe enough," Joanna said with contempt, "in the arms of the Church."

"I intend to be," Natan said calmly. "You could do worse than follow my example. Frei Jerónimo says those who whored on the ship may be saved if they repent."

"It is you who whore," Simon burst out indignantly, "hiding behind the priest's skirts. Do you think that Adonai cannot see you?"

"Hush, Simon," Joanna said, putting a hand on his arm. "We will not convince him, nor he us."

A shout from aloft, followed by excited cries and a general rushing to the starboard rail, interrupted their conversation before it could become any more acrimonious. The sailors were hauling in the sails and preparing to drop anchor, although the ship was still far out. The sailors went about their work grumbling about having to row the whole ship's complement to shore, although the ships risked running aground on hidden shoals if they did not. Many of the *degradados* climbed the rigging for a better look, in spite of the shouts of the sailors and soldiers trying to restrain them. They were barely close enough to the beach to see a huddle of people on the shore, a jumble of canvas tents and wooden huts behind them.

"There are not very many of them," Simon said.

A sailor with a coil of rope over his shoulder spat as he passed by.

"If this is Ponta Figa," he said, "the new governor is welcome to it."

Chapter Fourteen: Diego

Amir brought us into Toulon at night in the ship's boat. His oarsmen, skilled at sneaking into a hostile harbor from past forays along the coast, muffled the oars by wrapping them in rags to give us as silent a passage as if we had been under sail. His commander, in the end, had not demanded that I strip but been satisfied with my willingness to do so and the gold we had providently added to our purses in anticipation of being boarded. So our hidden gold and papers remained intact. When we parted, Amir insisted on giving me his direction in Istanbul.

"I thank you, my friend," I said, embracing him. "We are in your debt."

"No, the score is even," Amir said, embracing Hutia in turn and looking at Rachel as if he wished to hug her too. "Your family might fare worse than in Istanbul. Consider it if you find them not settled elsewhere."

I did not voice the thought that we might not find them at all, especially if they had not found a safe haven somewhere already.

Rachel, reading my mind, said, "We will find them!" with a bracing look and a lift of the chin that told me not to dare lose heart.

We found a night's lodging close to the docks in a tavern whose proprietor asked no questions. In the morning, we found that barely a horse remained in Toulon. All had been commandeered for Charles's expedition, except for those whose owners would have knifed us sooner than part with them and a few too broken down to make it to the next town. In the end, we set out along the coast on foot. We aroused no particular notice on the road or in the towns and villages along the way. At Nice or Nizza, a city with a thriving port, as Italian as it was French, we persuaded a fellow with a fishing boat to take us on to Genoa.

We arrived in the city that called itself *la Superba* on the sixth of July. It had been cool on the water, but it was a sizzling day on shore, ever hotter as we walked farther from the docks. It was too late to make inquiries at the Bank of St. George, but those we asked for its direction were uniformly incredulous that anyone in Genoa, even the newly arrived, could possibly not know. The Palazzo San Giorgio had been the city's crowning architectural glory for more than two hundred years, and the Genoese made little distinction between the bank's governors and the city's rulers, who were more or less one and the same. Having been raised in Spain's absolute monarchy, I still had difficulty comprehending the Italian cities' patchwork of republics, oligarchies led by doges like those of Genoa and Venice, duchies, and kingdoms.

"It is simple, Diego," Hutia said. "Each is a great village with its own *cacique* and council of *nitaino*. What they call themselves does not matter, for everyone knows who they are."

"That would be well enough," I retorted, "if each European *cacique* were content to stay in his own village, apart from the occasional raid on the village next door. You cannot tell me that the Taino have a word for 'empire,' as I know they have none for 'war.'"

"Please do not squabble," Rachel said. "I am tired and very hungry, and we must be alert in the morning when we present ourselves at the bank."

"Diego and I are but playing *batey* with words," Hutia said, "as Europeans do."

Lodging was hard to find, as Genoa was teeming with refugees from every town in the path of the French army, which had evidently left Naples in

May. King Charles had left a viceroy there in his stead, along with a substantial garrison, and set off north with his booty. According to a widespread rumor, he had borne off not only enough furnishings and decorative items to trick out every hall and chamber at Amboise, his vast château on the Loire, which it had long been his passion to rebuild, but three Italian architects, willy-nilly, to do the job to his liking. Now he was demanding passage through Italy back to France, which Venice and its allies were not inclined to grant him without a fight. We heard again about the slaughter at Mordano the year before and that even cities that had welcomed him, including Firenze, had come to regret it. The French soldiers, quartered on the citizenry, had eaten them out of house and home and pillaged the churches and palazzos so thoroughly that it would take them a decade to recover. The Genoese, who had diplomacy and luck to thank for having been spared a French visit on the army's march south, were flocking to their own churches to pray that their stout walls and the doge's militia would protect them if it came their way. But rumor had Charles and his troops not marching along the coast, but northeast toward Bologna and Parma, in search of provisions for thousands of hungry soldiers, fodder for their mounts, and perhaps a wider choice of routes out of Italy, whether or not they engaged the Holy League in battle.

Eventually, our gold bought us a cupboard in the stables of an inn, big enough for the three of us to stretch out, wrapped in our cloaks, on straw that smelled only faintly of manure.

"It be where we keep the pitchforks," the boy told off to lead us to it said, "but they all be taken up to use against the soldiers if the Frenchies come."

Not wanting to subject Rachel to the rough company in the taproom, I left her and Hutia to dine on bread that seemed to be composed partly of straw like that we were to lie on, cheese that smelled marginally worse than our dung-scented chamber, and sour wine. I elbowed my way through the crowd in the tavern, listening to every conversation I could catch. But I learned nothing to the point, except that those in the army's path were suffering from a new pox they were calling "the French disease," evidently spread by soldiers and whores to the respectable via the inevitable rapes of warfare and the hasty liaisons that occurred when soldiers were quartered in the homes of citizens. I was astounded to hear that some believed the pestilence had been brought by Admiral Columbus's sailors from the Indies, who had certainly visited as many whores as their Taino gold could buy on their return. But more attributed the outbreak and its rapid spread to the Jews, who had been driven from Naples in punishment. And that, though certainly untrue—most whores refused to service Jews, nor did Jewish girls give themselves to Christian soldiers—was nothing new.

In the morning, we woke before dawn, so we could use the horse trough for our ablutions without contesting it with either our fellow lodgers or the horses. For breakfast, we shared two wrinkled apples, in the barrel since '94 or even '93, for which I had paid as much as if they were golden apples of the Hesperides. When I said so, Rachel pointed out that Hesperides apples were almost certainly oranges. She had managed to untangle her hair with a comb left lying in a corner under the straw, no doubt last used on a horse's mane. Her cheeks were flushed, and she had managed to make a decent toilette, considering how far the gown she wore had traveled in her pack.

"I am glad to see you in good spirits," I said.

Her eyes sparkled.

"Today is the first time since we left Spain that we may hope to hear some real news of Mama and Papa!"

"Do not get your hopes too high," I warned her. "Your disappointment if they can tell us nothing at the bank will be the worse."

"On the contrary," Rachel said, "I will have the joy

of hoping for as long as I can and will not regret it if the bankers have no news for us."

Once we entered the imposing portal of the Palazzo San Giorgio, giving my name and those of Admiral Columbus and Doña Marina as references, Rachel stopped bouncing and began to look as nervous as I felt. She took my hand, hers warm and damp, as we sat on a bench in a cool antechamber paved in tile and pillared in marble awaiting a summons from whatever personage would deign to speak with us. Hutia sat crosslegged on the floor in his favorite position, running his hand over the tile as if marveling at how cool it felt, even though the morning was heating up to another scorching day. We had waited about an hour when a young Genoese with dark, curly hair and a harried expression came to lead us to an interview with one Signore Boccanegra, whom he seemed to hold in awe.

Signore Boccanegra, apparently of high enough rank to be friendly with whomever he chose, greeted us with more warmth than I had expected, shaking my hand and bowing courteously to Rachel. He cast a sharp glance at Hutia, who still insisted on presenting himself in public as a servant of deferent bearing, though both Rachel and I protested that there was no need and no point in doing so, since no one knew us or paid any attention to us.

"Let them ignore me," Hutia said each time we had this conversation. "It is best."

Everyone we had encountered thus far had done so. But Signore Boccanegra was cleverer than most.

"Andrea Boccanegra," he said, smiling warmly. "You, Signor Mendoza, must be one of our Genoese hero Colombo's sailors from the Indies. And this, no doubt, is one of the inhabitants of these marvelous isles. And the lady? Your sister? Signorina, your servant." He bowed again, this time with more of a flourish. "If we were not in the midst of chaos at the moment—no doubt you have heard the news!—I would ask you to tell me of your adventures. But alas, our tasks multiply with every fresh word that reaches the bank."

Rachel's eyes began to sparkle again, arousing a sympathetic twinkle in the Signore's. Next time she complained about being forced to resume being a lady, I must remind her of this moment, which she could not deny she was enjoying.

"You are observant, Signore," I said, before she could use up his no doubt precious time with flirting. "There is nothing we would enjoy more, but we are grateful for even this brief time, and we will not waste it. We seek news of our family. My father is the brother of Doña Marina Mendes y Torres. He and my mother and our two sisters have been living in Firenze, but we do not know if they are still there. Indeed, from what we have heard of the French occupation, we hope they are not, although it could have been much worse."

"So it could," Boccanegra said. "We have been exceptionally lucky so far here in Genoa. My great-great-grandfather was the first doge, you know, and a fine old rascal he was, by all reports. And now the Florentines have chased the Medici out and got themselves a republic at long last. The Medici would have done better to make himself doge and allow others to share his rule, as we do—Lorenzo, not Piero, who was always going to be a weakling. I wonder why families must always go up or down. Sons must either outstrip their fathers, like our great Columbus, or disappoint them, like Piero the Unfortunate and me. No, no, do not make polite noises, there is no need. I will never be doge, and I thank God for it. Let me send for someone who can look among the records and see what we can find of relevance to your quest."

"I cannot thank you enough, sir," I said. "Believe me, I can have no greater aspiration than to be exactly like my father. If only I can find him!"

"You are a lucky son, then, and he a lucky father," Boccanegra said. "Beppo, take this note to young Adorno and tell him to hop to it."

Beppo took the scribbled note. Though dressed like a banker in a highnecked brown doublet with a thin rim of fur around the collar, black hose, and a brown hat with complicated folds, he looked like any apprentice in his harried air and tendency to bob and scurry. He was nearly through the door when Boccanegra called after him, "And get someone to send in wine and pastries. And fruit as well—my guests and I are starving!"

Rachel and I had hardly finished exclaiming how grateful we were when an older servant brought in a tray heaped with food. Beppo had his master's measure to the extent that the tray held four glasses, making it clear that Hutia was considered one of the guests. Hutia expressed his own thanks for this courtesy. His Italian was coming on. Boccanegra's eager questions showed more sensitivity to how different a faraway land's culture and customs might be from his own than we had yet encountered since our return. Hutia responded willingly, but little time had passed before Beppo came running in, panting in his haste and fairly sliding across the floor.

"Signore! Signore!"

"Back so fast, Beppo? What did Adorno find? Is he coming himself to speak to my guests? They are anxiously awaiting the result of his research."

"News!" Beppo spoke on a sobbing breath and drew air into his lungs. "Signor Adorno is looking—says—will come presently. But there is news!"

We all leaped to our feet, agog but helpless until Beppo could compose himself enough to speak.

"Out with it, man!" Boccanegra said. "What has happened?"

"There's been a bloody great battle, sir!" Beppo's training in a banker's phlegmatic demeanor had deserted him. He was all excited boy. "At Fornovo—a village outside Parma—not a hundred miles from here." He drew several deep breaths and scrubbed at his sweating face with trembling hands.

"Don't stop now, boy!" Boccanegra exclaimed. "Go on! Who won?"

"No one knows, sir," Beppo said. "It was a bloodbath on both sides. The League is claiming the victory, and so are the French."

Chapter Fifteen: Joanna

Ҭһҽ ѕҽttlҽrѕ ѕtѳѳð on the beach, looking around them with dazed expressions. It had been a long day, with the *degradado* men pressed into service as rowers. The ship's boats shuttled back and forth, crammed to overflowing on each inbound passage. The folk on the beach who had gathered to welcome them numbered no more than two hundred. They assured an incredulous Captain Caminha, whom all must now call Governor, that they comprised the whole population of São Tomé. The huddle of tattered tents and lopsided huts, thatched with rotting fronds of palm, that they had seen when the ships dropped anchor was the settlement itself. The news spread like wildfire through the crowd of disembarkees.

"But where is the town?" Felicidade cried, her voice high and trembling. "Where are the shops?"

"Have you only now realized that Lisbon is dead to you?" Imaculada sniffed. "This is no worse than I expected."

For once, Joanna agreed with her.

"They said there would be blacks to do the work," Mateus said. "I have bleeding blisters from pulling on those cursed oars all day."

"Stop whining and shut up," Belmiro said. "If they have not brought in any Africans yet, the Governor will do it soon enough. Do you think the King would leave a rich trade like slaving to chance? Caminha is just the man to get it going, and I intend to get in good with him. Blacks and sugar—like so many sacks of gold for the taking, they'll be, if not now, then soon enough."

New canvas shelters, their folds stiff and smelling of tar, had been hauled to shore in the boats and piled on the beach. The soldiers now directed the newcomers to organize themselves into groups and select a leader as a spokesman for each group. This leader would report progress to the governor, carry instructions back to the others, and take responsibility for the whole group's workload. Belmiro and Mateus drew together, Belmiro assuming the leadership without discussion.

"We'll have to let a few of the others join us," Belmiro said, "or we'll be slaving all day and night ourselves. We need strong arms and backs."

"And stupid heads and weak wills," Imaculada said. "I've no intention of allowing anyone, man or woman, to interfere with my decisions. You, girl, get those brats together and drag those shelters over to the left of the huts, by that stand of palms. Move it!"

The couple cut a small knot of born followers out of the herd as skillfully as any shepherd. Reluctantly, Joanna was impressed. By nightfall, the shelters had been erected, a fire built, and the company's first freshly cooked meal in two months assembled. Dinner consisted of fish speared in the shallows, bananas from the broad-leaved plants that grew at the edge of the forest, and coconuts gathered from the ground beneath the tall palms on which they grew. Each group had been issued several knives, large and small, broad and narrow, smooth and saw-toothed, as well as a sickle and an axe. Belmiro kept these implements close at hand, allowing the men to use them under his supervision to cut stakes for the shelters, shape short wooden spears for fishing, and hack open the coconuts.

As followers, Imaculada selected women like herself, who apparently harbored no maternal feelings toward their charges. Joanna took charge of the augmented group of children, none older than seven, drying their tears of shock at this further change in their condition and making sure their bellies were full before they slept.

"In the morning," Belmiro announced, "as many of the brats as can will climb those trees and throw down more coconuts. Those who refuse don't have to share our food."

Joanna dared not risk asking what would happen if the children found they could not climb.

"Don't worry," Simon whispered. "I bet you we can shinny up it easily enough. We'll get a good view, and we'll be able to get coconuts any time we want."

If Joanna hoped to avoid attention, at least till morning, she was unsuccessful. When the fire had died to embers, the children's eyes drooping in sleep, and the adults either exhausted and already snoring or withdrawn into the shadows to couple in privacy, Imaculada stalked over to her.

"Now we're here," she said without preamble, "you'll have to work. Soon you'll have no time for whoring. But right now we need information. Go to that Pero, the Governor's cousin. He'll be near that fancy tent Caminha's got himself, if not inside it. Those like him who've got no families won't be pleased that that sorry lot that met us didn't have no slave girls waiting for them. He'll be glad enough to see you, and if you play him right, he'll talk. And don't bother saying you won't do it. Ship or solid ground, you're not the Queen of Sheba. You'll do as I say."

Joanna's wrath, tightly bottled for so long, blazed up. She drew a breath to spit out her true feelings, regardless of consequences. Before she could speak, Imaculada showed her the knife.

"I'll cut you if you answer back, so don't. I'm mistress here, and don't you forget it. Scoot. I need my beauty sleep now. You can report to me and Belmiro in the morning. And if you've got no news, the brats will get no breakfast."

Shaking with rage and fear, Joanna turned her back on the *degradada*. As slowly as she dared, she made her way past the newcomers' shelters. Once out of Imaculada's sight, she veered toward the beach and walked into the softly purling waves. The warm salt water caressed her feet and loosened aching muscles. She could see the governor's tent, illuminated by lanterns within and torches without, with soldiers standing guard. When she had stayed as long as she dared, she turned reluctantly toward the shore. She dreaded the humiliation of having to ask for Caminha's cousin and deal with the guards, who would know why she had come. Turning her back on the sea and the ships riding at anchor some distance out, she began trudging toward the lights, her feet slipping in the soft sand.

A man came down toward the water, unfastening his points as he walked. He came to a halt some distance ahead of her and pissed copiously on the sand. Creeping closer, Joanna saw with mixed emotions that it was the man she sought. Better to get it over with here, where no one could see.

"Sir," she said timidly, despising herself. "Dom Pero."

"Who's that?" he snapped. Pulling the folds of his clothing together, he whirled to face her, hand flying to the hilt of the dagger at his waist.

"It's me. Joanna." She wasn't sure he knew her name, but he had taken her often enough to recognize her.

Hand dropping from his dagger, he crossed the space between them in a single bound. He gripped her shoulders hard enough to bruise them. Then he grinned and took her by the chin, lifting her face toward his.

"Well, well. Did your mistress send you, girl? Has she not yet realized that coin will get her nothing in this place? Not unless she's rich enough to invest in a slave when those ships depart for the Guinea Coast. Or can you simply not get enough of me? No matter, I'm an obliging man. I'll take what's offered. Down on your knees, now."

Now his hand cupped the crown of her head, pushing down hard.

Die, you bastard, die now, she thought. If hate alone could kill, you'd be dead already.

It was over quickly. He uttered a shout of triumph and released her. She turned away to hide her face and take a moment to master herself. Mindful of Imaculada's threat to starve the children if she got no information, she could not simply leave. She stood, head hanging, until he grabbed at her hand and forced her to turn toward him.

"Not ready to leave yet, missy? You're a lusty girl. You're right, we've only just begun." He dropped to the sand and patted the ground beside him. "Come! Sit here and wait for me. Put your hand just so—that's right—and it won't be long."

"Sir, can we not sit and talk a while first?" She flushed with embarrassment. But he did not protest when she lifted her hand and placed it in her own lap. "What think you of this new land? Is it what you expected, sir?"

"Like hell it is!" He stared out to sea, his arms around his knees. "I begin to think this venture was a mistake. It's all very well for Alvaro. By the king's decree, he owns the lot of it. The last governor was an incompetent. No slaves brought in yet! No land cleared! No sugar planted! And the settlement placed where there is no harbor, when ships must come and go constantly for the slave trade to flourish. Alvaro swears he'll move it."

"What happened to the last governor, sir?" she ventured.

"Dead! Dead of fevers, and most of the colony with him, so there's no one to be held accountable, just one big mess to straighten out and not enough hands to do it. We'll have to crack the whip upon the *degradados*, that's for sure. And the sooner we get the first lot of Africans in, the better. Maybe they'll stand the season better than the whites, being used to this damned climate."

"Season, sir? It is very hot."

He gave a crack of laughter.

"The Ponta Figans tell us this is the hot season and that the island has but two seasons: hot and hotter. You'd better weave yourself a hat before the hotter season comes. Well, there's nothing to be done but make the best of it. It'll be a long time till a ship returns to Portugal. First they're bound to the Congo to round up the blacks, then back here, then to Elmina, the big fort on the coast that's the trade's clearing house. They'll sell off those we don't need and collect the money, our share as well as what Alvaro must send to the king. Alvaro has promised that should any ill befall him, I'll inherit the lot, provided the king approves. Seize the moment, girl, that's my philosophy."

Without ceremony, he tipped her onto her back and rolled onto her.

Chapter Sixteen: Diego

Signore Boccanegra advised us to do nothing until we had better news of the battle and its aftermath. In the meantime, the banker offered us the hospitality of his own palazzo. He bade the apprentice Beppo run to inform his wife, so the household could prepare for our arrival, while we refreshed ourselves and perused San Giorgio's excellent maps of the region and the lands beyond. Whichever route we chose, we were likely to find soldiers on it, and therefore trouble.

Signore Boccanegra withdrew to the other end of the room to speak with a colleague. We were still studying the maps when the two men crossed the room and came toward us. Signore Boccanegra took the other's arm and drew him forward.

"This is Signor Adorno," he said. "I must go about my duties, which will not wait, but Signor Adorno is at your disposal. Please do not hesitate to make your needs known. And young Beppo, when he returns, will be your messenger and porter while you remain in Genoa."

Signor Adorno bowed as I hastened to express our thanks and gratitude.

"If it is not too much of an imposition," Rachel said, with a dazzling smile, "may we have some kind of paper, along with quills and ink? My brother and I are both fair scribes, and if we might copy portions of these wonderful maps, having them would greatly increase our chances of success."

"Rachel!" I blurted. "Paper is expensive! Sir, I apologize for my sister's boldness."

Signore Boccanegra laughed.

"The Banco di San Giorgio is rich," he said. "We can easily spare a sheet or two of paper for the niece and nephew of a valued client. Giuseppe, see to it."

Signor Adorno bowed again. He had not taken his eyes off Rachel since she smiled. Hutia had also noticed, for he squared his shoulders and moved a little closer to her. He said nothing, but his eyes were watchful.

That evening, we dined sumptuously on soup made flavorful with herbs, a roast sirloin of beef basted with rosewater and the juice of oranges and dusted with sugar, a salad of leafy greens tossed with the vegetables of the season and bits of beef liver and kidney, an enormous fish that I did not recognize, fried whole, and cheeses, also sprinkled with sugar, which Rachel and I politely declined. The Palazzo Boccanegra was filled with marble, tapestries, and fine paintings, but Signora Boccanegra was a homely soul who hugged Rachel when she greeted us and exclaimed throughout the meal about our long journey and how hungry we must be. When Rachel inquired about the recipes for the soup and the sirloin, the lady herself whisked her off to the kitchens to be introduced to the chef and given a brief lesson in Italian cookery.

"I doubt we will have an occasion to roast a cow in the near future," I remarked to Hutia, "or make a soup that consists of more than an onion and a couple of turnips boiled over a fire in the woods."

"If thinking she might gives Rachel one evening free from care," Hutia said, "I am satisfied."

I looked at my friend and shook my head.

"You really are in love with her," I marveled.

Hutia laughed.

"Does it only now occur to you?" he asked. "I marvel at your blindness to her virtues."

"I know she has many virtues," I said, "but she is still my little sister, the snot-nosed brat who tagged along everywhere after her elders and was given to falling out of trees and leaving the door of the chicken coop unlatched."

"For which no doubt she was roundly scolded," Hutia said. "Today, she not only remembers to latch the coop but can catch a chicken on the run and wring its neck, a skill we may need. I doubt we will be offered abundant dinners like tonight's on the road. And the ability to climb a tree, which, as you failed to mention, must precede falling out of it, may well save her life some day."

On the third day of our stay in Genoa, Signore Boccanegra came to us with a smile of satisfaction on his face.

"I have news for you," he said.

"Good news?" Rachel asked.

With an avuncular pat on the shoulder, he told her, "The aftermath of a battle is never good news, I fear. But someone who knows far more than I do has returned to Genoa. I believe he can offer enough information to make it possible to continue your journey."

"Is he a banker too?" she asked, not at all abashed.

"No," he said. "He is a trader and a sutler to armies. His name is Niccolo Pesaro, a Jew of Venice and an old friend. If you will accompany me to the bank, I will bid Beppo escort you to his home, which is also his place of business."

It was the first time in years that either of us had heard any man named openly as a Jew without vituperation and denunciation immediately following. Rachel and I were struck speechless, leaving it to Hutia to express our thanks and interest in meeting Signor Pesaro as soon as possible. Indeed, once we reached the bank and Beppo was summoned, Rachel took the boy's arm and set a brisk pace through the streets to the trader's dwelling.

The gentleman greeted us warmly, whether out of regard for Signore Boccanegra or because, from our faces and our turn of speech, he guessed that we too were Jewish. His home was spacious, save that the rooms through which he led us were crammed to the ceilings with an astonishing assortment of objects, from full suits of armor and helmets stained with blood to tottering piles of books, many singed about the edges as if snatched from a fire. I saw wooden chests, also marked by fire, heaped with jewelry and household plate, enough clay jugs and barrels of wine and spirits to stock a tavern, and stacks of ladies' gowns, some fine enough for a princess with skirts of silk or velvet, sleeves dripping with lace, and bodices sewn with pearls or heavily embroidered in gold or silver thread. Atop a giant bell that might have come from a church tower perched a spotted cat as big as a child, stuffed in a realistic pose with back arched and predator's teeth bared in a snarl. I thought it might be a leopard, of which I had seen pictures.

"Forgive the mess," Signor Pesaro said, sweeping a tangle of tapestries and velvet hangings off a padded bench and gesturing for us to sit. "This is my stock in trade, which in times like these I have barely time to sort through and dispose of before more comes in. My palazzo in Venice is five times the size of this, but at the moment, Genoa is ideally placed for commerce such as mine."

"Signore Boccanegra said you were a sutler?" Rachel said on a note of inquiry.

"That is how I started out," he said. "Now, how can I help you?" He cocked his head and raised one eyebrow, his sharp eyes appraising us.

"We come from Seville," I said. "That is, it was once our home. Our parents settled in Firenze some time in 1492 or 1493, but we believe they must have left there. Our mission is to find them, along with our older sisters. That is why we have come to ask your help."

"I will aid you if I can," Pesaro said, "but I must caution you against undue optimism. Many have died since leaving Spain, and I must tell you that young women fare badly on the road."

"I will not travel as a young woman," Rachel said, eyeing a pile of tattered doublets flung over the back of an ornately carved chair. "Nor will I travel unarmed. I have weapons, and I know how to use them."

"I gather that you have traveled far since leaving Seville," Signor Pesaro said.

"That is true," I said. "I joined Admiral Columbus's expedition to the Indies in 1492 and have spent the past two years there as well, as has my sister."

Pesaro's eyes gleamed with interest.

"I would like to hear more of that at a time when you are not so pressed," he said.

"And we of how the Jews have fared in Italy during our absence," I said.

"That is a long and tragic tale," he said. "My friend Don Isaac Abravanel, our most distinguished scholar and champion, has lost several fortunes to the cupidity of kings. Most recently, he fled to Venice after his home in Naples was pillaged and his library destroyed."

"I know of Don Isaac as a great scholar," I said. "My father corresponded with him in happier times."

"The French soldiers burned books?" Rachel's lips tightened. As Amir had said, we were People of the Book. We had been brought up to revere books and treat them with great respect.

"So the Neapolitans would have us think. But I rescued these." Pesaro nodded at one towering pile. "And I can tell you that the Jewish quarter of Naples was attacked and looted before ever the French army marched into the city."

Rachel broke the ensuing silence.

"I am not exactly sure what a sutler is."

"Purveyors to the army," Pesaro said, "without whom armies and their train of camp followers could not survive. Most deal mainly in provisions, buying up supplies of meat, grain, and beer as well as cheese, onions, and strong drink and transporting them to where they can be sold at a profit."

"I see," Rachel said. "They buy up these staples in regions that are out of the line of march and bring them to the armies."

"Exactly," Signor Pesaro said. "I proved apt at anticipating events. Thus I could obtain my wares before prices were driven up too high. But there are many sutlers, and armies have rules concerning them. So I diversified. No one can prevent soldiers from looting. Indeed, allowing the sack of cities is kings' and commanders' favorite way of paying their troops. But how is an army to advance or retreat, burdened by such quantities of booty as you see here?" He waved an arm, the gesture encompassing the contents of the room. "Soldiers want cash, and I supply it. In any city that has been spared attack or occupation, as Genoa has in this war, I can find buyers for these orphaned luxuries."

Hutia shook his head. Pesaro, thinking he marveled at the scope and ingenuity of such trade, bobbed his head in a bow of acknowledgment. Rachel took Hutia's hand and squeezed it. She and I both knew that he was thinking of *matu'm*, the Taino virtue of generosity, which decreed that all possessions must be shared, not hoarded or sold. Even barter was not an exchange of value for value, but each giver's effort to be more *matu'n* than his neighbor. Even gold they valued chiefly as a potential gift. But European rapacity had won the day. The Taino were no more.

Rachel's eyes were bright with unshed tears as she steered the conversation back on course.

"We must cross Italy," she said, "no matter how perilous the road, for we will not abandon our search until we find our family. If your business brings you close to where sieges and battles have taken place, and if you have occasion to speak with those on both sides of the conflict, you must know what places we must avoid. We have maps. Would you be kind enough to look at them with us and help determine our route?"

"Willingly," Pesaro said, "but I cannot guarantee your safety on any route. Has any of you *seen* an army?"

Hutia glanced at me, eyebrows raised. I shook my head.

"Only raiding parties in the Indies," I said.

"Parties of savages?" He cast a speculative glance at Hutia.

"No," I said. "Of Spanish soldiers."

"Then you cannot imagine what you may encounter. If I thought I could dissuade you from continuing your journey, I would try. An army on the march stretches for miles in all directions. First come the troops and then those who serve and follow them: blacksmiths, bakers, wheelwrights, carpenters, apothecaries, and a host of other necessary artisans, as well as women and children."

"Loose women?" Rachel asked. "You need not hesitate to speak of them in my presence."

"Both these and the wives and families of soldiers," the trader said. "The camp followers can number in the thousands, even exceeding the tally of troops. In addition, the French have been drawing behind them artillery in wagons, as well as wagons filled with plunder."

"Cannon?" I said. "That must considerably slow their march."

"It does," Pesaro said, "but it accounts for the success of this invasion. We Italians find ourselves frequently at war among ourselves, but until now, we have left mercenary companies led by *condottieri* to do our fighting. The goal of *condottieri* is to take as much loot as possible, including captives who might be worth a goodly ransom, and to do as little killing as they can. These French have turned our way of making war upon its head."

"If they travel more slowly after taking this plunder you speak of," Hutia said, "it seems to me they must despoil more of the countryside as they go to keep their people fed."

"Exactly," Pesaro said. "The longer an army has been in the field, the wider it spreads its wings. Armies uproot and trample crops and regard the dozens or even hundreds of villages in their path as their rightful prey. Soldiers on the move are pitiless, rapacious, and often desperate. Since this latest battle at Fornovo, both the French and the Venetians and their allies wander the countryside. Some are wounded. All are unpaid and hungry. We will look at these maps of yours. But as to avoiding the war, you cannot, no matter which route you take. If you avoid the main roads and take to the mountains, you may not meet regiments, but you will still encounter soldiers. Some are merely trying to get home. Others are no better than bandits. Before you lies only a choice among dangers."

Chapter Seventeen: Joanna

Joanna hated São Tomé. She hated every vine and lizard, every shoot of cane. She hated every insect, crawling or flying, and every human being on the island except her brothers. She especially hated the masters, priests, and *degradados* and the king in Portugal, who had wantonly tossed away so many Jewish lives and thought himself a good man, beloved of God, for doing it.

Caminha chose to build a new settlement, farther east along the coast than Ponta Figa, overlooking a shallow but usable natural harbor. Beyond the beach lay a flat expanse of fertile land well suited to agriculture, which made it ideal for the cultivation of sugar cane. Everyone called the new site the Povoação, the Settlement. Perhaps they feared to tempt fate by giving it a grandiose name, as the inhabitants of Fig Point had done. On the other hand, the governor chose to name the modest stream that flowed through the settlement Agua Grande.

The governor could not imagine why this site had not been chosen in the first place. Once he had expressed his contempt for his late predecessor and the remnant of the first colony, his sycophants, led by his cousin Pero, repeated it incessantly. So did the *degradados*, whose self-esteem was raised by having someone to despise. No one but Joanna seemed to have an adverse opinion of the Povoação's location, alongside the pestilential swamp.

There was plenty of work to do. Caminha decreed that his people would not live in tents and commanded that huts be built for all. But this must wait until the first sawmill had been built and the first fields cleared and planted with sugar cane. They must fell enough trees for dwellings and storehouses, sugar mills, and more sawmills, for the island was to be completely self-sufficient, not dependent on supplies from Portugal. Fresh palm fronds must be cut to thatch the buildings. This would be an ongoing task for the children, as the intermittent torrential rains and the tendency of birds and lizards to peck at and burrow into the thatch meant the dwellings would have to be renewed from time to time. All the children, even the smallest, quickly learned to shinny up the trees. Belmiro, along with a few other *degradados* who particularly enjoyed exerting their authority over those weaker than themselves, spurred them on at first by cracking whips made of long strips of pigskin, raising raw welts on their calves and backs. The children soon learned to scoot up too high to reach. One defiant boy threw down a coconut on Belmiro's head, but his punishment, which involved the lash as well as fists and boots, deterred the others.

They climbed with knives or short sickles in their teeth, since no work could be done without them. But being armed, to Joanna's despair, did not lend them one jot of power. At least they would not go thirsty, as they had on board the ship. Thanks to the copious rainfall, there were many streams and small rivers on the island, essential to the sawmill and to irrigating the fields. Nor would they starve. There were coconuts and bananas for the picking. Joanna had seen no large animals so far except the pigs, which had been released to root where they would.

A small group of settlers from Madeira, who had been invited by the king himself to join the colony because they knew all about making and exporting sugar, swore that once the cane was growing and discarded husks available for the pigs to eat, their roasted flesh would taste unimaginably sweet. Joanna, hearing this, thanked Ha'shem that so far no one had proposed slaughtering a pig and challenging the newly baptized Christian children to show their sincerity by swallowing a food that all knew was forbidden to Jews. She did not know what she would do when that moment came. But it was not today's problem. She had heard that there were giant lizards in the swamp with teeth as sharp as a dragon's. But whether or not their flesh was good to eat, no one had yet mentioned.

The governor's house was built even before the first field was cleared. It boasted planks and roof tiles brought from Lisbon on the carracks. They were the final cargo to be offloaded, the day after the settlers' arrival. Then all six ships sailed away, heading east toward the Guinea Coast, a bare hundred miles from the island. It was apparent from the beginning that the favorite food of the Povoação would be gossip. Everyone knew the ship captains had been ordered to bring back as many slaves as they could cram into the holds as soon as possible. Those to be sold on would be shipped to Elmina, once the settlers had taken their pick. The settlement was charged with supplying the garrison at Elmina with fresh vegetables, fruits, and grain, so kitchen gardens must be planted and fields set aside for wheat or whatever would grow best.

It was also known that the governor's grant allotted him one *braço*, an arm, or in other words, one slave, for every sugar mill and sawmill built on the island.

"Imagine being paid in slaves!" Belmiro's small, piggy eyes gleamed at the thought. "I'll undertake any task they wish for such a currency."

In fact, the *degradados* were well motivated to work hard, although much of the actual labor devolved upon the slaves they had, the Jewish children, in anticipation of the slaves to come.

"It is up to you how much land you clear," Caminha said, having called a general assembly on the beach. "You will be issued canes that may be divided so they will root and grow. The first crop belongs to me, except for a small portion that you may barter for supplies to feed and maintain yourselves for the first few months. After that, the land you have cleared is yours. If you wish to become lord of a great *fazenda*, you may achieve it by industry."

"What about slaves?" Belmiro called out. "Can we trade in them too?"

The *degradados* standing near him laughed, for all the men who knew him from the prison in Lisbon or from the ship, especially those who had played at cards or dice with him, knew how he loved to dicker.

"He's lazy as a sow," Mateus called out, raising another laugh, "but he knows how to get the best of a bargain!"

"Sugar first," Caminha said, "then, with the first crop that is your own, you will be allowed to invest in the trade in blacks. There's an unlimited supply in the Congo, and Elmina's well set up for distribution, but the King intends that every African will first pass through São Tomé. And remember, a black is like a stalk of sugar cane: start with one little one, and they'll multiply and give you a good crop!"

All the *degradados* laughed at this. Joanna felt a hot flush of humiliation flood her, sweeping from her cheeks down the length of her arms and from belly to crotch. It felt as if their cruel laughter was directed at her own body. Their mockery reduced her to the status of property like the hapless blacks.

In fact, since the night on the beach with Pero, Imaculada had kept her away from the men most evenings, instead setting her tasks that kept Joanna busy from morning till night. Imaculada made sure the governor's companions and advisers knew she herself was available and that exceptional services would be provided for the right price. Joanna had heard her tell Felicidade that she hoped to amass enough coin to invest in slaves of her own, not merely in partnership with Belmiro. She knew that once the women slaves arrived, her usefulness would come to an end, as they would perform whatever acts the gentlemen required for free. But in the interim, she would make the most of it.

"You will do as you wish," Felicidade said petulantly. "You always do."

"What is the matter with you?" Imaculada demanded. "Are you breeding?" She sounded annoyed.

"Maybe," Felicidade said. She brushed a lock of hair off her damp forehead with a listless hand. "I have been vomiting, but not only in the morning. It comes and goes. And I ache all the time."

"We don't have time for babies!" Imaculada snapped. "If it were anyone but you, I'd throw you out of the compound."

The first shipload of Africans arrived within two weeks. Naked and chained together, clanking as they walked with shuffling feet and heads bowed, they looked even more demoralized than Joanna had felt on her arrival, though their voyage had been much shorter. Gossip said that the King of the Congo, an African himself, sold his enemies and perhaps even his own people to the Portuguese slavers. If that was true, they must feel abominably betrayed on top of their despair about the future. At least the Jewish parents, including Joanna's, had not consented to the seizing of their children. And no Jew other than an idiot would ever expect loyalty from any Christian king. So they could not be betrayed. Hate was better. It kept her strong.

"Do you hate the Africans?" Simon asked her one day as they hacked at the impenetrable thickets that set a limit on the size of the new plantations. It had become impossible not to allow the bigger children as well as all the *degradados* axes, saws, and knives. There was too much cutting to be done, too much land to clear, and no place to run.

"I am not sure yet," Joanna said. "They are slaves, like us, but they are adults and therefore bigger and stronger than we are. And they know nothing of Jews and Christians, so they have no reason to make common cause with us. We must wait and see how they treat us."

"And if they treat us neither ill nor well, but leave us alone?"

"Then I will try to hate them only a little," she said.

Chapter Eighteen: Diego

Signor Pesaro was right: there was no way to avoid the war. The straightest road out of Genoa was to Piacenza, eighty miles away. It led through mountains, an abode of bandits even in times of relative peace, and would lead us north as well as east. I doubted Papa would have chosen to go north, where the boot that Italy resembled on the maps broadened into a band of frilly petticoats that represented the Alps. Piacenza lay only forty-odd miles from Parma, itself a mere twenty miles from Fornovo, the site of the recent battle. Signor Pesaro had a remarkable grasp of distances, thanks to having traveled all these routes so many times. How long would it take to travel twenty miles? Signor Pesaro assured us that an army, dragging its tail of camp followers and foraging as it went, did well to cover ten miles a day. We would move faster, but so would single soldiers and small parties, especially if they had mounts.

It was becoming apparent to me that we would never be safe in Christendom, and I believed that Papa would have drawn the same conclusion. Any one of the eastern ports might have been their point of departure for Ottoman lands. To bear south and east, as our family had most likely done, we could start by following the coast. The farther south we went, the more the boot would narrow, until we might cross it with relative ease. But south meant Rome and then Naples, cities Charles had lately occupied. No one knew whether *all* his troops had joined the drive northward to engage the Italians and their allies at Fornovo. The battle over, with both sides weakened by losses yet declaring victory, French soldiers would be streaming north toward home and Italian soldiers south, toward *their* homes. Worse, from our perspective, their leaders might have rallied them to march on Rome and Naples, meaning to retake them by siege or battle at any cost. Little as we wanted to meet soldiers who had shed the yoke of discipline, still less did we want to meet an army.

We could deduce one certainty regarding the army's route: it must follow the existing roads or leave its wagons behind. Signor Pesaro smiled and rubbed his hands together when I voiced this thought to him.

"I count on it," he said. "One of my agents reports that the French have won their way northward but had to abandon the greater part of their booty. More details of the battle are trickling in. For one thing, it rained. The French could not keep their powder dry, so they lost the advantage of their mobile artillery. The Italian soldiers fought the harder for their leaders' promise that they would be permitted to loot. So if they had no wagons at Fornovo, they will have acquired them once the battle was over. Well, well, it is a pity, but war is war, and someone must profit in the end."

"We must avoid the main roads, then," I said. "We will strike out inland, bearing south and east toward Siena or Arezzo. If we reach the Adriatic coast too far south, we risk missing word of our family."

"Try Ancona," Signor Pesaro advised. "It is less than two hundred miles from Firenze, and our people are less unwelcome there than in other parts of Italy. Perhaps they have come to rest there, and your journey will be over. If not, it is likely that you will find word of them. There are synagogues in Ancona. Besides, many Byzantine Greeks settled in Ancona after the taking of Constantinople forty-odd years ago. They carry on a lively trade with the Ottomans these days. The Sultan has agents stationed permanently in Ancona, ostensibly for trade but no doubt to spy on Venice, his chief rival in the area, as well."

"That sounds promising," I said.

Against my better judgment, my heart leaped at the prospect of perhaps finding Mama, Papa, and the girls safe and happy. Even if they had moved on, they might have found someone to whom they could entrust a message. Rachel clapped her hands, her cheeks flushed with excitement. Hutia put his arm around her.

Signor Pesaro closed his eyes and held out his arms, palms raised, in prayer.

"*Baruch atah Adonai shomei'ah tefilah.* Blessed art Thou, Adonai, who hearkens to prayer. Direct our steps in peace, and grant that we reach our destination safely. Save us from enemy and ambush, from robbers and wild beasts on the journey, and from all the terrors that rage in the world."

"Amen," Rachel and I said along with Signor Pesaro, and Hutia joined in a moment later.

Three days later, we were following a sheep track that had probably not been used recently and seemed to consist largely of tussocks, rabbit holes, sharp, protruding rocks, and tree roots thrusting their way up through the earth. We led the horse we had obtained through Signore Boccanegra's good offices along with two mules. If any of them went lame, we would be in trouble indeed. I carried a sword and the arquebus the banker had insisted I take, tactfully calling it a loan. Hutia carried a crossbow and had two throwing knives tucked into his waistband. Rachel carried the Taino bow and red-fletched arrows, the only weapon the corsairs had left us, or rather, that Amir had confiscated, claiming them for himself and then returning them to us when we disembarked in Toulon. Signore Boccanegra had taken our letter of exchange on the Banco di San Giorgio and helped us provision ourselves for the journey, our mounts and my sword being the biggest expenses. We had discussed getting Rachel her own crossbow, which was very much a weapon of war by land or sea. But she had refused, saying that she could too easily imagine killing someone with it at close range.

"It would be a horrible death," she said. "I am not quite ready to be the cause of it."

"And if Diego or I were in mortal danger?" Hutia asked.

He placed his arm lightly around her waist and pulled her toward him. He took such liberties more and more frequently, and Rachel encouraged him. I had decided that I had enough to worry about without trying to check them. Once we found the family, as I allowed myself to hope we would, the pair would be Mama and Papa's problem, not mine.

"Then I would do whatever I had to," Rachel said.

Now the July sun beat down on us, causing rivulets of sweat to trickle down my face and arms as well as the back of Rachel's neck, with damp tendrils of hair escaping from her cap. Hutia led the way, Rachel walked between us, and I followed, leading the animals.

"This padded doublet is hot," Rachel complained. "Can I not take it off? I have a linen shirt underneath it."

"No!" I said. "The padding may not turn an arrow or a blade, but it will slow one down and keep it from going too deep. Is it worth your life to feel cool at this moment? Take a sip of water. We will stop and rest as soon as we come to a stream."

Rachel bent to retrieve her waterskin. So the bolt that sped out from behind the trees did not pierce her head but skewered her hat and sent it flying. Her long hair would have tumbled down, revealing her gender, had she not chopped it into a ragged bob around her ears before we left Genoa. I drew my sword with a shout, and Hutia raised his crossbow and sent a bolt flying in the direction from which the attack had come. Rachel also raised her bow.

Three men burst through the underbrush. One, a short, wiry fellow with ragged brown hair and skin pitted with pox marks, held his crossbow poised to shoot again. The other two held swords that showed signs of recent use. One of them was a tall fellow whose long reach would make defeating him a challenge. The other was stocky and of medium size. Older than the others, he held his sword as if casually, his eyes watchful. I surmised he was the most experienced of the three. As his eyes met mine, he grinned, baring stained and rotted teeth.

Out of the corner of my eye, I saw Rachel duck behind me, lowering her bow. I understood why when I heard a determined *thwack*, then another, followed by the surprised bray of one of the mules before all three animals, seizing their unexpected freedom, galloped off. If we won this fight, we would have the devil of a time retrieving them. But that was better than giving our enemies the chance to take them. Rachel's action had removed at least part of their incentive to fight us. The big man growled, and the crossbowman stepped to the side as if considering trying to outflank us and go after them.

"Don't!" I barked. "You won't catch them, and we are three to three."

I had time to think that Hutia had been clever to insist we put our bags of grain on the ground at our feet before allowing the horse and the mules to touch them, so they associated getting fed with us rather than with sacks on their own backs. The bags were almost empty, so soon they would be cropping grass, which even the stupider mule must realize did not require our presence. I leaped forward to meet the big swordsman's thrust and block it with my own blade. We disengaged and circled, each seeking an opening. I tried not to trip on the rough ground and hoped he would. Out of the corner of my eye, I saw the other swordsman moving toward me and heard a deep, humming *twang* as Hutia's bolt took him in the throat. I hoped that Rachel would not hesitate to loose her arrow before the crossbowman could shoot again. Then my world narrowed to my foe's weaving blade and the murder in his eyes.

Chapter Nineteen: Joanna

Within a short time, the coming of the Africans transformed the life of the island. The Povoação became a town, albeit a small one. Clusters of wooden houses with palm-thatched roofs on stilts to avoid flooding in the worst of the rainy season surrounded a roughly built church, a sawmill powered by the Agua Grande, and a sturdy building devoted to the administration of the island as well as housing the *fazenda real*, the royal treasury. Only half the wealth of the settlement was stored there, as slaves were a more common currency than gold. Even the priests were paid in slaves for their labors for the community, which included baptising the newly arrived slaves and instructing them in Portuguese as well as religion.

Before long, there were any number of *fazendas* stretching as far as half a day's walk from the settlement, planted mostly with sugar cane, although pepper grew well in large enough quantities to be exported. A few of the new *fazendeiros*, ambitious to increase their domains as quickly as possible, also grew vegetables and fruit for the Elmina garrison, taking payment in slaves who could be set to clearing and planting more fields. Ships came and went frequently between the harbor and the mainland, bringing newly captured slaves and shipping some of them on, along with the produce grown on the island, to Elmina. Less often, ships arrived from Portugal with news and fabricated goods and returned there loaded with sugar, pepper, and the Crown's share of gold and slaves.

Everyone knew that the slaves were there not only to work, but to breed. It was a slow way to build a labor force, but every African woman was pregnant within a short time of her arrival. Although Joanna was seldom called upon to service the Portuguese, she had not forgotten that the Jewish children were intended to mate with the Africans. Along with the anger that never left her, she carried a simmering dread that she would be ordered to leave the snug hut where Imaculada allowed her to live with her brothers and several other children young enough to need supervision and cohabit with an African man selected by Belmiro, who would own any children of the union. But most of the children were still too young for marriage to be an immediate prospect, so nothing had been done so far to implement this item on the king's agenda.

Natan was the only other Jewish child in the settlement old enough to copulate. As he had told Joanna he would, he quickly improved his status by becoming first scribe and record keeper, then plantation manager, to a young Portuguese who was willing to pay him for his services in slaves of his own and eventually hand over enough land for a small plantation. Joanna saw him at church every Sunday, since attendance at Mass was mandatory for the whole community. They seldom spoke, since Natan was always gossiping and joking with the younger planters he considered his peers and Joanna regarded his apostasy with scorn.

There was a communal celebration when the first sugar cane was harvested in conjunction with the opening of the first sugar mill. Several pigs were slaughtered to mark the occasion. Since all the Jewish children were now Christians, their participation in the feast was expected as a matter of course. The priests, who took seriously their task of keeping any of their flock from straying, kept a sharp eye on those children old enough to remember the tenets of their former faith. Joanna weighed her disgust at eating pork against her strong desire to avoid being conspicuous. She hardly knew why she so carefully husbanded her resources for survival, since escape was impossible. An island was a perfect prison, especially one whose forests were impenetrable and whose rocky heights, south of the settlement, were uninhabitable. But something drove her to acquire new skills, steal and cache tools, and avoid notoriety of any kind. So she chewed a few mouthfuls of the forbidden flesh, which was indeed sweet, thanks to the pigs' diet of cane husks, and managed not to gag on it.

Joanna was not completely invisible, because she took over from the priests the task of tutoring some of the slaves in Portuguese. While the *fazendeiros* could communicate all they wished to with the field hands by cracking a whip and gesturing, they also needed overseers, household servants, and craftsmen. Joanna volunteered to help so that her mind, deprived of books and rational conversation, would not atrophy. Being seen as a teacher also offered respectability, while concealing the real Joanna, the seething rebel that she knew herself to be. Another advantage was the special connection she hoped to make with some of the Africans. Along with her inchoate need for skills and tools for a goal not yet determined, she needed allies. She found one in a woman named Yenenga.

Yenenga already spoke some Portuguese when she arrived on São Tomé. A slaveship captain had kept her in his cabin for the length of several voyages before passing her on to the settlement. He had chosen her not only as a bedmate but because she was a *feiticeira*, a sorceress and healer.

"He sick," she told Joanna one day as they shared a meal of fried bananas and manioc root pounded to a heavy paste and spiced with pepper sauce. "He keep me for fix bad *juju*."

"What kind of *juju*?" Joanna asked. "The sweats? Ship fever? The squits?"

Yenenga had taught her this word for magic or any symptom or misfortune that might be caused by magic. Around her neck, Yenenga wore a *grigri*, a fetish or talisman consisting of a small leather pouch whose contents no one was allowed to see. She had carried it from Africa, moving it from hiding place to hiding place in the orifices of her own body.

The *feiticeira* furrowed her brow, trying to think of how to describe a condition for which she had no word. She pointed to her own crotch and pumped the air above it with her fist to convey the slaver's male anatomy. Then she pursed her fingertips and indicated several different spots on the imaginary member.

"He had sores," Joanna guessed. "Some kind of pox. Did they hurt?"

Yenenga shrugged.

"Just ugly. First dey go away for a while." She snorted with amusement. "He tink I got de power for real. Den body start to hurt."

She shook out her arms and legs, tossed her head from side to side, and moaned.

"He ached all over?"

"Yes. Den hair fall out, sore come back uglier. He get red here and here." She slapped her palms and the soles of her feet. "White *feiticeiro* come, bleed wit leeches, do no damn good. So captain beg me make bad *juju* go away."

"And did you?"

Yenenga shrugged again and spat.

"Not dat kind of *juju*. Dis ting go man to woman, woman to man. White man bring it, but it kill black and white. It go away again, so he tink he don't need me no more. It come back soon, den he die."

Thus Joanna was the first white on the island to hear, before ships from Portugal brought word of it, of what all of Europe called the French disease. It should have been called the Spanish disease, for Spanish sailors who had lain with the savages in the newly discovered Indies. But sailors go everywhere, and many who had served with Admiral Columbus had tired of eternal sunshine, limited supplies of strong drink, and the lack of pretty ladies who wore dresses and spoke civilized languages. Seeking new berths, they flocked to France, where King Charles was assembling a fleet for his Italian invasion, as did soldiers ready for real warfare after slaughtering the island folk for their fabled stores of gold. The dockside whores of Toulon and Naples, with their customers' enthusiastic cooperation, did the rest.

"Don't you go wid no men," Yenenga warned her. "Black folk get it from soldiers in Elmina, give it to dey own family. Soon everyone on São Tomé get it too. Dey all die."

Joanna shrugged in turn. She could only hope that the few Portuguese who still occasionally sought Imaculada out to buy her body did so precisely because they did not wish to lie with Africans. Most of the white men deemed the compliance of the black women among the chief blessings of the slave trade being based on São Tomé. Yenenga told Joanna that this compliance had little to do with slavery. Back in Africa, the men of many tribes insured young girls' docility by removing that portion of their genitals that the sailor who had taken Joanna's virginity had aroused so briefly. She occasionally achieved a shameful pleasure by touching it herself. The mutilated African women could experience no such sensation. Perhaps, Joanna thought, as if trying to imagine a city on the moon, if one had a husband one loved . . . But it was not worth thinking about.

The men of São Tomé regarded the pox as a tale of the troubles of faraway Europe, along with wars and the quarrels and alliances of kings. Their mission was to populate the island for the greater glory of Portugal, and the only way to do that was to couple with the women. Given the abundance of women slaves in the settlement, they did not think of the sailors' shore leave every time a ship came into port as affecting them in any way. Both settlers and sailors lubricated their desires with palm wine, which the Africans were skilled at making, another benefit of the slave trade. Joanna tried to warn Natan about the pox, but he would not listen. He had recently earned his first slave, a young woman seven or eight years older than he, who was teaching him the art of love, as he boasted to Joanna. So Joanna had to content herself with dire warnings to Simon, who had not gotten his growth spurt yet, but was beginning to look at girls. The glossy breasts and haunches of the black women were always on display, and some of the more modest Jewish girls were beginning to develop bosoms and cast demure looks from under their lashes at the older boys.

"I do not see," Simon said, cross at her for these repeated admonitions, "how I can die from touching Leah's breast. Anyhow, she wanted me to."

"You will understand when you are older," Joanna said. Having had her innocence torn from her, she was determined to let Simon hold onto childhood as long as she could, even though she knew the task was an impossible one.

"According to you," Simon said, "I'll never *be* older if I touch Leah's breast. I'm going to the swamp to spear frogs with Nissim and Caleb. You're no fun to be around these days."

Chapter Twenty: Diego

The explosion on my right, like a crack of thunder, startled me. I nearly lost my footing. Luckily, my opponent, startled too, fell back a pace. I heard a scream and the crash and clatter of the other swordsman's fall. Rachel had shot him with the arquebus that had been hanging from the horse's saddle. She must have secured it before she slapped the horse and sent it running off. We now had only one foe, but recovering quickly, he came at me with a snarl of rage. He had a longer reach and the seasoning of battle. I was tiring fast. I could not see what was happening behind me. The arquebus had a recoil like the kick of a mule. I had not thought Rachel had the strength to fire it, and she had probably been knocked to the ground in the process. Hutia would be trying to get in a crossbow shot at the soldier without hitting me.

A red-feathered arrow took my opponent in the leg, a crossbow bolt in the shoulder. As he faltered, I lunged, putting all my force into the blow aimed at his heart. Blood spurted as he fell. Trembling, I lowered my sword. I was bathed in sweat and so winded that I could barely draw a wheezing breath. Leaning on the sword, I turned. Hutia was just lowering the crossbow, still looking fierce although all three of our enemies were dead. Rachel sat on the ground, her face white. She was trembling even more than I. She had indeed been knocked over by the recoil of the arquebus but had had the presence of mind to drop it, seize her bow, and shoot from a seated position.

"We have all just saved one another's lives," I

said.

"I am about to be sick," Rachel said.

She held out her hands to Hutia and me, and we helped her rise and stumble several paces away from the carnage. As she bent and vomited up her fear and horror, a shaky hand upon the sturdy trunk of a tree for balance, my own gorge rose. I squared my shoulders and quieted my stomach by murmuring soothing words to Rachel until she was ready to compose herself.

"Water, please."

Hutia silently handed her his waterskin, which had remained slung across his shoulder throughout the struggle. She rinsed her mouth and spat, then swallowed one mouthful of water and handed it back.

"We must drink as little as possible," she said, "until we find a spring or a stream."

"First, we must find the horse and the mules," I said. "Hutia, are you all right?"

"I have killed before," he said. "Evil men, like these."

I knew he was thinking of the Spaniards Admiral Columbus had left at La Navidad, who had forced the Taino women and held them captive. One of them had murdered Hutia's sister.

"Were these men indeed evil?" Rachel said. "Now I wonder if we could have avoided bloodshed, if we should have tried to talk with them."

"Do not think it, Rachel," I said. "They were fresh from battle and well primed to kill and to take what they could: our food, our mounts, our weapons, and the gold they would have found on our persons had they killed us. Nor would they have spared you, had they discovered your gender. We did what we had to."

"It is well that carnage distresses you, Rachel," Hutia said. "After what happened in Quisqueya, my heart is like a stone—except when I think of what might have befallen you."

"As you saw," she said, "I can defend myself."

"We had better take their weapons with us," I said.

"Let us do as they would have done to us," Hutia said, "and see if they have valuables about their persons."

"I must find my hat," Rachel said, turning away, "and with it, one more crossbow bolt in case of need."

Hutia and I exchanged glances.

"Do not bother to retrieve my arrow," she added. "I can do that myself. I am not afraid of blood."

"We do not doubt your courage," I said.

Rachel indeed had enough stomach for this task, even cutting away the flesh to free her red-feathered arrow. But she averted her eyes from the ugly sight the ball from her arquebus had made of the second swordsman's head.

We found the mules cropping grass no more than a mile away, the horse a half mile farther on with its rein caught in a bilberry bush. The horse, having shaken off its saddlebags in its efforts to free itself, was placidly munching berries when we came upon it. Rachel ran to free the rein. It greeted her with a soft whinny and nuzzled her as she scolded it like an exasperated mother whose child has gotten into mischief. We found a stream shaded by alders not far away. All of us, animal and human, drank thirstily, and we were able to refresh ourselves and rid our clothing and the weapons of blood and dirt.

Three days later, we glimpsed the Adriatic in the distance, the horizon a blue blur where the sea met the sky. We led the animals down out of the hills, for the terrain was still rough underfoot. As we descended, the slopes were more and more thickly studded with trees about the height of olive trees, though the leaves were not silvery but a glossy dark green.

"These must be the strawberry trees Signor Pesaro told us of," Rachel said. "So the town we see is indeed Ancona. But I am disappointed. He said the tree bears fruit and flowers at the same time."

"It is the wrong season," I said. "Look, you can see the fruit just beginning to set and clusters of buds that will be the flowers."

"If we find your parents settled here," Hutia said, "you will be able to see this marvel in a couple of moons."

Rachel's face brightened.

"Do you really think they may be here? Let us mount, so we can get there faster."

Ancona nestled in a tumble of red tile roofs between two arms of the promontory of Monte Conero. It was beautiful, a city seemingly untouched by war, its streets thronged with citizens going about their business with an air of ease as well as purpose. The sky was as blue as any I had seen in Andalusia or the Indies. The sunlit air had that special clarity that blesses ports and villages built near water. The air smelled of jasmine and baking bread. We quickly found the white stone cathedral with its dome and the square white bell tower, also domed, rising above the rooftops. We made our way through the narrow streets toward these landmarks, from which Signor Pesaro had given us directions to the house where we might find his agent, Signor Bianchini.

We had to ask the way of a woman selling oranges and again at a tavern before we found the right house. It was a narrow building of the same white stone as the cathedral, crammed between two others on a crooked street with laundry festooned on lines across it at one end and a fishmonger's shop at the other. The door of the house we sought stood hospitably open, with a prosperous-looking orange cat sunning itself on the step.

"This is it!" Rachel kept her voice low, but she sounded excited. "Look!"

A *mezuzah* was fastened to the doorpost. I touched it lightly. Rachel did the same, her eyes filled with tears.

"What is it?" Hutia asked.

"It is a prayer to bless our comings and goings,"

Rachel said, "and it is holy."

"'Hear, O Israel, the Lord our God, the Lord is One,'" I said. "That is the prayer within the case. But it is more than that. The *mezuzah* says, 'This is a Jewish home.'"

"Knock, Diego," Rachel said.

I knocked twice, as hard as I could, on the wooden door. The orange cat rose, stretched elaborately, yawned, and strolled away down the street to the fishmonger's. I knocked again.

A man no more than ten years older than I emerged from an inner room. Well but simply dressed in dark green doublet and hose, he had freckled skin and auburn hair. As he approached us, his keen eyes taking in our faces and our disheveled state, he broke into a grin.

"You must be newly arrived from the west. And before that, from Spain? Or perhaps Portugal. Welcome, welcome! I am Aldo Bianchini. You will celebrate Shabbat with us this evening. Come in, come in! You are safe here."

That evening, for the first time since 1492, Rachel and I sat down to a true Shabbat dinner. Her face glowed in the light of the Sabbath candles as she regarded me across the table. Hutia sat beside her, so she could whisper an explanation of the unfamiliar aspects of the rite. Signora Bianchini had lit the candles, cut the challah, and was now bustling back and forth with heaping platters of fish, vegetables, and flat strings of flour paste boiled and flavored with fresh herbs and olive oil. Fruit and wine had been set out on the gleaming white linen cloth. The *signora* had already whisked away our clothes to launder and insisted on giving Rachel one of her own dresses. Four little Bianchinis, two boys and two girls, stared solemnly at us.

Signor Bianchini had asked no questions, insisting that we spend the time until sundown bathing and resting. He had sent a boy with the horse and mules to a stable the next street over, where he assured us they would be well cared for, and refused our coin.

"After dinner," he said, "you will tell me your story, and we shall consider how I may help you."

The children begged to be allowed to stay up late to see more of the visitors, but their eyelids were already drooping with fatigue by the time the meal was over. Signora Bianchini ordered them off to bed, promising them a story if they were good. The smaller of the girls insisted that Hutia carry her to her bed. The *signora* apologized for this liberty, but Hutia assured her that he would like nothing better. He held her tenderly, breathing in the clean scent of her soft curls as he bore her away to the chamber where the children slept.

Signor Bianchini shook his head when we asked if he knew the name Mendoza.

"There have been so many refugees. There may have been a family of that name. If so, they have moved on."

"What about Davila?" Rachel asked. "It is our mother's family name and that of cousins who traveled with them."

"I am sorry," Signor Bianchini said. "Our Jewish community is bigger than it was. For a while, our synagogues were packed with strangers. Many of the refugees from Spain and Portugal have gone on to Ottoman lands, not trusting any town in Italy to remain tolerant if trouble comes its way. Perhaps they did the same."

"They might have left a letter," I said. "They had no way of knowing where we were, so they could not send a message more directly. But neither had they any reason to believe that we would ever visit Ancona."

"Even if they believed us dead," Rachel said, "Mama would have written."

"Is your father a learned man?" Signor Bianchini said.

"Yes, he is," I said.

"We have two synagogues," he said. "Some of the refugees were nearly as starved for intellectual discourse of the kind that was forbidden in Spain as they were for bread. Rabbi Gershon is our most brilliant Talmudic scholar. I will take you to meet him in the morning. If he does not remember your family, we will visit the other rabbis. There are also Jewish merchants who outfit travelers to the Levant. Do not be discouraged. Among them, they will surely be able to give you news of your parents and much useful information if you wish to venture east. They are not all Turkish Muslims in the Sultan's realm, you know. There are Jews and Christians among them, as well as Muslims who were born Christian Serbs and Albanians."

"They are forced to convert, then," I said, "as we were?"

"It is not the same," he said. "Every year, the Ottomans take young boys from the towns and villages in the Balkan lands. Whether they consent or not—or whether the parents sell them, in years of poor harvest—is a matter of opinion, depending upon whom you ask. It is certain that after converting them to Islam, the Turks educate them in a special school in the Sultan's own palace in Istanbul. Once grown, they become either janissaries—soldiers in the Sultan's personal army, with the prospect of reward and advancement—or palace officials who may rise to greatness as his closest advisers, even his chief minister, or governor of a province with all its perquisites."

"That is astonishing," Rachel said.

"It is certainly different from the Christians' conversion of Jews!" I said. Amir had told us the same, but I wanted a Jewish opinion. "Having given them high office, does the Sultan not mistrust them, as the Spanish sovereigns suspect even the most sincere *conversos*?"

"From all I have heard," Signor Bianchini said, "once a man has embraced Islam, he is given the same trust and respect as a born Muslim. Certainly, there is no Islamic Inquisition."

"There must be some drawback," I said, "that is,

besides the genuine beliefs that make folk unwilling to cast off the faith of their fathers."

"And mothers," Rachel added.

Signor Bianchini grimaced and took a sip of wine.

"They say that every official and janissary, the grand vizier included, is considered a personal slave of the Sultan. That does not mean they can be sold as chattel or that they don't become rich and powerful through the Sultan's favor. He is clever to catch them young and treat them so well that it is said they are unwavering in their loyalty to him."

"I would rather be Jewish," I said.

"As would I," Signor Bianchini said. He lifted the wine jug, raising his brows in inquiry.

Hutia, who had said nothing but had been listening intently, had barely touched his wine. Rachel was enjoying hers and lifted her goblet eagerly to be refilled.

"You will have a headache in the morning," I warned her, "if you keep on. We must have our wits about us tomorrow. We have much to ask and much to learn."

"Diego, you worry too much," she said airily, knowing that I would not react as I usually did, by either growling or grabbing her and tickling her, in front of Signor Bianchini. "Besides, you will do all the talking tomorrow. I doubt that either the rabbis or the Turks will wish to converse seriously with a woman."

Signora Bianchini entered the room, smiling, with her cap over one ear and her apron half untied.

"You must be exhausted," she said, "and ready for your beds. I hope you will be comfortable."

"A good thought, my dear," her husband said. "You are right as always." To us, he said, "Is there anything more you wish to ask that cannot wait till the morning?"

"Nothing that cannot wait," I said, "but I had better ask the question on my mind now, so I will not forget it. Crossing the Adriatic would have been a great undertaking for my family, as would our doing the same in search of them. What is the likelihood of their having continued down the coast and found a safe haven in some other Italian city?"

"I do not think it likely," Signor Bianchini said. "There is Pescara, which is part of the Kingdom of Naples and thus unstable at this time. Bari has a bloody and confusing history and no particular fondness for the Jews. No, I am certain that since they are not in Ancona, you will find them in the Ottoman Empire."

The Last Letter

Ancona, November 1494

My dearest children,

May Adonai preserve you both and grant my fervent prayers that you will find your way to Ancona and seek news of us from Rabbi Gershon, who, if you are reading this, will have put my letter in your hands. Knowing Papa, you will guess that he would seek out the wisest man in Ancona! We are all well, *baruch Ha'shem.* After leaving Firenze, we spent many weeks on the road, not knowing where we would lay our heads each night and enduring many dangers and privations with which I will not trouble you. The girls have been very brave. Elvira has been a great comfort to me, and Susanna has put aside all her vanity and silliness. It makes me proud to see her grown into a woman, though I confess I sometimes miss her frivolity, her easy laughter, and even her pranks. Both of them, indeed all of us, grew thin and anxious on the road, although we have been much restored by our stay in Ancona.

We were fortunate indeed to reach this hospitable city in July, along with many other Jewish refugees. For a time, we hoped that we could make it our home. This hope found joyous expression in the wedding of Elvira and Akiva, which we celebrated in September. There were many women to accompany Elvira to the *mikvah.* Rabbi Gershon himself joined them in marriage. Both Miriam and I cried when we saw our children standing under the *chuppah* and again when Akiva broke the glass. It seemed a miracle that so many Jews could gather to cry *"Mazel tov!"* to the bride and groom and feast together without fear. Since then, the newlyweds have been billing and cooing like doves, although we cautioned them to wait before building too elaborate a nest until we were certain that things would remain stable.

Sadly, we were right. If Elvira had accumulated the household goods that give a new bride so much pleasure, bedding and dishes and pots, or filled her cupboards with stores of grains and spices, she would now be forced to abandon all these possessions. We have had terrible tidings of a place called Mordano, little more than a hundred miles from here and thirty miles from Bologna, much farther east than we thought the French invasion would go. The French army besieged the fortress, which had refused surrender when it was offered, and bombarded the walls until the fortress fell with cannon that they carried from France on wagons. Besides the garrison, all of whom were slaughtered, many folk from the surrounding area had sought refuge within the walls. Most of these were killed without mercy and other horrors visited upon those who survived. Much of the harvest was already in. The French seized the stores within Mordano and pillaged and trampled the fields for many miles around, so there will be famine throughout the whole region this winter.

It happened three weeks ago, and ever since, the few survivors have been straggling into the eastern coastal towns, Rimini and Pesaro as well as Ancona. These are Italian refugees, but they have surely suffered as much as Jews and deserve our compassion. King Charles now marches on Firenze on his way to Naples, of which he considers himself the rightful king. It is said that the Neapolitan army that opposes him consists of mercenaries under what they call *condottieri* who did not expect the savagery of the French. The Italians, it seems, with their constant quarrels between one city and the next, only play at war and expect their opponents to obey the rules!

Who knows where this invasion will end? And whether or not the French attack Ancona, we know all too well what frightened Christians do when faced with danger and adversity: they blame the Jews! Before that happens here, we must seek refuge in Muslim lands. We cross the Adriatic tomorrow. I do not say, "We sail," because we have booked passage on a Turkish galley. Its captain has assured us that the Sultan wishes more Jews to bring their knowledge and skills to his capital at Istanbul and already employs Jewish physicians, appoints Jewish tax farmers, and encourages trade with Jewish merchants. The journey will not be without its dangers, even if we make it under the protection of an Ottoman caravan, because not all of the Balkan lands are under the Sultan's rule. Bosnia, Albania, and Bulgaria are part of the Ottoman Empire, but Montenegro is not. Papa encouraged the Turkish captain to give him quite a history lesson, which he then passed on to me. He says the captain assured him that the Sultan would add Montenegro to his European possessions in the near future. Papa says we must all learn as much as we can about the Ottoman Empire and Islam, its religion, so that we can make the most of opportunity in our new home.

I cannot deny a lively interest in all we will learn and the new experiences we will have. It will be a great relief not to be looking constantly over our shoulders as we have these past few years. To my surprise, I am looking forward to the prospect of Istanbul, rather than feeling only that we are running away once more. If only, if only, my darlings, we had word that you are safe and on your way to Istanbul to join us, I might actually be happy.

All my love, Mama

Chapter Twenty-One: Joanna

Joanna sat on the beach, enjoying a rare moment of privacy as she watched the brief equatorial sunset blaze in a glory of reds and golds. At this latitude, one moment the sky was on fire; the next, night had fallen. So suddenly had her life changed three times now: from beloved daughter to neglected stepchild; from citizen of beautiful Granada to refugee in danger of torture or death; from disregarded but not uncomfortable maiden to violated slave, without hope of reprieve however long she lived.

She had just had a quarrel with Simon. All legs and Adam's apple and impatience as his voice cracked and changed, he was beginning to sound like Natan.

"Why can't you make up to a rich *fazendeiro*? You could be a planter's wife and live in luxury. Some of them must wish to beget white children and grandchildren. You have only to stop being so angry all the time. You could be pleasing to them if you tried."

She must stop trying to explain herself or reason with him. Unlike Shmuel and Benji, he could remember being Jewish once. But the memory of studying Torah and looking forward to becoming *bar mitzvah* held no appeal for him.

"What good did it do us?" he asked. "If I follow the teachings of the Church, I have a chance of making something of myself here. I have agreed to work on Saturdays at Ignacio Pereira's sugar mill. Don't tell Belmiro. Ignacio has promised to teach me the trade, and if I am diligent, in two years he will pay me one *braço*, maybe sooner if the mill prospers."

"A slave?" Joanna shrieked. "You would own a slave? Simon, what are you thinking?"

"That I would rather own a slave than be a slave. Besides, any I do not wish to keep can be sold on for gold. They say that Governor de Caminha has asked the King to consider manumitting any *degradado* who marries and bears children on a black. Why should he not do the same for us? You cannot say that you wish your children to be slaves!"

"There is no talking to you!" she said in despair as he stomped away, annoyed at her refusal to understand.

Shmuel too was growing and no longer came to her for comfort. All the surviving older boys shared Natan's and Simon's opinions, while the girls were growing up compliant: some timid and obedient, some striving to appear seductive at what Joanna considered far too young an age. Many had died of the mysterious fevers that plagued the island. Others had disappeared into the swamp, prey to the giant carnivorous lizards and poisonous snakes that made it their home. None of the *degradados* would venture into the swamp. They sent the children to spear frogs, whose legs made a delicious dinner, net crabs, and fish. This was not one of Joanna's usual duties, but she preferred to accompany the boys. She liked to keep an eye on Benji, who was still small enough to be cuddled and might listen when she cautioned him about the dangers of the swamp. He usually obeyed her, but he became reckless when the older boys were present. It was natural that he wanted to be one of them. She would lose him too before long.

After her argument with Simon, she was not sure if he would wake her before dawn as he had promised. But gray light was filtering into the hut and parrots beginning to scream when he shook her shoulder and whispered her name.

The air was humid. It smelled of rotting vegetation and swamp lilies whose spidery blooms brushed against Joanna's cheeks as she parted their tall stems, squidging barefoot through the wet, sponge-like floor of the swamp. The thick miasma made it hard to breathe. As the sun rose, mosquitoes began to whine around her ears. Simon, Shmuel, and Benji slapped at them as they attacked the boys' arms and legs, necks, cheeks, and foreheads.

"The mosquitoes aren't biting Joanna," Shmuel said. "It's not fair!"

"Yenenga gave me an ointment to keep them away," Joanna said. "Do you want some?"

"I don't need it," Simon said. "I don't believe in *juju*."

"Neither do I," Shmuel said.

"Do you see me having to slap away mosquitoes? Benji, what are you doing?"

Benji was staring in fascination at a mosquito perched on his outstretched finger.

"Look at this bug," he said. "You can see its body, and it's turning red."

"Stop that!" Joanna swiped at the mosquito.

Benji jerked his hand away, the insect still clinging to his finger.

"Let it go, Benji! That's your blood it's feeding on. Kill it."

"But it's interesting," Benji protested.

"You'll get sick."

"No, he won't," Simon scoffed.

"No, I won't," Benji echoed.

"It's just a little blood," Simon said.

"Benji's got lots more," Shmuel added.

The mosquito, sated, flew away.

"Come on, Benji," Joanna coaxed. "Let me put some of Yenenga's ointment on you."

"Let me see it first," he said. "Ew, it looks disgusting."

"You won't even see it once I rub it in," Joanna said. She grabbed his arm and smeared a dab of sticky ointment on the back of his neck.

"Come on!" Simon said impatiently. "The frogs hide when the sun gets too high. Follow me. I found a sort of pool last time with lots of frogs."

He led the way under towering trees dripping with mosses and past murky waters covered with bright green scum. Simon, surefooted, forged a path between stands of grasses by pushing them aside, disrupting the business of insects bright as jewels and stilt-legged birds poised to snap up the unwary frog or fish. Shmuel followed him, then Benji, Joanna bringing up the rear.

"We're almost there," Simon called over his shoulder. "We just have to skirt around this pond, toward the tree trunk sticking up with the two trees just beyond it."

Looking at the landmark he indicated, Joanna was not paying attention when Shmuel said, "Why skirt around the pond? Look, there's a short cut, I'm stepping on this log."

Then everything happened at once.

"Wait, Shmuel!" Simon cried.

Shmuel screamed.

Benji tripped and fell back against Joanna, who flung her arms around him and squeezed him tight.

The log rose up, a knobby muzzle, the same murky gray-green color as the swamp, yawning wide to reveal dripping spikes of teeth in a cavernous jaw. The creature's powerful tail smacked down with a tremendous splash.

Shmuel screamed again as he fell, arms windmilling in the dark water.

"No!" Joanna gasped on a quick intake of breath. She forgot to exhale as Shmuel floundered and Benji struggled in her arms.

"Crocodile!" Simon screamed.

"Help me!"

Shmuel twisted frantically, trying to paddle toward the edge of the pond, where he might pull himself up by grasping the tangle of vines and grasses. The crocodile seemed to be everywhere, lashing its tail, turning the water into a whirlpool, blocking the boy's every move. It gnashed its huge teeth, the great jaw snapping closed and opening again without ever losing its dreadful smile.

Malevolent yellow-green eyes seemed to take in not only the terrified boy but the others: Simon lying on his stomach holding out his wooden frog spear, too short for Shmuel to reach; Benji punching and kicking at Joanna as he screamed his brother's name; Joanna unable to do anything but prevent Benji from getting away.

Blood spurted as the beast's dripping teeth clamped down on Shmuel's arm. The boy uttered one agonizing howl of pain, then went limp. He's fainted, Joanna thought. Her lips, unbidden, shaped a *b'rucha* and repeated it over and over. The crocodile's jaws shifted, opening and closing, to get a better grip on Shmuel. The water frothed and bubbled as it fed. Shmuel's head was underwater now, his legs flopping as the beast crushed his body in its jaws. A dark stain of blood spread slowly outward on the water.

"Don't look, don't look, don't look."

Joanna pressed Benji's head to her chest and bent over him, burying her face in his hair. He squirmed frantically, still sobbing out his brother's name. She felt a hand on her shoulder and a gust of warm breath at her ear.

"Let us go," Simon said, "now, while it pays us no attention. We can do nothing for Shmuel."

"We should try! If I could get Benji to calm down—"

"Do you want to die?" Simon snapped. "Benji!" He slapped the hysterical boy hard on one cheek, then the other. "Shut up! Do you want the crocodile to get you too?"

"Simon, don't—"

"Shut up, Joanna. We have to go *now*. I'll take Benji." He pried the boy from her arms and hoisted him over his shoulder.

With a strange, dreamy detachment, Joanna thought, He will never be *bar mitzvah*, but he's become a man anyway.

"Let's go!" Simon said in an urgent tone. *"Run!"*

As they neared the settlement, Joanna wondered

sluggishly what she should tell Imaculada. Would the *degradada* believe her account of what had happened? Would she accuse her of conniving with Shmuel to escape? She might even beat both Simon and Joanna for failing to bring home the promised frogs. But she found Imaculada in a languid state, complaining of headache and nausea and in no mood either to eat frogs or to care how many children had gone to the swamp that morning and how many had returned. Joanna made broth and stayed at her bedside as she sipped it, the cup slipping from her hand as she fell into an uneasy doze. An hour later, she woke, tossing off her blanket with a petulant twitch of the hand.

"I am burning! Bring me water." She put her hands to her flushed cheeks. "The night is hot."

Joanna cautiously laid the back of her wrist against Imaculada's forehead.

"You have a fever," she said. "Do you want me to get Yenenga?"

"The witch-woman?" Imaculada's dry throat produced a cackle. "I don't need a *bruxa*. Get me water and sit by me."

Joanna obeyed. Half an hour later, Imaculada's teeth were chattering, and she complained that she was cold. Her blanket failed to warm her. Joanna must fetch another. Felicidade had stolen Imaculada's extra blanket a month ago. Ask her, the selfish sow. She thought the world revolved around her.

Joanna found Yenenga sitting with Felicidade, who was sleeping, her cheeks streaked with tears and her shift rucked up and bloody.

"What happened?" she asked.

She lose a baby," Yenenga said. "Not so bad ting. She have dat pox."

"The French disease?"

Yenenga shrugged.

"Her man he go wid Congo woman, Congo woman go wid sailor. I tole you, dey all get it soon. I hear you meet de dragon's cousin in de swamp. Too bad about your boy."

"How did you know?"

Yenenga fingered the *grigri* that lay between her breasts.

"I have fast ears, hear everyting soon. What you need?"

"I came for a blanket. Imaculada has chills and fever." She shuddered. "The dragon's cousin is an apt name for that monster. How do you know about dragons?"

"Blanket in dat corner. I know crocodile. Crocodile bad ugly beast, dragon ugly beast dat be worse. However bad is bad, dere be worse, and worse will come. You know dat."

"Yes," Joanna said. "I have seen bad, and I have seen worse come. What should I do for Imaculada?"

"Dat woman have chills dat come and go, den fever? Head and body hurt all over? She puke?"

"Yes, all of that."

"Dat bad fever," Yenenga said. "Come and go, you tink it finish, den come and go, come and go again."

"Will she die?"

"Maybe yes, maybe no."

"Will you come and see her?" Joanna asked. "Can you ease her?"

"Can't do much," Yenenga said. "I know a bark, but dere be none here. When she fever, you cool her down wid water. When she chill, you cover her up. She sweat, you wipe her dry. All dat come every tree days, dat be de fever dat I know."

Within two weeks, two-thirds of the colony had the relapsing and remitting fever, including Simon and Benji. More whites were stricken with it than blacks, and their symptoms were more severe. Joanna felt achy and nauseated most of the time, but she had not yet shown signs of chills or high fever. Ill as she felt, she tended her brothers with devotion. Whenever she tried to catch a few hours of sleep, she found herself reliving Shmuel's terrible death. She would wake to find she was grinding her teeth and muttering aloud, "I should have done *something.*

I should have done *something*."

When she could spare the time, she did what she could for Imaculada: fanning her with a palm frond, helping her change a sweat-soaked shift for a dry one, and bringing her water, for she complained constantly of thirst. Prolonged and debilitating illness had drained the *degradada* of her authority. She no longer intimidated Joanna, who ignored her threats and obeyed her orders when it suited her.

Yenenga tried to bring the fever down with various roots and barks, shaking her head and regretting the remedy she could not give, because the tree needed did not grow on the island.

"Dis island plants and animals all wrong," she said. "Dis island too alone, she got she own ideas bout how tings grow."

"They're different from European plants and animals too," Joanna said, momentarily interested, though she had not had a thought unconnected with Simon's and Benji's misery for weeks. "Maybe some of the living things on São Tomé exist nowhere else in the world."

"Dat what I say," Yenenga said. "Dis island too alone. Nuttin get on, nuttin get off."

It was a bleak thought. Joanna dismissed it and turned back to Simon, who became delirious when the fever was upon him. In his ravings, he roamed with Mother in the gardens of the Alhambra, as Joanna had on the ship, but it brought him no peace. He constantly reproached her for leaving him alone.

Benji's chills and fever were less severe, but his constitution was more delicate. Yenenga said they must try to build up his strength. She concocted broths for him that she gave to no one else. But he could not keep them down, retching till he was faint with exhaustion when he had nothing to bring up. On a night when the moon was halfway between new and full, Joanna sat holding his hand and humming a lullaby that her mother had sung to her, though she could no longer remember the words. He had just been through a round of fever and was catching what sleep he could before the chills began again.

Simon was feverish and moaning, begging her, or perhaps Mother, to make it cool. She had fanned him with a palm frond till her wrists ached. She could bathe him with cool water on a cloth. But Benji would not let go of her hand. It was late, and the settlement was quiet. This island is deficient in love, she thought. Who else in the Povoação cared for another human being as she did for Simon and Benji? The slaves who tended their masters slept whenever their charges did, unless an overseer was watching. But the overseers too were sick.

Was love enough to sustain her through years and years, a lifetime, in this dreary tropical prison? Simon's illness had made him sweet and childish again, grateful in his dependence on her. But it would not last. Benji's affection would wane as he grew up. When Portuguese sailors had first discovered São Tomé twenty-five years before, it had been uninhabited, completely bare of human life. It could have been the Garden of Eden. But the King of Portugal had chosen to populate it with slaves, guaranteeing that it would become a travesty of paradise. The sweetness of sugar, the innocence of children: the ingredients were there, but combined into a bitter brew, a taste of hell.

She came out of her reverie with a start. Benji's hand lay slack on her knee. Simon still moaned and tossed. He paid no attention as she gripped Benji's shoulders and shook them with increasing roughness.

"Benji! Wake up! *Benji!*"

He was dead. The bloom of fever had drained away. His face, once chubby and rosy, was gaunt and pale. She forced herself to touch him, to close his staring eyes, to kiss his cooling forehead. Then she laid her head upon her knees and wept.

"Mama?" Simon sounded fretful. "Why are you crying? Mama, I'm thirsty!"

Now she had only Simon. She tended him with

redoubled watchfulness, forcing her heavy eyelids open when she longed for sleep. Exhaustion was preferable to nightmares in which Shmuel's dark blood spread on the slimy surface of the swamp and the crocodile, smiling, turned its gaze upon her. She left Simon only to fetch water, for unremitting thirst made him miserable, whether he was delirious or lucid.

One night, when Simon seemed to lie more quietly, she took up a bucket and stepped out of the hut, thinking that if she hurried, she could reach the spring and return before he became restless again. The air was cooler outside, and she held up her damp, flushed face to a passing breeze. The moon was almost full. Having filled her bucket, she walked quickly, water slopping over the sides as the bucket banged against her leg. When she reached the hut, she set it down, poured water into a drinking bowl, and hurried to Simon's side.

She could not hear him breathing.

"No," she whispered. "No, Ha'shem. Do not take him too."

They were alone in the hut. The other children had been sent to work and live on the plantations or died of fevers, snakebite, and infected cuts. Joanna laid her ear close to Simon's mouth. No breath. She felt his hands and forehead. Colder than flesh should be. He was gone. So was her anger. She searched within herself for grief and could not find it. She felt nothing.

As if in a trance, she left the hut where her brother lay and made her way to Belmiro and Imaculada's hut. Belmiro had not spent a night there since Imaculada fell ill. He would be in the quarters of the slaves held in common by the settlement, getting drunk on palm wine and slaking his lust in the bodies of the slave women, who also felt nothing. Imaculada was flushed and snoring. Joanna could see the sweating phase of the disease was upon her. But she would not wake. A jug that had held palm wine lay on its side under her hand. Yenenga said that spirits were an ill remedy for fevers. But Imaculada never listened to Yenenga. Joanna would miss Yenenga, who had offered to teach her midwifery and the art of poisons. But it was not enough. Yenenga did not offer love.

She moved slowly and steadily around the hut. Imaculada and Belmiro had made themselves comfortable, building up stores of all they would need when they rose to be *fazendeiros*, as they firmly believed they would. Imaculada had thrown off her blankets. Joanna spread them just inside the door and began piling upon them items she would need: flints to make fire, a pot to boil water, a coil of rope. An old pair of leather boots that Belmiro had discarded caught her eye. She threw them onto one of the blankets. A moment might come when going barefoot proved unwise. A bundle of net. Needles and fish hooks. A hank of linen thread. A fist-sized lump of wax. A small lantern. A sealed jug of oil. A whip. She wrapped a leather belt, also Belmiro's, twice around her waist. She knew where he hid his knives. She snatched up several of different sizes and stuck all but one into her belt. With the remaining knife, she cut off a length of rope. She bundled up the blankets and knotted one end of the rope around each of them, making herself a rough pair of what might have been saddlebags if she had been a mule.

When she could carry no more, she left the hut. The moon shed its silver light on the path before her. No one was stirring. The huts and houses she could see were dark. She made her way down to the beach. She would walk along the shore as far as she could. When dawn came, she would seek the shelter of the forest and find a place to sleep. Then she would consider her options: the coast, the forest, the mountain. There were no ships in the harbor, no horses in the settlement. No one would come after her. She started walking. She did not look back.

Chapter Twenty-Two: Diego

𝔐𝔶 𝔥𝔞𝔫𝔡 𝔱𝔯𝔢𝔪𝔟𝔩𝔢𝔡 as I handed Mama's letter back to Rabbi Gershon, who had tactfully left the room while I read it aloud to Rachel and Hutia. He returned, followed by his housekeeper bearing a tray laden with fruit, pastries, and wine, to find Rachel sobbing in Hutia's arms and me so overcome with emotion that I could hardly speak.

"Please read it, Rabbi Gershon," I said. "We would be grateful for your counsel."

"It is good news, then?" He produced a device consisting of two round pieces of glass connected by metal wire and held them to his eyes, peering through them at my mother's words. "I do not see as well as in my youth, but these spectacles make all clear, *baruch Ha'shem*. They make them in Firenze."

"My mother writes that they planned to leave for the Balkans on a Turkish galley in November. It is a great relief to have certain news of them, but I fear they might have encountered storms on the passage at that season."

Rabbi Gershon smiled gently. Stooped and shrunken with age, his hands white and wrinkled with but a thin layer covering a network of greenish veins, his white beard falling almost to his waist, he had the kindest eyes I had ever seen.

"I believe the Turkish galleys, with their oarsmen and shallower draft—is that the correct term?—are bolder on the sea than Christian vessels. That is the sum of my knowledge on the matter. I do not remember hearing of any great storm last fall."

Ask what questions we might, there was only one way to ascertain whether Papa and Mama had arrived safely at their destination.

"Whatever the risk," I said, "we must leave for Istanbul as soon as possible."

"That may not be as difficult as you fear. The Republic of Ragusa is Ancona's ally. Once you get there, you must find a merchant caravan going to Edirne, as many do. Forty years ago, the Sultan made the Greek Jews of Edirne resettle in Istanbul, but now our numbers there are growing again, as Jews from Spain and Portugal find their way there."

"Might Papa and Mama have changed their minds and gone no farther?" Rachel asked.

"Not after telling us to look for them in Istanbul," I said. "But if there is a Jewish congregation, it will surely have news of them, perhaps even another letter."

"The distance from Edirne to Istanbul is no farther than from here to Bologna," the rabbi said. "I have no doubt that your father will do all he can to make sure you find them."

"Do you remember my father, sir?" I asked. "Efraín Mendoza of Seville?"

"I do," the rabbi said. "An intelligent and well-read man. We had an interesting discussion about whether the Inquisition, in making the Spanish *conversos*—the convinced converts—the main object of its persecution, is pursuing Christian heretics, as it thinks, or rather Jews who have lost their way."

I could not help grinning.

"That sounds like Papa. He loves a good debate. What did you conclude?"

"Only that the Inquisition is iniquitous," the rabbi said. "And intelligence is hardly needed to come to that conclusion. I met your mother as well."

"Really?" Rachel left Hutia's side and linked her arm in mine, beaming at the rabbi.

"She invited me to dinner," the rabbi said, with a reminiscent smile. "You look very much like her, my dear. And before we parted, I begged her to send my housekeeper her recipe for veal loaf cooked with eggs and white beans. It was quite delicious."

Rachel laughed and clapped her hands.

"I am sure it was on your doorstep the next morning, with a packet of leftovers made up for your supper."

"No, she pressed that on me before I left that very evening."

"It does me good to hear these stories of Mama and Papa," Rachel said, "behaving so very like themselves here in Ancona, in spite of the many hardships they endured before they got here. I cannot help believing now that we will reach Istanbul safely ourselves and find them well and safe when we arrive."

"It will be as Adonai wills," the rabbi said. "I will do everything in my power to assist you."

"We must leave as soon as we can find a ship."

"You must be properly outfitted," the rabbi said. "Your host, young Bianchini, will help you there, I am sure. Since you travel among the Turks, you must leave your horse, which only Muslims may ride. They have many rules."

"I will give the Bianchinis my horse," I said, "to thank them for opening their home to us so unstintingly. We are grateful to you too, sir. How can we thank you?"

"Would you have any use for a mule?" Rachel asked. "A galley captain might not want to transport mules."

"My children," the rabbi said, "every member of our community here in Ancona, so fortunate ourselves, is well aware it is a *mitzvah* to shelter a fellow Jew. Each small act toward reuniting a Jewish family is a *mitzvah*. Your need gives us the opportunity to perform *mitzvaot*, so pleasing to Adonai."

"He has *matu'm*," Hutia said in Taino. He had been silent throughout the visit except for the initial courtesies on our arrival and whispered words to Rachel once we knew the contents of the letter.

"Among the Taino," I explained, "our friend's

people in the Indies, all they do is governed by generosity. It is their guiding principle."

"A spiritual people, then," the rabbi said, with a friendly nod to Hutia.

"So they were," I said.

"Give me half an hour," the rabbi said, "to write a few letters that you can present to certain people whom I think you will find helpful. If you wish no more refreshment, you might like to pass the time in the garden. It belongs to the synagogue, and all are welcome to enjoy it, but you will almost certainly have it to yourselves at this hour if you wish for privacy."

The three of us did not speak as we filed down the passage the rabbi indicated toward an archway that gave onto the gardens. We stepped out into brilliant sunlight. Rachel drew a long breath. I realized that I too had been so caught up in emotion that I had barely breathed since we had learned Papa and Mama's destination.

"We are going to find them!" Rachel exclaimed. "They are alive! We will see them again!"

"Did you not think you would, *nanichi*?" Hutia asked. "You have given no sign that you ever lost heart."

"I tried not to," Rachel said. "I did not want to discourage you, Diego, or make my worst imaginings real by speaking of them."

"It has been the same for me," I admitted. "Let us sit down. I don't know why joy should be exhausting, but I feel drained and limp, like an empty wineskin."

We sat on the nearest bench, its pink marble, veined in green, cool under us in spite of the heat of the day. Across from us, an elaborate fountain played, its waters providing pleasing splashing sounds that complemented the birdsong all around us. An occasional breeze sent a cooling mist our way. Formally clipped shrubs created ornamental screens and mazes. Columns and more fountains carved in stone were separated by the slender spears of cypress, trees of so dark a green they seemed almost black against the cloudless, burning sky.

"This is very different from the gardens of Seville," I said. "Ours had palm trees," I told Hutia, "not this severe cypress. In the gardens of the Alcazar, the arches and columns were Moorish work, elegantly curved and scrolled. Mama used to take us, Rachel. Do you remember? The paths were paved with glazed tiles in rich colors, and a profusion of flowers cascaded over walls and around corners. In comparison, this Italian garden is formal and lacking in color. It is peaceful, though. I suppose it is a matter of getting used to it."

"It is a new fashion," Rachel said. "Signora Bianchini was telling me. It started in Rome and Firenze, and now everyone in Ancona wants an Italian garden. They are based on classical Greek and Roman models. She said that some of the statues and fountains were not suitable for children. I know what she meant, because I got up early this morning and slipped out to explore their garden. In the farthest corner, there was a small clipped maze, a thick mass of shrubbery that you couldn't see through or over, so I went in, and at the center of the maze I found a marble statue of a fat little angel boy, what they call a *putto*. He was a fountain, and guess where the water came out?"

"Rachel!" I tried to sound stern, but I had to laugh. "You will have to practice guarding your tongue before we arrive in Istanbul. The freedom of speech you learned in Quisqueya will not do for Mama and Papa, not to mention a respectable Jewish congregation."

"How can you say that I cannot guard my tongue?" Rachel demanded. "I kept the secret that I was Jewish and a girl from 1493 to 1495. You will not meet another girl my age with such discretion in all of Europe or the whole Ottoman Empire. And in Quisqueya, nobody thinks of such silliness as respectability or having to watch what you say even to people you love. Don't you agree, Hutia?"

Hutia stood up and reached out his hands,

drawing her up beside him.

"Let us not quarrel," he said.

"*You* never quarrel, Hutia," she said.

I had opened my mouth to say the same. But arguing with Rachel was a futile exercise, as I knew by long experience. And I was happy. Even squabbling in jest was out of place today. I stood.

"Let us stroll and explore the garden," I said. "Do you think we will find a urinating *putto* hidden away in a corner?"

Rachel chuckled.

"Not in a *synagogue* garden," she said.

She danced down the path, which was made of pebbles that crunched agreeably underfoot. Hutia and I followed her. We passed down a long alley of tightly clipped shrubs that met overhead to form arches. I breathed in the slightly astringent spiciness of the shrubbery.

"I do not understand all this clipping and confining of what is meant to grow freely," Hutia said. "Indeed, I am just beginning to understand the idea of a garden."

"Quisqueya itself is a garden," Rachel said.

Rounding a corner in the hedge, Rachel, in the lead, almost ran into a man standing stock still in the middle of the path. He wore *tallit* and *t'fillin*. It seemed an odd place for anyone to say his prayers. He must have supposed himself alone in the garden, as we had. He was elderly and gaunt, his sunken cheeks visible above the rust and gray strings of his unkempt beard. He wore a black robe that looked as if it had seen better days and traveled many roads.

Rachel stammered out an apology for interrupting him. I echoed it, but he ignored me. Slowly, he lifted one hand and stroked Rachel's flushed cheek with his finger. I had never seen sadder eyes.

"'O daughter of my people,'" he said, "'gird thee with sackcloth, and wallow thyself in ashes.'" His voice was cracked but still vibrated with a faint sonority, as if it had been beautiful in his youth.

"'Make thee mourning, most bitter lamentation, for the spoiler has most bitterly come upon us.'"

Rachel took his hand.

"May I help you, sir? My name is Rachel, Rachel Mendoza. Would you care to sit and talk with us? Will you tell me your name?"

She drew him into an arbor that shaded a marble bench and down onto the seat beside her. I raised my brows at Hutia. He shrugged. My sister would do what she would do and say what she would say. I could hardly wait to hand the care of her over to Mama.

"I am Moshe Nahman," the old man said. "Like Moshe, I have wandered in the wilderness. Do you know what Nahman means? 'The Lord will console.' But Adonai cannot console me. We are cursed in His eyes." He raised his head and shook his fist at heaven. "'Thou hast given us like sheep appointed for meat and scattered us among the heathen.'"

"Did you come from Spain, sir?" Rachel asked. "We are from Seville, and we seek our parents."

"From Girona, and then from Portugal," Moshe Nahman said. "'And the Lord shall scatter thee among all people, from one end of the earth even unto the other; and there thou shall serve other gods, which neither thou nor thy fathers have known.'"

"We have just learned that our parents have gone to Istanbul," Rachel said. "It is said that the Sultan of the Ottomans allows Jews to live in peace in his lands."

"'And among these nations,'" Moshe Nahman said, "shalt thou find no ease, neither shall the sole of thy foot have rest: but the Lord shall give thee there a trembling heart, and failing of eyes, and sorrow of mind.'"

"You must have suffered greatly," Rachel said, stroking his hand. "I am so sorry. Did you fall into the hands of the Inquisition?"

"No." He held her hand in both of his, which were twisted and begrimed, the joints swollen and bumpy. "'Thou shalt beget sons and daughters, but thou shalt not enjoy them; for they shall go into captivity.'"

"I am so sorry!" Rachel repeated. "They took your children?"

The old man released her hand and tore at his beard. Tears spilled from his red-rimmed eyes and ran down his furrowed cheeks.

"'Thy sons and thy daughters shall be given unto another people, and thine eyes shall look and fail with longing for them all the day long.'"

"Oh, no!" Rachel cried. "It is unbearable! How did it happen?"

"The King of Portugal, cursed be he, stole our children and sent them to the Isle of Crocodiles." He shook his fist at the sky. "Adonai! Adonai! 'Thou hast sore broken us in the place of dragons and covered us with the shadow of death.'"

PART TWO
Istanbul

Chapter Twenty-Three: Diego

We reached Istanbul just before sunset. We had bought appropriate garments in Edirne: comfortable baggy trousers and long surcoats for Hutia and me, a long-sleeved underdress, a simple light brown overdress, and an enveloping robe and headscarf for Rachel. After some discussion, Hutia and I chose nondescript caps. The dazzling white turbans we saw everywhere once we entered Ottoman lands were reserved by law for Muslims. A stiff red cap like an overturned flowerpot caught Hutia's eye, but the vendor told us that they were made in Fez, a city of the Saadi sultanate in southern Morocco, and only foreigners wore them. We sold our doublets and Italian hats, along with Rachel's dresses, for ready money in the Ottoman silver *akçe*. While we remained ignorant of the rules that governed Jewish behavior here, we could not afford to be conspicuous.

The vast dome of Hagia Sophia dominated the city. Built by the Byzantines to be the world's greatest cathedral, it had been transformed into a mosque upon the conquest of Constantinople. At this hour, the light turned it into a great bowl of gold. We could see two minarets that the Turks had added, the slender towers from which the men known as muezzins called all Muslims to prayer. We could see many more minarets rising above the roofs of the city. As we looked, the call of the muezzins rang out in a melodious chant.

"Allāhu akbar . . . Lā ilāha illā-Allāh."

The call to prayer was in Arabic, the language of Islam. "God is the greatest . . . there is no God but God." A Turkish trader had been kind enough to tutor us on the road. We had left the caravan with enough mastery of Turkish to manage on our own while we made our way from Edirne to Istanbul. The road was very well traveled. We had never been alone or lacked for someone to ask if we needed anything or saw something we did not understand. We had grown accustomed to the sight of Muslim men unrolling their prayer rugs, as they did now, and prostrating themselves, turbaned heads bowed to the ground.

I moved my mule up to stand beside Rachel's, jerking on its rein when it tried to nip its companion. I put my lips close to Rachel's ear and sang the Shema.

"Sh'ma Yisrael, Adonai Eloheinu, Adonai echod."

"Hear, O Israel, the Lord our God, the Lord is One."

Jewish prayers and Muslim were not so very different. And if what we had been told was true, this Shabbat might find us in a synagogue, hearing a cantor sing these words aloud. As night fell, the Muslims, prayers completed, rolled up their prayer rugs and went about their business. Those with tents and wagons started fires by the roadside, while veiled women, who had withdrawn into the shadow of tent or wagon to pray, emerged and began to prepare their evening meal.

"Let us find a caravanserai," I said. "We will begin our search for Papa and Mama in the morning."

When we reached the inn, Rachel was relegated to the harem, the women's quarters, while Hutia and I shared a bed in a room assigned to *dhimmi*, the Turkish term for non-Muslims in their territories. Most of those with whom we shared the room were Christians. We soon fell into conversation with the only Jew, a trader in textiles from Salonica who knew no one in Istanbul except those engaged in his own business.

"We have a thriving Jewish community in Salonica," he said. "You might consider settling there if you find Istanbul too big and bustling for your taste. We have a booming textile industry. We also have Jewish printers in Salonica as good as any in Istanbul." He lowered his voice. "Would you believe that there would not be a single printing press in the Ottoman Empire without the Jews? It is against the Turks' religion to reproduce the written word in Arabic characters, that is, to print Turkish, Arabic, or Persian text. Their calligraphy is considered a holy art. It is beautiful, of course. But the net result is that the works we are allowed to print, in Hebrew as well as in the Latin alphabet, are those that will endure."

"We seek my parents," I explained. "They may have arrived months ago and established themselves so well that we have only to rejoin the family to feel at home in Istanbul. But I will remember your words about Salonica, just in case. Can you at least tell us where to find the Jewish quarter?"

"There is no Jewish quarter as such," he said. "There are many neighborhoods where Jews are welcome, as long as they do not build their houses too close to mosques or to the homes of Muslims. That too is prescribed by their religion."

"But there must be a synagogue," I said.

He laughed.

"There are many. The oldest is the Ahrida Synagogue in Balat, to the east, not far from the Bosphorus. That has been here since before the Ottoman conquest. But your people, the Jews from Spain and Portugal, have formed their own congregations. Not all of them have built their own synagogues, since the construction of new houses of worship by the *dhimmi* is against the Sultan's law as well."

"So many rules," I said, because I knew Rachel would have said it, had she been present.

"We may repair those that exist," the man from Salonica said. "And we are not forbidden to gather in a building the congregation designates for community use. So in fact, we do have synagogues, as long as we do not build conspicuous houses of worship to rival the mosques. To tell the truth, sometimes the rules are enforced, and sometimes we can do what we will for a while, until the wind changes."

"Can you direct me to the congregations of the Spanish Jews?" I asked.

"There are many of those too by now," he said. "You might start by seeking out Gerush, which was established when the first Jews from Spain arrived."

"A congregation of the exiled," I said. "The name is apt."

We set out the next morning, after swallowing a hasty breakfast of bread and dried figs, retrieving our mules from the stables, and loading all our possessions on their backs.

"How do you find something whose direction is *away* from any mosque?" Rachel demanded. "There are mosques everywhere!"

It was true: wherever we looked, we saw minarets thrusting up toward the sky. And those we could not see, because of some accident of the terrain, we heard five times a day when the muezzins called their people to prayer.

The innkeeper had advised us to keep Hagia Sophia on our right as we proceeded eastward to the central part of the city, which lay along the Bosphorus, the strait that divided Europe from Asia. As a guide, it left us a lot of territory to cover.

"It is also difficult," I said, "to look for buildings large enough to hold a congregation that do *not* display the Star of David anywhere."

"We must eliminate folk who cannot be Jews," Hutia said, "and question all the rest."

Rachel sighed.

"It will take *forever*," she said.

"It is the best idea we have," I said. "We need only ask those who are likely to know. We can eliminate men in white turbans."

"And women with their faces and bodies completely veiled," Hutia said. "Diego is right, Rachel."

"We need not accost anyone wearing a cross around his neck," I said.

"Very well," Rachel said. "Let us try it."

After carrying out this program for several hours, we were footsore and thirsty.

"We are closer to the Bosphorus," Rachel said, reaching for her waterskin, "and Hagia Sophia is still on our right, but we are no closer to finding Mama and Papa."

"We can find ourselves lodging and a meal and take up the search tomorrow," I said.

"No, let's keep trying for just a little longer," Rachel said.

As she spoke, a skinny, curly-headed boy dashed by almost under her mule's nose. He was too young to grow a beard and wore neither turban nor cross. We could hear the muezzins beginning the afternoon call to prayer, but the boy did not stop to pray.

"Hey!" Rachel said. "You, boy!" She encouraged her mule to shift its hindquarters, blocking the boy's way forward. "I just want to ask you a question."

The boy looked up at Rachel. He patted the mule's nose and reached out to scratch it behind its long ears.

"Nice mule," he said. "Does she like carrots?"

At Rachel's nod, he produced a purplish-black carrot from about his person and fed it to the mule.

"What do you want to know?" he asked.

"Can you tell us where we might find the Jews of Istanbul?" she asked.

"Sure," he said. "Which Jews do you want? The Iberians, the Germans, or the Greeks?"

"The Iberians," she said.

"We have heard that a congregation called Gerush," I said, "might know of the people we seek."

The boy produced another black carrot for my mule, which had moved closer as we spoke, pushing its muzzle forward.

Rachel gave him a sunny smile.

"We are from Seville ourselves," she said.

"Oh, in that case," the boy said, "you don't need to

ask at Gerush. There's a Seville congregation. They started it last year."

"Can you take us there?" I asked.

The boy looked not at me, but at Rachel.

"Sure," he said. "Will you give me a ride on your mule?"

An hour later, I stood with my fist poised to knock on the door of a house two stories high, made of wood and brick with a roof of ceramic tiles and a *mezuzah* fastened to the doorpost. I recognized the *mezuzah*. The small silver case with its filigree pattern of vines and roses had hung in our doorway in Seville. The house had no windows on the street. The rooms must face an inner courtyard, for I knew my mother could not live without light. Rachel was trembling with excitement. Hutia hung back, suddenly shy, with one hand on the gathered reins of the mules.

"Knock!" Rachel urged me. "Go ahead. Do it!"

I banged on the wooden door hard enough to make my knuckles tingle. I could hear voices within the house, not loud enough to make out words or recognize voices. I thought two people called to one another. Then one voice fell suddenly while the other got louder. Someone must be coming to the door. It swung open. A young man I did not recognize, wearing a *tallit*, peered out at us, squinting as if nearsighted.

"Yes?"

Then I heard my sister Elvira's voice call out, "Akiva? Who is it?"

A girl with a mop of hair as unruly as Rachel's came flying out of an inner room, shrieking, "It's them! It's them!" My sister Susanna flung herself upon me, arms tight around my neck and legs clinging to my waist. "Mama! Papa! Come quickly! Diego and Rachel have come home!"

And then Rachel was sobbing in Mama's arms, and Papa was lifting Susanna down so he could hug me himself, his beard wet with tears as it brushed against my cheek, or maybe the tears were mine.

"My boy, my boy!" Papa said. *"Baruch Ha'shem!* Thank God you're home!"

Chapter Twenty-Four: Rachel

In the morning, Papa and Diego left the house early to pray with the *minyan*, the men of the Seville congregation. Mama wept a little as she fingered Diego's begrimed and tattered *tallit*. Along with his *t'fillin*, it had accompanied him since he first sailed with Admiral Columbus in 1492.

"I will launder it," she said, "and Diego must have a new one. Fine silk cloth can be found in the Bedestan. But none will find the state of this one lacking in respect for Adonai. Every Jew in Istanbul knows a symbol of survival when he sees one."

Once they were gone, she turned to Hutia, who sat in a corner looking as if he hoped to remain unnoticed.

"Hutia, you must speak up if there is anything you need. You too have had a long journey and survived many dangers and sorrows. Will you spend the day with me and my daughters?"

Hutia leaped to his feet and bowed with a flourish he had learned from Signor Bianchini in Ancona.

"Doña Elena, I thank you for this invitation and for your kindness and hospitality."

Mama smiled with pleasure at this form of address, while Rachel laughed.

"Hutia, you bow like an Italian. It goes better in doublet and hose. Mama, how do people greet each other here?"

"Rachel, do not be rude to our guest. One says, '*Asalamu alaykum*,' and if you are greeted first, you may respond '*Alaykum asalaam*.'"

"But not at breakfast," Susanna said, spreading honey on her bread and licking her fingers.

"I do not mind Rachel's teasing, Doña Elena," Hutia said. "I am used to it."

"Anyway, I already know that greeting," Rachel said. "We heard it everywhere in the Balkans. It is Arabic for 'God's peace be upon you,' and the response is, 'And upon you also.' It was the first thing our Turkish tutor taught us."

"You studied Turkish?" Elvira asked. "Why? Most of our Jewish women do not learn it."

"Why not?" Rachel said. "Wherever I go, I like to be able to speak to the people I meet."

"Rachel speaks several languages fluently," Hutia said, "including Turkish, Italian, and Taino, my native tongue."

"Huh." Susanna's tone indicated that she would rather not be impressed. "Say something in Taino, Rachel."

Rachel grinned at Hutia. Her face softened as she said tenderly in Taino, "You will never forget your native tongue, *nanichi*, as long as I am alive to speak with you."

"Well, if Hutia says it is really Taino, so it must be," Susanna said. "What does it mean?"

"Nothing much," Rachel said. "What are we going to do today, Mama?"

"Would you like to go shopping?" Mama asked.

"Oh, Mama!" Rachel flung her arms around her mother and did her best to twirl her around. "Yes, yes, yes! I have not had a new dress in so long, unless you count the dress that Signora Bianchini gave me in Ancona, but nothing of my own, not for *years*."

"I will come too," Susanna said. "I love the bazaar."

"I had better go along," Elvira said, "to keep you all from being too extravagant. You too, Mama! I know you are dying to shower Rachel with pretty clothes."

"Hutia, will you come?" Rachel asked.

"No, thank you," Hutia said. "I would only be in the way."

"You mean you would be terrified," Rachel said, "to spend the day in the bazaar with four women bent on a bargain."

"Truly," Hutia said, "I find Istanbul itself overwhelming. You know that I am not used to cities. I can best conquer my unease by exploring the town on my own until I have become accustomed to it."

The Bedestan was a massive stone edifice of domes and great arched passageways, thronged with shoppers haggling over a dazzling variety of wares: silks, brocades, and velvets, gold and silver jewelry set with pearls and rubies, spices, glass, and weapons, leather goods, luxurious furs, elaborately carved wooden furniture and chests, embroidery and carpets, ribbons, buttons, and shoes.

"The Bedestan is only the covered market," Susanna said, skipping along beside Rachel. "The Grand Bazaar itself is far larger. We can go to the sweetmeat seller's, Mama, can we not, the one who makes the best Turkish delight? Rachel has never tasted it."

"We'll see." Mama linked her arm in Rachel's, as if she feared she would wander off and disappear. "Most of the Jewish shops in the Grand Bazaar are in the uncovered market, but gradually more Jews are being allowed to rent shops in the Bedestan."

"The shops are called trunks," Susanna said. "The vendors keep their goods in trunks that are locked at night, with guards to make sure that none disturb them."

"Elvira!" Mama said. "Do not get too far ahead."

"We will not get lost, Mama," Rachel said. "The girls obviously know the bazaar well, and I have been to the Indies and back without getting lost."

"Oh, my sweet girl!" Mama exclaimed. She stopped and embraced Rachel, oblivious to a group of turbaned men who were trying to get past. "I thought I had lost you forever."

"Even folk who know it well get lost in the Bedestan," Susanna said. "Mehmet the Conqueror, he who took this city from the Byzantines, designed it to be a city in itself. There's a mosque, though of course we can never go into it, and public fountains from which all may drink."

"I will not leave your side, Mama," Rachel promised. "Of course, when I sailed to the Indies, I had Admiral Columbus to make sure I did not get lost! Whatever his flaws, he is a very great navigator."

"I had forgotten you knew Christopher," Mama said. "He was a friend of Papa's, you know, when we were all young. How is he?"

"Mama!" Rachel cried. "Are you blushing?"

"What's this?" Susanna cried. "Elvira, come! We must hear this. Mama, was the Admiral your *novio*? Were he and Papa rivals for your hand?"

"Don't be silly, Susanna," Elvira said. "Columbus isn't Jewish. But do tell us more, Mama."

"He had bright red hair," Mama said, smiling reminiscently, "and a strong Genoese accent. But he had presence. You could tell he would do great things. And so he has, though I assure you, girls, I would never have married anyone but Papa. What is he like now, Rachel?"

Rachel grinned.

"He has lost the accent," she said. "His hair is white, and he forgets to comb it, for he always has some great work in hand: a town to build, a course to chart, or a letter to write to the Queen. And he suffers from the gout."

"Oh, no!" Mama said. "Ah, well, nobody stays young forever."

"The first time I met him," Rachel said, "in Seville, he said that I reminded him of you."

"Ask Papa," Mama said. "He will say the same. You spoke of flaws, and I do not think you meant a neglect of grooming."

"He was always very kind to me, Mama," Rachel said. "Indeed, he kept me safe. And he was fond of Diego, showing him much favor. But Hispaniola changed him. First, he wanted to make all the Taino

Christians. You may talk to Hutia about it, if the Jews' experience is not sufficient proof of what is wrong with that! But then he came to believe that there was gold in Hispaniola. Well, there was, but only in the rivers. The Taino do not value it. Their whole virtue is generosity, and they gave it to us freely, once they knew we liked it. The Admiral came to believe there was a mine and that the Taino were keeping it secret from him. But there was not! He had them tortured, Mama, so they would tell him where to find the gold. And then he became obsessed with what he owed the King and Queen for supporting his explorations and how he must repay them by sending the Taino as slaves to Spain, since he could not send sufficient gold."

Mama pinched her lips together and shook her head.

"Slavery is a cruel practice," she said, "and I am afraid you will see much of it here. Even some Jews have slaves, which Papa and I deplore deeply. Papa says what he can to make the congregation speak out against it, but so far, without success."

"You must be very kind to Hutia, Mama, and so must Papa. We have lost much, but we still have each other, and here in Istanbul, the Jews as a people have a chance to rebuild. Hutia has lost everyone, Mama! The Taino are no more."

Mama kissed her.

"We will do all we can to help your friend make a new home here, my dear, for Diego's sake and for yours."

"I want to talk to you about that," Rachel began.

Susanna had flitted off to browse among the wares on display in the nearest shops. "Rachel!" she called out. "You must see this."

The moment was lost. Susanna was holding up a pair of oddly shaped objects made of leather on which strips of silver leaf had been laid in intricate patterns around an inlay of mother of pearl, with pegs extending downward.

"Are they shoes?" Rachel asked. "They look like

tiny six-legged tables."

"They are shoes," Susanna said, "made for ladies of the harem."

"You know about the harem, do you not?" Elvira said. "The Muslim ladies do not go out, but live in special quarters, where they are not allowed to see any men except their fathers and brothers, and of course their husbands when they marry."

"In the inn where we stayed the night before we found you, I slept in a sort of harem, except that there were not only Muslim women, but Christian women as well, besides me. I found it very relaxing. I have not been much in the company of women since I left the convent in Barcelona, except for a few months in '93 with a family in Seville that had many daughters. I did not realize I missed it."

"And now you have us!" Susanna said, beaming.

"I see women in the market who are completely veiled," Rachel said, looking around her. "So Muslim ladies do go out."

"They are probably servants or the poorer class of women," Elvira said. "Shoes like these, raised high above the ground so the wearer's feet never get wet or dirty, are for the Sultan's wives and concubines or the wives of the very rich. You will not see such ladies in the market, even in the richest quarters of the Bedestan."

"Come, girls," Mama said. "We must move on. Rachel needs shoes, but less expensive ones."

"Oh, Mama," Rachel said, "may I have a pair of red leather slippers with pointed toes? I saw them at the inn, and they are adorable. It is *so* long since I wore something pretty."

Mama being inclined to indulge her newly restored daughter, Rachel soon owned two pairs of flat slippers with pointed toes, the second in a sensible brown leather, and three dresses with gathered waists and buttons. Two were plain, but dyed a deep ochre and a rich red, with silk buttons. The third was blue and heavily embroidered in a floral pattern. Mama had said a firm no to a cream-colored silk gown embroidered in gold thread, calling it unsuitable for an unmarried girl who was not a princess.

"Or a sultan's concubine," Rachel said. "That's all right, Mama, I didn't really think you would let me have it. It is beautiful, though."

"We need to get you several of the long-sleeved underdresses, Rachel," Mama said. "Everybody wears those, Muslim and Jewish women alike."

"It is as well you did not fall in love with the green gown," Susanna said. "Green is a color that only Muslims may wear."

"You must have a hat or two," Elvira said, "perhaps a couple of these cup-shaped caps in the colors of your gowns, with a twist of scarf around it like a sort of turban."

"Can I have a *şalvar*? They are not only for men. Look, there is a Turkish woman with the trousers showing under a shorter overdress, more like a tunic."

"We don't usually—" Mama began.

An unveiled woman with a dark cloak and scarf over her hair stumbled into her. Mama reached out to keep her from falling.

"Malka! Is it you?"

"Elena! I am so sorry. I tripped and lost my shoe."

Rachel started forward, recognizing the mother of a childhood friend from Seville, though much altered by suffering. She was Mama's age, but she looked twenty years older. Elvira held Rachel back, grasping her arm in an iron grip.

"Don't ask about Naomi!" she whispered. "In fact, come. We will look at hats while Mama talks to her."

"But won't she want to—"

"No! Come away. I'll explain later."

It occurred to Rachel that Malka must be their neighbor here as well and a member of the Seville congregation. Susanna had also recognized their former neighbor. Rather than greeting her, Susanna too had turned away and was making a great show of shaking out silk and satin scarves and holding them up against the bright-colored caps to see if their colors complemented each other's.

"Is there some reason we must shun her?" Rachel asked. "If so, why is Mama being so friendly?"

A quick look over her shoulder showed her that Mama had turned her back on her own daughters as if to protect them from the sight of Malka, or perhaps Malka from them, since she was talking to the woman in what seemed to be a sympathetic fashion, nodding and reaching out now and then to touch her arm.

"It's not that," Elvira said. "You might as well pick out your scarves and caps. We'll tell you once Malka is gone."

Fifteen minutes later, Mama joined them.

"Poor Malka!" she said.

"Why were we not to speak with her, Mama?" Rachel asked. "What happened to Naomi?"

"I did not want to cause her pain," Mama said, "by reminding her that I have beautiful, healthy daughters who are a source of pride and comfort to me. Naomi is dead, and so are her brothers and her little sister."

"All of them? How terrible! What happened?"

"Poor Malka! She and Avram went first to Portugal in '92, to Lisbon, as many Jewish families did, thinking it would be more like home than Italy. The Portuguese took them in, but then they changed their minds, and the King sent the children to the lizards—all four little ones, and Naomi was killed trying to stop them. She was too old to be taken herself, the same age as you, but she tried to intervene. The soldiers killed her right there on the docks. Malka is half mad with grief and Avram not much better."

"How terrible! Sent to the lizards! Is that the same as the Isle of Crocodiles? We met an old man in Ancona who had lost his children. It had driven him mad as well. He could hardly speak sensibly. He kept quoting Bible verses: 'Thou hast sore broken us in the place of dragons and covered us with the shadow of death.' Psalm 44: I asked Rabbi Gershon, and he told me. He said it was as pertinent a comment on the situation as any a rational man could utter."

"Rabbi Gershon is a good man," Mama said. "We might none of us have gotten here without his help. But now you will see why you must be betrothed immediately and married as soon as possible. Even Papa no longer thinks early betrothals a bad thing— not that yours would be an early betrothal, you are as old as some of the widows in our congregation. We have lost so many children! We must rebuild, or Israel will be lost and forgotten. It is your duty, all of you, to regenerate the Jewish people. Family has always been important to us, the most important thing after love of Adonai. Indeed, they are the same. I have been meaning to discuss this with you ever since you arrived. We must lose no time, for all the parents feel the same, and the rabbis agree that it is a matter of urgency. There are several nice boys in our congregation. Some of them are children you played with in Seville. You must meet them all as soon as possible. Papa and I are prepared to respect any preference you have, for we want you to be happy."

Rachel listened, appalled. She could not wait for a quiet moment to break her news to Mama. She must speak at once.

"Mama! Stop! I too have meant to talk with you. If I had known you and Papa had such ideas about my betrothal, I would not have delayed one second. Hear me now, and please, please try to understand. Hutia is not only Diego's friend and mine. He is far more. He is the man I plan to marry, and I will not, I cannot have another."

"Rachel!" Susanna screeched. "Are you out of your mind?" She clapped a hand to her mouth, eyes round with shock.

"You cannot disappoint Papa with such a mad idea." Elvira frowned in disapproval. "If you drop it now, he will not even need to know. Akiva, too, would be shocked. I will not tell him. You are my sister, and I do not wish to see you shamed."

Mama shook her head and reached out to smooth Rachel's hair off her forehead. Rachel's heart sank to see her look of sorrow. Anger she could have braced herself against.

"Rachel, oh, my darling," Mama said. "What have you done?"

Chapter Twenty-Five: Diego

"Sh'ma Yisrael, Adonai Eloheinu, Adonai echod.*"

I felt a thrill run through me as the strong male voices rang out. I had kept faith with Adonai for so long without a *minyan*. In the crow's nest of the *Santa Maria* in the uncharted Ocean Sea, in the depths of a tropical paradise in Hispaniola when it put my life at risk, in the shadow of a ruined castle on the dry plains of Spain, I had prayed alone. Whispering or crying aloud to God, I had counted on the raging winds to conceal my voice from men to whom my Jewish faith was an abomination. My blood sang to hear my brethren declare so boldly that the God of Israel is One.

Papa and I sat to one side of the crowded room, where we could see both the Ark of the Covenant and the *teba*, the platform from which the rabbi conducted the service and from which the weekly portions of the Torah and Haftorah were read. It was my first Shabbat in Istanbul, but I recognized some of the men from the daily *minyan* and others, familiar faces I had never thought to see again, from my boyhood in Seville. I let the familiar prayers wash over me, feeling for a moment Adonai's presence and a deep sense of home.

The gabbai made his way down the rows of congregants as the rabbi and cantor approached the Ark. He stopped beside us, leaned over, and whispered in Papa's ear.

Papa turned to me and murmured, "You are being honored. The rabbi invites you to help carry the Torah. Our sons do not often return from the dead."

He stood so I could squeeze by him. I followed the gabbai to the front of the sanctuary, where the rabbi and the cantor were gently lifting the holy Book out of its resting place. I kissed one corner of my *tallit* and touched it to the Torah. The whole congregation did the same as we carried it around the room. I wondered if the other men felt the same joyous awe that I did. Women were not allowed to touch the Torah, so we did not carry it to where they sat, a side room from which they could hear but not see the rabbi. I wondered how Rachel felt about that.

Every morning after we had prayed with the *minyan*, Papa showed me more of the many sights of Istanbul. These hours of walking and talking were precious to me. One day, he took me to see the Sultan's Palace, a vast complex of buildings and courtyards, domes and towers. Set high on a hill overlooking the Bosphorus, it looked more like a European walled city than a residence.

"It is far more than a residence," Papa told me. "All the business of the Empire is conducted here. They say no event is too small, no person too humble to engage the Sultan's attention. After all, even the grand vizier and the commanders of his army and navy are considered his personal slaves."

"I do not like the sound of that," I said. "And we?"

"Let us put it this way," Papa said. "He does not buy and sell either viziers or Jews, but he has the power of life and death over all his subjects, and he expects total loyalty. It is never wise to take any action without considering his will."

We came to a monumental arched gate supported by two conical towers and a thick section of crenellated wall. It was well guarded by janissaries dressed in uniforms of red and gold, consisting of *şalvar*, the loose Turkish trousers, tucked into high boots, tunic and vest, and a tall conical hat with a rectangular flap of cloth hanging down behind it. All of them had dark mustachios that added to their air of menace. A curved sword hung at each janissary's waist. Those nearest the gate held arquebuses as well.

"Fierce, are they not?" Papa murmured. "All born Christian in the Balkans, taken as boys, and educated in an inner courtyard of this very palace. Our Jewish countrymen extol the Sultan's benevolence to the Jews. But make no mistake. The Sultan's welcome has its foundation in the *cizye*, the poll tax levied on all who are not Muslim."

"Who collects the taxes?" I asked, trying to look through the gate without getting too close to the janissaries. I could see handsomely clothed and mounted troops falling into ranks, their horses prancing and shaking out their manes.

"We do," Papa said. "The congregation is taxed collectively, and the rabbi is responsible for paying it out."

"It is a clever system," I said. "The Sultan does not borrow from Jewish bankers and get rich by defaulting on the loans and banishing the lenders as the sovereigns did in Spain, but finances his empire through taxation and gets the taxed to collect it."

"If you wish to become wealthy here," Papa said, "one way to do so is to seek an appointment as a tax farmer. Indeed, the tax farmer has to start out rich enough to purchase the office. For a sizable sum, the Sultan authorizes the tax farmer to collect the revenues of some substantial office such as a mint or a port where there are all sorts of taxes on trade. The Sultan takes a portion of the revenue, while the tax farmer keeps the rest. If any difficulties arise, the problem is the tax farmer's, not the Sultan's."

"It is not an occupation that appeals to me," I said. "I want to prosper, but I have seen what can happen when men make their most important decisions on the basis of a desire for riches."

I could see the horsemen circling on the grassy expanse of the courtyard and forming up into two bodies facing each other. Each held a short wooden javelin loosely couched.

"Are Jews allowed inside?" I asked, gesturing toward the gate.

"Anyone may enter the outermost courtyard," he said. "It is like a park, as you can see, with administrative buildings set around it. One of them is the imperial mint."

"Let us enter," I said. "I would like to see what the horsemen are doing. It looks like some kind of sport or military drill."

The janissaries neither acknowledged nor stopped us. When I looked back, those closest to the gate were casting quick glances at the activity inside.

"What do you want to do with your life, Diego?" Papa asked. "You do not want to remain a sailor, do you?"

"I never intended to," I said, "though I have come to love the sea. I am a skilled seaman, given a sailing ship on the Ocean Sea. But I am no expert when it comes to Muslim galleys upon the Mediterranean."

"There are other trades involving the sea," Papa said, "shipbuilding and commerce. Trade between Istanbul and lands to be reached by ship is growing and will increase further as the Sultan seeks to extend Ottoman influence to the Maghreb, besides having his eye on Venice."

"I would like some time to think about it," I said.

Two groups of twenty horsemen each now faced each other at some distance. Each team, for so they must be, had a flagbearer. One team flew a green banner, the other a blue. One of the green players picked up his reins and galloped toward the blue team, calling out a single word as he threw his javelin. The game had started. A single player on the opposing team responded, guiding his horse away from the speeding javelin and calling out as he threw his own. Before long, both teams were fully engaged, wheeling and galloping as they cast their javelins. The object seemed to be to hit an opposing player. When a blue player hit his opponent's horse, his own teammates as well as his opponents jeered. After watching for some time, I realized that each player called out the name of his chosen opponent before letting the javelin fly. Several times, the most skillful players actually caught the javelin aimed at them in one hand. The horsemanship was dazzling. The players hardly touched their reins, but guided their horses with their knees. More and more riders broke away from the groups. One blue player lured three green players to pursue him to the far end of the field, taking pressure off his teammates.

A crowd had gathered, cheering on one team or the other and furtively making wagers.

One loser, flipping a gold ducat at a grinning winner, said, "It is written: 'The sin is greater than the profit.'" He then cast a sharp look around. Only my father and I and a gangling youth of about fifteen in a white turban and silver-embroidered vest over white garments stood near enough to overhear what I suspected was a blasphemous quotation from the Quran. The man's gaze passed over us dismissively. I could see the boy noticed that he had been snubbed. His shoulders drooped, and he hung his head with a sigh.

"*Asalamu alaykum,*" I said, nodding at the boy.

"*Alaykum asalaam.*" His face brightened. "They play well, do they not? I support the greens. Which team do you favor?"

"I have no preference," I said, "because I have never seen this game played before. I don't even know what it is called."

"How is that possible?" the boy asked. "Everybody knows *cereed.*"

"I have but recently arrived in Istanbul. My name is Diego."

"I am Hasan. Where are you from, that you do not know *cereed*?"

"I am originally from Seville, in Spain, but lately I have been in Italy, and, before that, in the Indies, far across the Ocean Sea. Will you tell me about the game?"

"The *cereed* is the javelin. It is a very ancient game. They play it in the army to stay fit between battles and at festivals like the end of Ramazan. The team gains points by hitting a player or catching the *cereed*, also by retrieving javelins from the ground with the curved cane they carry. They lose points if they hit the horse or injure it or if they ride out of bounds."

"Do you play *cereed*, Hasan?" I smiled at him.

The boy drooped, all the animation in his face and bearing leaching away.

"I am not allowed to bear weapons, even in sport," he said.

"Why is that, if I may ask?"

The boy looked sideways at me through his dark lashes.

"You are not a Muslim, are you?"

"No, I am a Jew."

"I thought so," he said. "Then I will tell you, and perhaps you will not regard me with disgust."

"I am sure that I will not," I said.

"I am the son of Prince Cem," he said. "I should not be alive."

"Why not?" I asked. "Are you ill?"

"You have not heard of my father? That is hard to believe." He added hastily, "Though I do believe you!"

"As I said, I have just arrived," I said. "I am still learning about my new home. Tell me about your father."

"My father was Prince Cem," he said, "the brother of our Sultan Bayezid. He is dead now. When my grandfather, Sultan Mehmet, died, the Grand Vizier tried to make my father the Sultan. But the janissaries were loyal to Bayezid. They killed the Grand Vizier and declared my uncle the Sultan. For a time, my father ruled in Bursa, hoping to share the empire. But the Sultan marched against him. After my father lost his final battle, he had to flee. He hoped the Christian Knights of Rhodes would help him regain his throne, but instead, they held him captive for many years. I was born after he fled, so I never knew him. Later on, he became the prisoner of the Pope. They say Sultan Bayezid paid the Pope much gold to promise never to release him. The

Sultan has held me hostage all my life. Cem died earlier this year, but he thinks it safer not to release me, in case I should try to usurp the throne. I am not allowed to learn the art of war. But I must be grateful. Everyone knows that when Bayezid fought my father, he said, 'There is no kinship between rulers.' It is normal for a sultan to behead his rivals or to have them poisoned or strangled with a silken bowstring. But he lets me live. So I must never seek to rule."

"I am sorry," I said. "It seems unfair that you cannot even play *cereed*. Look, the game is over. Your team has won. Did you have a wager on the game?"

"No," he said, "I am not allowed to have coin."

It seemed a sad life for a boy. The players were clapping each other on the back and making rude remarks as grooms came to lead away the horses. They reminded me of my Taino friends after a game of *batey*. How differently the Turks and the Taino regarded sport. Here, the game was played with weapons and considered preparation for war. The Taino had no word for war, played with a bouncing sphere that would harm no one, and used the game to resolve disputes and honor the gods.

"I have a friend you might like to meet," I said to Hasan. "If I may come and visit you again, I will bring him."

"Another Jew?" Hasan asked. "I would welcome him, for I have no friends. Nobody wants to be suspected of conspiring against the throne."

"He is neither Jew, Christian, nor Muslim," I said, "for he comes from a faraway land across the Ocean Sea. His name is Hutia. I have seen him spear fish and small animals, and I think he could match any of those players at throwing the *cereed*. But when I first met him, he had never seen a horse. He says he is getting used to them, but I think he still does not quite like them."

"He would like my horse," Hasan said. "I am allowed to ride, and my mare, Esinti, is both swift and sweet-tempered. She is gray, and her name means 'breeze'. Please do come to visit me, and bring your friend Hutia with you. You may ask for Prince Hasan, and someone will fetch me. There is usually a game of *cereed* at this hour. If you come then, we can watch it together. If anyone questions you about your business with me, you may say that you have come to tutor me in—what skills do you have that I might study with you?"

"How about Hebrew," I said, laughing, "and navigation?"

"Those will do," Hasan said. "Please come back soon. I am very happy to have met you!"

"That poor boy," Papa said as we passed out through the great arch and made our way through the winding streets toward home. "What a lonely life he has."

"You heard all he said?" I asked.

"Yes, I could not help hearing," Papa said, "though I tried to stay out of your way. Of the thousands of souls who inhabit that Palace, I think you have befriended the one who cannot offer you any advantage."

"Then it is a good thing you raised me not to consider advantage in choosing my friends!" I said. "Hasan seems younger than his age, do you not think so?"

"That is what living without a sense of purpose will do to you," Papa said. "Think of that when you are tempted to put off choosing your life's work."

"Yes, Papa." I regarded him with affection. "Oh, Papa, I am so glad to be with you again! You cannot imagine how many times I longed for your counsel. Indeed, you were often present in my mind, adjuring me to behave far more wisely than I would have on my own."

"I am glad to hear it," he said. "*Baruch Ha'shem*, you are not like that poor fatherless boy. The blood of Mehmet the Conqueror flows in his veins, and the only guidance he has ever received is that he must not be a warrior, a statesman, or a visionary. Did you notice how adept he was at conspiring to make sure your presence in the Palace would not be questioned? I suppose an Ottoman prince imbibes intrigue with his mother's milk."

Chapter Twenty-Six: Rachel

When Mama asked Rachel if she might have behaved so recklessly as to need to marry in haste, she refuted the suggestion so indignantly that Mama had ended by offering an unprecedented apology, with Rachel in floods of tears. She had not been able to return home until she had bathed her swollen eyes at one of the convenient public fountains in the bazaar. By common consent, neither Mama nor the girls brought up Rachel's revelation or the matter of her marriage again. If they talked of it among themselves, she did not know of it. Nor had they mentioned it to Papa, or he would certainly have insisted on discussing it with Rachel, most likely calling a full family conclave without delay.

Rachel longed for a good talk with Diego, who would surely understand her feelings and might advise her how to approach Papa and persuade Mama to support her. But life in Istanbul differed from the cameraderie of the road, the even greater liberty of life on shipboard, where Rachel had passed for a boy, and the glorious freedom of the Taino *yucayeque*. There, Rachel had shared in the constant but agreeable work of keeping the village fed and comfortable and been given unstinting love and whatever else she asked for without a moment's hesitation. She missed bare limbs and freedom of movement, the easy social intercourse between men and women, and the joy of throwing herself into a game of *batey*, not to mention the elation of winning and the delicious exhaustion at the end of the day, when a flower-scented breeze rocked her *hamaca* and sent her untroubled dreams.

It was never quiet in Istanbul. The houses in their street were crammed close together, the stars looked pinched and feeble instead of glowing and beckoning as they did in Quisqueya, and no matter how late she lay awake, there was always a couple arguing or a baby crying, if not both at once. Men and women lived such separate lives here that she could never find an opportunity to pour out her troubles into Diego's ear. He was always gone, either at synagogue with Papa or running all over Istanbul, going wherever he wanted and looking at whatever he wanted to see, secure in the knowledge that his family trusted him to define his own destiny and shape a productive future for himself. They weren't even pushing him to marry! Or if they were, they were probably telling him he had plenty of time, and of course he had to get himself established in some trade and wait for those eligible little girls to grow up enough to make acceptable wives.

Worse, she did not dare talk about all this to Hutia. He did not understand jealousy or envy. She would be ashamed for him to hear her whine about her petty discontents. But it would not be petty if they made her marry someone who was not Hutia! She could not bring herself to tell him that her family opposed the match, because she wanted him to love them, not to resent them. Maybe she could get Hutia and Diego between them to broach the topic of Hutia's conversion, letting Papa and Mama get used to the idea of a Jewish Hutia before mentioning betrothal.

This she thought she had accomplished one evening when, the evening meal over, the family sat together making the most of the time when various tasks could be performed before the light failed. Elvira and Akiva had gone home, and Susanna had gone with them. The newlyweds lived next door with Cousin Chaim and Cousin Miriam, although it was a family joke that one would never know it, they spent so much time at the Mendozas'. Mama was mending one of Papa's shirts. Rachel herself was embroidering a vest in colored silks, a task she enjoyed and would have done more if it had not so often led to someone asking if the pretty garment was for her wedding. Papa was mending a shoe. Diego was poring over the Torah portion he was supposed to read on Shabbat; the rabbi had let him take the precious parchment home because it was so long since he had read Hebrew. Of course he wanted to make the family proud. If only she too could make the family proud simply by reading! Hutia was oiling and sharpening a knife and humming under his breath.

She had pulled Diego aside just before they all sat down to eat and begged him to say something to Papa about Hutia's desire to convert. But now he was absorbed in study, his finger traveling from right to left across the page and his lips moving as he silently pronounced the Hebrew words. If he did not take care, he would turn into a stuffy old man like Cousin Chaim, who locked himself into his study, saying that every Jewish man was commanded to learn Torah as the highest form of *mitzvah*, and emerged hours later so rumpled and dazed that it was obvious he had done nothing but nap all afternoon. Meanwhile, Cousin Miriam worked from morning to night, cleaning and cooking and baking not only for her family, but to sell her delicious fig tarts in the bazaar and bring in a little extra money for a bottle of wine for Cousin Chaim or a new silk *tallit* for Akiva. That is what women do, Mama told her when she said it wasn't fair that Cousin Miriam did all the work and Cousin Chaim did none. It was not the life Rachel wanted. Susanna liked nothing better than to have Mama impart a secret recipe that her own mother had handed down to her. And Elvira was downright smug these days. If she didn't want anyone to know yet that she was expecting a baby, she should not be knitting tiny caps and blankets where everyone could see.

"Diego? Diego!" When he looked up, Rachel cast a meaningful glance at Hutia and jerked her head toward Papa.

"What? Oh." Diego shook his head and pulled himself together, smoothing out the page of Torah and folding a clean cloth over it before putting it carefully on a shelf where it could not get damaged.

"Papa," he said, "Hutia and I wish to have a serious talk with you and Mama. That is, Hutia has a request, and I have promised to help him explain and ask for your support."

Mama exclaimed sharply and sucked at her finger. She had stuck herself with the needle.

Did Mama think that Hutia was about to ask her hand in marriage? Rachel hurried into speech, not trusting what any of them might say.

"We have all been talking about Hutia's conversion for some time."

"Hadn't Hutia better speak for himself?" Papa said.

Hutia squared his shoulders.

"Yes, sir, I will. Don Efraín, Doña Elena, you know that I am far from my home and that my people are dead or dying. Until I met Diego and then Rachel, I had never heard of Adonai. The Taino knew nothing of the One God. We knew only the *cemi*, our gods of earth and sky, of storms and death. But I have left the *cemi* behind. Indeed, I believe they too are dead or dying. Does not a god die when all who heard his voice are gone? Is that not why you left Spain, so the voice of Adonai would remain strong?"

"Something like that," Papa said. "Go on. I am listening."

"A man is made of spirit," Hutia said, "as well as flesh and bone. He must believe in something, or he will despair. The Spaniards brought a proud man and a weak man to persuade the Taino to follow the Christian way."

"Fray Buil and Fray Pane," Diego said. "I agree. I knew them, and nothing they did and said could have recommended Christianity to either Taino or Jew. Hutia is saying he hungers for a spiritual home, Papa."

"I know what he is saying, my son," Papa said. "What do you wish to do, Hutia?"

"I wish to become part of your family as a Jew," Hutia said. "To convert."

"We Jews are not like the Christians or the Muslims," Papa said. "We do not encourage conversion. The rabbis would have to consent, and they will not do so easily."

"I understand."

"Jews are the People of the Book. You would have to learn to read Hebrew and study Torah and Talmud."

"I understand that too," Hutia said. "I will learn."

"He is very quick at languages, Papa," Diego said.

"Hutia is good at any task he undertakes," Rachel said.

"It is to your credit, Hutia," Papa said, "that my children think so highly of you. But that is not enough. You would have to be circumcised. Do you understand that fully? Are you willing?"

"I understand, and I am willing."

"I have lived more than fifty years," Papa said, "and I have never met a convert. Not a soul I have known would choose to be a Jew, were he not born to it. But I know your history, and I hear your sincerity. Every man needs a community. No man should have to live alone. You ask to join our family as well as the community. Very well. Let me think about it, and in the meantime, you may begin your studies, if Diego is willing to help you."

"I am, Papa," Diego said.

"I will help too," Rachel said.

She heard Mama draw in a quick breath.

"Elena? What is your opinion? Please speak."

Rachel held her breath.

"No, no. I agree with you, but Rachel has her household duties to keep her busy. How can any but a Jewish man teach Hutia to be a Jewish man? It is for Diego to provide this assistance."

Please, Ha'shem, no more, Rachel prayed. It is enough. Let them leave it for now, with all of us in accord.

Mama picked up her needle. Diego stood.

"Then we are all agreed?" Papa said.

"No, sir," Hutia said. "That is, yes, I thank you, and I will do all you ask while you consider whether I am worthy. If I am not, you will not speak for me before the rabbis. If I am, I hope you will. But there is more. The quality we Taino value most in a man or woman is *matu'm*. You would call it generosity. My people loved Rachel and Diego because they are *matu'n*. They give always with an open hand and a full heart. Since then I have met other Jews in whom I have seen *matu'm*, those whose joy it is to do what you call *mitzvaot*. I have also learned to recognize another quality, one that you, Don Efraín, have in full measure: integrity. I must show you that I have equal integrity by waiting no longer to tell you that I love Rachel. I wish to marry her. I know you wish her to wed a Jewish man. I will prove that I am worthy of her by becoming such a man."

"Elena, did you know about this?"

"I told Rachel she must not think of it. I hoped that would be enough."

"Hutia is the finest man I know, Papa," Diego said. "He has behaved with great honor throughout our difficult travels, and I would rejoice to make him my brother and see Rachel happy."

"Don Efraín," Hutia said, "this is not some bargain I make with Adonai for the sake of winning Rachel. When I become a Jew, Adonai will be my God."

"It is not Adonai, but the Seville congregation, that will oppose this match, I fear," Diego said, "and the conversion, too, if they learn of both at the same time."

"Hutia, *nanichi*, my beloved," Rachel said, her eyes swimming with tears, "you should not have spoken. Why did you not ask me first? I would have told you to wait."

"My darling Rachel," Hutia said. "I could not wait, for I cannot bear to lose you. Please do not ask me to leave you, for wherever you go, I will go, and wherever you live, I will live. Your people will be my people, and your God will be my God."

Mama gasped. Papa's eyebrows shot up.

"I did not tell him to say that," Diego said. "I swear it. He has never read the Book of Ruth."

"What?" Hutia said. "What have I said?"

"It is written," Diego said, "in the Book of our people, the Book for which we have suffered so much. One of our foremothers said exactly what you did. You uttered Ruth's very words."

As if against her will, Mama said softly, "'Entreat me not to leave thee or to return from following after thee. For whither thou goest, I will go, and where thou lodgest, I will lodge. Thy people shall be my people and thy God, my God.'" Her eyes met Papa's. "It is something true lovers say."

"Please, Papa!" Rachel, her eyes now streaming with tears, held out her hands to Hutia. "You must see that we are meant to be together."

"I believe that God is telling us not to reject Hutia's suit out of hand," Papa said. "More than that I cannot promise you."

"Thank you, thank you!" Rachel cried. "It will be all right, Hutia, I know it will."

She would have embraced Hutia, but he took her hands and clasped them firmly, holding her a little away from him. Papa gave a nod of approval.

"Do not get ahead of yourself, Rachel," Papa said. "I make no promises."

Chapter Twenty-Seven: Diego

𝔐onths later, I was no closer to finding an occupation that I could believe would engage my mind and heart for a lifetime. Nor had Mama and the matchmakers of the Seville congregation succeeded in finding me a wife. I could not take seriously the prospect of joining my life to that of any of the twelve-year-old nice Jewish girls they trotted out for my inspection. While not as sheltered as they would have been had we all been able to remain in Spain, they were docile and content with the prospect of spending their days managing a household and, eventually, children, going to the *mikvah*, and looking forward to a new dress for Pesach or a family wedding. Papa and Mama, who had married for love, allowed me to reject these prospects, regardless of what advantages might be obtained by marrying into the family of one girl or another. Everybody else, from Cousin Miriam to Rabbi Eliyahu, the chief rabbi of the congregation, told me with complacency or conviction that love came after marriage. But I could not forget the beauty of the love I had shared with my Taino sweetheart. Having known Tanama and traveled with my sister Rachel, I wanted a marriage of the body, heart, and mind that none of these unfledged girls could provide.

As to Hutia's conversion and marriage to Rachel, the battle still raged. Papa and Mama, living under the same roof as the thwarted lovers, could not help but see Hutia's many virtues and how miserable Rachel would be if forced into an arranged match. They came around to a degree of acceptance of the marriage insofar as they refrained from proposing any of the youths of the congregation as a husband. But the rabbis were inalterably opposed to letting Hutia convert, much less dilute the blood of Israel by allowing Rachel to marry him and bear his children.

Hutia refused to be discouraged. He impressed even my conservative brother-in-law Akiva by learning, with Rachel's help, to read and write Hebrew characters and puzzle out the meaning of the words they formed. He learned to read and write Latin characters as well, insisting that to be worthy of Rachel, he must be literate in Castilian. I discovered by chance that he could also write the beautiful script of Ottoman Turkish, which I doubted many of our Jewish scholars, if any, had mastered.

"You are full of surprises, Hutia," I said when I came upon him practicing the flowing characters one evening. "As the People of the Book, we take such pride in our intellectual brilliance that it astonishes me the rabbis are not begging you to become one of us. Where did you learn to write Turkish?"

"At the Palace," he said. "Through Hasan, I have become acquainted with all sorts of interesting people: imams and janissaries, dervishes and poets."

"I never dreamed your visits to the palace had any purpose but to watch *cereed* with Hasan."

The very day after my first meeting with the young prince, I had brought Hutia to meet him and watch a game of the remarkable sport. Hutia had enjoyed it immensely, as I had known he would. Since then, I had not returned, since I could not neglect my obligations to the Jewish community. Papa had started to invest in trading ventures between Istanbul and other lands, both westward to Venice and Ancona and eastward along the silk route. While importing and exporting luxury goods such as spices, perfumes, dyes, and the finest textiles did not strike me as the vocation I sought, I gave him whatever help I could. In the meantime, Hutia had gone his own way.

"Hasan's tutor," he said, "who has Sufi leanings, is

encouraging me to learn Persian as well, so that I can read the poet Rumi in the original."

"Who is Rumi?"

"He was the greatest of the Sufi poets, who lived almost three hundred years ago."

"Can you recite any of his work," I asked, "in a language that I understand?"

Hutia pondered for a moment, then grinned and declaimed:

"Leap up, my heart, place wine in the hand of the soul

for such a time has befallen, it is time to be roistering,

to go hand in hand with the garden nightingale,

to fall into sugar with the spiritual parrot."

"You have surprised me yet again," I said. "I thought Muslims did not drink wine."

"It is not meant to be taken literally," Hutia said. "The Sufi are mystics. He is talking about spiritual ecstasy."

"Have you recited this stuff to Rachel?"

Hutia laughed aloud.

"Rumi wrote many love poems as well," he said. "Do you wish me to astonish you further?"

"Please do," I said. "More poetry? Or have you gained access to the harem? It would be perfectly safe, as you have no interest in any woman other than Rachel."

"Do not make jokes like that in front of any Muslim," Hutia said, "not even Hasan. The only males admitted to the Sultan's harem are eunuchs. No, this is something completely different: I am learning to ride a horse."

"Away, demon!" I said. "What have you done with my friend Hutia? Very well, I am truly astonished."

"They are marvelous creatures," Hutia said, "and since I do not wish to live in the past, I decided I must lose my fear of them. The *cereed* players have said they will allow me to play if I can attain the necessary level of horsemanship. Do you not think it a worthy goal to strive for?"

"An ambitious one," I said, "but I have never seen you fail to meet a challenge. Let me know when you have succeeded. I must be there to cheer you on when you first play *cereed*."

"The players of *cereed* are skillful," he said, "but the *sipahis*, the cavalry, do something even more remarkable. I have seen troops of mounted archers loosing their arrows at a moving target while galloping full tilt. It is an extraordinary sight."

"I would back your skill at archery against even the best trained Turk," I said. "Shooting from horseback—as in *cereed*, you would not have a hand free for the rein. I would give much to see you do it."

"The archers' practice is a purely military exercise," Hutia said. "It is one thing to join a *cereed* team for a game, another to participate in training for the Sultan's wars or even to bend a bow within the palace. But some day I would like to try it."

It occurred to me that by performing so many astounding intellectual and physical feats, Hutia might be trying to balance out his lack of power to bring about his marriage with Rachel. I wished that I could make the rabbis change their minds, but I could not. I could only offer him my friendship and my considerable admiration for his resilience.

At home, the family was in a high state of excitement over two impending events that all could celebrate without ambivalence. Elvira's child would soon be born, and Susanna was betrothed and soon to be married. It was hard on Rachel to be drawn daily into the collective frenzy of wedding plans and preparations for the coming baby. As a woman of the household, she had no choice, and since she loved her sisters, she tried to do so with a willing heart. But I could see her struggling to maintain her cheerfulness. My freedom and Hutia's to go where we pleased must also be difficult to bear. On the rare occasions when we had a moment alone, I would hug her, praise her forbearance in a difficult situation, and encourage her not to lose heart. It was not enough, but since the rest of the household, indeed, the whole neighborhood, had no inkling that she was not delighted without reservation to participate in these joyful family events, I hoped my understanding eased her burden at least a little.

Susanna's betrothed, Nahum, and her future father-in-law were printers. Their status in the congregation was high, since they had recently undertaken to print the *siddur*, the prayer book of which so many copies had been lost, and the Haggadah, which was essential to the Seder on Passover. By doing this, they earned the whole congregation's gratitude. It was comical to see how Susanna and Elvira squabbled over whether a printer's wife or a rabbi's merited more esteem. In truth, most of the congregation's enthusiastic interest in my sisters' welfare was based on delight that both of them would soon be producing Jewish babies. The only shadow over the community's festive mood was the recent arrival of several more families from Seville by way of Portugal. Their children, like the others we had heard of, had been "sent to the lizards," and the daily reciting of Kaddish was made both more heartfelt and more depressing by their presence.

I liked to go down to the Bosphorus and spend time around the harbor, which bustled with shipping. Not only did the Sultan encourage trade and seek to expand his empire, but he was also engaged in building up a navy that could challenge Venetian hegemony in the eastern Mediterranean. Not all the building of ships for the imperial fleet took place where any casual observer could see. The Sultan, naturally, did not want his enemies to know how big the fleet was and with what munitions each ship was furnished. But his admiral, Kemal Reis, had a recently built flagship that was the buzz of the waterfront. The *Göke* was a magnificent four-masted galley big enough, it was said, to carry seven hundred soldiers. I had the luck to see her coming into port one day, bright red banks of oars flashing in perfect unison and pennons snapping in the wind.

There were plenty of other galleys to see, the hulls of many of them painted in the Turkish blue-green that Europeans called turquoise, a beautiful color like that of the waters off Hispaniola. I also saw trim galliots, galleys rigged for sail as well, and numerous smaller fishing boats. Slender caïques only three feet wide, built to be rowed in either direction, were everywhere, as they were the chief means by which those who had business on the Asian shore crossed the strait.

I made the acquaintance of a Jewish tax farmer whose revenues came from dock and wharfage fees. He told me that the Sultan commissioned naval vessels by the hundreds and fielded armies of sixty or seventy thousand who might be transported by sea to wherever they needed to fight. Considering how proud I had been of having helped to outfit Admiral Columbus's fleet of seventeen ships for the second voyage, I was impressed. Papa warned me against growing too complacent about the Sultan's benevolence toward the Jews. But I could not help a comfortable feeling that in coming to Istanbul, we had backed a winner.

One day I was watching a fishing boat unload its catch when I heard someone call my name. Whirling, I saw Amir grinning at me. I remembered guiltily that I had promised to seek him out if I ever came to Istanbul. But not thinking at the time that I would ever find myself there, I had not troubled to remember where his home was located.

"Diego Mendoza! *Asalamu alaykum.*"

"Alaykum asalaam," I responded.

The Moor laughed in delight at hearing me return his greeting.

"So you have come to Istanbul, Diego Mendoza. It is fate that brings us together once again. I am on my way to the *hammam*. Nothing clings like the stink of fish. I do not want to bring it home with me. Would you care to accompany me?"

"I would be honored," I said. I had not yet been inside a *hammam*, the bathhouses that Turkish men frequented not only for cleanliness but as a congenial setting for much of their social life. "Have you become a fisherman, then?"

Amir laughed.

"I have a fleet of fishing boats. I own the fish you were gazing on with such fascination. In addition, I do favors for the navy now and then."

"Every time I see you," I said, "you have risen further in the world. What is your ultimate ambition? To be Grand Vizier? Admiral of the fleet?"

"Neither. Viziers are taken from the *devşirme*. Admirals can be Muslim born, but I like my independence too much to dream of bearing responsibility for such a bureaucracy as the Royal Navy. Come, let us go. In the *hammam*, you will tell me how you have fared since we last met, and I have much to relate as well."

I felt a lively interest in what Amir would say. Whenever the Moor's path crossed mine, something unexpected happened. After months of behaving exactly as a dutiful young Jewish man ought— barring my failure to marry or commit myself wholeheartedly to my father's business—I was ready for a touch of the unexpected.

Chapter Twenty-Eight: Rachel

"I do not understand, Mama," Rachel said, "how you can be so incurious about all that happens in Istanbul outside these few streets that surround the Seville congregation." She pushed a strand of hair back from her forehead with a floury hand, for she and Mama were making bread.

"I do not think that I am incurious," Mama said. "I am interested in what your brother tells us of the dockside and the Palace. And only today, Papa visited a carpet warehouse, for he thinks of investing in a trading venture. He examined carpets that will travel far, to be trodden on by strangers in Antwerp and London."

"But do you never wish to see these places for yourself?" Rachel demanded. "Not only the warehouse and the docks, but Antwerp and London?"

"I cannot say I do," Mama said. "If I did not stay home to manage the household, your father would wear torn shirts and eat crusts, and that would never do. Besides, our own travels were exhausting, uncomfortable, and frightening. I am content to stay home."

"Well, I am not," Rachel declared. "I am glad to be home and grateful for my family." She flung her arms around her mother's neck, spraying a fine mist of flour on them both. "But I cannot say that I am content."

"I do not see," Mama said, "how you can say that I never leave the neighborhood, when only yesterday we spent hours in the Bedestan."

"Yes, but that is the *only* place you ever go. Do

you never wish to see the janissaries play *cereed*?"

"I understand that it seems strange to you, but no, dear, I do not."

"Then why can't I accompany Diego next time he visits the palace?"

Rachel knew well enough that Hutia, not Diego, continued to visit the palace. I am not *really* trying to deceive Mama, she thought. Nothing I said is untrue.

"It would not be seemly, dear," Mama said. "We must never forget that we are here on sufferance. For now, the Sultan allows our women to go about with uncovered faces. But that could change. If you visited the palace with Diego, I am afraid you would not be treated with respect."

"It's not fair," Rachel said, knowing she sounded sulky and feeling ashamed of it. Now that I am under my parents' roof again, she thought, I behave like a spoiled silly girl instead of a woman. "I am sorry to complain, Mama. When I had a job to do, such as being the Admiral's scribe, it made me happy. And I enjoyed pounding yuca and making hutia stew in the *yucayeque*. I do not know why kneading dough and peeling onions in Istanbul should not feel equally satisfying."

"In different circumstances," Mama said, "you might make candles or embroider linens and sell them in the Grand Bazaar."

She means if I were married, Rachel thought. We tiptoe around each other these days. It is unbearable.

"Darling Mama," she said, "I did not mean for it to be like this. I am sorry to make things more difficult for you and Papa."

"Nonsense." Mama gave Rachel a quick kiss on the cheek. Her lips were slightly sticky, and she smelled of honey and raisins. "Our distress is for you. We only want you to be happy."

"You would think those rabbis had never been young," Rachel said. "They confuse stubbornness with wisdom, at least when it is their stubbornness and not that of someone who merely wants to live the life she chooses."

"Oh, Rachel, think of all that they have sacrificed, how much all of us have suffered, that the Jews might not die out as Hutia's people have. How can we not wish you to bear your part in the survival of our community? We do respect Hutia."

"It is not enough!"

"Please, darling, try to understand."

"I wish Akiva respected Hutia," Rachel said. "He called Hutia a savage the other day when he thought no one but Elvira could hear him."

"Akiva is too easily swayed by what the neighbors think," Mama said.

"I do not know which is the more pigheaded," Rachel said, "an old rabbi or a young rabbi."

"I promise such concerns will play no part in our final decision," Mama said. "In the meantime, try to be grateful that you have more freedom than the Muslim women who spend their whole lives sealed off from the world. And I promise I will try to think of something to add savor to your days."

A few days later, Rachel returned from the Davilas' house next door to find Mama sitting in their own tiny courtyard eating dates and oranges with a woman Rachel had never seen before. Rachel was not eager to make polite conversation with a stranger. Elvira had complained of the heat all morning and needed frequent rubbing of her aching back, for she was very near her time, with a belly big enough to carry a calf. Susanna had chattered on and on about her wedding, making plans so extravagant they would have suited a queen, had half of them been carried out. But Mama called out to her, so she summoned up a welcoming smile and joined them in the courtyard.

Mama extended a hand to Rachel and drew her close so she could give her a kiss and brush a wayward strand of hair back from her forehead.

"*Kira*, this is my daughter, Rachel, about whom I have been telling you. Rachel, this is Kira Chana. We met in the Bedestan this morning, and she was kind enough to come and take refreshment with us. As we have been talking about what occupation a Jewish woman might follow in Istanbul, if she finds that keeping her home is not activity enough, I think you will be interested to hear what she does."

The lady was small and plump, with shining dark hair coiled up under her cap. She had twinkling brown eyes, looked to be a few years younger than Mama, and was beautifully dressed in silk with a pale blue brocaded overrobe.

"I am pleased to meet you, Doña Kira," Rachel said.

The visitor laughed.

"*Kira* is not my name, but the title I am known by," she said. "*Kira* is a Greek word for 'lady.' My name is Chana."

"My apologies, Kira Chana," Rachel said, returning the lady's friendly smile. "You are not from Spain, then?"

"No," she said, "my family lived in Turkey for three generations before the Byzantines were overthrown. I was born in Edirne, where my father managed the family business, but we were relocated in '54. Do you know about the *sürgün*? Sultan Mehmet wanted to rebuild Istanbul, which had been badly damaged by the time the war ended. He moved people around like so many chess pieces, not only Jewish families but many others. It was not meant as a punishment. He was convinced that the presence of Jews with our abilities would help his new capital prosper. Our family has always thrived by cooperating with the current ruler, so I grew up in Istanbul and have raised my own family here."

"May I ask what the family business is," Rachel asked, "if it is not rude of me?"

"Not at all," Kira Chana said. "We are merchants."

"Mama said that you engage in business yourself," Rachel said. "Do you have a trunk in the Bedestan?"

"No," she said. "I am a purveyor to the Sultan's harem in the Palace."

"The harem!"

"I said you would find it interesting!" Mama said with satisfaction.

"So I do!" Rachel said. "How did you have the luck to obtain such a position? Are you the only one, or are there others? What do you purvey? And I long to hear as much as you are willing to tell me about what the harem is like!"

"There are two or three of us at any given time," Kira Chana said. "They refer to all of us as *kira*, whatever our origins. My aunt was a *kira* before me. She trained me by allowing me to visit the harem with her from the time I was old enough to keep my mouth shut and my eyes open, not only so I would learn, but because discretion is a key requirement for the job. If I had proved to be a chatterbox, she would have sent me home and taken on one of my cousins instead. By the time she retired, I was ready to take over."

"Does that mean you cannot tell me anything about your work?" Rachel tried to suppress her disappointment.

Kira Chana laughed.

"Not at all. As you have probably guessed, since the Sultan's ladies cannot go to the Bedestan, I bring the Bedestan to them. They are always eager for the latest bauble or plaything. They are given many luxuries in the palace, but some things must be sought in the bazaar. I act as their banker if they wish to exchange a jewel for gold, and I carry out whatever commissions they wish, such as buying medicines and cosmetics on their behalf or summoning just the right poet or instructor—they must be women, of course—to the palace. But some of the ladies also wish me to purvey information, and that is where the discretion comes in. I am their eyes and ears on the world, and I would not last long if they ceased to trust me."

"It sounds very exciting!" Rachel said. "And I am glad the harem women are not so confined that they cannot have any dealings with the outside world, as

I imagined. I have pictured them as sad and lonely prisoners, no matter how many of them there are."

"They are anything but sad and lonely," Kira Chana said. "Of course there are always some who are not there by their own choice and remain unhappy, even when the Sultan favors them. But most have been brought up to consider it a great honor. Do not forget that most of them are Muslims, so they would spend their lives in some man's harem, if not the Sultan's. It is a comfortable life. There is a lot of laughter in the harem."

"Oh, please, tell me more," Rachel said.

"I can do better," Kira Chana said. "Would you like to accompany me to the palace?"

"Oh, *kira*!" Rachel cried. "I would love to! Mama, I may go, may I not?"

"Of course, dear," Mama said. "I am delighted for you. Kira Chana, thank you so much for giving Rachel this opportunity. Please put her to work as you will. Rachel is a doer, not a spectator. I know she will not disappoint you."

Chapter Twenty-Nine: Diego

𝔏𝔦𝔨𝔢 𝔬𝔱𝔥𝔢𝔯 𝔭𝔲𝔟𝔩𝔦𝔠 𝔟𝔲𝔦𝔩𝔡𝔦𝔫𝔤𝔰 in Istanbul, the *hammam* was a massive stone edifice of lofty vaulted ceilings and arched doorways, slender pillars and lacy grillwork. Lanterns and thin shafts of daylight slanting in from high up on the walls lit the reception area. When Amir and I entered the outer hall, we were invited to exchange our clothes for *peştamal*, sheets of thin silken cloth big enough to wind around our whole bodies, and *nalin*, wooden sandals elevated several inches off the slippery floor by pegs protruding from the soles. The attendant greeted Amir by name and offered him a more elaborate pair of elevated clogs inlaid with mother-of-pearl.

"I come here frequently," Amir said, "so it is convenient for me to leave my own bath shoes with the attendants. You might consider doing the same. The Sultan himself endowed this *hammam*, and it is the best in Istanbul, at least outside the palace. Let us go immediately to the hot room. Once we have been bathed and massaged, we can take refreshment in the cold room."

The hot room was a spacious atrium under a dome, its central feature a series of fountains surrounding a vast marble stone so big that eight or ten men might lie upon it. It was untenanted when we entered the room, and Amir indicated that we were to do exactly that.

"Be careful," he cautioned me. "The *göbek taşı* is hot. You will find it very relaxing once you get used to it, but first lay a fold of your *peştamal* on the stone, then lower your belly cautiously onto it."

I did as he suggested. Within a short time, I felt my muscles relax. It occurred to me that I had been tense for many months, ever since we left the Indies, even, perhaps, since 1492. When I closed my eyes, the stone under my belly, comfortably warm, evoked a vivid memory of Quisqueya: lying on a rock in the sun with Tanama below the waterfall where we had first made love. For a moment, the low murmur of men's voices speaking Turkish and the hiss of steam that filled the air and released a cleansing sweat on our skin became the cries of parrots and other tropical birds, the chitter of small creatures high in the forest canopy, and the rushing descent of the waterfall.

I was almost asleep when I heard a soft voice inquire in Turkish whether I was ready to be bathed. I opened my eyes just long enough to see that the attendant was young, no more than a boy, and let my eyelids droop again. Amir answered for me, evidently ordering the full range of services for both of us. Then skillful hands took charge of my body, soaping, scrubbing, and kneading until I felt boneless and inert. I wondered if I would ever move again and decided that I would not mind it if I never did.

It might have been as long as an hour before Amir's voice roused me. With his amused encouragement, I gathered myself together and followed him to the cold room, where we were given clean robes and shown to couches where we could talk while we ate fruit and pastries rich with honey and crushed nuts and drank cool sherbet that tasted of roses and aromatic spices.

Amir insisted that I recount all our adventures after his leaving us in Toulon. In turn, I asked what had happened to our unfortunate shipmates after we parted. He much relieved my mind by telling me the French girls had been ransomed and returned to their kin undamaged except for memories of their terror when they had been captured and uncertain of their fate.

"I understand that men must be ruthless in war," I said, "but I do not like the idea of children being enslaved and torn away from their familiar surroundings and all who love them. Do you scorn such softness?"

"On the contrary," Amir said, "I am deeply thankful that you hold that opinion, or I would still be a miserable slave in Seville. In the Quran, it is written: 'Neither kill nor destroy yourselves, for surely Allah has been to you most merciful.' He who attempts or commits suicide is trying to do God's job. But in the time between the fall of Granada and when you and Rachel rescued me, I thought often of ending my life. I did not think that Allah had been merciful. Yet, as it turned out, my life had barely begun."

"I too," I said, "have had glimpses of wisdom when I believe that whenever we think it is the end, it is simply another bend in the road. Speaking of rescue, did you complete your mission to Spain?"

"We did," he said. "We found a number of wretched Jewish men and women hiding in sea caves on a rocky stretch of coast. Some of them were so close to starvation and others so feverish with untended wounds that they died before we reached Istanbul. These folk had fled from Spain to Lisbon and other Portuguese cities. When the Portuguese king pronounced that they must convert or die, they could think of nothing to do other than to return to Spain and hope for a miracle."

"It would seem that you and your crew were that miracle," I said.

"Too little and too late, I fear," he said. "Except for a couple of boys of fourteen or fifteen, there were no children among them."

"I am not surprised," I said. "I have heard this story before."

"You have heard of the lost children of São Tomé?" Amir said. "It is not common knowledge."

"São Tomé? Is that the island's name? I have only heard it called the Isle of Crocodiles. But the story is well known among the Iberian Jewish parents who endured it and those who must witness their despair. The Portuguese tore their children from their arms, two thousand of them, and sent them to be slaves on an uninhabitable isle, where all of them perished. I have met a father driven mad with grief, and my mother shows what kindness she can to a poor soul who is a mother no more. Among ourselves, we say such children were sent to the lizards. Some say the island harbors dragons that belch smoke and that, from time to time, rivers of liquid flame pour from the monsters' mouths. They say that all who step ashore fall dead within a year."

"It is a terrible tale," Amir said. "From what I can ascertain, the Portuguese certainly stole away a host of Jewish children and sent them to a fever-ridden isle near the Guinea Coast. Whether or not the isle is uninhabitable, it was uninhabited when Portuguese navigators first discovered it a matter of twenty-five years ago. That is why the king conceived his scheme of planting sugar and importing slaves to work it, expecting an easy success since it required no war of conquest."

"Some day," I said, "I must tell you of my time in the Indies with Admiral Columbus. 'War' is too inflated a word for how Christians armed with steel and mounted on horses deal with folk who have never seen either before, especially if they are trusting by nature and generous by conviction. My father says that dragons are a myth. I am inclined to agree, since we sailed to the edges of the known world, beyond the compass of any map, and saw none. Papa thinks the smoke and fire might be a volcano like those in Italy, Etna and Vesuvius."

"Turkey has its share of volcanoes, including Ararat, but none has erupted within men's memory. Did you know that we consider your Noah a prophet? In the Quran, we call him Nuh. Istanbul, or rather, Constantinople once had an earthquake and could have another, they say."

"Earthquakes do not trouble me as those children

do," I said, draining my cup of sherbet. "Rumor has a way of gaining conviction as it is repeated, until it is hard to know what to believe."

"You have a good heart," Amir said. "But you can do nothing. The children are all dead."

"So everyone says," I said. "That is precisely what bothers me. How can anyone know for certain?"

Chapter Thirty: Rachel

Three days after her visit, the *kira* returned to take Rachel with her to the Palace. She was accompanied by a boy who led two mules yoked to a wooden cart, its wheels creaking with the weight of a trunk as big as those in which the vendors in the Bedestan stored their goods.

"This is my youngest son, Solomon," Kira Chana said. "He will not be allowed anywhere near the harem, of course. In fact, he will leave us at the outermost gate of the palace, the Imperial Gate. The courtyard within it is open to the public, but the mules would not be welcome. The janissaries on guard will send someone to inform the Kizlar Agha, the chief eunuch of the harem, that we have arrived. He will send a eunuch to escort us and slaves to carry the trunk, first through the Gate of Salutation and through the middle court, then through the Gate of Felicity to the inner court, which is the Sultan's private residence. There will be a delay when they see that I have brought a stranger with me. You will be asked some questions, but you have only to answer respectfully and honestly, and there should be no problem."

"Have your daughters come here with you?" Rachel asked. "Do they not want to take over your job when you wish to work no more?"

"Believe it or not," Kira Chana said, "neither of my daughters has any interest in becoming a *kira*. Both are married to good men and interested only in raising their own families. And I have no nieces, only nephews, so there is no one in the next generation to take the position on. I am afraid that all my knowledge of the harem and the network of connections I have built up between the ladies and the outside world will be lost when I am gone."

Rachel sparkled.

"Oh, they must not! They will not, if you are willing to make me your apprentice. I can imagine no more fascinating job."

Kira Chana laughed.

"I like your spirit," she said, "and I will certainly consider it. But let us first see if you like it as well as you imagine you will, before either of us commits herself."

"That is just what Mama would say," Rachel said.

A slender, fair-skinned young man clad in red and white came to escort them across the first courtyard and a succession of others, while servants lifted the heavy trunk from the cart and showed Solomon where he and the mules and wagon might wait.

"Is he a eunuch?" Rachel whispered.

Kira Chana nodded almost imperceptibly and held a warning finger to her lips.

Their beardless guide looked no different than any other clean-shaven young man to Rachel's eyes. He led them past well armed janissaries on guard through a second imposing gateway.

"The Gate of Salutation," Kira Chana said.

"It is a town within a town!" Rachel exclaimed. "Please, sir," she said to the impassive eunuch, "will you tell us what the buildings are?"

"It is not permitted," the eunuch said. The note of regret in his high, clear voice suggested that he was not entirely immune to Rachel's charm.

"I believe it houses the janissary barracks," Kira Chana said, "as well as stables, a hospital, and kitchens."

"Were I permitted to speak," the eunuch said, relenting, "I would tell you that the imperial council meets in the middle courtyard, and that the Sultan himself sometimes holds audience here."

"Thank you," Rachel said, "you are very kind. I will ask you no more. I do not wish to get you into trouble!"

"Here I must leave you," the eunuch said when they had crossed the vast courtyard. "You stand before the Gate of Felicity. Beyond it is the *enderun*. Here you must wait, for this is the home of the Sovereign of the House of Osman, Sultan of Sultans, and Emperor of the Three Cities and the lands beyond."

Seated on a low marble bench, they waited. Two janissaries stood by them, while a black eunuch was sent to report their arrival. Half an hour later, Rachel had inveigled the janissaries into a lively discussion of *cereed* when two eunuchs more elaborately dressed than any they had yet seen glided up to them, soft-footed on pointed slippers embellished with red embroidery.

"The Kizlar Agha comes," one of them announced.

The janissaries sprang to attention.

A mountain of a man with skin of deepest ebony approached them with dignified tread. He wore a dazzling white silk underrobe and turban, with an overrobe so thickly embroidered with gold thread that only a glimpse of the white satin beneath it could be seen. Its full sleeves and long folds were trimmed in fur of a hue almost as dark as his skin. His white satin turban added a foot to his height, with a red velvet cap peeking out of its upper folds. He wore elevated sandals that flashed with rubies, pearls, and diamonds. Rings of the same jewels covered his hands. Rachel thought that even without the embellishments above and below, he must be more than six feet tall. His massive body would have seemed grossly fat had he not carried himself with such an air of authority, even menace.

Kira Chana bowed and indicated with a lift of her eyebrows that Rachel should do the same.

"*Kira,*" the Kizlar Agha said. His voice was pitched high but full and resonant. "Who is your companion?"

"This is Rachel Mendoza, *effendi,*" she said. "If it pleases your excellency, she will be my apprentice."

"I would hear her speak," the Kizlar Agha said. "Account for yourself, Rachel Mendoza."

The *kira* nodded encouragingly.

"I am Jewish, *effendi*," Rachel said, "born in Spain and lately come to Istanbul with my family, drawn here by reports of the benevolence of Sultan Bayezid, Sovereign of the House of Osman, Sultan of Sultans, and Emperor of the Three Cities and the lands beyond."

"Are you married?" the Kizlar Agha asked.

"No, *effendi*," Rachel said.

"Or betrothed?"

"No, *effendi*."

"Why do you wish to enter the harem as a *kira*?" the Kizlar Agha asked. "Is it out of curiosity, or do you seek riches and advantage for yourself?'

"Neither, *effendi*," Rachel said. "I seek to be of service."

"And why," the Kizlar Agha demanded, "is marriage to a man of your people, keeping his home, and bearing his sons not service enough for you?"

"My father and mother, *effendi*," Rachel said, "have asked me the same question. I was brought up to use my mind and value the qualities of a man, such as courage and responsibility, as well as the virtues of a woman. In order to respect myself, I seek occupation beyond being a wife and mother, though indeed I wish to fulfill my woman's destiny as a wife and mother too. I believe that Kira Chana's service here has merit, and I would learn from her."

"Very well," the Kizlar Agha said. "You may enter the *enderun* and visit the seraglio, where only women and eunuchs may go. We shall see how you comport yourself. Do not think the harem lacks its own dangers. Never forget that you serve neither the *kira* nor any of the seraglio's inhabitants. You serve the Sultan."

Without farewell, he turned and made his stately departure. Rachel drew a deep, shaky breath. She held out a trembling hand to Kira Chana, who clasped and squeezed it, her own hand cool and firm.

"You did well," the *kira* said. "If you can keep your wits about you in the harem as well, you will be on your way to becoming a *kira* yourself."

As the janissaries wheeled and headed back the way they had come, two more black eunuchs appeared, bearing the *kira*'s trunk. A third eunuch, more richly dressed, led them deep into the inner courtyard to the entrance to the harem.

Not knowing what to expect, Rachel had told herself not to be surprised if the ladies of the harem were naked, like her Taino friends in Quisqueya. But they were not. Most were clad in *şalvar*, the loose trousers that both men and women wore, of varying degrees of transparency, with bodices and overshirts ranging from a twist of sheer silk supporting the breasts to tunics elaborately embroidered in gold thread. Several wore loose silken robes and sashes. The floor of the room into which the eunuch led Rachel and Kira Chana was covered with what seemed like acres of carpet so thick that their feet sank into it as if they walked on grass, dyed in rich shades of blood red, indigo, and ochre. The carpet had been cut away to reveal tile in brighter shades of the same colors surrounding a series of marble basins in which fountains played. The insides of the basins were lined with chips of tile arranged in mosaic patterns of flowers, vines, and leaves in emerald, gold, black, and the turquoise blue that Rachel knew was the Ottomans' most favored color.

None of the women were veiled. Some had blue or green eyes and white or rosy skin, their long hair falling to their waists in glossy waves from palest flaxen to gold to a coppery red. A few had creamy skin with a golden tinge and hair as straight as Hutia's, though shining where his was coarse, and of a black so deep it was almost blue. These had black eyes shaped like almonds and set in demure folds that concealed their lids. Others ranged in tones from golden to rich brown of skin, hair, and eyes, while several had the midnight skin of Africans, their tightly curled black hair arranged in elaborate braided patterns with pearls, diamonds, or rubies threaded into the braids.

Framed by the ornamental fretwork around the arched doorway, they made a highly decorative picture. Several were having their hair combed or their fingernails and toenails filed and painted by slave women more scantily clad than the ladies, though wearing no less than Rachel had on certain occasions in the *yucayeque*. Some were singing, playing musical instruments, or reading. Two were playing chess. A group of girls who looked years younger than Rachel were laughing at the antics of a monkey decked in a red turban and a little coat with pearl buttons. When Rachel and her companion entered, followed by two eunuchs bearing the *kira's* wares, the women all dropped their activities and converged on the newcomers, laughing and squealing with delight.

"Kira Chana! Kira Chana! What have you brought us today? Did you bring the lovebirds I asked for? Did you deliver my message? Did you find ivory bangles in the bazaar? Who is this? Has she come to entertain us? Does she sing? Is she your daughter?"

The eunuchs set down the trunk, bowed, and withdrew. The *kira* flung back the lid, and the women fell upon its contents with glad cries.

"They are like finches squabbling over a pan of millet," Kira Chana said. "Don't be alarmed. We can say what we wish here. Neither the women nor the eunuchs speak Hebrew."

"I am glad to know that there are no Jewish women in the harem," Rachel said.

"We do not sell our children," the *kira* said. "Nor do we have villages that can be raided and burned, like those of the Balkan peasants."

"That is where the janissaries come from, do they not?" Rachel said.

"And some of the eunuchs as well," the *kira* said.

Rachel looked around the room, which had become as lively as a bazaar, the contents of the trunk strewn all over the carpet as the women tried on the clothing and jewelry and snatched up treasures ranging from books to mirrors.

"I see only blacks," she said, "other than the women."

"Ordinarily, only black eunuchs serve the harem," the *kira* said. "White eunuchs serve the Sultan. If you return to the palace, you will eventually meet the Kapi Agha, who is the chief eunuch of the Gate of Felicity."

"Is he as frightening as the Kizlar Agha?" Rachel asked.

The *kira* laughed.

"You have nothing to fear from either of them," she said, "as long as you remain vigilant."

"Vigilant against what?" Rachel asked. "What did the Kizlar Agha mean when he warned me of dangers?"

"The ladies of the harem will charm you," the *kira* said. "They are trained to be charming in the best school in the world. Do not make friends of them."

"May I not be friendly, when they themselves are so friendly?" Rachel asked.

"Of course. Be friendly to all, but guard your heart against attachment to any one of them. It could be fatal to become involved in their intrigues. Believe me, they will try to draw you in."

"What kind of intrigues?" Rachel asked.

"The most dangerous would be a love affair, which is punishable by death for both parties as well as anyone who abets them. If one of them asks you to carry a message or a token to a lover, you must refuse. There are jealousies and rivalries among the women too. Each of them wishes to be highest in the Sultan's regard and in favor with the Kizlar Agha. Their sole ambition is to bear a son to the Sultan and for that son to become Sultan in due time. If you are asked to buy poison in the bazaar, make any excuse you must. Say you could not find the herb or root they sought."

Rachel looked at the ladies, who were chattering

with much merriment and animation. Some sat with their arms around each other's necks. One fed sweetmeats to her companion, who opened her mouth like a baby bird and licked honey off her lips. As she watched, the latter licked the other's fingers. Both laughed hilariously.

"You are saying they would kill each other out of jealousy or ambition? It is hard to believe."

"Believe it, for it has happened. Many would kill one who rises too high, first in the Sultan's bed and then if he shows too much favor to the son she bears. Or they might kill a rival's children."

"That is terrible!" Rachel said.

"What do you think happens to a new Sultan's brothers and nephews," Kira Chana said, "once he gains the throne?"

"My brother has met a nephew of the present Sultan," Rachel said. "It is said his father, the Sultan's brother, was held in captivity by the Christians for many years with the Sultan's consent."

"Then he has been exceptionally merciful to this youth," the *kira* said. "When you Sephardim have lived here long enough to know more Ottoman history, you will no longer be surprised. But we must not talk of these matters here. I have already said too much."

"One more question," Rachel said, "and I am done. What exactly would befall a woman here who took a lover?"

"If the Sultan were particularly fond of her," Kira Chana said, "she might be strangled with a silken bowstring. Ordinarily, she would be bound, placed in a sack weighted with rocks, and thrown into the Bosphorus. If you wish to be a *kira*, you must harden yourself to such things."

"I understand," Rachel said. "I have much thinking to do."

Chapter Thirty-One: Diego

"Diego, I have a serious matter to discuss with you," Hutia said.

"Very well, my friend," I said. "I am listening."

It was some time since Hutia and I had spent a whole day together. He was usually busy with his studies, which went more slowly than they would have had the rabbis allowed him to join the congregation's class of boys who were preparing to become *bar mitzvah*. Or else he was slipping off to spend time with young Hasan and the *cereed* players at the palace. He did not say much about these excursions, beyond mentioning that the janissaries who had befriended him had received a remarkable education in the palace school. Perhaps he thought the family wished him to devote the whole of his mind to Judaism. But I thought someone must have been giving him riding lessons, because he sat his mule with a careless ease that I had not seen in him before. We both rode mules, horses being forbidden to us, for we had decided to pass beyond the city walls into the countryside that lay inland from Istanbul. The farmlands we saw looked well tended and prosperous. I observed with special interest that they included numerous olive groves, the low trees, with their silvery leaves and twisted trunks and branches, heavy with fruit. It was a pity that Bayezid, more conservative than his predecessor, enforced such rules as forbidding the *dhimmi* to purchase land. The Romaniot Jews who had lived here during the reign of Mehmet the Conqueror said that such infractions had been winked at, the transactions sweetened with bribes to local officials.

"I ask you to listen," he said, "with an open heart. Do not speak until you have heard me out."

"Now I am getting worried," I said.

For once, he did not make the usual joke about my worrying too much that both he and Rachel still found amusing. I began to worry in earnest.

"It concerns my marriage to Rachel," he said.

"You have not changed your mind, have you?"

"Never," he said. "I love Rachel with all my heart. I have been patient and striven to please your parents and the congregation by becoming a man they can give her to without reservation: in short, a Jewish man. I know many of your stories now. If I had to, I would wait seven years for her as Jacob did for his Rachel."

"We will not make you take her older sister first, you know," I said. "Susanna is already pledged to her printer and has her wedding plans well in hand."

"Why must you jest?"

"I do not know," I said. "Perhaps because I am afraid I will not like whatever it is you wish to tell me."

"I share your fear," he said. "But I must tell you. Diego, I do not think the rabbis will relent. They do not wish me to become a Jew. Or rather, they believe that no matter how hard I study, no matter how sincerely I pray to Adonai, I will never truly be a Jew."

"They are wrong!" I said. "Their narrow minds cannot get past their prejudice against you."

"They are not wrong," Hutia said, "for I have come to agree with them."

"What are you saying?"

I reined in my mule, and he did the same. We had reached the summit of a grassy hill overlooking the domes and minarets of Istanbul, with the sea a misty ribbon of blue beyond it.

Hutia dismounted, and I did the same. We loosed the mules to crop the sun-warmed grass, well seasoned with wildflowers, and stood gazing out at the view.

"I have been studying your Torah and your laws. It has become clear to me that what makes a Jew is not only what he believes, but what he is. You are a true son of Abraham and Isaac. I am not. You are Jewish in the same way that I am Taino. I will always be Taino, even if, as seems probable, I am the sole Taino left in the entire world."

"I cannot claim that I do not understand what you are saying," I admitted. "We have always been a people as well as a religion. Perhaps it is that duality that has helped us survive being scattered and hounded from place to place, generation after generation. But what is the alternative?"

"I must become a Muslim," Hutia said.

I was at a loss for how to respond.

"I see I have shocked you speechless," he said.

"I promised I would hear you out," I retorted. "Have you mentioned this to Rachel yet?"

"No," he said. "I thought it might be easier for her to accept if you already had some understanding of my plan."

"You mean that you are more afraid of Rachel than you are of me," I said, "and wished to practice on me first before explaining it to her."

"If you can still joke," Hutia said, "I hope it means that you are not so angry that you no longer wish to be my friend."

"I would never deny our friendship!" I said. "But I admit I do not understand."

"I met an imam at the palace," Hutia said. "He has encouraged me to study the Quran."

"I thought you were only playing *cereed*," I said.

"I have already said goodbye to the gods whose voices my people could hear," he said. "Adonai or Allah, Torah or Quran: are they so different? It is you who taught me, you and Rachel, that God is One. Think about it, Diego. Muslims come from every race and people. The first Muslims, those who heard Muhammad preach and followed him, were Arabs and Turks and Berbers, the ancestors of the Moors of Iberia, Christians and perhaps even Jews. Instead of distrusting its converts like Christianity or refusing to accept them like Judaism, Islam welcomes its converts wholeheartedly. It has no Inquisition expecting them to backslide and eager to destroy them if they do. In Portugal, Jewish children were converted and sent away to be slaves. Here, Christian children, the boys of the *devşirme*, are converted and treated like young princes, educated to rise to the highest positions of trust. "

"I don't know what to say," I said.

My mule, tiring of cropping grass, came up and nuzzled me. I stroked its nose and gazed at the distant city.

"What do you see out there?" Hutia asked.

"A great city," I said. "Istanbul."

"What kind of city is Istanbul?"

"A city that welcomes folk of many races and religions," I said.

"A city," Hutia said, "in which Muslims are superior by law to even the richest and most elevated *dhimmi*. I have been studying *şeriat* law and talking to the kadi."

"You surprise me once again," I said. "Our kadi?"

The kadi was the judge of the Ottoman district court. Our local kadi was a man with a reputation for integrity and fairness. The rabbis and the men of the Seville congregation, including Papa, held him in such esteem that from time to time, when some dispute brought before the rabbis was not resolved to the satisfaction of both parties, they would take the case to the kadi for another ruling.

"You know the kadi will hear cases between one Jew and another," Hutia said, "and his rulings are considered fair. Did you know that if a case is brought before the court in which the dispute is between a Jew or Christian and a Muslim, he is required *by law* to rule in favor of the Muslim? Do you not think I will be in a better position to protect and provide for Rachel if I belong to the favored faith? Do you not think that having a Muslim in the family will be to the advantage of the Mendozas and all their kin?"

"If there is a flaw in your logic," I said, "I cannot detect it."

"Think, Diego," he said. "If I were a Muslim, there is so much I could do for you all. Jews are not permitted to buy land, but I could. Jews are not permitted to add a second story to their homes or live in one of the pleasant Muslim neighborhoods, but I could. Why would I wish to do these things, if not to share them with your family? I could buy olive groves and give them to you. I could buy horses, and you and Rachel could ride them, at least outside the city, on our own land."

"You could ride them yourself and even play *cereed*," I said.

"I have been playing *cereed*," Hutia admitted. "As a Muslim, I could join a team."

"Really? I was only teasing you. Have you overcome your dislike of horses to such an extent?"

"Do not mince words, Diego. I feared horses and loathed the part they played in the destruction of my people. But the horses here are of a different breed and put to a different purpose. I have missed playing *batey* since we left Quisqueya. It was so much more than sport. It gave me a sense of balance, a way of being a man. When I play *cereed*, it is somehow similar."

"It is a pity that we no longer have the *batu*," I said. The ball had been a casualty of our encounter with Amir's corsairs. "We could organize a game, janissaries against Jews." I flung out my hands in a gesture of frustration and bafflement at my own impulse to jest. "I am sorry, Hutia. A demon has taken control of my tongue today."

"You are disappointed," Hutia said. "I understand. But to me, continuing to fight to become Jewish makes no sense, while I keep thinking of more and more benefits to becoming Muslim."

"At least I know you are not rejecting Judaism to avoid circumcision," I said, "since you will have to be circumcised in any case to follow Islam."

"I am not looking forward to it," he said. "But consider this. As a Jew, I would be circumcised by a disapproving *mohel* who is more accustomed to cutting babies who may bawl for a moment but then fall asleep and have forgotten it by the time they wake. For Muslims, the rite is a coming of age, since boys are not allowed to pray in the mosque until they are circumcised. The imam has assured me I may participate in a circumcision festival at the palace, in the company of princes as well as the future governors, viziers, and janissary captains of the Empire. I might even share the experience with a future Sultan, since no one knows which son of the present Sultan will be his heir."

"Now I understand," I said. "The Muslims give a better party after the *brit*."

Hutia grinned.

"I cannot deny it, for the festivities will last for several weeks, and the Sultan himself takes a keen interest in the magnificence of the celebration. Do you not think all doors of the palace will be open to me then? Truly, Diego, I am not ambitious on my own behalf. I wish to serve the family."

"And you wish to stop knocking your head against a wall," I said, "as you have been doing with regard to these obdurate rabbis. I cannot blame you for that."

The afternoon light was waning, turning the fields and groves to gold and giving the city the lambent aura of a mirage. I drank from the waterskin at my saddle and tossed it to Hutia, who tilted it to his mouth, draining it.

"We had better head back," I said, "if we wish to get home before dark."

I took a final look at the view before turning my attention to the road. The great dome of Hagia Sophia with its attendant minarets glowed as gold as the setting sun. The mules began to clop along, having no inclination to hurry.

"You have not mentioned the greatest obstacle to your plan," I said. "Rachel will not turn Muslim."

"I know that," Hutia said, "and I would not ask it of her. I have discussed it with the kadi."

"And?"

"A Muslim man may take a non-Muslim wife. There are restrictions. She will not be able to inherit from me, nor I from her. But we can settle all that when we marry. Of course I will provide for her! In fact, where a Jewish bride must bring her husband a dowry, it is a Muslim man's duty to pay a *mehr*, a bride-price, to the woman's family."

"And what about the children?"

"By law, they must be raised Muslim," Hutia admitted. "But we have overcome worse obstacles."

"I am not so sure you have," I said. "Obtaining my parents' blessing may be the most daunting task you have yet undertaken. They have journeyed far and suffered much for Adonai. They would wish their grandchildren to share their faith in Him."

"I know it will be a blow."

"I do not envy you the task of telling Rachel of this plan, much less my parents. In Judaism, the children follow the religion of the mother, so it will be unexpected."

"I fear greatly that she will not consent," he said, "but it is the only solution that I see for us. As you and Rachel have often told me, Adonai does not wish for new worshippers, but only for those He already has to remain faithful."

"When you break the news to Papa and Mama, " I advised, "give them some time to grow accustomed to it before mentioning that the children must follow Islam. The prospect of one Muslim in the family will be shock enough."

"I pray constantly for their consent," Hutia said. "I cannot bear to lose Rachel."

Hutia had already lost so much. It was unthinkable that their love might break upon the rock of their unborn children's religion. But I could not find within myself enough certainty to reassure him.

"To whom do you pray?" I asked.

"To Allah," he said. "To Adonai. If God is indeed One, perhaps He will listen."

Chapter Thirty-Two: Rachel

Before long, Rachel was accompanying Kira Chana to the harem twice weekly. She looked forward to these visits, for she liked the women, even sulky Adile, vain Gülizar, and volatile Nesrin, who had hysterics if she broke a fingernail or could not find her pet kitten. They called her Kira Rachel and soon started coming to her with their small commissions and demands. She was called upon to hunt for Seyhan's scattered pearls when the string snapped, hold up a mirror so Melike could see her back hair while she preened, and search the Bedestan for an inlaid gold button to replace one that had been lost from Ulviye's favorite vest.

The Kizlar Agha ruled the harem, but he seldom appeared when Rachel visited. The chief wives, those who had borne the Sultan's eldest sons, dominated its daily life. Bülbül Hatun, the mother of the eldest, Şehzade Ahmet, was aloof. The younger women stood in awe of her. When she needed to transact business outside the palace, she dealt with Kira Chana in a dignified fashion. She never spoke to Rachel. Nigar Hatun, the mother of Şehzade Korkut, loved to relive the period of glory when she had produced the Sultan's son.

"Do not listen to Nigar," Hanöm, whose name meant "merry," whispered the first time Rachel heard Nigar describe in great detail the birth pangs and all she had thought and felt through every moment of her labor. "She will tell it all again tomorrow; it is her great topic of conversation."

"How old is Prince Korkut?" Rachel asked.

"He is eighteen!" Hanöm disclosed on a cascade of

giggles.

Rachel found Ayşe Hatun, the mother of Şehzade Selim, as intimidating as the Kizlar Agha. She doted on her son, and it was believed throughout the harem that she would do anything to assure his succession to the throne. The more spiteful girls swore that Ayşe was not above poisoning her rivals, if they threatened her ambition, and counseling her son to do the same. Those more inclined to think the best of everyone scoffed at this, saying she might seek to protect Selim and weaken his brothers through the use of amulets and charms, but no more. All the ladies set great store by talismans. The *nazar*, the blue and white glass ward against the evil eye, was one of the most popular items in the *kira's* stock in trade.

"Would Ayşe really poison anyone?" Rachel asked Kira Chana.

"I would not put it past her," the *kira* said, "if she found a way to do it without getting caught. But the true obstacles to Selim's becoming Sultan one day are his brothers, not their mothers. The women do not have much access to each other's sons, for the young men are forbidden the seraglio. Ayşe may go unveiled in the *haremlik* when her own son and the Sultan are present. But to allow any of his other sons to behold her beauty would be to put the fox in the henhouse, as they see it. Nor would a woman, even heavily veiled, ever be permitted to converse privately with another woman's son. Still, you must be on your guard. If Ayşe ever asks you to visit the seller of herbs and medicines for her, tell her that I have said I would dismiss you if you took such a commission without first consulting me. She knows better than to try such tricks with me."

When Ayşe did have a commission, she summoned Kira Chana to attend her in an inner room of the seraglio.

"You had better come along," the *kira* said. "She might as well get used to dealing with you as well as me. It is likely that she has a large commission rather than a dangerous one today. Ayşe Hatun has expensive tastes."

So it proved.

"I wish to have a sword made as a gift for my son Selim," the lady said. "It must be of the highest quality. More, it must be magnificent and unique. I do not wish it to be made in the palace, for it must be a surprise."

"That is not the true reason," Kira Chana told Rachel later. "The Sultan wants his sons raised to be warriors who will fight his enemies. But if they show too great an interest in weapons or have a gift for leadership that might seduce the loyalty of the pashas or the troops, he will suspect them of plotting to usurp his place. The gift of such a sword as Ayşe Hatun asks for might displease him, but it will send a message to her rivals and Selim's."

Having visited the best swordmaker in the Bedestan, Rachel arrived home bubbling with excitement about the magnificence of the sword that the *kira* had ordered and the life story of the artisan who would create this work of art.

"Two of Mustafa's sons are armorers in the palace," she told Diego and Hutia, "and both began as his apprentices, so he is very proud of them. It will be a beautiful sword! The blade will be made of Damascus steel, the hilt of ivory. The guard and scabbard will be gold, set with jewels and worked with patterns of curvetting horses and verses from the Quran. Mustafa had a casket as wide as my forearm is long filled with pearls and diamonds, rubies and emeralds. Kira Chana let me help her choose the jewels for brilliance and lack of flaws and match them for size. Ayşe Hatun must approve them, so next time we visit the palace, we will ask for janissaries to escort us from the bazaar to the palace and back to the swordmaker's when she has made her selection. Hutia, you are not listening. Are you not interested?"

"Speaking of the Quran," Diego said, "Hutia has something he wishes to tell you."

Rachel heard Hutia's proposal first with disbelief, then with dismay.

"I do not understand," she said. "How can you suddenly believe that Allah is the only God?"

"Rachel, *nanichi*, you know better than that. If God is One, then it does not matter by what name I call him. And if I still believed, as the Taino do, that there are many gods, I could not help observing that Allah, not Adonai, is the stronger in this place and better able to protect me and those I love."

"And what about me?" Rachel said. "Does this mean you wish me to bow down five times a day and spend the rest of my life immured in a harem or so wrapped in cloth that I can barely move? Will my face and my hair and my limbs belong to you instead of to myself?"

"No!" Hutia said. "I would never ask you to turn your back on Adonai, and I know how much your freedom means to you. You would still be Jewish. It is permitted. The kadi says so."

"I do not like my future happiness depending on the kadi's opinion," Rachel said, "no more than I do the rabbis muttering in their beards about us. Would marrying me not mean that you remain an outsider in the eyes of other Muslims? Being an outsider is very wearing."

"I know that, my love," Hutia said. "It seems to be our destiny, all three of us, to be outsiders: you and Diego among the Christians, I among the Europeans and the Jews. But I believe that Islam offers me the best chance to belong somewhere, to be accepted to some degree. And I will have no wife but you."

"I should hope not!" Rachel said. "Muslims may have two wives or even more, I know, but do not even think of it!"

"I swear I never will," Hutia said.

"Papa and Mama will never agree," Rachel said. "They would be more likely to accept our marriage if you remained a Taino whose gods are far away."

"I hope to make your father understand," Hutia said, "that having a Muslim in the family will greatly improve the family's position in Istanbul."

"I would never let material advantages weigh with me," Rachel said, eyes flashing, "and neither would Papa. I am surprised that you would suggest it."

"I am thinking of your safety," Hutia protested. "If you do not know by now that I care nothing for material things, then you were deaf and blind in Quisqueya."

"Stop, both of you," Diego said. "It will not serve either of you to become angry at the other, and it makes me profoundly uncomfortable. We have talked enough about this for today. Tomorrow will be time enough to discuss it with Papa and Mama."

"Such a discussion would be premature," Rachel said. "I need time to think about whether I care to marry a Muslim. Until I support this plan with equal conviction, there is no point in Hutia pleading his case to Papa and Mama."

"You will not marry anyone else, will you?" Hutia looked miserable and sounded uncertain.

"Will you convert to Islam even if I refuse to marry you?" Rachel countered.

"I refuse to consider that possibility," Hutia said.

"Do not bait him, Rachel," Diego said. "You know that Hutia adores you."

"Then it is a shame that so many rabbis and imams have been dragged into our private business," Rachel snapped.

She burst into tears and ran out of the room.

Chapter Thirty-Three: Diego

As the streets of Istanbul, its waterfront, and its many beauties became familiar to me through my wanderings, I ceased to regard them with wonder. To my shame, my sense of gratitude for this safe haven and the restoration of our family diminished. All the industry and purpose around me came to seem but a chorus of reproach for my own lack of these essential qualities. The great shipbuilding yards, the caravans departing east along the Silk Road or west through the Balkans to Ancona and Venice, the merchants in the Bedestan, the Jewish scholars poring over Talmud: all men had goals and occupation, pride and satisfaction in their work. Only I had none.

I thought often of Admiral Columbus, not the ailing, gold-obsessed destroyer of the Taino, but the fearless visionary who had first ventured on the Ocean Sea. *Adelante!* Onward! he had cried, inspiring us to press on regardless of whatever lay ahead, danger or reward, but above all, the unknown. The tragedies and terrors of the past still haunted my dreams: Tanama with the Spanish soldier's knife in her breast as I struggled to reach her, Rachel in the cruel grasp of the Inquisition, the emaciated, naked bodies of Taino captives hitting the water, discarded like so much offal while I looked on, powerless to prevent or even to honor their deaths. But Jewish memory, not only mine, was haunted by specters such as these and a thousand more. My sufferings were slight compared with those of Moshe Nahman and Malka, whose children had been snatched away and sent to the Isle of Crocodiles. Why could I not move on?

As the debate over Rachel's future raged through the household, I thought my own discontent would go unnoticed. But in that, I underestimated both Papa and Mama.

"What troubles you, my son?" Papa asked one evening. "It is not this matter of your sister's marriage, is it?"

We sat alone in the tiny courtyard at the heart of our house, in shadow as the day's light receded but still warm and sweetly scented with the blossom of one orange and one lemon tree in pots and jasmine climbing the walls. In the house, we could hear the clatter of the women clearing away the remains of our evening meal. Ordinarily, bursts of chatter and peals of laughter would have accompanied this nightly ritual. But since Hutia had announced his decision, the whole family had found that the best alternative to quarreling was silence. Rachel greeted not only opinions but even attempts at sympathy for her dilemma with snarls of resentment. Susanna sulked at the withdrawal of attention from her wedding. Elvira, always inclined to officiousness as the eldest, was at her sanctimonious worst. Rachel and Susanna were united only in declaring that if Elvira uttered the words "Akiva says" one more time, they would kill her.

"Hutia is a good man, Papa," I said, "the best I have ever known except for you. Whatever his faith, he is devoted to this family and will make it his mission to serve us. And whatever doubts Rachel may struggle with now, she will choose him in the end. She will never be happy without him. Rachel is not the good Jewish daughter you sent off to a convent in Barcelona to keep her safe, Papa. She has been marked by experiences that set her apart forever."

"You are not saying she is unfit to be a wife," Papa said.

"On the contrary! She has been forged and tempered into a stronger and more flexible mettle.

No ordinary man could handle her." Or satisfy her, I added silently, that point being more than a son could say to his father.

"Or satisfy her," Papa said, proving once more that to this father, this son could say anything.

"I love you, Papa," I said, words that too often went unspoken.

"And I you, my son," Papa said. "And I perceive that you are unhappy."

"It would be ungrateful of me," I said, "to be unhappy when I have so many blessings and there is so much suffering in the world."

"I do not think you ungrateful," Papa said. "I am as proud of you as any father could be, not least for having the heart of a true Jewish man. We are the only religion that teaches compassion for the suffering of others as a guiding principle."

"The Christians would not agree with you, Papa."

"It is their blind spot," Papa said. "Their compassion is confined to their co-religionists. In our Proverbs, it is written: 'Rejoice not when your enemy falls.' And in the Talmud, a *midrash* relates that when the Egyptian soldiers who pursued Moses and his little band of Jews were drowning, God rebuked the very angels who wished to sing out praise of the Almighty. 'My creations are drowning in the sea, and you wish to sing praises?' So to this day, at our Seder on Passover, when we recite the plagues of Egypt that resulted in our liberation from slavery, we remove a drop of wine from the cup for every plague. Our cup of happiness is never full while there is misery in the world."

"Oh, Papa, I wish I were half as good as you!" I said. "If I am unhappy, it is because I am afraid I will always disappoint you. I fail in knowledge, in forgiveness, in providing for a family, in every possible way."

"Do you think so, Diego?" Papa said. "Yet in Spain I stood by helpless as our people burned. If this house were attacked tomorrow, your fighting skills, not my scholarship, would save us. You have saved lives, and not only Rachel's. She has told me much that passed in Hispaniola. I cannot think of anything I have done to further *tikkun olam*, the repair of the world with which all Jews are charged. It is no great good to be a merchant."

"You are mending our family's fortunes!" I said. "All I have contributed so far is gold that rightfully belonged to the Taino."

"Which you refused," Papa said, smiling, "until your Taino friend persuaded you to take it by pointing out that it would increase his *matu'm*."

"Oh, Papa," I exclaimed, "don't you see what a good son Hutia would be to you? In some ways, he is more like you than I am."

"As it happens, I do. I tell you in confidence, Diego, that I plan to give my consent."

"Papa!"

"Do not discuss this even with your mother," he said. "She loves Hutia already, and she understands Rachel very well indeed. But she needs time to accustom herself to the thought of Muslim grandchildren. Oh, yes, I have thought of the point that you all so carefully avoid mentioning. And Rachel must make up her own mind, however long that takes."

"What if the rabbis expel Rachel from the congregation? What if they expel us all?"

Papa's eyes twinkled.

"Then we will build our own synagogue. The Sultan forbids the Jews to erect new synagogues. But my Muslim son-in-law will be free to build whatever edifice he chooses. However, once again you have managed to deflect the conversation from yourself. I fear I have tried to turn you into an accountant. I cannot blame you for not liking it! Perhaps you would prefer to serve as my agent on a caravan or trading vessel. Either would make better use of your skills."

"It is not that, Papa," I said. "You are right. The family business would make better use of me in such ventures than in the counting house. But I will do whatever you think fit."

"Any man works better," Papa said, "when he loves his work."

"I can see that," I said, "when I hear Akiva spouting Talmud. He is a true scholar. And Nahum has such enthusiasm for his trade that one would think his veins ran with printer's ink. Believe me, Papa, I consider constantly how best to employ what skills I have. I could sail a merchant vessel or build ships. While I could never be a captain in the Ottoman navy, I have thought of volunteering as an oarsman to learn the ways of galleys. The Turks do not use slaves, at least in the navy, but consider rowing an honorable profession. You can see it in the way the galleys slice through the water, as like to birds flying upon the sea as the trimmest caravel. But first, I would like to do something more. I would honor *tikkun olam*. I would like to make the world a better place somehow."

Papa chuckled, patting my shoulder to indicate that he did not mock me.

"Oh, my son, and you fault yourself for lacking ambition! You have already made the world a bigger place, indeed, twice as big as men thought. Men begin to speculate that our friend Columbus did not find the Indies, as he believes, but a new land altogether. While evil has come out of it already, much good may also come as time goes on. Perhaps one day Mendoza trading vessels will bring marvelous new merchandise to our shores."

"We told you of the Taino game of *batey*," I said, "and the bouncing ball we used to play it. I would be glad to be the first to import the bouncing substance, which could be put to a variety of uses. I must warn you, though, that Rachel would insist on teaching all the girls to play *batey*."

"Then my Muslim son-in-law will have to purchase land outside the city," Papa said, chuckling again, "and build a court, so that my daughters and granddaughters can run and shout in privacy."

"That will not be the end of it," I said, "for if I

know Rachel, she will bring it to the Sultan's harem itself."

So separate were men's lives from women's here in Istanbul that it was more difficult for Mama to arrange a private conversation with me. But it did not take her long to find a reason for me to accompany her to the bazaar.

"Diego, you have nothing fit to wear to Susanna's wedding," she said one morning. "You must accompany me to the Bedestan. No, girls, I do not wish you to come. You will only distract us with your chatter. I have not had a moment to give your brother my full attention since he arrived in Istanbul. Thank you, Efraín, I need neither a mule nor a cart. The walk will do me good, and Diego is perfectly capable of carrying whatever purchases we make. In any case, our main objective is for the tailors to measure him for a suit of clothes that will not disgrace the Mendoza name when he stands holding his corner of the *chuppah* with the whole congregation looking on."

She took my arm in a determined way.

"Come along, Diego," she said, "do not dawdle."

"No, Mama," I said meekly.

"We have much to accomplish this morning."

"Yes, Mama."

She gripped my arm a little tighter.

"Are you laughing at me, my son?"

"No, Mama, I would not dare to."

I kissed her cheek without slackening the brisk pace she set. It was a beautiful morning, the air sparkling, flowering vines spilling over the tops of the walls that concealed the domestic life of the city's inhabitants, minarets soaring toward the sky, veiled women chattering as they filled their pitchers at the public fountains.

"Diego, I wish you to be completely frank with me," she said. "What do you think of this business of Rachel and Hutia?"

"You cannot keep them apart, Mama," I said. "Rachel will never change. As for Hutia, had it not been for his love of Rachel, he would have chosen to die with his people. Tell me this, Mama. If you and Papa had been merely courting, rather than long married, when the Edict of Expulsion was pronounced, suppose your parents had decided it was better to embrace Christianity than lose all they had. Would you still have embarked on this journey? If your family and all your friends had chosen to stay, would you have followed Papa? "

"I would," she said. "I do not deny the fears and misgivings I had before we left, even as his wife, especially as a mother with children to protect. But I could not have borne to be parted from your father."

"And Rachel is your true daughter," I said.

"It is not only of Rachel that I wished to speak," she said. "I am worried about you, my darling."

"About me? You need not be."

"I see the puzzlement and longing in your eyes," she said, "as you search the city for something you cannot find because you cannot even name it. It has occurred to me to wonder whether you might not be jealous of Rachel and even of Hutia."

"Jealous?" I stopped dead, bringing her to a halt. We blocked the narrow street as I stared at her in astonishment. Behind us, a donkey brayed. We stepped aside to let the animal and the cart it drew pass us.

"But we have just been talking of the frustration and disapproval that Rachel has been forced to endure. And Hutia has lost everything, besides embarking on the perilous course of conversion to Islam, with who knows what outcome. He does not even know if Rachel will marry him, even if you and Papa give your consent."

"They both know what they want," Mama said. "Indeed, you have convinced me that we must allow them to wed. Rachel has found work that suits her perfectly. Hutia has not yet chosen among all the opportunities that will open up once he has become a Muslim. But choosing among a multitude of possibilities does not dismay him as it does you."

237

"Hutia is good at everything he does," I said. "I am not jealous, Mama, truly. I admire him more than I can say."

"I know, my love," she said. "As he does you, for you too are good at whatever you turn your hand to. Yes, you are, so do not contradict your mother."

She smiled up at me. It had not occurred to me before that I had grown since leaving with the Admiral and now towered over her.

"Along with her children's happiness," she said, "what any mother wants most is grandchildren. Elvira's first is on the way, and I have no doubt Susanna will do her part as soon as she and Nahum are wed. But it would give such joy to your Papa to have grandsons to carry on the Mendoza name. It is time you began to think of marriage."

"Mama!" I protested. "How can I become a husband before I have a settled life to offer a wife? I thought you understood that."

"I did not press you," she said, "when you were newly arrived and needed to get your bearings. But thirteen-year-old *bar mitzvahs* who have done no more in life than learn their Torah portion are marrying, and so must you."

"Mama, I will not marry a twelve-year-old girl!" I said. "Is this because you fear that Rachel's children will be lost to you?"

"They will not be lost to me," she said, "although Rachel and Hutia will be required to raise them in Islam."

"How do you know that, Mama?" I asked.

"When Hutia made his announcement, I went to see the kadi."

"Mama!"

"He is a remarkably tolerant man," she said. "I liked him. I asked him exactly what will be required. For one thing, he assured me that as long as Rachel does not convert, she cannot be forced to live in seclusion. She might find it more convenient to wear a veil in public, but I have no doubt she will become a respected *kira* to the Sultan's harem, taking Kira

Chana's place one day. I did *not* see any need to tell him that no grandchild of mine will grow up without a full understanding of its Jewish heritage. They will learn our history and traditions in the privacy of our home, along with the teachings of Islam. When they are old enough, they may choose for themselves what to believe and how to worship God. And like Jewish children of your own generation, they will learn to keep the family's secrets."

"Oh, Mama," I said, laughing, "you have thought of everything. You make it sound completely possible."

"And so it will be," she said, with a complacent smile. "It is all a matter of interpretation."

"Interpretation being the essence of Jewish thought," I said. "Mama, you will make the most marvelous grandmother who ever lived. Will you be content if I promise solemnly to give you grandchildren, without saying precisely when?"

"My darling Diego," she said, "if you will also promise to be happy, I will be delighted to seal the bargain."

Chapter Thirty-Four: Rachel

During the weeks following Hutia's surprising announcement, Rachel went about her business at home and abroad nursing a sense of grievance, exacerbated by her feeling that no one understood. Kira Chana said, "There are plenty of other boys. Your parents will not let you go without a husband." Susanna, who was besotted with her Nahum and counting the days till her wedding, said, "Of course you must marry him. What does it matter what his religion is?" Elvira said, "Of course you must not marry him. This is what comes of being headstrong and thinking you can always have your own way. It has gone on long enough, and Akiva says the same." Neither Papa nor Mama would commit themselves. Looking grave, they said that they had no power to prevent Hutia from becoming a Muslim, but that it would take much thought and discussion before they would be prepared either to forbid Rachel to marry him or to give the union their blessing. Diego, who Rachel had feared would side with Hutia, refused to give his opinion, saying that it was Rachel's life and only she could decide how to live it. She was grateful for his forbearance but found his point of view burdensome rather than comforting. As for Hutia, it seemed to her that he avoided her, making her wonder whether his decision had already driven them irreparably apart.

As she tried to weigh the strangeness of wedding a Muslim against the joy she had always expected to find in marrying Hutia, her thoughts tainted her pleasure in visiting the harem, which seemed less of an exotic playground and more of a gilded cage as she imagined herself one of the sequestered women. Hutia assured her over and over that she would live as a Jewish wife, if not in the freedom of a Taino woman, which they both knew she could never have expected. But once the imams got hold of him, who knew how he would change and what he would come to believe?

She still enjoyed her visits to the Bedestan, where the colors, the smells, and the cries of vendors and shoppers swirling around her took her out of herself. The need to concentrate on finding the exact perfume that Gülbahar Hatun wanted and making sure that the pegs of Ferahşad Hatun's jeweled sandals were precisely the height she had specified took her mind off her troubles for a while. It was Rachel's task to visit Mustafa the swordmaker at least once a week to ascertain what progress he had made on the creation of Prince Selim's sword.

"Asalamu alaykum, effendi," she would say. "How is the most magnificent sword ever made coming along?"

"Alaykum asalaam, my daughter," he would reply. "Such work cannot be rushed. The sword must be perfect."

Then he would bring out the sword, whose blade, he said, must be sharp enough to slice through a butterfly's wing, and she would watch him polish a gem to be set in the hilt, then hold it up so they could both admire how its fire caught the light. Then he would offer her an orange or a handful of dates, or she would fetch them squares of baklava, still hot from the baker's oven, and they would sit together, munching the sticky pastry as she admired the beautiful objects on display and listened to his stories about the artisan's life and especially about his family, of whom he was clearly very fond.

Her pleasure in the making of the sword did not incline her toward liking for Selim. She had never met him, for even if the rules of the harem had permitted it, he was far too grand to take notice of a humble Jewish maiden. But Ayşe Hatun, who doted on him, said "Selim says" as often as Susanna said "Nahum says" at home. Rachel kept that observation to herself, sighing as she remembered how eager she would once have been to share it with Hutia. She missed the freedom to say whatever popped into her head. She missed the laughter between them.

One day, as some of the ladies examined the *kira*'s wares while others lay nearby on couches having their bodies depilated and their hair elaborately dressed, Rachel heard a name she knew. These rituals were accompanied by a torrent of chatter that always reminded Rachel of a flock of sparrows in the orange trees of Seville. Ordinarily, she let the prattle wash over her. But the name "Hasan" made her prick up her ears. She had not met the hostage prince herself, but she knew that Diego liked him. However, Hutia's interest in Islam dated from his first meeting with the boy, so she could not feel kindly toward him.

"He is finally allowing young Hasan to be circumcised," Seyhan said. *He* in the harem was always the Sultan. "He mentioned it in bed last night."

"Don't be smug," Nigar Hatun snapped. "I doubt he said it to a pretty nitwit like you."

"Well, no," Seyhan admitted. "He told the Kapi Agha to inform the boy. But I was right beside him when he said it."

"It is long overdue," stately Bülbül Hatun pronounced. "My Ahmet had his done at eight years old."

"And my Selim at seven, in the same ceremony," Ayşe Hatun said. "The festival went on for weeks. None of your sons were even born."

"My Korkut was," Nigar said, "and circumcised the very next year, with just as great a festival. *He* said he had never seen the janissaries put on a better display of archery."

"I do not approve of his allowing the boy to live," Ayşe said. "Selim says, 'A carpet is large enough to accommodate two Sufis, but the world is not large enough for two kings.'"

"Then he had better look to himself," Bülbül said, unusually heated, "and remember that Şehzade Ahmet is the eldest."

"And Şehzade Korkut the most able," Nigar added, "because he does not waste his time writing Persian poetry."

The younger *hatuns* giggled at this until Ayşe's glare silenced them.

"*He* writes poetry himself," she said, "and is proud to have one son who shares his gift."

"What was that about?" Rachel asked Kira Chana as they made their way home with their depleted stores. "Are Muslim boys not circumcised soon after birth, like Jewish boys?"

"On the contrary," the *kira* said. "It is their coming of age ceremony. A boy cannot pray at the mosque with the men until he has been circumcised. The royal circumcision festivals involve hundreds of performers, military displays, lavish feasts, and a degree of spectacle that you cannot imagine."

"He would not put on so great a show for Prince Hasan only." Rachel laughed. "*He*. I am beginning to sound like them. I mean the Sultan, of course."

"Of course not. As many as a dozen younger princes may participate. But hundreds of others will undergo the ritual as well, mostly boys of six to ten. It is a great honor to be invited to share a royal circumcision."

"I wonder," Rachel said, "why the Sultan is allowing Hasan the privilege of manhood now, after denying it for so long."

"It is because his father is dead," the *kira* said. "Cem had many supporters in the West. Indeed, the Knights of Rhodes and then the Pope held him poised like a sword over the Sultan's head. Hasan has no allies, either here or in Christendom. He is no longer a threat."

"How did Cem die?" Rachel asked.

"He supported the King of France's invasion of Italy," the *kira* said, "or, more likely, Charles took him along as a useful pawn. He died on the march."

"I cannot fathom how bloodthirsty these people are," Rachel said, "killing their relatives without a second thought to secure the throne. Bayezid must be more softhearted than most, as he kept Cem alive and then Hasan too."

"He killed his viziers fast enough," the *kira* said, "when they supported his brother. After Cem escaped to Rhodes, he could not touch him. And one could argue that drawing Hasan's claws as he did was more cruel than killing him outright. But let us talk no more of this—at least, not in the street."

That night, as Rachel sat embroidering a silk shawl as a wedding gift for Susanna by the light of a guttering oil lamp, Hutia came up and knelt before her. He laid a gentle hand over hers, stilling the needle.

"Rachel, we must talk."

Rachel's heart thumped wildly. Her stomach fluttered. Raising her head, she saw that they were alone. She had been too absorbed in her work to hear the others leave the room. Was he going to tell her that he must take a Muslim wife? Would he ask her to convert? Would he take her refusal for granted and say that all was over between them?

"I am here. It is you who have been avoiding me." She could not meet his eyes but kept hers lowered to their joined hands. She felt his hand tighten over hers. "If you are going to tell me that we cannot marry, please do it quickly."

"No, *nanichi*, never!" He grasped both her hands and held them to his lips. She felt his warm breath on her fingers as he said, "Rachel, you are my beloved. I will never have another. I did not wish to sway you. I thought you wanted me to stay away while you thought it over. I am asking much of you, I know. I am still tempted to use any argument to persuade you. But you would never forgive me did you not come to me wholehearted. You would not be my Rachel if you did not choose me of your own free will."

Rachel's breath caught on a sob that turned into tears of laughter.

"I thought you did not want me. Men!"

Somehow her arms were around his neck and he was pulling her close with his lips soft upon hers. He unclasped one of her hands and held it to his breast.

"Can you feel my heart pound? It is loud as the drums of Juracán, so fiercely do I want you. I would make you my wife this minute if I could, and all the rabbis and imams and fathers in the world could not stop me."

Rachel drew back, though she allowed him to go on kissing the inside of her arm. It felt remarkably pleasant.

"Then what is stopping you?" she asked.

He let her go then and straightened his back, though he still knelt before her.

"Your knees must be killing you," she said. "There is a stool behind you."

He laughed at that.

"Oh, Rachel, you are so practical, and I love you so." He drew the stool toward him and sat, still facing her, his face growing grave.

"What is it, Hutia? It is unbearable when I see doubt in your eyes. If you do not tell me, I cannot help you overcome it."

"It is not doubt, sweetheart," he said, "not of my love for you."

"Or mine for you, I hope."

"I have already asked so much of you. And now I ask more."

"Not that I convert!"

"I would never ask that. I understand the price you have paid to remain Jewish, and I honor your choice."

"Do you wish me to live in seclusion after all? Or to accept that you may take a second wife?"

"Never. Of course not."

"Then I cannot imagine what you might wish to ask me that would be so terrible," she said.

He smiled at that but remained silent.

"Hutia?"

"Do you remember why they named me Hutia?" he asked.

"Yes, of course," she said. "When you were little, you were quick like the hutia in the forests of Quisqueya. And furry."

"I was not furry!"

"Very well, not furry." She reached out and ruffled his hair, which was still thick and smooth.

"Would you say," he asked, "that I still resemble a small animal in any way?"

She considered it, regarding his well-made body from top to toe. She shook her head, her gaze returning to his face. His eyes were pools of blackness flickering with fire.

"The imam has suggested that I take a new name, a Turkish name. Would you hate it?"

"It would depend on the name," she said. "Do you have one in mind?"

"I do," he said, "in fact, two names: the personal name by which all would call me and a new name for our family, ours and our children's."

"Don't stop now," she said. "What are they?"

"My personal name would no longer be Hutia, but Ümīt. It means hope."

"Ümīt. Ümīt," Rachel said, testing it on her tongue. "Hope. It is a good name. I like it."

"Truly, sweetheart?" Hutia cried. "You do not mind? You will be able to call me by it and hold Ümīt in your heart as you have Hutia?"

Smiling, Rachel cupped his face in her hands and drew him forward so she could kiss his lips.

"I love you, Ümīt," she said. "You must have faith in me as well as hope. Now tell me our new family name."

"Gezgin," he said. "Is it all right?"

"That word I know," she said. "It means wanderer. It is appropriate for both of us, though I hope it does not mean we will be forever homeless."

"You are my home, and I am yours," he said. "And I hope that Istanbul will truly become our home, ours and our children's. I hope we will not be wanderers any more. *Gezgin* also means voyager or one who is well traveled."

"Not our destiny," she said, "but our history. It is certainly apt. You and I, along with Diego, have probably traveled farther than anyone else in the world. Now are we through with surprises for this evening?"

"I have one more piece of news to tell you," he said. "I do not think you will mind. If it hurts anyone, it will be me, not you."

"Of course I mind if you will be hurt!" she said. "Who could possibly wish to hurt you? I will not let them!"

"My brave Rachel!" Hutia—Ümīt—smiled. "It is not like that. I have been invited to take part in the royal circumcision ceremony. It is a great honor and will make a good start to having influence at the Palace, in case we find we need it to keep the Mendoza Gezgin family safe and prosperous."

"The Mendoza Gezgin family," Rachel repeated. "I like the sound of that. So we will both have some influence at the Palace. But Hutia, I mean Ümīt, we must go cautiously. Influence at court is a dangerous path to tread."

"So far," Ümīt said, "I have done no more than play *cereed* with the janissaries. But I promise to be careful."

"Good," she said. "Ümīt, tell me, how did it come about that you were invited to share the princes' circumcision? Was it Hasan who put your name forward?"

"Yes, it was his idea. The young princes liked it, though. They are mad for *cereed*, and I am becoming skilled enough to make an impression. It was they who proposed me to the Kapi Agha, who is the chief organizer. Why?"

"If the princes did not mention Hasan to the Kapi Agha, it will be all right. Hasan is being allowed to reach manhood, but he is not in a strong position. It would be unwise, perhaps even unsafe, for your name to be too closely associated with his."

"Where do you learn such things, my love?" Ümīt asked. "You sound like a courtier!"

"In the seraglio," Rachel said, "and I am deadly serious. Ottoman politics are not a game of *batey*! In Quisqueya, the *caciques* respected the bounds of the game and accepted rulings based on it. It is different here. The path to power in the Palace is strewn with blood and silken bowstrings. I am learning that influence is neither easily won nor easily kept, and there are few whom you can trust. Before, I would have advised you to speak to the rabbis and tax farmers, even the physicians, Jewish courtiers who have experience in treading this maze. Now, you must find your own mentors and test their trustworthiness well before you confide in them. Your kadi sounds like a decent man. Perhaps you can seek his counsel, but carefully, carefully!"

"My wise darling," Ümīt said, kissing her, "in Quisqueya you would be a *cacique* already. Here, you will make a formidable *kira*. I will heed your words, I promise. In any event, it seems that our life as the Gezgins of Istanbul will not be dull!"

Chapter Thirty-Five: Diego

𝔄mír an𝔡 𝔍 quickly fell into the habit of meeting frequently at the *hammam*. I came to enjoy his companionship greatly once we knew each other better. I found I could talk more freely with him than with anyone I knew except Hutia, as if the differences between us opened up my full awareness of the man I was, shaped by my experience as well as my heritage. Before long, he honored me by inviting me to visit his home.

"Please tell me what to expect," I said. "I do not want to be rude out of ignorance or commit any social errors that would offend your wife."

Amir laughed.

"You will not meet my wives. There are two of them, Fatma and Salime. They do not leave the harem. They will prepare mint tea for us, and the maidservant, veiled, of course, will serve it. Fatma's mint tea is the most delicious I have ever tasted, and if we are lucky, Salime will have made fresh pastries. I am a very happy man, with two such wives."

"Do they get along?" I blurted out the thought that was uppermost in my mind. "Forgive me! Now you will not believe I care about being polite."

"Do not distress yourself," he said. "It is the first question the *dhimmi* have, whether or not they are bold enough to ask it. Fatma and Salime love and depend upon each other. They are close in age, and I am careful not to favor one above the other, so they have no cause to be jealous. Domestic harmony is the greatest gift that women can give a man. I set a good example by not setting the children of either wife against the other's, and they follow suit."

"According to my sister, the women of the Sultan's harem would benefit by your example." I could feel my face turn red. "I am sorry, Amir! The steam of the *hammam* has relaxed my tongue to the point of indiscretion. I meant no disrespect."

Amir grinned.

"I enjoy your Western directness," he said. "Nor do I forget that I owe you and Rachel my life."

I looked forward to the visit, and I was not disappointed. Amir's hospitality was faultless. We sat on thickly piled carpets strewn lavishly with cushions and drank mint tea that was indeed rich and sweet and almost as thick as honey, while the pungency of the mint expanded my nostrils and cleared my head as if without it I had never breathed fully. Amir's sons, three small boys, bowed solemnly when introduced and then proceeded to laugh and whoop as they darted in and out through the beaded curtains between the room where we sat and the interior of the harem. Four little girls, all eyes and giggles, peeked at me through the curtains, not abashed by Amir's scolding, delivered in indulgent tones, or their mothers' sharper threats.

"I would like to show you my pigeons," Amir said, when we had drunk our fill and smoked relaxing poppy in a bubbling water pipe. "They are on the roof."

We emerged from the dimly lit interior of the house to a flat roof bathed in dazzling sunlight. Around us stretched the roofs of Istanbul. A cage in one corner of the roof was crowded with pigeons in constant motion, rustling their feathers and emitting a symphony of gurgling chirrs, throaty trills, and melodic coos. When Amir released a catch, the door of the cage swung open. The pigeons jostled each other as they crowded toward it. A whirling flood of feathers resolved itself into an airborne river of pigeons that wheeled in unison, circling the rooftop. The birds spiraled outward to swirl around the dome of a nearby mosque and its slim minaret.

Amir held out his arm and emitted a piercing

whistle. In response, the pigeons tightened their spiral, returning to circle the still point of his slim form and outstretched hand. Circling tighter and tighter, they wheeled once around the roof and dropped to the ground. In a moment, they were pecking at the grain Amir poured from a sack stored in a great urn beside the cage as composedly as if they had never taken flight.

"Magnificent, are they not?" Amir said.

Holding the sack at arm's length inside the cage, he shook out a generous portion of grain and coaxed the pigeons in after it with a persuasive mixture of whistles and coos.

"Impressive," I said. "You seem to have mastered the language, too."

"We have an understanding, my birds and I," he said. "Would it surprise you to learn that they communicate over distance as well?"

Picking up a pigeon, he held out its leg so I could see the band around it, to which a small tube was attached.

"Messenger pigeons!" I exclaimed. "I have heard of them but never seen one."

"Yes." He produced a scrap of parchment and showed me a thin line of writing on it in the flowing Arabic script. He then rolled it into a minuscule scroll, which he inserted into the tube on the pigeon's leg. "They know home, you see. Every pigeon that I breed knows that this rooftop is its home. Wherever they are released, they will brave foul weather and extraordinary difficulties to find their way back here."

"And when you send them out? How do they know where to go?"

"Each one was carried by ship or caravan to the place where it was first released. That place becomes their second home. For some it is al-Andalus, my lost Granada. For some, it is Gibraltar, for others, the cities of the Maghreb: Tunis, Algiers, Fez, and Meknes."

"How do you know which pigeon to send where?"

"They are marked. See the dots on the band? They form a code that only I and those I trust can read."

"What happens when you are far from home?"

"As when I met you in the waters of the Mediterranean? I carry a cage of pigeons to sea with me. Fatma and Salime come up here to seek messages. When they find one, they send word to the imam, who sends someone to read it to them."

I forbore to comment that the process would be simpler did he but teach his wives to read. As I watched, he tossed the pigeon into the air. It took wing immediately, circling once, then heading west toward the sun, which had become a glowing orange ball as the day waned. A cool breeze blew its soft breath across my skin.

"May I ask to whom that pigeon bears a greeting?"

Amir's grin bared teeth as white as his turban.

"My grandfather in Tunis. I told him to expect me within the next few months."

"On me? What do you mean?"

"Domestic harmony can pall," he said, "when one is accustomed to danger and uncertainty. I have a new commission from the Sultan. I am to be his eyes and ears in the coastal regions and on the seas beyond his borders. He craves intelligence of the sultanates of the Maghreb and what lies beyond them along the western flank of Africa."

"I am not sure I can claim domestic harmony," I said, "but I cannot deny that I am restless. Both my parents have recently accused me of discontent. I was forced to admit that the daily life of a dutiful Jewish man holds little appeal for me. Yet I have thus far failed to find a worthwhile venture to put in its place."

""Come with me, then," Amir said. "I would welcome your company."

"Would the Sultan not object?"

Amir laughed.

"I may choose what men I will. I would even

share command with you."

"It is a tempting offer," I admitted. "Yet I cannot imagine explaining to my family that my mission is to spy for the Sultan. Indeed, I would surely be bound to secrecy on this point."

"That is true," he said. "So let me propose another mission that we can pursue at the same time. You have spoken to me about the Jewish notion of repairing the world, which I find both foolish and noble."

"*Tikkun olam*," I said. "Yes."

"Would it serve this directive if we sailed to São Tomé?"

"São Tomé?" I repeated stupidly. "But the children who were sent to São Tomé are dead."

"Are they?" Amir raised his brows and cocked his head. "All of them? As you said yourself, how do you know? Let us go and find out."

"It would be two months' sail across the Mediterranean to Gibraltar and another two months down the coast of Africa. And in the White Sea, the Mediterranean, are the Turkish navy and the Knights of Rhodes, corsairs all, and the Venetian fleet as well. And farther east are the Spanish, with yet another fleet. And should we make it through Gibraltar, there are the Portuguese, who consider the waters down the coast of Africa their own."

"I hear your objections," Amir said. "At the same time, I observe that you already have much necessary knowledge of the route."

"Have you heard of the Tordesillas Meridian?" I asked. "The Spanish and the Portuguese, without a by-your-leave from anyone but the Pope, have divided the world between them. The Mediterranean and the western lands the Spaniards continue to discover, Spain considers its own. The southern Atlantic, down the coast of Africa and around it to the rich trading in the true Indies and far Cathay, the Portuguese have claimed, along with whatever new lands may be discovered to the west and south of the meridian."

"They may own an imaginary line," Amir said. "For that is all a meridian is, is it not? As for the lands themselves on either side of it, the peoples of the world may have something to say about the matter. It would suit the Sultan to know more of what the Portuguese are about."

"Exploration and the trade in slaves," I said, "by all accounts."

"Then let us go and see for ourselves," he said.

Chapter Thirty-Six: Rachel

𝔓rince 𝔖elim's sword was finished. Rachel woke early that morning, for Ayşe Hatun was impatient to receive it and planned to present it to her son that very day. Shivering in the pre-dawn chill, Rachel scrubbed and splashed herself with cold water into a rosy state and braided her hair with trembling fingers. She had hung up the blue flower-embroidered dress, still her best, the night before to shake out any wrinkles and made sure her finest *şalvar* and blue leather *babouches* were clean. It was no small thing to please a *hatun* whose son might one day be Sultan. Kira Chana would present the sword, of course, and do the talking, but she had promised she would inform Ayşe Hatun that Rachel was equally responsible for making sure the gift was worthy of its purpose. If all went well, perhaps the *hatun* would charge her with commissions on her own, coming to see her not as Kira Chana's negligible, practically invisible servant but as a *kira* in training on whom she might rely, at least in small matters.

Kira Chana's mule would carry no wares for the seraglio today. Solomon had vowed to curry it within an inch of its life and braid jasmine into its mane in honor of the occasion. They would go first to Mustafa's shop in the Bedestan for the sword, then to the Palace, where the Kizlar Agha himself would escort them to a chamber in the *haremlik*, to which Ayşe Hatun would be free to summon her son once she had approved the beautiful object. And it was beautiful! Rachel had seen the completed weapon the day before. Mustafa had run his hands over it lovingly before wrapping it in a silken cloth and promising to have every facet of the jeweled hilt sparkling and every inch of the bright steel blade glinting like sunlight on the Bosphorus before they came to collect it.

"Are you not sorry to let it go, *effendi*?" Rachel could not resist asking.

Mustafa smiled.

"This beautiful thing is made for use," he said. "See how sharp the blade is." He held up a strand of silk and sliced through it with one quick swipe, so suddenly that Rachel jumped back. "Şehzade Selim will use it to smite the Sultan's enemies."

"More likely his own brothers when the old man dies," Solomon muttered under his breath, fortunately in Hebrew.

His mother shot a quelling look at him.

"The sword is worthy of the Sultan himself, *effendi*," the *kira* said. "Perhaps when he sees this weapon of his son's, he will commission one for himself."

"I am the Sultan's slave," Mustafa said.

Afterward, Rachel asked, "When does Mustafa get paid? Will we not need to give him gold before we take the sword?"

"You heard him," Kira Chana said. "He is the Sultan's slave, as indeed is every subject of the Empire, including ourselves. Once Ayşe Hatun has approved the workmanship and the quality of the jewels and the *şehzade* has indicated that he too is pleased, eunuchs from the Palace will deliver his fee in silver *akçe* or in gold. Mustafa will be rewarded, never fear."

Now, hearing the clop of equine feet on the still quiet street, Rachel ran to the door and flung it open. There was the mule, clean as a janissary's horse and duly adorned with flowers. There was Solomon, also clean and looking as if someone had curried him with the same brush as the mule.

"Where is Kira Chana?" Rachel cried.

"Sick," Solomon said. "You must go alone."

"Oh, no!" Rachel said. "She can't be! What is wrong? Will she be all right?"

"Did you not know she has a weak heart?" Solomon said.

"No," Rachel said. "She has always seemed a tower of strength to me."

"So she wishes everyone to see her," Solomon said. "I am not surprised that she did not tell you. From time to time she has spells like this morning's, when she suffers from shortness of breath and becomes weak and dizzy. Do not look so tragic. She will take her usual remedy and be better by tomorrow. But Ayşe Hatun cannot be asked to wait. Mama said to tell you she has every confidence in you."

"But I *can't!* It is not only Ayşe Hatun, who can be frightening enough when she is displeased. But the Kizlar Agha will be there, and Prince Selim himself might appear. I do not know which is more terrifying."

"You must," Solomon said. "There is no one else. You know very well that I cannot enter the harem, nor can Mustafa. Mama said to remind you that you are the girl who stowed away on Admiral Columbus's flagship and were the first European woman to reach the Indies. I had not heard that story before. Did you really do it?"

"Yes," Rachel said, "but that was different. I *wanted* to sail to the Indies."

"You want to be a *kira*, do you not?"

"Yes," Rachel admitted.

"Then take the next step," Solomon advised.

He had more of his mother's brains than Rachel had supposed.

"Very well," she said, "let us go. Mustafa will be waiting."

Having survived this ordeal—with flying colors, as Hutia, Diego, and Kira Chana all assured her afterward—Rachel found that her status in the seraglio had indeed gone up a notch. This meant further demands on her time, as the senior *hatuns* all began to give her small commissions whenever Kira Chana was not close at hand.

"It is not about immediate reward," the *kira* said when Rachel had to empty her own purse to pay an old lady in the Grand Bazaar who embroidered exquisite linen handkerchiefs and would not believe Rachel's assurance that their price would come directly from the Palace. "You are establishing yourself as a *kira*, a trusted purveyor to the harem. It is a long game. If you find yourself too greatly out of pocket, ask more in reimbursement. If a *hatun* demands your services and then puts off paying you too long or too often, go to the Kizlar Agha. He will make sure that you get your due. And do not tell me that you are afraid of the Kizlar Agha. One reason I agreed to take you on is that I suspect that you are not afraid of anything."

"That *might* be true," Rachel said cautiously, "at least now that I am beyond the reach of the Inquisition. And know how to use a sword. And shoot an arquebus. Why are you laughing, *kira*?"

The *kira* wiped her eyes with a handkerchief almost as fine as those commissioned by Bülbül Hatun.

"I see why everybody loves you," she said between chuckles. "Even my Solomon is smitten, and he is much too young."

"You must be mistaken," Rachel said. "Anyway, I am pledged to Ümīt Gezgin. But you are right, I can see I need not be afraid of the Kizlar Agha. He is a man like any other, only sadder and more powerful than most."

"Ah, you see the sadness," Kira Chana said. "You have a good heart, Rachel. That is the other reason I wanted you as my apprentice."

As time passed, Rachel became more and more at home in the seraglio, while exclaiming nightly, especially to Ümīt, how miserable she would be to lead such a life herself. One day, while Kira Chana was engaged in reviewing a long list of requested purchases with Nigar Hatun, Ayşe Hatun beckoned to her from the bath, where she was soaking her still supple body in milk and rosewater while four slave women painted her fingernails and toenails.

"*Kiracik!*" she called.

I cannot expect her to know my name, Rachel thought. "Little *kira*" is progress indeed.

"Yes, *hatun*," she said, bowing. "How may I serve you?"

"You are she who brought my son's sword," she said languidly. She looked Rachel up and down as if she were a new species of animal.

"Yes, my lady."

Ayşe turned her head a fraction of an inch and caught the eye of another slave woman, one of two standing by with thick towels.

"I wish Armaghan to massage my head. Fetch him. And you! Let down my hair."

Rachel could not repress a start of alarm before she realized that "you!" was the other slave woman, not herself. The woman knelt and began to remove long, wicked-looking pins from Ayşe's thick, lustrous hair, the color of mahogany with streaks of red that might be henna covering silver, but perhaps not. If the *hatun* dyed her hair, she did it in secrecy.

"Do you know flowers?" the *hatun* demanded. "I mean you, *kiracik.* Speak up. I do not think you are stupid. In fact, I know you are not."

"Yes, lady, I do." What kind of a question was that? "I have spent many hours in the flower market. I have set myself to learn the names of those that grow nowhere but in Turkey."

"Do not babble, girl!" the *hatun* said sharply. "I have heard enough."

She is deliberately trying to intimidate me, Rachel thought. There is no reason for it. Flowers are a small matter, and she knows I will do her bidding. It must be a matter of policy with her.

"How may I serve you, lady?" Rachel repeated.

"My son will visit the *haremlik* tomorrow," Ayşe said. "I wish to deck the chamber where we will meet with flowers, and the eunuchs will be occupied with other tasks. I wish you to visit the flower market at dawn, when the blooms are freshest, and bring them to me. There must be an abundance of them, all that will fit in two mules' packs. Can you do this?"

"Yes, *hatun*." The task sounded easy enough. "Do you wish a particular kind of flower?"

"Tulips, of course," the *hatun* said. "They are the glory of the Ottomans. Yes, yes, I can read your face, our tulip gardens here in the Palace are unparalleled. But those must not be cut. Their destiny is to bloom only for the Sultan's pleasure and die where they are planted, like our master's *hatuns*. You may pick out strong and violent colors to suit the nature of my son. For fragrance, lilies and jasmine. And *yüksükotu*, do you know it? It is my son's favorite flower. White and purple bells on a stalk with dark spots in each bell's throat."

"Yes, my lady, foxglove. I have heard them called fairy fingers or fairy's gloves."

Ayşe laughed.

"Is it so? I must tell my son. It will make him laugh. Those are poor names for a warrior's favorite flower."

"What could I do but bow and agree?" Rachel asked Ümīt that evening, as she told him about her day. They had taken to spending at least an hour together, no matter how tired they were or how busy they had been. "I am not certain even she knew what she was talking about. What is so funny about fairy's gloves? I would have asked Kira Chana, but she felt ill again this afternoon. She must rest at home tomorrow. Solomon will meet me at the flower market at dawn with two mules, and once I have delivered Ayşe Hatun's flowers, I can do whatever the ladies wish for the rest of the day."

"It will be a long day for you," Ümīt said.

"I am proud that Kira Chana trusts me," Rachel said.

"You need not walk through the streets before dawn alone," he said. "May I escort you?"

"Of course, *nanichi*," she said. "I will be glad of your company. And thank you for not saying I *must* not walk through the streets alone."

Ümīt grinned and ruffled her hair.

"I am learning tact," he said, "another quality of which the Taino had no need."

Chapter Thirty-Seven: Diego

"What do you know about the western end of the Mediterranean?" Amir asked.

"Very little," I said. "When I first boarded a ship in 1492, I was not a seaman but a frightened boy who knew only that he would be killed if he did not leave Spain that very day. Since then I have crossed the Ocean Sea four times, three of them with the best navigator in the world. On the Mediterranean, I have been only a passenger who encountered first a storm, then corsairs. That one of those corsairs was a friend, I thank God."

Amir waved a hand as if to say that saving our lives and our freedom had been but a trifle. We sat on cushions in the cool room of the *hammam*, a low table between us. This held not only a tray of pastries and glasses of mint tea but also maps and charts, for Amir had thrown himself enthusiastically into the venture he had proposed.

"And of what manner were your ships?"

"The *Santa Maria*, our flagship on the first voyage, was a carrack, a lovable tub."

"Oh, yes, slow to catch the wind but undaunted in a storm and with a belly fit to hold a regiment of soldiers or provisions for an army."

"The others were caravels," I said. "Then you know sailing ships as well as galleys?"

"When I escaped from slavery," he said, "I knew I must make up for lost time and acquire as many skills as possible—especially those that might assist me to quit any place I did not wish to be! Your big ships will be no use to us, as we have not the men to crew such a vessel."

"We have no men at all," I pointed out.

Amir flashed the white teeth in a dark face that made his smile so dazzling.

"I have many friends. Will Ümīt not join us?"

"He is no sailor. In any case, he will not leave Rachel, now that they have reached an accord and my parents given their blessing. His latest ambition is to take part in the *sipahis'* demonstration of equestrian archery before the Sultan at the circumcision festival."

Amir laughed aloud.

"He is optimistic indeed if he thinks he will be able to sit a horse, much less shoot a bow at a gallop and swing down beneath the belly of his horse to avoid the others' arrows, directly after being circumcised." He took a pastry, bit into it, and licked his fingers, sticky with honey.

"He assures me," I said, "that the demonstrations are scheduled for well after the ritual itself."

"We too will be busy," Amir said. "We have much preparation ahead of us."

"I agree," I said. "First, we must find the right ship. She must be swift, for she must outrun any who pursue or try to stop us. She must require a relatively small crew. Her draft must be shallow enough to hide in coves and enter any harbor, but deep enough to brave the ocean off the Guinea Coast. An oared vessel would serve us best as we pass through Ottoman waters, but the ocean demands sail. I cannot imagine such a vessel."

"You underestimate yourself," Amir said. "You have never seen such a vessel, nor have I, but we can imagine it. We need a very small galliot, more like a caique or fishing boat in size, but with two masts for sail, rigged to require the smallest possible crew, with no more than six banks of oars, and so efficiently designed that it can get us through the roughest waters. I know a shipbuilder who can build us the very ship we need."

"Commission a ship?" I shook my head. "The cost would be prohibitive."

"This shipbuilder and I have done business together for some time," Amir said. "I have brought him ships to repair such as the captured vessel on which you and I met again, and that is only one part of our association. He and I will come to an agreement. In fact, I can propose the vessel as a prototype to be presented to the Sultan for his navy, once we have tested it by completing our voyage successfully."

"It takes time to build a ship," I said. "We cannot count on leaving until the spring."

"Will such a delay trouble you?" Amir asked.

"Not as long as I have employment," I said. "What I have lacked in Istanbul is a sense of purpose, and this venture provides it."

"We will both have much to do," Amir said. "I will recruit the men."

"You can leave the provisioning to me," I said. "In '93, I not only learned to estimate and supply the needs of twelve hundred men, but wrote down with my own hand every biscuit and barrel the Admiral's fleet carried, under the two most cantankerous masters who ever bullied an apprentice."

"Two?"

"The other was an Archdeacon," I said, "a high official of the Church. Columbus and he, sailor and counter of beans, were at daggers drawn the whole time we were outfitting the fleet."

"Let us hope we do better as joint captains," Amir said. "We will need a helmsman, a cook, a dozen rowers, and the same number of sailors. You to speak with any Spaniards we might encounter, I to speak Turkish and Arabic. And in me you have a Moorish corsair with a commission from the Sultan. How is your Portuguese?"

"Faulty. Once we pass Gibraltar and turn south, we will meet none but Portuguese on the sea. We would do better to include a native speaker. What language do the Knights of Rhodes speak?"

"There is no short answer to that question," he said. "They come from many lands and speak the tongues of those lands: German, French, the *langue d'oc*, Italian, English, and the various tongues of Spain, Castile and Aragon not being as united in the Knights' hearts as in those of Ferdinand and Isabella. And Latin, of course."

"I can manage in all but English and the *langue d'oc*," I said. "Let us hope that we meet no English Knights. If we do, we will have to shoot first and try to communicate later. Shall we carry cannon?"

"Even one bombard will weigh the vessel down and compromise its speed," he said. "If we are accosted, I think our best strategy will be to run and hide. I know the coast on both sides of the Mediterranean, and I will alert my many cousins to expect us."

"It seems to me," I said, "that the most risky part of the voyage will be getting through Gibraltar. I confess I have not studied the geography of the area. The Admiral led us west of the Pillars of Hercules, straight from Cadiz to the Canary Isles."

"Let us look at our maps," Amir said. He snapped his fingers, and a boy appeared to bow and remove the tray. "On the north, the coastal towns belong to Spain: Gibraltar itself, Algeciras, and Tarifa. However, Algeciras is in ruins, and that is to our advantage. A hundred years ago, a Sultan of Granada destroyed it so that the invading Spaniards would get no benefit from it, and they have yet to rebuild it."

"I suppose you have cousins there," I said, "and pigeons that know the way."

"Of course." Amir smiled.

"And on the south? Dare I hope that Ceuta and Tangier are in Muslim hands?"

"Alas, they are not," he said. "The Portuguese hold them both. Even if they were, neither the Persian nor the Moroccan ruler is a friend to Bayezid, rightly believing that he eyes their empires with a view to expanding his own."

"So we will have enemies at every hand on land and sea."

"Do not discount our allies in the Maghreb," Amir said.

"Cousins. And pigeons."

"And a stout crew. We have only to recruit them, build our ship, provision it, and embark."

"There is no booty to be gained on this voyage," I said. "What incentive can we offer the crew?"

"Most of those I have in mind are retired pirates," Amir said cheerfully. "They will come for the adventure."

"I seem always to choose companions more optimistic than myself," I said. "You, Ümīt, the Admiral. Do you know Rachel's favorite remark to me?"

To my surprise, he said, "I do. My desire to escape slavery made me alert to every word spoken on that journey. I will not quote her, but say to you on my own behalf, Diego, you worry too much."

"And if we reach the Isle of Crocodiles only to find that all the children are dead or that for some reason we cannot rescue the survivors?"

"Then we will have tried," he said.

"Very well, I will set my doubts aside," I said.

"This is your mission," he said. "What will you name our ship?"

"Let us name her *Esperanza*. Hope."

Chapter Thirty-Eight: Rachel

After delivering Ayşe Hatun's flowers to the Kizlar Agha, who unbent sufficiently to compliment her on their freshness and color, Rachel continued through the now familiar corridors of lacy stonework and tiled passages to the seraglio, chatting with the eunuchs who escorted her. They were brothers, white, unusually for the seraglio, but Bülbül Hatun doted on them, calling them her white bullocks. Ulviye, the youngest of the *hatuns* and the least discreet, had told Rachel they had been rendered fit for service to the harem at Bülbül's direct request. Kira Chana had refused with tightened lips to tell her what that might mean. Mama, who did not believe in evasions or watering down the facts, had said that she supposed there were degrees of gelding in the making of a eunuch and that those allowed to serve the women had more of their private parts cut off than those who attended the Sultan.

"That is so cruel, Mama!" Rachel had exclaimed.

"We cut our boys at the *brit*," Mama said, "as Ümīt will be cut along with the Turkish princes. Is that cruel?"

"You cannot think circumcision is the same as gelding, Mama!" Rachel said. "Oh, I know, you wish me to think."

Mama smiled.

"When a woman learns to think, it doubles her power."

"You always say that," Rachel said. "I love you so much, Mama. I missed you all that time that we were apart."

Mama stroked a curly tendril of Rachel's hair off her forehead.

"And I you," she said. "You will need all the wits you can muster to be a *kira*. We cut our fingernails and toenails. Is that cruel?"

"I see," Rachel said. "You are suggesting it is a matter of degree. Circumcision is a gesture of obedience to Adonai."

"And cleanliness," Mama added.

"While a man's parts are a natural part of him and his ability to father children, so it is wrong to take them from him. How can the Turks do it?"

"They do not do it themselves," Mama said, "thus demonstrating that they know it is wrong. Muslims are forbidden to perform the act. They leave the cruelty to their Balkan subjects and buy the eunuchs afterward."

"That is—what is that word that Papa uses when Akiva advances an unsound opinion simply for the sake of argument?—sophistry!" Rachel said indignantly.

Mama laughed and bent forward over her sewing to kiss Rachel very tenderly.

"I need not worry about your capacity to think, my daughter," she said, "or your feeling heart, which is even more important."

Since then, Rachel had made it a point to learn all the eunuchs' names and thank them for the tiniest courtesy. She did not pry, but when they let fall snippets of information about their history and their likings, she listened. The white bullocks were Dīrenç and Doruk. Doruk, the elder brother, was built like a minaret, slender and tall enough to soar far above the others in any company. Dīrenç was barely taller than Rachel, with a stocky body that looked as if it had once been muscular, though harem life tended to render all the eunuchs flabby and some were grossly fat. When she ventured to ask Doruk about his name, he told her willingly enough that it meant "mountaintop" in Turkish and that it had been given to him by others in the early days of his captivity.

"My birth name was Dragomir," he said. "I do not often think of it. To endure life, one must live in the day."

"That is very true," Rachel said, "and easier to say than do, is it not?" She kept to herself the pity aroused by the idea of perceiving life as something to be endured.

"My brother was Duşan," Doruk said, "but do not ask him about his name or our life in Serbia. Dīrenç means "resistance." He fought like a tiger when they captured him and again when they put us in the ground."

"In the ground?"

"They cut us and then buried us in sand for three days," Doruk said. "It is the custom. Only the strongest survive. I am sorry, *kira*. I did not mean to trouble you with that story. You have a sympathetic face. We both survived, and our life here is pleasant. We have every luxury and no danger."

Horrified, Rachel said no more. But after that she sought ways of showing the brothers any small kindness she could.

"Doruk," she said, trotting to keep up with his long-legged gliding strides, "do you still have the rheum you suffered from last week? I have brought you mint and chamomile. You must make an infusion and drink it before you sleep." She turned to Dīrenç, holding out a small casket. "Have some of these sweetmeats. They are sugared rose petals. Seyhan Hatun asked for them, and I know she will not share even with the other *hatuns*, so I got extra."

The eunuchs exchanged a look.

"Seyhan Hatun has a craving for sweets lately," Doruk said.

"Except when she demands sour fruit or cherry juice," Dīrenç said.

"Although sometimes she cannot keep down the delicacies she demands," Doruk said.

"Especially in the mornings," Dīrenç added.

"Do you mean that she is breeding?" Rachel asked, hoping they would not be curious about how an unmarried maiden knew such things. All the Taino women in the *yucayeque* learned midwifery, and Rachel had attended several births.

"It is the only explanation for her megrims," Doruk said. "Or for her new jewel, a ruby the size of a date that the Sultan has bestowed on her."

Rachel found that Seyhan's condition was the chief topic of conversation in the harem, since the *hatuns* lived for the possibility of bearing the Sultan's sons.

"I know it is a son," Seyhan declared, fingering the ruby that hung between her breasts on a delicate golden chain. "I can feel him *here*." She pressed a shapely hand to her belly, which looked no more rounded than usual to Rachel's eyes.

"Foolish girl," Nigar said. "Son or daughter, it will not kick for months yet. When I awaited my Korkut, I carried him high, so I knew I had made a little prince. Your hips are narrow, so you will carry low, and it is likely to be a girl."

"More than likely," Bülbül agreed. "If you do not take better nourishment than sweetmeats, she will be a puny thing, unlikely to live long. But why waste my breath? You will do as you wish. In any case, my Ahmet is a man grown and high in his favor, so why make a fuss about another insignificant harem brat?"

"He is not an insignificant brat!" Seyhan said, defiantly stuffing a fistful of rose petals into her mouth. When she could speak again, she added, "You are simply being spiteful, and I will tell him so when he sends for me yet again tonight."

Seyhan retched, and two black eunuchs hurried to her aid, one holding a basin, the other guiding her tottering steps to the nearest couch. By mutual accord, the other *hatuns* turned away and began chattering of other concerns. They had their own ways of establishing privacy in this strange existence. Rachel thought that lacking the freedom to be alone at will would be unbearable. Seyhan looked pale and weak, reeling as if she were dizzy.

She lowered herself to the couch with the eunuch's help, her breath coming in short gasps. Resisting the eunuch's attempt to persuade her to lie back, she pressed one hand to her chest and, with the other, summoned the eunuch who stood holding the basin, which he had emptied and rinsed. Her long hair fell forward as she once more made copious use of it.

"The other basin," she said faintly, "quickly."

Her hand clutched at the ruby on its dangling chain, holding it aside from yet another spurt of vomiting. Another eunuch hurried forward with a chamber pot, yet another eased it under her, loosened her *şalvar*, and spread the folds of her tunic around her. The first attendant held her hair back, and the second knelt, resting the basin on his knee. Rachel, realizing that the way all the other women were now ignoring Seyhan must be protocol, turned away.

The next day, Kira Chana returned to work, riding in the cart as both Solomon and Rachel insisted she must.

"I hope Seyhan Hatun is better today," Rachel said. "She seemed very ill yesterday, more than one would expect with morning sickness."

"The Sultan has fine physicians," the *kira* said. "Most are Jewish. Our medical knowledge is one of the skills Bayezid values us for most highly."

"Will they let a Jewish physician attend the *hatun*?" Rachel asked.

"It is unlikely," the *kira* said. "They complicate things with this inability to trust the integrity of any whole man. You will grow accustomed to it. The eunuchs will describe the symptoms to the physician, who will prescribe a syrup or potion. The Sultan will no doubt send for holy men as well. He is known for his faith in the efficacy of prayers and charms, and nothing is more important to him than his children, however many he has."

But they found on their arrival that Seyhan Hatun was worse. Her couch had been curtained off. She was now suffering morning and night from vomiting and diarrhea, Ulviye whispered to Rachel. From behind the curtain, Seyhan could be heard moaning that she would now disgust the Sultan, who would no longer wish to take her to his bed, and begging her attendants to assure her that her son would still be born safely. Dervishes had been stationed well outside the harem to dance and chant for her recovery. The younger *hatuns* looked anxious and whispered in corners. Rachel heard enough to know that while some feared that if illness could strike one of them, it could strike them all, others speculated on which of them the Sultan's next favorite might be and what measures they might take to improve their chances of pleasing him.

The older *hatuns* maintained a calm and dignified demeanor but were concerned enough, Rachel pointed out to Kira Chana, to offer tinctures and decoctions made with their own hands, which the eunuchs administered whenever Seyhan was briefly able to keep them down. Kira Chana, in her turn, pointed out that a eunuch was required to taste each offering before it touched the suffering *hatun*'s lips. The *hatuns* also added silver from their own purses to the Sultan's no doubt generous reward for the dervishes' services.

"He has said that if she lives," Hänom Hatun, another chatterbox, told Rachel, "and the child is safely brought to term, he will increase his endowments to the Sufi orders. The dervishes are very holy, you know."

"So I understand," Rachel said, wondering for a moment whether there were any similarities between Sufi mysticism and kabbalah and how perplexed Hänom would be if she uttered the thought. Unlike Mama's daughters, the *hatuns* were not encouraged to think.

"Do you think Seyhan will recover?" Rachel asked the *kira* as they made their way home at sunset. Her shoulders relaxed and she breathed a sigh of relief when they left the palace behind, entering the greater world where they could talk freely.

"I think she will die," Kira Chana said. "I have thought she may have a weak heart, as some of her symptoms resemble those I occasionally suffer from, though less severely. If they believe she has been poisoned, I fear they will start torturing the eunuchs."

"I don't understand. Why would the eunuchs wish to kill Seyhan?"

"It is not they who might wish her ill, but the other women. Some are always jealous of a favorite, and Seyhan has boasted of it without even a show of modesty or tact. But the real threat is her pregnancy. The reign of a favorite never lasts for long. It is the custom for a bedmate to be dismissed once she has borne him a son. But the mother of a son has status that endures as long as the Sultan lives and outlives him if her son inherits."

"That is horrible!" Rachel said. "And they would torture the eunuchs to see if they had conspired to poison her but not question the *hatuns* themselves?"

"The eunuchs are expendable," the *kira* said. "Ordinarily, the Sultan's ladies are not, although if he comes to believe one of them killed his child, he will have her strangled or thrown into a sack and drowned, as he would if she took a lover. Do not forget, my dear, that we are expendable too. I hope you have heeded my advice not to accept commissions for drugs or spells."

"I have indeed," Rachel said, "though in fact, none of them have asked me to obtain any medicines or even spices. I have purveyed nothing less innocent to the harem than sweetmeats and flowers."

"Flowers? I do not remember any such commission. The palace gardens are one of the wonders of the Empire. Why, it is said that every species of tulip that exists blooms within the palace walls. Who made such a request?"

"Ayşe Hatun," Rachel said. "Solomon did not tell you? She wished to surprise her son Selim by decorating a chamber in the *haremlik* with his favorite flowers for his visit. You were ill that day."

"It is no surprise," the *kira* said, "that Ayşe's indulgence of her son knows no limits. But flowers? That does not sound like either of them. What did she say his favorite flowers were?"

"She asked for an abundance of tulips for color and lilies for scent," Rachel said, "but she said his very favorite flower was foxglove. You know, fairy's fingers."

"Rachel!" Kira Chana stopped dead, turning white as her hand flew to her throat. When she spoke again, her voice was hoarse. "Do you not know that foxglove is a specific for the heart? I take it myself. In small doses, it has healing properties."

"No, I did not know." Rachel's eyes widened in horror. "What does a large dose do?"

"It kills." The *kira*'s hands gripped Rachel's shoulders so tightly that she gave a little cry of protest. "I have heard it called deadman's bells."

"What shall we do?" Rachel breathed.

"Nothing. Or rather, let us pray that Seyhan recovers. In the meantime, say nothing to anyone, not even your mother."

"I must tell Hutia, I mean Ümīt. There can be no secrets between us."

"Your betrothed? You must not! What man can keep a secret?"

"There is not a man like him in the whole world," Rachel said. "I will tell him the whole story in Taino, a language that no one survives to speak except the two of us, and tell him to lock it within his heart."

"And your brother?"

"Yes, Diego too speaks Taino. He too would keep the secret, but I will not speak of it to him, I promise. Soon he will be far away from Istanbul. Besides, if he knew, he would try to insist that I give up being a *kira*."

"Then you still wish to be a *kira*?"

"I do," Rachel said firmly.

The next day, when they reached the gates of the palace, grim-faced janissaries stopped them.

"You cannot go in today," their captain said. "Our

master's favorite, Seyhan Hatun, has died. The palace is in mourning."

That evening, she poured the whole tale out to Ümīt, sobbing by the time she reached the end. He put his arms around her and let her cry upon his shoulder.

"She was vain and silly," Rachel said, "but she did not deserve to die, nor did her baby. That I had an unwitting part in it is a burden I must bear."

"I am glad you have allowed me to share it, sweetheart," Ümīt said, rocking her back and forth. "It is a great burden, but I agree that you can do nothing but bear it in silence. Any other course would be disastrous. Are you sure that you still wish to be a *kira*?"

"Yes," she said. "Kira Chana asked me the same, and I have been thinking ever since about why. I cannot be nothing but a Jewish wife, whether my husband be Jewish or Muslim. I must have occupation. I must have purpose. Ha'shem has given these ladies into my charge, if it does not sound puffed up so say so."

"It does not, *nanichi*," Ümīt said. "I understand you perfectly. God has shown you that by serving them, you increase *matu'm*."

"Exactly," Rachel said. "It is *so* comforting to know you see it just as I do. And if I continue to serve them, perhaps Ha'shem will show me how I may do them good to make up for the harm I have done."

"*Inşallah*," Ümīt said.

"*Im yirtzah Ha'shem,*" Rachel said. "I *knew* you would understand."

PART THREE
The Pillars of Hercules

Chapter Thirty-Nine: Diego

Esperanza skimmed through the water, the rowers' strokes commanding the waves as the long oars rose and fell in unison. The oarsmen's arms, burnished with sweat and sun, pulled and thrust in an unvarying rhythm. At the tiller, the Moorish helmsman kept them in time by singing a nasal, hypnotic tune that evoked lost Andalusia. Two nimble Tunisian sailors, cousins of Amir's, held stations at the foremast, tending the single sail we used when under oars. An Anatolian sailor from Amir's rescue mission to the Iberian coast balanced on the bowsprit, calling out our depth and speed. We had a smooth sea and a light wind, perfect conditions for the little *galliotçik*, as the men had taken to calling her.

I had always delighted in being under sail. I remembered vividly my first days on the *Santa Maria*, when I had discovered the sanctuary of the crow's nest and climbed the rigging whenever I could to feel the wind in my face and praise Adonai out loud. This was a different but equal joy. As captain of the vessel, I could go where I would. Amir and I had agreed to alternate command between one watch and the next. But we found that we worked together in such amity that we could share responsibility without keeping to an inflexible schedule.

I had loved every vessel I had shipped in: the homely *Santa Maria*, elegant *Mariagalante*, and the staunch little *Niña*. But *Esperanza* was mine, and I loved every plank and yard of cable of her being. We had not dared to fashion her with the long beak of a

Turkish galley, for fear she would prove too recognizable as of Ottoman make, tempting to the Christian corsairs who patrolled the western Mediterranean and alarming to the Portuguese we might encounter off the coast of Africa. But I loved to stand upon the prow with the wind in my face and only sea and sky between me and the horizon. My mind was usually busy with the day's duties, the vessel's course, the men's comfort, the weather, and the need to be alert to the slightest possibility of danger in the form of other ships, whether Ottoman or Venetian or vessels of the Knights of Rhodes. But by forcing myself not to think too far ahead, not allowing myself to worry, as Rachel would put it, beyond the day's compass, I found a peace that had eluded me in Istanbul.

We ate well, for there was nothing to stop us from resting the oars and dropping anchor to cast our nets at will. Several of the sailors were Turks drawn from the fishing fleet of which Amir was part owner. Our cook was Greek, well versed in preparing the sweet-fleshed fish of the Mediterranean: *lavraki*, which the Turks called *levrek*, red *barbounia*, and the tiny silver *sardeles*. Once we reached the deep waters off the coast of Africa, we would not be sure of fresh food, so for the moment, we enjoyed the fish, glistening with oil and redolent of dried herbs, that he produced under our cramped shipboard conditions.

Most of the crew were Muslim, so we carried no wine or spirits, a great saving in space and a source of relief in terms of discipline. Nor did our provisions include salt pork, which it had so taxed my ingenuity to find excuses not to eat on the Admiral's ships. We carried a good supply of salt beef and dried peas, and I had found a Jewish baker in Istanbul willing to make us a great quantity of ship's biscuit, that tasteless but durable staple of seamen's fare. I found that Amir shared my belief in the efficacy of oranges and lemons to prevent tooth rot. We insisted that all the men partake of them and replenished our supplies at every port.

"What if an infidel corsair seeks to board us?" Amir snapped at one of the Tunisians, who had complained that lemons puckered his mouth. "Or fires a broadside at us? How much use do you think you will be if you are howling with the toothache? You are my cousin, but I am your captain, and do not forget it. Now will you eat a lemon, or must I force it down your skinny throat?"

"You'd better obey the captain, Saláh," advised another cousin, "or next time it will be an orange up your backside."

"That will do," Amir said with what dignity he could muster, since all the men within earshot were snickering and even I had trouble repressing a smile.

In reality, Amir ruled the crew with firmness, charm, and a gift for inspiring loyalty. Indeed, they followed him blindly, because he had persuaded me not to tell them at the outset where we were going and why.

"That is how it was when we got the Jews out of Spain," he said. "If they had known, they would have had opinions, which are all very well in a court of law but not on board my ship."

"I wish I had your gift for command," I said to him one day as we watched a school of dolphins at play in *Esperanza*'s wake.

"Do you not know how much the men admire you?" Amir asked.

"What do you mean?"

"They admire your fortitude and your legendary travels," he said. "Besides, they think you are more intelligent than I."

"What gives them that idea?"

"You understand their needs to the last dried pea in the hold. You speak more languages than I. You are always reading or writing, which impresses them greatly. I am not sure that, did we both fall overboard, they might not rescue you ahead of me."

"You must tell them to save you first," I said. "For I can swim, and you cannot."

In short, I was happy.

For the first few weeks of the voyage, we remained in Ottoman waters. We stopped to augment our provisions in Izmir, which the Greeks called Smyrna, and again in Athens. This route had the advantage of keeping us clear of Rhodes. Once we passed between the southern coast of Greece and the isle of Crete, which was ruled by Venice, we entered the broadest reach of the eastern Mediterranean. We took care to keep closer to the Maghreb than to the Italian shore. We passed Venetian ships, both galleys and round ships. The Ottomans were not currently at war with Venice. Still, we always heaved a sigh of relief when they had gone on their way.

"In two or three years," Amir said, "it may be a different story. The Sultan and Venice both have empires. They wish to expand, and they seek ever greater trading opportunities in the east, since your Spaniards seem set to gobble up the lands of gold to the west."

"They are not *my* Spaniards," I said with a grimace of distaste. "What about the Portuguese?"

"The Portuguese are determined to find a spice route to the Indies by sea around the tip of Africa," Amir said. "Do you not think they too will seek gold to the west, below that imaginary line the Christians have drawn? But their real trade is slaves. We will have to beware of slavers between Gibraltar and São Tomé. It is an ugly business."

"I have seen that ugliness at first hand," I said, thinking of the wretched Taino.

"And I have lived it," Amir said.

"We have been lucky," I said presently, "to have time to test the ship's mettle and to forge the crew into an admirable working team."

"The true challenge will begin," Amir said, "as we pass Malta and approach the Strait of Sicily, which marks the gateway to the western Mediterranean."

"Before we reach that point," I said, "let us send a pigeon back to Istanbul to reassure our loved ones that all is well, while we can still say with sincerity that so far, nothing has gone wrong."

Rachel and Ümīt had insisted that they would await my safe return before they married. I had protested in vain.

"What if I never return?" I asked. "You cannot wait for me, denying yourselves, year after year. Let us set a term, not to despair of my safety but simply to accept that you must hold the wedding without me. Surely six months will be delay enough."

Rachel and Ümīt exchanged glances, consulting each other without words as had become more and more their habit. Then Ümīt nodded.

"We will wait for a year," Rachel said.

"It is too much!"

"It is not enough," Rachel said, "but we will compromise to please you. And we will pray for you every day."

"To both Adonai and Allah," Ümīt added.

The worst mishap we had between Istanbul and Malta was that Amir's cousin Saláh, who was charged with feeding the pigeons their daily allotment of millet, carelessly left the door to their cage unlatched one evening, and by the time it was discovered, a number of pigeons had escaped. I added several curses I had never heard before to my Turkish and Arabic vocabulary as Amir examined each of the remaining pigeons' coded leg bands to determine the destinations toward which the escapees were winging their way with empty message tubes. Saláh was in his bad graces for a week afterward. The Tunisian also had to endure the teasing of his fellows, as his punishment was to swab *Esperanza*'s already spotless deck. The sailors, almost as fond of the gallant little ship as Amir and I, kept her groomed like a prize filly.

"We will put in at Tunis," Amir said, once he had finished taking inventory of the remaining pigeons. "Luckily, the second home of one of the remaining birds is my grandfather's rooftop. But if we are pursued by corsairs as we near Gibraltar and must hide in the coves and ruins of Algeciras, we will have no way of summoning help. I can only hope that my kin there will not read the arrival of pigeons bearing no messages as a sign that I have met with disaster. They know that if my ship were ever boarded or sunk, I would free the pigeons rather than see them drown or, for that matter, be eaten by my enemies."

"And the birds that remember only Istanbul?" I asked.

"Five of them remain," he said. "We will still be able to send a message home."

It occurred to me that we might reassure Amir's kin in Algeciras by telling his family to send a pigeon from Istanbul explaining the mishap. But considering that our journey had barely begun, it would not do much good to report that we were safe. By the time the pigeon bearing such a message arrived, it might well no longer be true.

Chapter Forty: Joanna

They called the huddle of huts in the dusty clearing the encampment to distinguish it from the Portuguese settlement. The muddy spring in the forest was close by. Joanna liked being the one to fetch the brimming buckets of water for common use, especially when the encampment baked in the midday sun. It gave her a precious moment of solitude and a chance to bathe her feet. It was always cool in the forest. Joanna was taller than Yenenga now, strong enough to carry heavy buckets and spend hours pounding manioc for what the African woman called *foutou*. Her arms were ropy with muscle from hoisting the heavy pestle and slamming it down to crush the tubers, bland but filling, that formed an important part of their diet.

Joanna had struggled to survive alone when she had first escaped. She had had to claw her way upward through the slopes of the thick, tangled forest to find the spring. She had lived on bananas and berries, discovering by trial and error which made her sick and which were edible. Yenenga had been the first to join her, still carrying the bloody knife with which she had killed the Portuguese master who had committed one outrage too many on her body. Yenenga had shown her how to dig roots from the earth and prepare the poisonous ones to make them safe to eat. She had helped Joanna fashion spears and taught her how to lure and skin the small animals of the forest. She had shown her how to turn over a rotted log and eat the grubs and insects on its underside.

For coconuts and fish, they made their way down

to the coast. Yenenga could make nets and baskets from the vines of the forest and the leaves of the palm trees. Joanna's baskets were neither as beautiful nor as tightly woven, but they served. She was already adept at climbing the tall, prickly trunk of a coconut palm and shaking or cutting down the fruit, with its crunchy white flesh and its heart of sweet, milky juice. They had trapped a pregnant sow that had wandered far from the Povoação, and now they had a growing herd of pigs, half feral but too lazy not to be caught at need. Joanna had grown accustomed to eating pork. She no longer feared that Adonai might smite her for doing so. Meat gave her strength, and she thought God owed her a dispensation.

Unlike Joanna, Yenenga had not been wandering blindly in the forest.

"I follow your track," she said, grinning broadly as she displayed the treasures she had brought: an axe, a coil of bowstrings, extra flints, a precious package of salt. "Not hard—for me. No fear! Masters tink you dead."

"That is what I hoped," Joanna said. "How did you know I survived? I myself expected to be dead."

"Be good at knowing," Yenenga said, fingering her *grigri*. Rumor in the small community of escapees whispered that her fetishes included the dried and shriveled *bolas* of her late master.

It had been fortunate indeed that Yenenga was the first to join Joanna, for the next half dozen were African men who bolted from servitude under cover of night in ones and twos and made their way up the mountain. With Yenenga at her side, they treated her respectfully from the start and had since become comrades. But it might have been otherwise had they found her alone. None of the slave women had escaped for the first year or two, not least because every one of them had borne children either to the Portuguese, *fazendeiro* or *degradado*, or to the older Jewish boys like Natan who had not only become New Christians but eagerly adopted Governor

Caminha's policy that they embrace accelerated manhood and breed.

Now the small band included several women whose *metiço* children had all died in the recurrent waves of fevers. They chose partners from among the men, thus relieving much tension in the community at large. For those who did not wish to have more children, only to risk losing them, Yenenga made decoctions of various barks and herbs that so far had achieved their purpose of preventing conception. Yenenga's body was her own to bestow, which she did rarely, as far as Joanna knew. No one troubled Joanna herself, who still struggled with disgust of any hint of bodily pleasure. Once or twice, Yenenga, who seemed to regard Joanna as a daughter, brought up the topic. But seeing how silent and shuttered Joanna became when the matter was mentioned, she eventually left her alone.

Not a single Jewish child had joined the escapees. The latest arrivals, a handful of African couples, reported that only the strongest still lived. Most were dead of swamp fever, snakebite, and crocodile attack. As the Portuguese settlement spread, and more and more forest was hacked down to make way for fields of cane, the settlers made no attempt to tame the swamp but sent Jewish children to raid its resources. The Africans were considered less expendable, as they could labor for many hours in the cane fields or be set to felling trees, a task beyond the children's strength. The surviving Jewish girls, as soon as they reached puberty, were to be mated with African slaves, the priests performing the rites of Christian marriage and baptizing the children who resulted. They could look forward to a life spent toiling within the confines of a colony that could bite only so much out of this circumscribed speck in the ocean, which remained essentially wild. As Joanna and her companions discovered, the mountainous thickets in the interior could not be cultivated except in small patches and with great difficulty.

No one ever pursued the escapees.

"Dey tink we drowned or eaten or dead," Yenenga said with a grin to each fearful new arrival. "I make sure dey get no different idea in dey dreams."

As the men grew comfortable with freedom, they began to discuss the possibility of raiding the Povoação to improve their condition or even inciting a general slave revolt. These conversations, which took place around the communal fire where they shared the evening meal, could become heated, but so far had not led to any action.

"I would rather steal what we need than fight," Babune said in the patois the group had developed, a blend of Portuguese and the survivors' tribal languages, although Yenenga, for some reason, liked to amuse herself by speaking plantation pidgin to Joanna. "Metal implements, axes and shovels, bigger knives, maybe even a gun."

"Why a gun," N'goran asked, "if we do not mean to fight? I say we take many guns and take the plantations from the white men. The others will join us. They do the work. Why should they not benefit from the harvest?"

"You say 'take many guns' like a fool." Fafale spat into the fire. "Before we could beat down one door of the strong hut where they keep their arms, they would be upon us. We would only end up dead. Better we sneak in by night and take sacks of that sugar cane that they stick in shit to take root." He held his hands apart to indicate a short length of cane. "That way we start our own plantation."

"What," Kwaku scoffed, "and build a mill and sell cones of sugar to the Portuguese to take away in their ships? You are crazy."

"We don't need that white man sugar," Mawuwo said. "Chewing cane, that is plenty sweet. Let us sneak in and steal some palm wine. We are free men, we should get drunk."

"You will be dead men if you get drunk in the Povoação." Yenenga, who had been sitting quietly with Joanna and the other women, all engaged in weaving baskets or mending nets or their few ragged garments, spat into the fire in turn. "I would not trust one of you to bring palm wine safely away from the settlement without sampling it within a hundred paces. We can make our own palm wine, though I do not recommend it. Drunken men are careless men, and careless men are dead men. I am going to sleep. There is work to be done in the morning." She rose and stalked away from the firelight toward her hut.

When the big storm started, Joanna, Yenenga, a young woman named Brou, and Brou's husband, Nunke, were making their way down the mountain to the beach to collect coconuts. It was raining, as it rained every afternoon. Brou carried her baby curled up in a length of cloth tucked around her waist, his cheek against her back, his moist mouth hanging open as he slept. Yenenga trailed the others as she scanned the area around the barely visible track for useful plants and barks, a sharp knife ready in her hand.

"This island's two seasons are not hot and hotter, as they say." Joanna wrung out her hair, which, like her clothes, was drenched. "They are wet and wetter."

A forked crack of lightning split the air, followed by a rumble of thunder and the sound of branches breaking.

"Yenenga? Maybe climbing trees is not a good idea this afternoon."

"Dat lightning not so near," Yenenga said. "Tunder come far behind. When he catch up, den time to worry."

"Should we turn around?" Brou asked, twisting to see the baby's face.

"We're almost there," Nunke said. "You want to give him to me?"

As he spoke, the baby woke, squalling as a fat raindrop hit his nose.

"Never mind," Brou said. With a practiced

movement, she swung the cloth around to position the baby's head beneath her breast and thrust her nipple into his mouth. The baby subsided with a grunt of satisfaction and started to suck.

"This wind will throw plenty of coconuts to the ground," Yenenga said with one of her sudden shifts into fluency. "We will not have to climb any trees to get a good haul."

"We cannot get any wetter," Joanna said. "We might as well go on."

Cracks and peals of thunder punctuated their journey as Joanna squinted through the torrential curtain of rain, picking her way down the overgrown path. When a flash of lightning illuminated the scene, she enjoyed its strangeness, her companions looking like colorless ghosts and the massive vegetation all around her transformed from its everyday green lushness into the stuff of dreams.

They came out on the beach and stood under a dripping canopy of palms. The trees' trunks creaked and groaned as they swayed, and the wind shrieked as it tossed the flapping fronds from side to side. The tide was abnormally high, leaving only a sodden ribbon of beach. Towering rows of breakers rolled in toward the shore. The vast sky suddenly lit up, as a simultaneous crash of thunder overrode the ceaseless roar of the waves.

"That was close!" Joanna could not hear her own voice over the howling of the wind.

Brou crooned to the baby, jiggling him and walking in circles as he flailed his tiny fists and wailed inaudibly, his mouth stretched wide. Yenenga was laughing, face and arms raised to the heavens as she exulted in the power of the storm.

Nunke shouted something, pointing out to sea. Peering toward the horizon, Joanna could see nothing but the roiling of the baleful ocean. Though it was only midafternoon, the sky was almost black. A jagged spear of lightning ripped the sky with a crack of thunder on its heels, then a broad flash lit up the whole expanse of sea and heavens, with a growl so long and loud that Joanna's ears rang.

"Look! A ship!" Joanna hurried over to Yenenga and tugged at her arm to get her attention. She drew Yenenga over toward Brou, who stood staring with the baby, enveloped in the now sopping cloth, clasped tight against her breast. Only the top of his head peeked out. Nunke, hunched over as he bucked the wind, hurried to them. He put his arm around Brou and laid his cheek against hers so that their two heads tented together, protecting the baby.

Yenenga also put her arm around Brou and beckoned to Joanna to huddle close.

"It is a slaver," Yenenga said. She spoke quietly, but with their four heads touching, the others could hear. "That last bolt of lightning has dismasted it."

"Kheboso the lightning god does not like his people enslaved," Nunke said. "That is how he makes his opinion known."

Fires had broken out on the ship. Joanna could make out the tiny scurrying figures of sailors trying in vain to extinguish them. Another flare of lightning showed that the ship, unable to maneuver, had slammed into the jagged rocks that could only be seen at the lowest of low tides. It began to break up.

Brou gave a cry of anguish.

"The devils, the devils! Look what they are doing!"

Sailors hauled a long string of limp and cowering figures up out of the bowels of the ship: Africans who had been chained together in the hold. As the broken masts and booms swung wildly, they hauled the Africans to the rail, still chained, and hoisted them overboard. As they did so, the fire spread until the whole hull was alight.

Yenenga raised her arms again, her expression wrathful now, and began a sonorous chant in her own language.

"I ask the Sky God to curse the slavers," she broke off to say.

"I think it is working," Joanna said. "It is hard to make out at this distance, but it looks as if some of the slaves were not chained. They are picking up burning brands and fighting the slavers."

"The Lightning God has done his part," Nunke said with satisfaction. "Look, the whole ship is burning as it sinks."

"They must stop fighting if any are to escape," Joanna said.

"If they do, they will drown," Brou said. "Even if they can swim, they will not reach the shore."

A towering wave, driven by the wind, crashed on the shore, spilling a foaming field of seawater that ran forward so close to their feet that they jumped backward. The surf ebbed slowly down the beach to meet the next mighty breaker.

"Do you care if they escape?" Yenenga asked.

"I hope the slavers do not!" Joanna said. "If they discover the encampment, I do not know what will happen."

"If they do," Nunke said, "we will kill them. They will be half dead already if they manage to swim this far."

"There is no hope for the chained Africans," Joanna said, "but those who seized the brands and fought—I could not see if any jumped."

"A few leaped into the sea," Yenenga said, "but they must still swim a great distance in violent seas. If they do not know how, or if they are burned or wounded, there is little hope for them."

"We must help any who manage to reach us," Brou said. She kissed the top of the baby's head. Replete with milk, he had gone back to sleep. "Between death and life, I am for life."

"I am for death to slavers," Nunke said, "and freedom for slaves."

"*B'ezrat Ha'shem,*" Joanna said. "God's will be done."

Chapter Forty-One: Diego

𝕿𝖍𝖊 𝕸𝖊𝖉𝖎𝖙𝖊𝖗𝖗𝖆𝖓𝖊𝖆𝖓 𝖜𝖆𝖘 a convivial sea compared to the empty ocean I had crossed with Admiral Columbus. When we met galleys flying the crescent flag of Islam, we hailed them and exchanged courtesies. More often than not, Amir knew their captains, and the men could sometimes hail acquaintances among their crews. More circumspect when we encountered the well-armed ships of the various lands of Christendom, we withdrew our oars, made sure no flag flew from our masts, cast out our nets, and took on the semblance of a simple if somewhat over-equipped and over-crewed fishing boat. In any case, the approaching vessels could see that *Esperanza* carried no ordnance and therefore considered the *galliotçik* harmless.

As it happened, the first moment of peril we encountered came not at sea but on land. Shortly after we passed Malta without incident, two of our water casks sprang leaks. It was imperative to replace them while we could. The farther behind we left the Ottoman Empire, the less leisurely our voyage could be and the more filled with potential dangers that might force us to implement our "run and hide" strategy without regard to the needs or condition of *Esperanza* or the crew. Luckily, Tunis was not far. I looked forward to setting foot on land and getting my first glimpse of the Maghreb.

Tunis was a jumble of boxlike houses, all dazzling white with blue doors and shutters that echoed the color of the sea. Short, stubby palm trees bristling with fronds could be seen behind the walls of dwellings, and an occasional smooth white dome thrust upward from a larger building toward the cloudless sky. As we made our way through the winding, narrow streets, we could see through arched doorways into courtyards decorated with elaborate tilework of pale turquoise, ochre, indigo, and white. The air smelled of jasmine.

We left the pilot in charge of *Esperanza* with two sailors and two oarsmen to guard her. One sailor and one oarsman escorted us. The cook accepted a pouch that held coin enough for abundant provisions and disappeared in the direction of the produce, meat, and spice bazaars. The men would eat well tonight. Amir and I would be offered his family's hospitality, not only for the evening meal but overnight. We gave the remainder of the crew a few hours liberty, along with a small amount of coin.

"Even a Muslim city like Tunis," Amir said, "has its share of dockside whores and establishments where they can gamble and get drunk. However, they know that I will flay them if they are not aboard and ready to depart when we return in the morning."

Amir led the way. As we walked single file through a narrow alley blue with shadows, he said, "My grandfather's home is not far, and I have sent a pigeon, so the household will be expecting us. There is a public fountain not far away. My *jaddi*'s men will take charge of obtaining water barrels and transporting them to the ship, so we need only rest and enjoy ourselves. Musa and Kemal can take refreshment and then join the others or return to *Esperanza* as they choose."

At that moment, the oarsman Musa, who walked last in line, gave a startled cry. I whirled to see him fighting off two ruffians robed in black. I clapped my hand to my waist and drew out my dagger, regretting that I had left my sword on the ship. As I leaped to Musa's aid, a shout from Amir and a string of curses from Kemal alerted me that three more villains were coming at us from the other end of the alley. I cast a quick glance upward on the chance that more enemies were poised to leap down at us from a rooftop or creeping toward us atop a courtyard wall. I saw none. That meant we were not too heavily outnumbered.

Each of our enemies had a knife in either hand, but so did Kemal and Amir, who were already forcing the trio before them back step by step. None bore a sword, whose length might indeed have proved more hindrance than advantage, so narrow was our battlefield. I kicked an attacker's knife away from Musa's throat. Panting, he retrieved it as I slashed at the villain's forearm. A quick breath on the back of my neck warned me that the other man we fought had come up close behind me. I ducked in time to avoid his lunge. But his knife took Musa, rising and turning too slowly with a knife in either hand, in the shoulder. He gave a cry of pain and dropped both knives as he clapped his other hand to the deep slash, already oozing blood.

I moved to shield him from our attackers, scrabbling to seize one of the fallen knives and kick the other away without losing a moment. We would have been quickly overcome had not a flying knife taken one of the ruffians in the throat. I cast a quick glance behind me to see Amir already launching a second dagger through the air. It whizzed past my nose as I leaped back. My second opponent fled back the way he had come. Amir's knife caught him high in the back but did not bite deeply enough to stop him. In the meantime, a band of men in white turbans had appeared, blocking the far end of the alley. The bright steel of their drawn swords caught the light as they advanced. The three ruffians who had engaged Amir and Kemal brushed past me as they howled and fled.

"Cousins," Amir panted, grinning as he dropped his arms, chest heaving.

Within minutes, we were installed in great comfort in a luxuriously carpeted chamber in Amir's grandfather's home, responding with all the courtesy we could muster to apologies from the patriarch himself for our having encountered brigands in his city.

"It is not your fault, *jaddi*," Amir said. "There are brigands everywhere. They must have seen us come ashore and followed us, considering sailors at liberty a promising source of coin."

"Brigands in broad daylight, only paces from our door! It is a disgrace!" His grandfather's eyes flashed. "It shames me, as it would any householder in Tunis. I will send men to the docks to make sure your men have not been attacked as well."

"Thank you, *jaddi*. They were in a larger group, and Diego and I probably caught their eye as promising richer pickings. But it cannot hurt to check."

"I have already sent for a physician for your crewman," his grandfather said. "The knife must have nicked a vein, as well as cutting through muscle. It will need stitching. And he has lost enough blood that he must rest. You must all stay here tonight."

"You do me too much honor, *effendi*," Musa said. His voice was weak, and he was pale with shock. "It is nothing. I can return to the ship."

The wound had already been bound with a white turban cloth. Kemal knelt by Musa as he lay propped on cushions, pressing the wound with both hands to discourage the flow of blood.

"Don't be a fool, Musa," Amir said. "The wound is serious. You will let the physician clean and stitch it. Then you will accept a nourishing broth and a good night's rest. It will be many days before you can pull an oar."

"Captain! No!" Musa protested. "I must row. You need me."

"Unfortunately," Amir said, addressing me rather than the oarsman, "that is true. Nonetheless, he cannot row. It is a problem we must solve."

"I do not like the idea of recruiting a stranger," I said, "at this point in our venture. I don't suppose one of your cousins here can row?"

"Those who have a taste for adventure," Amir said, "like me, are no longer living under our grandfather's roof. Let us see if one of our sailors can be persuaded to trade tasks with Musa until he recovers fully."

"I will do it, Captain," Kemal said.

"You are too skinny," Musa scoffed. "A rower's arms must be thicker than his oar at the very least."

Kemal was indeed a wiry fellow, adept at climbing the rigging, as well as a knowledgeable seaman, attuned to wind and sails. While we did not need a precise number of sailors, as we did of oarsmen, I would be loth to lose his skills.

"Perhaps one of our sailors," I said, "has experience at the oars. We will hold you in reserve, Kemal, and the offer does you honor."

"There is one," Amir said, "but here comes the physician. Let us discuss it later."

"Miguel is a fisherman by trade," he told me when we were alone, "but he has rowed. He has not much experience of larger sailing vessels, but he is intelligent and willing. I took him on because Portuguese is his native tongue. He will make a good spokesman when the time comes."

"I had no experience at all when I shipped on the *Santa Maria*," I said. "But if he is no sailor, why did he not sign on as an oarsman?"

"Because he got his experience as a slave," he said, "chained to an oar on a Muslim pirate's galley. I got him in trade and freed him. I share the Sultan's opinion that voluntary oarsmen make better rowers."

"In that case," I said, "he may yet be unwilling to row, and I would not blame him. We must give him the option of refusing and take up Kemal's offer if he does."

Fortunately, Miguel had no objection to rowing, since it served the expedition.

"I owe the captain my freedom," he said, "as well as my employment in a strange land. For that I must be grateful. I am willing to be put to whatever use you can make of me."

Slavery and suffering had clearly taken its toll. Miguel was not young. His face was deeply grooved and his eyes the saddest I had ever seen. Neither freedom nor gratitude had restored his happiness or any liveliness he might once have possessed.

"How came you to be captured by corsairs," I asked, "if you do not mind my asking? It must have been hard indeed for a Christian to endure."

"I was bound for Istanbul," he said, "so it is an irony of fate that in the end I got there."

"A miracle, surely," I said lightly.

"I do not believe in miracles," he said. "Nor did I care, either before or after my enslavement, in what place my body came to rest. And I am not a Christian."

"What!" I could not conceal my surprise. Looking into his eyes, I wondered how I could have missed the familiar despair deep within them. "You are Jewish then, as am I."

"Am I indeed?" Miguel said bitterly. "I am by birth and blood. But tell me, can a man call himself a Jew when he hates and mistrusts Adonai?"

"You lost someone dear to you," I said.

"My only son," he said.

"On the docks in Lisbon, perhaps?" I said.

"You know what happened, then. They tore him from my arms. Two weeks later, my wife in her despair took poison. Since then, I have neither prayed nor wept. The corsairs but chained a man already dead. Not even freedom brought me joy."

"I cannot offer you joy," I said. "But it may please you to know, as all the crew soon must, that we go to seek survivors of that terrible abduction. We are bound for São Tomé."

Chapter Forty-Two: Joanna

$\mathfrak{T}$hree men emerged from the foaming breakers and staggered through the surf, their dark skin gray with exhaustion. One of them fell to his knees, buffeted by the succeeding waves every time he tried to rise. He inched forward on his belly, using his elbows to drag himself along. Another, limping, supported his fellow. The latter, head hanging, had his arm slung around the lame man's neck. Joanna ran forward to help them, the others at her heels. A quick glance showed her that the ship was gone. Not even a broken spar remained. No heads bobbed in the water. The sky lit up one last time. With a final rolling growl, the storm departed, though the torrential rain still fell. The survivors of the wreck were so drenched that it was impossible to see their wounds until the party had made its way, with painful slowness, to the shelter of the trees.

"Let us take a look at you," Yenenga said.

Joanna and Brou, the baby still tightly wrapped to her back, cleared the ground of coconuts, broken branches, and other debris and laid down giant palm fronds for the three strangers to lie upon. Nunke and Yenenga helped them to lie down. One looked dazed and kept shaking his head, which streamed with blood. Another screamed aloud when Nunke inadvertently touched the burns on his hands. The third winced with pain every time his foot touched the ground and moaned when Yenenga laid an experimental hand on his ankle.

"You are safe now," Yenenga said. "We will help you. Lie still now."

"What are your names?" Nunke asked. He

repeated the question in several languages. Then he pointed to himself. "Nunke." He pointed to each of his companions in turn. "Brou. Yenenga. Joanna."

The man with the head wound closed his eyes and did not respond. The burned man nodded weakly but did not speak. Finally, the man whose ankle was injured pointed to himself and to his companions in turn.

"Mishambo. Nkonde. Shanda." He added in Portuguese, "The gods were angry."

"The gods saved you," Yenenga said. "You are safe here."

"The ship? The whites?"

"Gone. They drowned."

"Good."

One of the others asked a question in his own language.

"Our people?" the spokesman asked.

"Also drowned," Yenenga said.

"We are sorry," Joanna added.

"Rest now," Yenenga said.

Days passed before the strangers were well enough to be helped up the track to the encampment. By that time, all of the others had come down to the beach to see the newcomers at least once. A few had common languages with the strangers, who talked eagerly when they found they could tell their story and seemed to recover more rapidly once they knew that they had reached not only safety but also freedom.

"How did it happen that you were not chained?" Joanna asked Mishambo one day. He had the best command of Portuguese and was quickly learning the hybrid language of the band.

"Their greed undid them," Mishambo said. "They took more slaves than they had chains, for the slavers at Elmina complained constantly about the cost of the iron they must replace when they ship their captives on."

"You were fortunate," Joanna said. "We are all survivors."

"I knew I would not drown," Mishambo said, "once the fires broke out. I am a child of flame. That is the meaning of my name."

Some brought the rescued men gifts: a hunk of smoked fish wrapped in banana leaves, a cowrie shell, or an article of clothing from the community's small store. This generosity, after having waited, hopeless, naked, and starving, in the dark hold and then enduring the fury of the storm, expecting death at any moment, moved the newcomers to tears. Joanna shuttled back and forth, bringing whatever Yenenga needed, since the *feiticeira* would not leave her patients.

Finally, there came an evening when the whole augmented company could feast around the fire in the encampment. By common consent, a pig was killed and an abundance of bananas and coconuts laid out. Mawuwo and Fafale, grinning, brought out a small store of palm wine with whose manufacture they had been experimenting in secret.

"It has not had time to age," Fafale said.

"But it will make you sing," Mamuwo added. "All but Fafale, who cannot sing no matter how drunk he is."

"He cannot," Kwaku agreed, "no matter how strong the palm wine is. I have heard him try."

When all had eaten and drunk their fill, Kwaku and N'goran drummed on instruments made of pigskin stretched over lengths of hollow log. The others danced around the fire, singing praise to their various gods. Joanna watched, sitting on a log, her foot tapping to the drumbeat. She smiled when she saw Brou's baby fast asleep, still bound to his dancing mother's back.

Still later, all sat in a circle, firelight illuminating their gleaming faces as the flames crackled and danced on a bed of glowing red coals.

"Let us remember our homelands," Yenenga said, "and the people we were born to, though we may never see them again. I am Yenenga. I am Mossi."

"I am Kwaku. I am Ewe."

"I am Babune. I am Ewe."

"I am N'goran. I am Baule."

"I am Brou. I am Baule."

As those in the circle named themselves and their tribes, they seemed to Joanna to sit taller, their eyes to grow brighter. The newcomers sat together.

"I am Mishambo. I am Mbunda."

"I am Shanda. I am Mbunda."

"I am Nkonde. I am Mbunda."

Now all the others had spoken. Everyone looked at Joanna.

"I am Joanna. I am Jewish."

The enlarged community continued to flourish. But all seemed reluctant to call the encampment a settlement, and not only to avoid reminders of the hated Povoação. Some of the men continued to urge a foray to the settlement, either to raid it or to instigate a slave revolt. Others talked of building rafts and striking out for the mainland, where they might find their way back to their various tribal lands.

"How hard can it be to build a raft of logs and vines?" Babune asked.

"Not as hard as making it carry you over a hundred miles of ocean in the direction you wish it to go,"N'goran said.

"Or swimming fifty miles to shore," Yenenga said, "if it sinks in the middle of the sea."

"Even half that distance is too far to swim," Mawuwo said, and several of the others nodded in agreement.

"Do you know how to swim, Babune?" Joanna asked.

"No, but I can learn," Babune said with a broad grin that bared his broken teeth and set the tribal scars on his cheeks to dancing. "Mishambo, you will teach me."

"It is all very well for you," Nunke said, "but I have a baby to consider. And I do not have Mishambo's *juju* against drowning."

"After the passage here," Fafale said, "I vowed I

would escape or die before I let them put me in another slave ship. Drowning is not the alternative I had in mind."

"Mishambo, if we do this thing," Babune said, "are you with us?"

"I am not ready to trust myself to the great water again so soon," Mishambo said. "Good *juju* can run out."

The other Mbunda nodded assent, as did several of the others. A man of powerful presence, Mishambo had gradually taken on a leading role that only Yenenga had held before his arrival.

"First, I must see this settlement," Mishambo said. "We must consider our brothers and sisters who are still enslaved. Why have they not risen and killed the whites? Perhaps they lack only a leader. I am a warrior!"

"You are a fool," Yenenga said. "Have you not yet learned that we cannot stand against the white men's guns and swords?" Mishambo folded his arms across his chest and glared at her.

"Yet I am here," he said, "and the white men who carried me across the sea are not. We would take the guns and swords before attacking."

"Easier said than done," Yenenga said. She spat into the fire.

"Why can we not stay," Brou asked, "and make this a true village, make it our home?" She wiped the baby's milky mouth with a corner of her cloth and tucked her breast into its folds. "The whites do not even know that we are here."

"Is that true?" Shanda asked. "How can that be?"

"The forest is thick," Nunke said, "too hard to clear for their plantations, and the mountain lies between us and the settlement. They have never come after us, not even on the beach. If they knew, they would."

"And when people disappear," Nkonde asked, "as you did?"

"They think us drowned in the swamp," N'goran said, "or killed by the cursed creatures of the island:

venomous snakes, lizards with teeth like knives, insects whose sting gives deadly fevers. Stay far away from the swamp. There is no good in it."

"Stay far away from the settlement, I say," Mawuwo said. "It would be folly to let them know that we are here. Now that we make palm wine, we have everything we need. The people there are weak and frightened. They would not rise. If they had any warrior spirit left, they would at least have seized their freedom, as we did."

"You did not seize it," Mishambo said, "you crept away like lizards."

"There speaks one who has not seen the Povoacão," Babune said. "Even if you could take it and kill all the whites, which you cannot, you would still be stuck on this cursed island. It is better to build rafts and leave."

"I say build no rafts," Nunke said. "Even if they do not sink, what if the current brings you ashore on your enemy's doorstep? It was not white slavers who raided my village. First I was taken captive in war, then I was sold to the whites."

"You would rather cower in this clearing for the rest of your life?" Babune said. "I say let us build a raft and try. Who is with me?"

"To leave while so many black men and women remain in bondage," Mishambo said, "is the coward's way. Who is with me?"

At this point, the men started shouting. Joanna slipped away. She entered her hut and sat huddled with her arms around her knees.

"Ko ko ko." It was Yenenga's way of knocking at a hut that lacked a door.

"It's all right, Yenenga." Joanne tried to put welcome into her voice.

Yenenga ducked through the doorway and crouched beside her. She laid her hand on Joanna's knee.

"You are discouraged," Yenenga said. For once, she did not tease Joanna by speaking plantation pidgin. "It is hard for you to be here. You are the only white. You are farther from all you have ever known than any of us. And you do not have a man."

"You don't have a man," Joanna pointed out.

"I do not suggest you get one," Yenenga said. "But you are lonely."

"It is not that," Joanna said, "or not entirely. After all they did to me on the ship and in the Povoação, it is a relief to be alone. But what is my purpose, Yenenga? Did Ha'shem put me here to eat and sleep and perform the tasks of survival from day to day and nothing more? It is not enough, Yenenga! Yet there is nothing more and no way out. This island will be my grave."

"You are not inclined to join Babune's venture?"

"Of course not. Even if it succeeded, which I cannot believe it will, what would I do in Africa?"

"And what about Mishambo's plan?"

"If he attacks the settlement," Joanna said, "he will get himself killed and jeopardize the safety of every one of us. Do you think he is just talking, or will he try?"

"I do not know," Yenenga said.

"Why do you let him take charge the way he does?" Joanna demanded. "Everyone listens to him now. You are a natural leader, Yenenga, and you have much more common sense."

Yenenga grinned and patted her knee.

"Of course I do," she said. "I am a woman. And having common sense, I prefer healing and even sorcery to being a leader. I do not wish to spend my time trying over and over to get a pack of fools to change their minds."

"Do you not think he will tear the group apart?" Joanna asked.

"Were you frightened when they started shouting?" Yenenga asked.

"Not frightened, but it made me feel discouraged. If we must stay here, we must become a village, as Brou said. We must have accord. If that does not happen, our future looks bleak indeed. How do you keep your spirits up, Yenenga? Have you never fallen into a melancholy, a mood of despair?"

"What you call melancholy is a luxury, child," Yenenga said. "I have never had a moment to spare for it. Come." She stood gracefully, extending her hand to Joanna. "Let us go and pound *foutou*. It will put your muscles to work and your mind to sleep. And men must eat. Let them use those active mouths to chew and swallow, not to argue."

Chapter Forty-Three: Diego

Our days at sea fell into a rhythm. We rowed. We fished. The Muslims among us unrolled their rugs five times a day and prayed, facing the stern, for we were now northwest of faraway Mecca. When a brisk breeze arose, we hoisted our sails and scudded along for a while, giving the oarsmen a needed rest. We also sailed at night. The incessant rippling gurgle of the ship cleaving the water and the beauty of the bellying sails under the great bowl of a starry sky reminded me of nights aboard the *Santa Maria*. This too was a voyage into the unknown. With the stars to reckon by, only the helmsman need stay awake at these times. Miguel told me that on the corsair galley, the slaves had been chained to their benches in pairs, that one might sleep where he sat while the other rowed.

As we drew nearer to Gibraltar, tension mounted. All aboard *Esperanza* now knew that we planned to pass through the Pillars of Hercules and sail south upon the ocean. We would brave waters unknown to any save Portuguese navigators and slavers, for even Amir had never heard that any of the tribes south of the Great Desert were seafarers. I had not passed the gateway to the Mediterranean before. Cadiz, where we had embarked for the Indies, lay beyond it, and we had sailed south to the Canary Isles, set in the ocean off Africa's northwest shoulder, before heading west. Spanish Gibraltar faced Portuguese Ceuta across the strait, guarding the only entrance to the Middle Sea. The strait itself was only nine miles wide at its narrowest point. The question was not whether we would encounter other vessels but how many and whether they would accost us or let us pass.

The first galley to bear down on us flew the flag of the Knights of Rhodes, a white cross on a red ground. We had taken care to display no insignia ourselves, and none of the men wore turbans.

"Keep rowing," Amir ordered, "but do not increase your speed."

"We do not wish them to think that we are fleeing," I added. "Let us do nothing to arouse their suspicion."

Once they came near enough, they hailed us in Italian, Spanish, and English.

"Declare yourselves!"

"The *Esperanza*," I shouted back in Castilian, "out of Cadiz and on our way home with a cargo of fish and a quantity of soap from Marseille."

"Soap?" Amir, beside me, raised his eyebrows.

"You once knew the same soapmakers that I did," I said, "the Espinosas of Seville. If they have questions, we can answer them, and I doubt such a cargo will arouse their cupidity."

"That ship you've got there is a little beauty," one of the Knights shouted, also in Castilian. "What do you call her?"

"An experiment," I called back. "My cousin the shipbuilder swore he would buy our whole catch if we tested her out for him."

"I know Cadiz," the Knight shouted. "What's your cousin's name, and what chandlers do you use?"

I laughed under my breath as I called out a string of names. I had dealt with all of them while outfitting the Admiral's fleet.

A shout from his own ship's stern distracted my interlocutor's attention from *Esperanza*. A larger galley with a couple of masts had appeared on the horizon.

"From her size and shape," Amir said, "she's a merchantman out of Venice, perhaps carrying spices, silks, and gunpowder to the Venetians' Spanish allies. If the Knights have piracy in mind, that's a far better cargo than fish and soap."

The Rhodian ship was indeed coming about and setting a course for the Venetian.

"They might simply greet her as an ally," I said.

"Or that might be what the Rhodians want her to expect," Amir said. "Those Knights are a rapacious lot even for Christians."

A shout from *Esperanza*'s bow drew my attention from the ships behind us to a round ship under sail approaching us from the west.

"Another merchant ship," Amir said, "this one Portuguese. She might be carrying sugar from Madeira or almost anything from Lisbon to Ceuta."

"Do you know every vessel on the Mediterranean?" I asked.

Amir grinned.

"Akdeniz, the White Sea, is my *hammam*," he said.

"Hail her, Miguel," I said. "Ask her what's the news from Lisbon."

"Look to port!" Musa cried. His arm still being weak, he often served as lookout.

Two galleys with the distinctive long beak and painted hull of Ottoman vessels appeared from the direction of the African coast. Both were moving fast, oars flashing. Ignoring us, they separated, one making for the Venetian merchant ship, the other for the Portuguese.

"Hoist all sail!" I cried. "Let us make a run for it while they are distracted."

The men leaped to obey.

"You said that Venice and the Empire are not at war," I said to Amir. "Is this to be a boarding or a battle? In either case, let us put distance between us as quickly as we can."

"War is never far away in these times," Amir said. "Venice has been the Sultan's trading partner in the past. But they have fought as well. Venice led the league that chased the French out of Italy, calling it but a prelude to using the alliance to fight the Turk. The Sultan will not tolerate that for long."

"Captain!" Musa cried. "The Knights come after

us!"

The Rhodian galley had abandoned the fray to pursue us, rowing hard.

"The pious corsairs will not defend their fellow Christians," Amir said. "Men, I want every square inch of those sails filled with wind!"

"Why do they pursue us?" I said. "We have no guns, no riches they can seize, no passengers to hold for ransom."

"They covet *Esperanza* herself," Amir said. "We have designed too well. What a corsair she would make!"

"One adventure at a time," I said. "Ask me again when we have returned safely from this one."

"I would be pleased if I thought you meant it," Amir said.

At that moment, the Venetian ship emitted a loud boom and a puff of smoke.

"The merchantman is armed!" Musa cried.

The ball fell short, rocking the water around it.

"We must go faster!" I said. "At whom are they shooting? The Rhodian or the Ottomans?"

"It does not matter," Amir said, "if we are in the way. Venice did not gain an empire by waiting to be attacked."

I called out to our Moorish helmsman to take evasive maneuvers, which indeed he had already begun, while the sailors leaped to anticipate the swing of the sails as we tacked.

The foremost galley rolled out its own bombard, set in the bow, whereas the Venetian's cannon was mounted amidships. Their maneuverings brought them ever closer to us, though not within range of their artillery.

Amir uttered a curse in Arabic.

"If the next Venetian-Ottoman war begins right here, we are indeed in trouble."

Musa, clinging to the rigging high above the deck, shouted, "The Venetian carries bowmen! Look up in the fighting top!"

As I squinted upward to follow Musa's pointing

finger, the Moor cried out and dropped his hand from the tiller to clap it to his shoulder. For once, *Esperanza*'s responsiveness served us ill, for she reacted at once to loss of the helmsman's guidance. I leaped to take the tiller, with only a quick glance at the Moor. The arrow that had pierced his shoulder was still quivering, and blood leaked out from between his fingers. One of the oarsmen seized a discarded turban that lay on the bench beside him and ran, crouching low, to the stern to help the Moor. I felt *Esperanza* dance beneath my hand.

"Let us get out of here!" I said.

The sailors tightened the sheets. *Esperanza* flew through the water.

Amir leaped up into the rigging for a better view.

"Do not slack off!" he said. "The Rhodian still pursues us, and now one of the galleys comes after them. Now the Ottoman bowmen are shooting at the Rhodian."

I ducked as an arrow sped past where my head had been a moment before.

"They are still shooting at us!" I said. "Or else their aim is not up to the usual standard of Turkish archers."

"They are shooting from a greater distance than it seems," Amir said.

An arrow whizzed through the rigging an inch from his nose. He jerked his head back.

"Keep her tight to the wind!" I shouted to the men. "Amir, can you not signal to the Ottoman to shoot only at the Rhodian?"

Amir laughed and swung out from the rigging, holding on only by one hand and a foot tucked into a twist of rope.

"What, are you not enjoying this? Look, we are pulling away from the Rhodian."

"And the galleys?"

"They cannot catch us," Amir said. "We are too light and swift for them."

"I hope you are right," I said.

"They will turn back once we are through the

strait," Amir said. "Oars are of no use upon the ocean."

Sure enough, as we ran before the wind and shot through the strait, our pursuers fell back, giving up the chase. As the Mediterranean gave way to what men were beginning to call the Atlantic, sea met ocean in an indescribable blend of blues and greens. Higher seas than I had seen since the storm on our voyage from Barcelona rose before us, rocking the little ship below a cloudless heaven.

The men cheered, even morose Miguel and the helmsman, who was wincing with pain as one of his fellows dug out the arrow, which, luckily, had not gone deep.

"We did it!" I exulted.

"We have taken the first step," Amir said, grinning in elation. "Now let us see how we do when we pass Tangier, which remains in Portuguese hands. After that, if we continue to hug the Moroccan coast, we must still be on the lookout for pirates. On the other hand, the odds are in favor of any pirates we meet being friends of mine."

"If you wish us to reprovision in the Canaries," I said, "I can go ashore and get us whatever we need. If necessary, I will use the Admiral's name. The lady who rules the isle of La Gomera was once his inamorata."

"That does not guarantee that she will remember him kindly," Amir said. "On the contrary, perhaps."

"I will be cautious," I said. "I did not meet Lady Beatriz myself, nor will I seek to, unless I get into trouble."

As it happened, my brief visit to the port of San Sebastian went smoothly. Two of the Serbian sailors, Muslims who could pass easily for Christians, accompanied me to shore in the ship's boat, for we decided to moor as great a distance out as possible. We did not need a second lesson in the curiosity the *galliotçik* might arouse. As I stood on the bustling docks, where the native Guanche who labored under overseers' whips seemed both sadder and less numerous than before, I was reminded vividly of my previous visit, when I watched the same scene with Rachel and the Taino Cristobal, Ümīt's father. My errands were quickly done. In all probability, I would not set foot on land again until we reached São Tomé.

Among my purchases in San Sebastian were oil and oranges. That evening, Amir and I sucked sections of the sweet fruit as we pored over our charts by lantern light.

"Africa is vast," Amir said. "Among Europeans, only a handful of Portuguese navigators have reached its tip. We must sail south for many days before we reach what they call the Gulf of Guinea."

"When we do, we must turn east," I said, running my fingers along the map, "to continue along the coast. But how will we locate the island?"

"We need only locate Elmina," Amir said, "the fort that serves as center of the Guinea slave trade. We lie offshore, so that we may observe activity in the harbor without attracting attention. Then we wait. It should not be long until one or more slavers emerge, bound for São Tomé. We have but to follow them to reach our destination."

"It sounds risky," I said. "What if well armed naval ships escort the slavers?"

"My guess is that they do not," Amir said. "The Portuguese have no competition on the sea this far south. Nor will they have any other destination than São Tomé, whose whole purpose is to serve as a depot for slaves and sugar."

"Elmina must be the epitome of wretchedness," I said.

"São Tomé may not be much better," he said.

"We cannot relieve the misery of the captives on the mainland," I said. "There is at least a chance that it will be otherwise on the island."

"Inşallah," Amir said. "By the way, if you wish to tell your family that you are safe so far, now is the time. We must loose the remaining pigeons. They cannot cross the Great Desert, though if we released them south of it, they would try."

Chapter Forty-Four: Joanna

As Joanna had feared, the argument between Mishambo and Babune left the whole encampment in a state of discontent. The women, at least, were united in their opposition to both plans.

"I am not putting my baby on a bundle of sticks in the great water," Ekuwa said.

Crouching by the fire, she stirred pepper into a pot of sauce that she was making to spice up the *foutou* for the evening meal.

"I have told my man that I will deny him my body," Aminata said, "if he so much as speaks in favor of this foolish plan to attack the settlement. Warriors indeed!"

She held up a large banana, then thrust it into the bowl she was using as a mortar and ground it into mush with her wooden pestle as the other women uttered shrill cries of amusement.

"Babune has demanded that I teach him to swim," Joanna said. "He says that Mishambo is no good as a teacher, he does not know how to explain."

The women's raucous laughter greeted this remark too.

"Will you do it?" Lumusi asked.

"I do not mind helping Babune," Joanna said. "Do not worry. It will be long before he swims enough to trust himself to a raft in the depths of the ocean. Perhaps never. He squinches up his face like a baby when I tell him he must put it right into the water and let out his breath."

"But does he do it?" Kamina asked.

"No," Joanna said, "and when he tries to float, he sinks. Oh, it feels so good to laugh. Why must the men try to ruin everything?"

"They are men," Yenenga said. "It is their nature."

Had Joanna not been on the beach enjoying a moment of solitude, she would not have seen the little ship, and, in all probability, it would have passed that spot by. She had been giving Babune his swimming lesson, along with a few other men who thought it might prove a useful skill. A couple of the women had come to cheer or jeer but shyly joined in the lesson at Joanna's urging. Earlier, they had retreated to the shelter of the trees upon seeing three slaving ships pass by on their grim way to the Povoação.

"It is lucky we have no natural harbor," Babune said, "or they would be coming ashore to search for water and telling the Portuguese they have found the perfect site for a second settlement."

"Chas v'shalom!" Joanna said. "God forbid, in the language of my people."

"I may have trouble learning to swim," Babune said, "but I am not a complete fool."

"I did not think you were," Joanna said. "Must you really try to leave the island?"

"Do you really wish to stay?"

"My choices are limited."

Joanna said no more, and shortly afterward, the others retreated toward the encampment. But Babune's question resonated in her head as she paced back and forth, her bare feet digging into the wet sand and scattered pebbles and bits of shell of the foreshore. A breeze from the sea lifted strands of her hair from her neck and forehead and fluttered the faded red shawl she held wrapped around her shoulders, a treasured gift from Lumusi, whose baby she had helped Yenenga deliver. She was so absorbed in thought that she failed to see the small ship approaching in time to retreat into the shadows. That someone on board had caught sight of a moving figure in red was evident, for the ship's slow progress ceased. She could see scurrying figures lowering sail and dropping anchor. As she watched, sailors drew the small boat that bobbed off the ship's stern in close enough for two figures to drop into it, reach up for what looked like water buckets and casks rather than weapons, and begin to row toward shore.

Joanne watched them draw near, her feet planted in the sand, hair and shawl flying in the wind. An odd mood of fatalism came over her. There was no point in hiding now. They had seen her. If they meant her harm, she could run. She would not make for the encampment, but lead them away from it. They must not find the others. If they threatened to assault her person, she would climb a tree. Even were they agile and light enough to follow her, they could not rape her at the top of a coconut palm. As they climbed the trunk, she would brain them with a coconut before they could reach her and dislodge her from her perch.

They had been following the same route as the slavers, but the vessel appeared too small to be carrying slaves or any significant cargo. The ship itself was of a kind she had never seen. She could not fathom its purpose. Now the boat came close enough that she could see the rowers, their backs bent to their task. One had long iron-gray hair, the other tight dark brown curls above a sun-browned neck. When he cast occasional quick glances over his shoulder, she could see that he was young. He wore no shirt. Now they had almost reached the shore, close enough for her to discern sweat gleaming on the muscles of his back and arms. As she watched, thinking that she must flee but curiously unable to do so, he leaped from the boat and splashed through the water. Seizing a rope trailing behind it, he began to pull the boat to shore. The other man laid down his oars and climbed more cautiously over the side. He gripped the gunwale and began to push, hunched over with his head still bent. Joanna could not make out his features, but she could tell that he was old. The hull of the boat scraped over the slope of wet sand with a hissing sound toward the rim of seaweed that marked high tide. The young man gave the rope he held a final tug, looped it around his hand, and stood erect. His eyes met hers. Improbably, he smiled and bowed.

"Good afternoon, lady," he said in Castilian. "I am Diego Mendoza, formerly of Seville and now of Istanbul. Please do not be afraid." He added, *"Shalom aleichem."*

Two hours later, Joanna and Diego sat side by side on a log eating grilled fish and drinking coconut milk. As they ate, they cast sidelong glances at each other. The older man, Miguel, sat with them. The rest of the ship's crew had come ashore and addressed their own meal at a fire a hundred yards down the beach.

"I do not wish them to alarm you," Diego said. "They are good men, and they know to treat you with the utmost respect. But you need not have their eyes upon you as you eat your dinner."

"I am not alarmed," Joanna said. "I can run faster than they and fight fiercely if I need to. And perhaps they have never climbed a coconut tree?"

"I do not know," Diego said gravely, his mouth twitching. "It is a question I must ask them."

"And you say they are Turks?"

"Turks and Muslims from the Balkans, who are also subjects of the Sultan, and some are Maghrebians from North Africa."

"If they are not Portuguese," Joanna said, "they are not the men I most despise."

"I *was* Portuguese," Miguel said, removing a small bone from between his teeth.

"That is different," Joanna said. "You are Jewish."

"It is a miracle that we have found you," Diego said. "Everyone told us that all the children were dead."

"Then why did you come here?" Joanna asked.

"Because I refused to believe it," Diego said, "without the evidence of my own eyes."

"Had you nothing better to do?" Joanna asked, wondering why she was snapping at this polite young man.

"Many pursuits to occupy me," he said, showing no sign of offense, "but none that seemed more worth doing. Are the others all dead?"

"No," Joanna said. "That is, when I left, many had died, but some had survived and converted."

"And did that better their condition?" Diego asked.

"If they married Africans by the Christian rites, both they and their spouses were to be manumitted and allowed to benefit by their labor on the plantations. They were to be given land. I do not know how well those promises have been kept."

"But they were children!" Diego said.

"The ambitious marry young," Joanna said drily.

"And forgive me," Diego said, "but you are not a child. How old are you?"

"I do not know," Joanna said. "What year is it?"

"It is 1497."

"What month?"

"September, by my reckoning. We have been at sea for a while."

"Then I am sixteen," she said.

"If I may ask, why did they take you? You must have been older than the rest."

"I was," she said. "I was twelve and should have been safe, but my stepmother made sure I was taken so that I could care for my little brothers. I did not blame them. I comforted and cared for them, and they loved me in return. I wish only that I might have saved them from fear and suffering."

"You speak of the past," he said. "They are not with you now?"

"They died."

Casting a keen glance at her shuttered face, Diego asked no more questions.

Presently, Miguel said hesitantly, "My son was taken on the Lisbon docks. He was older too, eleven, but small for his age. Perhaps you knew him. His name was Natan."

"Natan," Joanna said. "Eleven, born in Lisbon. Yes,

I knew him."

Miguel's eyes shone with hope. His clasped hands trembled.

"Does he live?"

"When last I knew," Joanna said, "he did."

"*Baruch Ha'shem!*" Miguel said.

"*Baruch Ha'shem!*" Diego echoed, beaming at Miguel. He frowned as he looked at Joanna's expressionless face.

"He has converted," she said. "He was one of the first."

Chapter Forty-Five: Diego

"We must go as quietly as ghosts," Mishambo said.

The big Mbunda led our party, which consisted of himself, his fellow tribesmen Nkonde and Shanda, Miguel and me, and two escaped slaves who knew the settlement, Nunke and Kwaku. Amir and some of the hotheads in our crew would have liked to join us on this adventure, but I did not wish to risk a single one of them.

"If some ill befalls me," I told Amir, "who but you could lead them on the journey home?"

With some reluctance, Joanna had volunteered to join the party.

"There is nothing I wish less than to revisit the scene of my captivity," she said. "But why should the children listen to strange men who tell them to run away after all this time, even men who claim to be Jewish? You need me, so I will come. It is my duty."

Mishambo failed to persuade the tall black woman named Yenenga to join us, though the ex-slaves all agreed that she alone had the authority to persuade the women slaves to consider revolting.

"As a *feiticeira*," Joanna told me, "she is respected by the men as well."

"We do not mean to fight," Mishambo said, "but to gather support for an uprising later on."

Yenenga herself scoffed at the notion that she should lead the women in rebellion.

"Women not need leaders," she said, "because women not go do anyting foolish."

"Do not mind Yenenga," Joanna said. "If she comes to trust you, she will reveal her powerful intellect in fluent Portuguese. She is also the wisest of us all, which is not the same thing."

"I hope you will come to trust me too," I said, finding within myself a powerful desire for her to do so.

"Like Yenenga," Joanna said, "I do not give my trust lightly. For the moment, I believe that you are who you say you are and that you mean me no harm. I admit it is a pleasure to converse in Spanish for the first time since my brothers died. Are you sure you cannot dissuade these men from returning to the settlement?"

"I cannot," I said, "although I truly wish to please you. Miguel will not rest until he has spoken to his son."

"I fear he is doomed to disappointment," Joanna said. "Natan is one who took the first opportunity to remake himself in the image of our captors. I suggest we have a strategy for a quick escape if he betrays us."

"I cannot tell Miguel that," I said. "When I proposed this journey, he was in a state of complete despair. Would you deprive him of hope one moment before you had to? What would you wish for your own parents?"

"My mother is dead," she said, "and my stepmother could easily bear to lose me, since she did not give a fig for me. My father no doubt despaired when he lost his children, but he would never undertake a journey of thousands of miles on the chance of rescuing us. He was too ineffectual to protect me from her malice, much less from the King of Portugal's soldiers."

"I am sorry," I said. "I hope one day you will meet my parents, who are otherwise."

"If you truly wish that," Joanna said with a crooked smile, "you will abandon this expedition to the settlement."

"I cannot," I said. "I do not do this only for Miguel. What brought me this long way was a vow to save as many Jewish children as I could."

"I think we will find very few survivors," Joanna said, "and that none of them will wish to be saved."

"I hope that you are wrong," I said. "And I will take to heart your warning that Miguel's son might betray us. I will insist that Mishambo, Nunke, and the others approach the slaves and you and I the Jews before Miguel reveals himself to Natan. Thus little will be lost if we have to get away quickly."

We approached the settlement from the rear, circling from the beach into the thick woods beyond the most recently cleared cane fields. As we waited for dark, we observed what appeared, at least on the surface, to be tranquil scenes of plantation life. We saw blacks sweating in the sun amid the cane and booted whites in broad-brimmed hats supervising their labors. The whites held whips but did not use them while we watched. We identified a sawmill and a sugar mill, both powered by the flow of a small river that ran between the fields. The black workers included heavily pregnant women and others with babies on their backs, held safely by a twist of cloth around the mothers' waists. The babies were evidently accustomed to this position, for many slept, awaking only to suckle at their mothers' breasts, which the women whipped out casually, swinging them around without ceasing to work the cane.

We did not see a single young person, black or white, between the ages of six and fifteen.

"I was the eldest of the children," Joanna said, "and Natan the next, as far as I know. The Portuguese brought along no children of their own four years ago, nor did the first shiploads of slaves include children, though some of the women were pregnant. What the Portuguese call *mestiços*, born of mothers impregnated by the masters here, would be no more than three years old and those fathered by Africans on Jewish mothers even younger."

"Are you saying that Jewish girls bore children?" In Istanbul, most girls married at twelve or betrothed even younger were allowed to delay the consummation of their marriages. "How could they be old enough to bear?"

"They were not when I left," Joanna said, her jaw set. "But not all of them escaped rape. Do not forget that the king's purpose in transporting us here was not only to rid his kingdom of Jews but to breed us before working us to death."

"I am sorry," I said, spreading my hands in apology for the inadequacy of my words. "You must have endured terrible things."

"I might have borne a child to slavery myself," she said, "if not for the cupidity of the degradada who controlled me and, later, Yenenga's skill with herbs."

I did not let my horror show on my face for fear that she would think I condemned her. No wonder she had difficulty trusting any man. She was younger than Rachel, and her experiences made the dangers Rachel had faced appear trivial in comparison. I doubted that Rachel's sunny spirit and capacity to trust every soul she met, provided they were not coming at her with a weapon, would have survived the treatment Joanna had undergone. Rachel had courage. Joanna surely had more, for her sufferings had not broken her.

"You have good reason to be angry," I said.

"Anger has kept me strong," she said.

"Yet you do not approve of Mishambo's plan to incite the slaves to rebellion."

"I am practical," she said, "as I have needed to be to survive so long. Having refused to die of despair, I have no desire to throw myself headlong at death as Mishambo intends to, whether or not he knows it. I wish to live, especially now that you offer a way to escape this pestilential island."

"I will get you out of here," I said. "I swear it."

Her eyes met mine, still wary but with grim humor lurking in their depths.

"Then let us make sure not to get ourselves killed before you have a chance to keep your promise."

When night fell, we ventured deeper into the settlement, moving as softly as we could. Joanna, who had left the place behind three years before, betrayed by a quick intake of breath or a tightening of her lips signs of how firmly established the settlement had become.

"The king's plan prospers," she said bitterly as we rested briefly, crouched in the cover of a deserted cane field. "Did you see the fine house of the owners of this field? He is a *degradado*, she a former slave. And did you see the slave huts set apart from the house? This couple has accepted payment in slaves for the sugar they have sold to the Crown." Lowering her voice so none but I could hear it, she added, "We may find that Natan has done the same."

"In Istanbul," I said, "you will find Jews who hold slaves."

"But none who have experienced slavery themselves," she snapped. "I loathe the very thought."

"As do I and all my family," I said.

It was nearing dawn when we found Natan at last. As Joanna had predicted, he had a fine house of wood through whose window we could see him sleeping in a great bed with a pregnant black woman beside him. His fields lay relatively close to the center of the settlement, with a well-worn path leading toward it that I judged to have been in daily use for years. Another track led to slave quarters less ramshackle than most we had seen, another sign that the owner's prosperity was of long duration. On seeing his son, Miguel would have cried out had I not clapped a hand across his mouth as he opened it. Joanna seized his arm, stretched out as if he would have touched his sleeping child through the window. Together, we dragged him back. Crouching low, we withdrew to the shadows.

"Soon it will be day," I said. "Miguel, you can do nothing now."

"You whites must remain in hiding," Mishambo said, "while my brothers and I sound out the slaves. We can pass among them freely as long as we can be seen to labor."

"Will not the overseers notice unfamiliar faces among their workers?" I asked.

Nunke responded with a smile that did not reach his eyes.

"Do you not know that all black men look alike?"

"They do not to me," I said. "Will you ask those you speak with about the Jews? If we see no white children again today, it is at least possible that they no longer labor in the fields but can be found within the houses and mills."

"You are an optimist," Joanna said. "I have no reason to believe that swamp fever, snakes, or crocodiles changed their nature when I left."

"You may be right," I said, "but we will not know unless we try. I have come too far to give up now."

While Miguel and I waited in hiding for Natan to wake, the Africans canvassed the slave quarters, waking the sleeping slaves and whispering to them of freedom. Joanna elected to remain with us.

"I do not wish to come face to face with my tormentors," she said.

"Do you not fear that those the men approach will raise the alarm?" I asked. "It would only take one to betray us, and they do not know Mishambo."

"Shared suffering makes a bond," she said, "that resignation is not strong enough to break." She cast a quick glance at Miguel, who was pacing impatiently, biting at his fingernails, and spoke more softly. "His son is the one I fear will betray us. His loyalty to Adonai broke easily, and at no time did he show a trace of sympathy for anyone else's pain. If his father ever spoke to him of *tikkun olam*, he did not listen."

"I can only guess at what Miguel was like in happier days," I said, "but I do not think he taught his son the selfishness you describe by example. It is far more likely that he adored and indulged him, allowing the boy to perceive himself as a little prince."

"Had he been a little princess," Joanna said bitterly, "that illusion would have been shattered on the ship that brought us here. But he managed to escape the worst and quickly ingratiated himself with the masters, climbing on the backs not only of the children but of the *degradados* to whom we had been given."

The beginning of this speech aroused once more my worst imaginings about the horrors that must have befallen her. Since it was clear she would not welcome even the most kindly meant invitation to tell me more, the return of the Africans provided a welcome distraction.

"Our success has been limited so far," Mishambo admitted, "though we confined our visits to the huts of those who knew Nunke and Kwaku."

"We had no success," Kwaku said bluntly, "in recruiting rebels for an uprising. The settlement grows, the whites grow rich on slaves and sugar, and ships come from Portugal with weapons and fighting men. If one *fazendeiro* dies of the fever, two more spring up in his place."

"Not many of those we knew still live," Nunke said, "and those who have replaced them are treated so brutally by the slavers that they are thoroughly cowed by the time they get here. We told them little of our own encampment, since what they do not know, they cannot betray. But a few begged us to take them with us when we leave."

"What did you say to that?" Joanna asked.

"That we would discuss it."

"I am against it," Mishambo said. "These men who are willing to flee but not to fight would mill about and bleat like a flock of sheep and bring the white men down on us."

"We were planning to bring children back with us," I said, "who surely would have been more unruly, so it is not impossible. I do not like to leave men who long for freedom in slavery."

"What did they say of the children?" Joanna asked.

"As we supposed," Nunke said, "most are dead. The few who remain have been married and manumitted or adopted and treated well enough to forget the past. They go to church on Sunday and cannot be trusted. You must forget them."

"Can we not tell those who wish to escape where to find us," Kwaku asked, "so that they may choose their own moment to make their way to us? Even you, Mishambo, must concede that if they are stalwart and clever enough to reach the encampment through miles of untracked forest, they are worthy to join us."

It seemed to me that Mishambo read implied criticism of his simple swim to freedom into this, for he said quickly, "Let us hear what Shanda and Nkonde think. Nkonde? Shanda? Where have they disappeared to?"

The other two Mbunda were indeed missing.

"They could not have gone far," I said. "We must find them quickly, for our time is running out."

As I spoke, a shaft of sunlight struck my face, dazzling me so that for a moment, I could see nothing else. Then the sun rose, spilling light everywhere. I saw Shanda and Nkonde running toward us, both laughing. Shanda held something that squealed and squirmed between his hands. Nkonde had his arms wrapped around something inside his shirt that wriggled and grunted.

"Look!" Shanda cried. "Piglets!"

"Good eating for us all!" Nkonde tightened his arms around his prize.

We all stared, openmouthed.

"You idiots!" Joanna snapped. "Do you want to bring the soldiers down on us? Drop those piglets at once and be silent, or you will get us all killed!"

I thought her words had gone home, for the two Mbunda's eyes grew round, and they both dropped their piglets. The little creatures scampered off, still squealing, in the direction they had come from. But Nkonde and Shanda were staring not at us, but at something behind us.

A cold voice spoke.

"Do not move. I have an arquebus pointed at your

backs, and I will not hesitate to use it."

We froze.

"If I but shoot it in the air, men will come running."

Mishambo, Nunke, and Kwaku, closest to our captor, obeyed literally his command not to move. I slowly turned.

"Slaves who steal are hanged, but no one will mind if I spare them the trouble. They may even pay me a bounty of slaves to replace you."

The speaker was little more than a boy, but he held his arquebus as if he knew how to use it. I had already seen his face in repose, while he slept. Waking, it was stern, as if he were accustomed to authority, and faintly sneering, as if he enjoyed it.

Joanna pushed past me and stepped forward between Nunke and Mishambo to confront him.

"Natan. Will you really shoot me or see me hanged?"

"Joanna! But you are dead."

Behind her back, Joanna made a pushing motion with her hand. I caught Mishambo's eye and jerked my head at the others. I took a stealthy step backwards.

"Am I really?" Joanna said. "Are you sure that is it not you who are dead? Dead to Adonai, to Torah, to humanity?"

"I have merely seen the truth of Our Lord Jesus Christ, who conquers all. Only a fool would cling to the losing side."

"Christ in whose name your masters kidnap children. Christ in whose name you have no shame in owning slaves and even in impregnating them."

Slowly, we moved backward, away from that menacing gun. Only Miguel stood stock still, staring at Natan. When I put my hand on his arm to draw him backward, he shook it off.

"Do not blaspheme!" Natan scowled. "And do not presume to speak so of my wife."

"Whom you had to marry in order to be manumitted yourself." Joanna's voice rang with scorn. "Yet you boast of acquiring yet more slaves. Are you rich yet? Do they pay you in gold for the bloodstained sugar you grow without lifting a finger? Or is all your compensation in human lives? You must be very proud!"

Natan's hands trembled, whether with rage or because Joanna's words cut too close, it was impossible to tell. The arquebus shook, and Joanna reached out and pushed it contemptuously aside. She held Natan's eyes with hers. I did not want to leave her, but I motioned to the others to get out of sight.

"Run!" I mouthed.

All of them took to their heels and ran for the concealing trees at the edge of the field.

"I am proud!" Natan snapped. "I am a *fazendeiro*! I am a survivor who had the wit to live when all the others died!"

"Do you really think it was your wit that caused the fever to pass you by? Do you think your Jesus told the snakes and crocodiles not to bite you? Blind luck saved you, boy, and your own capacity for self-deception and playing the lickspittle did the rest. Jesus may forgive your selfishness, but could you face Adonai with your choices and the deeds you have done? Could you face your father?"

"Adonai is dead to me, and so is my father!" Natan spat out.

I pushed Miguel forward. Joanna stepped aside, revealing him to Natan.

Miguel, his face a mask of tragedy, held out his arms, tears running down his cheeks.

"Oh, my son, my son!"

"Papa?"

Natan's face went white with shock. The gun dropped from his hands. He started forward as if to submit to Miguel's embrace, but then dropped to his knees, clutching at the cross around his neck.

"*Pater noster qui es in caelis, sanctificetur nomen tuum.* Deliver me from evil, deliver me from evil." His eyes squeezed shut. His whole body shook.

"Jesus save me, Jesus save me," he gabbled. "*Pater noster qui es in caelis.* I am dreaming, I am dreaming. You are not real!"

"Come!" Joanna said. "Now!"

Joanna and I each seized one of Miguel's arms. For a moment he resisted.

"My son, my son," he sobbed.

Then he allowed us to pull him toward the shelter of the forest.

Chapter Forty-Six: Joanna

When they had withdrawn to a safe distance, Diego called a halt. Mishambo was engaged in giving his compatriots a blistering scold in their own language. Nunke and Kwaku, half disappointed and half relieved that their plan to foment rebellion had come to naught, looked to Diego for direction. Miguel, face averted and back hunched, was sobbing. Diego knelt beside him, his arm around the older man's heaving shoulders, murmuring words meant to comfort by tone rather than sense, as one would soothe a skittish horse. Joanna stood apart from all of them, arms folded across her chest. Diego cast a puzzled glance at her stony face.

"His heart is broken," he said. "Are you not moved by his pain?"

"My heart turned to ice when I was taken on the Lisbon docks," she said. "That day I saw thousands of parents bereft as he is without any mitigation of their loss. He at least knows that his son still lives and, moreover, that that son has proved unworthy of his grief. Losing my family is the least of what I have endured since that day. The only emotion that still burns within me is anger, and that is a fire that cannot melt my heart."

Mishambo flung himself away from the other Mbunda with an exclamation of disgust.

"Thanks to these fools," he said, "we cannot linger here."

"We cannot count on Natan not to sound the alarm," Joanna said, "once he has recovered from the shock."

"I agree that you must go, Mishambo," Diego said.

"It is not safe for any of you to stay. Miguel, I am sorry, but you too should leave. There is nothing for you here. For myself, I will always regret it if I do not speak with at least one Jewish child. Joanna, will you remain with me? I will not urge it if you think the danger too great. I can complete my mission alone."

"Except for Natan," Joanna said, "I do not believe any Jewish child who knew me and still lives will prove a threat to me. Certain Portuguese are the folk I must avoid."

"Those who would recognize you as a fugitive, you mean," Diego said.

Joanna's knife flashed in her hand as she turned on him a baleful smile that brought the words "the wrath of God" to his mind.

"Those whom I would be hard put to forbear from killing should I encounter them again," she said.

Diego's look of compassion brought a scowl to her face.

"Do not dare to pity me!" she snapped.

He hastily rearranged his expression.

"I would not so presume," he said. "You may accompany me or not as you choose, but the Africans must go as soon as possible."

"I will stay," Joanna said. She beckoned to the others. "Nunke, Kwaku, when I escaped, I walked a long distance along the beach. None followed me, because I left when the fever was at its height, but that route would leave you too exposed today. Have you a better one?"

"Brou and I struck south through the forest," Nunke said, "which gave us ample cover. More land has been cleared since then, but if we go silently and skirt the new plantations, I believe we can remain hidden."

"Go quickly, then," Joanna said. "We will follow you as soon as we can."

Miguel, no longer sobbing but dazed and trembling, still knelt in the dirt as the Africans prepared to depart.

"Miguel," Diego said, "you must go with them. I will join you shortly."

"I should try to speak with him again," Miguel said. "He is still my son and a child of God."

"You must leave him to God," Diego said, "for there is nothing you can do. If you approach him, you endanger us all."

That argument striking home as an appeal to seek his own safety would not have, Miguel allowed Kwaku to take his arm and lead him away, the whole band crouched and hunched close together as they moved off. Diego and Joanna watched them out of sight.

"How shall we proceed?" Diego asked. "I defer to your experience of the settlement."

"The children and *degradados* who arrived with the Governor," Joanna said, "lived in compounds near the heart of the settlement. If those huts still exist, we may find the children who did not die there. If they have moved on, it will most likely be to the earliest cleared plantations. I suggest we start at the Povoação and search outward from the center."

"Would not the eldest of the children be the most likely both to remember you," Diego said, "and to have been married, freed, and given land of their own?"

"Natan and I were the eldest," Joanna said. "But you are right. There were boys of nine or ten who would be *bar mitzvah* by now if they had not converted and might conceivably have fathered children if they were given wives among the older slave women. Even though the Portuguese thought Jews fit to be slaves, they would value *metiço* offspring as improving the breed of the blacks."

"The very thought of human beings being bred like cattle is repulsive," Diego said. "It is hard to believe not one would choose a different life if it were offered."

"You would be surprised to know how completely one can accept the intolerable," Joanna said. "After a time, it is but a trick of the mind to

334

convince oneself at one and the same time that it is normal and that it is not happening or is happening to someone else."

"You speak as one who has been obliged to perform this mental feat," Diego said, "and I am sorry for it."

"You need not be," Joanna said. "I am no longer obliged to live daily with the intolerable, and I have locked those memories away."

"I wonder," Diego said, "if such a lock can hold indefinitely. At the least, the memories must come back to you in dreams. But I do not mean to press you. If you ever wish to talk of it, I would be honored by your confidence."

"I will not," Joanna said. "The other girls were too young to be treated as I was. But at the age of twelve, they would have been considered women even had they remained at home, although my father considered that age too young for a betrothal."

"As did mine," Diego said. "My sister is seventeen, and she is but newly betrothed. However, I must tell you that most Jews in Istanbul are marrying their children younger and younger in an effort to rebuild the Jewish people."

"So the rabbis themselves," Joanna said with a sardonic twist of the lip, "consider us breeding stock?"

"It is not the same!" Diego said. "Well, in a sense, perhaps it is, but I can understand it, can't you?"

"Having lost my freedom completely," Joanna said, "I will allow no one to trifle with it again. The day that we were taken, rabbis performed some hasty marriages on the spot, as if to bind the children to Judaism and prevent them being forcibly married to Africans or Christians later on. But the priests did not consider those marriages binding, so they did no good. And girls of twelve today were eight at the time of the abduction, young enough to have forgotten they were ever Jewish by now. The priests did their best to make sure of that."

"In Spain, as you know," Diego said, "though

many of us converted, in every city there were some who went through the motions but secretly never forsook our faith. My family were among those they called *marranos*."

"Mine fled to Portugal," Joanna said, "in order to avoid having to do just that. In the end, it did us no good."

By late that afternoon, they had found only a handful of children and none with whom they thought it safe to speak. Joanna had recognized three boys tilling garden plots of their own, all three with pregnant young African women working alongside them and toddlers playing at their feet.

"They look happy," Joanna said reluctantly. "Look, the biggest child is white. Perhaps this boy was allowed to marry a Jewish girl who then died in childbirth, being too young to bear safely, and whom he then replaced with this black girl. From the King of Portugal's point of view, I would say his plan to populate the island is succeeding."

The rough huts Joanna remembered were gone. The settlement had grown populous enough that they found a graveyard behind the church, with neat rows of wooden crosses and ample room for more within a mud-brick enclosure.

Joanna walked up and down along the rows, reading the inscriptions.

"Ha! So Imaculada and Belmiro did not survive," she exclaimed. "I am glad of it!"

"Who were they?" Diego asked.

"The *degradados* to whom I was given," Joanna said, scowling. "I was told the King intended them to be my Christian parents, but their own intent was to profit from degrading me. May they rot in hell, if such a place exists!"

"Come away," Diego urged. "They are gone and cannot hurt you now."

"No, I cannot go yet. I must see— Oh, no!" Joanna dropped to her knees, her face a mask of pain. "The villains! See what they have done!"

Diego knelt and peered over her shoulder. Three

names were burned into a single cross. The inscription read: "Simon, Samuel, Benjamin—of the household of Belmiro Furtado."

"Who are they?" he asked.

"My brothers," she said through gritted teeth, clenching and unclenching her fists. "They buried them as Christians in a single grave, to be remembered by a single name, like animals. See how they say "of the household," designating them as slaves rather than as sons. At least they got Belmiro's name right: Belmiro the Bastard!"

"I am truly sorry, Joanna," Diego said.

"Simon was my full brother and such a dear, conscientious boy," she said. "Shmuel and Benji were my stepmother's children. When I had to mind them at home, I considered them a nuisance, but I came to love them dearly here, where all we had was each other. Shmuel was the reckless one, Benji the sweet one. He was just a baby! Shmuel is not actually buried here. A crocodile ate him in the swamp. The other two died of fever. It was after that that I left."

"Would you like me to say Kaddish for them?"

"At least it is a prayer that Adonai is likely to hear," Joanna said. "I prayed so many that were disregarded, prayers for my brothers' safety. Do I shock you?"

"My father," Diego said, "who is the wisest person I know, says that all anger, from whatever cause, is to some extent anger at God."

"And what are we supposed to do about it," Joanna asked, "when God does nothing?"

"Exactly what we are doing now," Diego said. "*Tikkun olam.* Whatever we ourselves can do to repair the world. Let me say Kaddish for your brothers, Joanna."

Joanna shrugged.

Taking that as assent, Diego closed his eyes and spoke the familiar words in an undertone.

"*Yit'gadal v'yit'kadash . . .*"

Afterward, Joanna insisted on reading the inscription on every cross in the graveyard.

"Many whom I know to be dead are not buried here," she said. "Their names have already been forgotten. I suppose you will say that Adonai remembers them."

"I believe He does," Diego said, "but I neither can nor wish to compel you to believe the same."

"That is refreshing," Joanna said, "in a world in which it sometimes seems that the powerful have nothing better to do with their power than compel others to believe as they do."

As the afternoon waned, they made their way toward the outskirts of the settlement.

"We had better find the others before dark," Diego said. "I hope they have found a spot where we can lie concealed and get a few hours' sleep."

"We must hurry, then," Joanna said. "Sunset never varies here. The sky is ablaze for a few minutes, then night falls like a curtain coming down. There is no winter when the days get shorter or summer with a lingering period of twilight."

The workers in the fields had laid down their tools and were moving in the other direction, towards their dwellings and cooking fires.

"At least we need not worry about being discovered," Diego said.

At that moment, Joanna, pushing through the cane, came face to face with a Jewish boy and girl of eleven or twelve who were walking hand in hand. The boy had wiry brown hair much like Diego's own, but the girl's thin face was framed in a mop of coppery curls. The children and Joanna uttered simultaneous exclamations of surprise. The girl dropped the boy's hand and looked apprehensive, as if detected in committing an infraction, while the boy squared his narrow shoulders and looked belligerent.

"Mira!" Joanna said. "Do you not remember me? I am Joanna. We lived together in the children's hut when we first came to São Tomé."

"I do not remember you," the girl said. She took the boy's hand again as if he lent her courage to

338

speak to this stranger. "And my name is Maria. I live on a *fazenda*. My parents will be worried if I do not return by sunset."

Joanna and Diego exchanged glances, both noting that she had said "worried" rather than "angry."

"You are happy, then?" Joanna said.

"What do you mean?" the girl said. "Of course I am. And if I am good and pray hard to the Blessed Virgin, Cristiano and I will soon be betrothed."

"You do not have to tell them all that!" the boy said. "Who are you to question us? I have not seen you before. Where do you come from?"

"Hush, Cristiano," the girl said. "You will not tell anyone you saw us, will you? We are not supposed to slip away alone like this."

Diego suddenly spoke to them in Hebrew. Both the boy and the girl looked blank and shook their heads.

"I am someone who used to know Maria," Joanna said. "We mean you no harm, and we will not tell anyone we saw you if you will promise the same. Do you not remember the ship? Or that you once had another name?"

"We do not know what you are talking about," the boy said. "Come on, Maria, we must run."

He tugged at her hand. Giggling and looking over her shoulder, she allowed him to pull her along until they vanished into the concealment of the dense green forest of cane.

"We had better do the same," Diego said. "They were probably lying under a tree and kissing. They were more concerned about whether anyone would tattle about their misbehavior than about who we were."

"She would have been seven when we arrived here," Joanna said. "Her name was Mira. I did not know the boy, but I am very certain that his name was not Cristiano! So the King of Portugal's purpose is fulfilled. They have forgotten that they were ever Jewish."

Chapter Forty-Seven: Diego

We returned to the encampment at dusk three days later to find that Amir had insisted that a watch be kept in our absence, on the chance that our visit to the settlement might bring the Portuguese down on us. The whole community, my crew along with the Africans, quickly gathered, eager to hear our story.

"I see no children with you," Amir said. "Are they all dead after all?"

"The few who remain are dead to us," I said. "The younger ones have forgotten who they were, and the elder have thrown in their lot with the Christians and aspire to nothing more than to be planters rich in slaves and land."

"What about the rebellion?" Fafale asked.

"It will not be the work of a day to rouse the captives from their stupor," Kwaku said.

"All we spoke to," Nunke said, "were either fearful or apathetic."

"They will never rise," Shanda said.

"Do not say never!" Mishambo glared at Shanda. "We must have leaders from among ourselves who are not fools, thinking only of their bellies instead of our mission. We must build our store of weapons, making some and stealing others. We must recruit the captives by helping them escape, speaking of an attack on the town only when they are strong and confident again. In short, we must have a plan."

"Where is Miguel?" Amir asked. "Did he find his son? You have not lost him, I trust."

"Miguel is safe," I said, "but things went badly with his son. He went down to the beach, for he did not wish to be questioned or hear it spoken of. Who is on watch on *Esperanza*?" I scanned the familiar faces of my crew. "Kemal? Miguel will relieve him."

Our safe return brought new energy to the encampment, although the Africans were still divided between those who wished to leave the island and those who wished to build a permanent community. Those who dreamed of rebellion allied themselves with the latter.

"Let us build something for our enslaved brethren to run to," Mishambo said, "rather than merely effecting a bloodbath with no notion of what comes after."

"He takes charge as if he had been here all along," Joanna grumbled.

"What does it matter?" I asked. "You will come with us when we leave, will you not?"

"I suppose so," Joanna said. "Yes. Of course. I will be glad to leave this cursed island behind me. Since I have no place in the world and no people to call kin, I might as well try Istanbul as anywhere."

"It seems to me," I said, "that you have the very dilemma Mishambo has stated. You know what you are running from, but not what you are running toward. Please do not think you will have no kin in Istanbul. My parents will welcome you with open arms, and my sister will stand your friend. You will like Rachel, I think. Like you, she has been tempered and honed by experiences far beyond the lot of an ordinary Jewish girl."

"So I have been tempered and honed, have I?" Joanna said. "I feel bone weary, as if I am a blade that has been beaten into submission too many times."

"You strike me as anything but submissive," I said, smiling. "And I am sure you will regain your edge once you no longer have to fight for each day's bare existence and come to believe that you once more have a future."

"What makes you think your Rachel will like me?" she asked. "I have been consumed by anger for so long that I have no kindness or sweetness in me to offer a friend."

"I do not believe that," I said. "Your sweetness has simply gone into hiding. Perhaps having a sister will encourage it to venture forth."

"Are you to be my brother, then?" she asked.

Tanama, my lost Taino love, would have said it with a sidelong glance and a teasing lilt to her voice, her body engaged in a silent conversation with mine beneath the light exchange of words. Joanna seemed to be oblivious to me as a man. I found I wanted to change that. That she had a capacity for passion, I knew, for I had seen her angry. I believed she had known love, for I had seen her face when she beheld her brothers' grave and heard the tenderness and yearning in her infrequent mentions of her mother. But with respect to men, on the few occasions when her guard had slipped, only fury, fear, and bitterness peeked through. I did not know if I could win her. It would take patience and compassion. But I wished to try.

"I am to be your friend," I said gently. "If you ever call on me for help or understanding, I promise never to let you down."

"I have learned to need no help," she said, "and as for understanding, I fear that it is I who would disappoint you if you truly knew me."

"Only by failing to trust me," I said. "Nothing you could tell me would disgust or shock me. I have seen much cruelty in the world, Joanna, and myself experienced the ugly feelings anyone must feel on witnessing it without having the power to stop it. I saw my first auto da fé when I was ten years old. My best friend is a man without a country, a man more stripped of kin than you, for we saw Admiral Columbus's Spaniards slaughter and enslave his entire people." I hesitated, then decided that I could elicit frankness in her only by demonstrating it myself. "I saw my lover raped and murdered before my eyes, and I could do nothing. That is, I killed the soldier who assaulted her, but I could not save her."

"You have killed," she said. "I have wished to,

many times, but lacked either the power or the opportunity at those moments."

"I am not proud of taking human life," I said. "But I have done what I had to."

"I admire you for it," she said.

After this, we talked more freely. We had time to do so, though we spent many hours working, for there was much to do. With some relief, those who wished to leave the island abandoned the project of building rafts, for I offered to carry any who chose to return to the mainland with us on *Esperanza*. The ship must be provisioned with food and weapons for the return journey. The villagers helped us dry fish and make arrows, and in return, *Esperanza*'s crew helped those who wished to stay raise sturdier houses and fashion bows and spears for both hunting and defense. Whether they were ever used to arm a slave revolt, I told Joanna, was none of my business. For now, turning the encampment into a village and providing for its protection was a task in which I willingly participated.

"This is becoming a community with a sense of purpose," I said.

Joanna and I were watching the spectacular equatorial sunset on the beach. She preferred gazing out at the open sea to being hemmed in by forest, and I liked to keep an eye on *Esperanza*. I would have liked to hide her from view, but Joanna told me there was no way to do so. The Portuguese who had discovered and circumnavigated the island swore its whole coastline was smooth and even, without coves or natural harbors except for the one next to the swamp, where they had built the Povoação.

"We all need a sense of purpose, do we not?" she said. "If the Jews had not been driven out of Spain, I suppose I would have found mine in being a dutiful wife and mother. It is hard to imagine. I was angry and rebellious from the day my father brought my stepmother home. And you?"

"I certainly would not have become a sailor," I said, "had the Jews not had to flee. In Istanbul, we are allowed to worship openly and work at whatever trade we choose. But after my adventures, I am equally ill suited to being a dutiful Jewish man, studying Torah and complying with the rabbis' rulings on everything. I cannot deal in absolutes, having met and even loved people whose beliefs and ways were so very different from mine."

"Is there no place where one can live happily without having to choose?" she asked.

I grinned.

"The best such place I know is in the bosom of my family," I said. "At least, so it will be soon enough, for the Taino friend I told you of, Ümīt, has converted to Islam and will marry Rachel. Their children must be raised as Muslims, but Rachel refuses to live in seclusion, indeed has found work that takes her weekly to the Sultan's palace, and my parents are determined that their grandchildren must understand their Jewish heritage and choose whatever beliefs they will once they are grown. So it will not be a conventional household."

"Is what you describe permitted?" Joanna asked.

"What happens behind the closed gates and high walls of a dwelling in Istanbul is no one's concern but the family's."

"It sounds lively," Joanna said wistfully.

"You will be part of it," I promised. "And it will not be dull."

A full moon rode high in the sky by now, casting a silvery track along the water from *Esperanza* to the shore. The canopy of palms whispered secrets from frond to frond. Gently rounded waves rolled toward shore, then broke without great violence but with a pleasing crash, sending broad strips of foam toward the beach. I stood and held out my hand to her.

"Come, let us cool off. The sea is calm enough."

She did not take my hand, but unfolded her legs and stood easily. She followed me as I waded in up to my knees. The water was warm and silky.

"Do you swim?" I asked.

Her face lit in one of her rare smiles.

"Do you not know I am the encampment's swimming instructor? I was recruited to improve Babune's and the others' chances of surviving their voyage to Africa on rafts."

"Come," I said.

As the next breaker rose before me, I dove headlong into the wall of water with its crest of foam. Without hesitation, she did the same. We both came up laughing.

"Again!" she said.

We dove again and again, saying little but exchanging delighted looks at the sheer pleasure of it. As a variation, we breasted our way deeper into the water, where we could soar high on the rollers before they broke.

"I am smiling like a dolphin," she exclaimed after flying through a particularly exhilarating wave.

I wished I might risk telling her how beautiful she looked wet and smiling. But I did not want to spoil the moment, when she had lost her wariness and was unselfconscious and happy.

The sea was getting up, the waves rising higher and breaking more sharply.

"Are you getting tired?" I asked.

"Yes," she said, "but I do not want to stop."

"Look at how beautiful the beach is in the moonlight," I said, "almost as bright as day."

Smiling at each other as we turned to look toward shore, we did not see a wave higher than the rest until it towered over us. It crashed down before we could turn to dive through it, tumbling us helplessly toward shore. I spat out seawater and tried to right myself, my feet touching the sand and then sending me head over heels through the surf again. I cannoned into something hard: Joanna's body, legs and arms flailing as she struggled to find her balance. Her wet, slippery arms came up around my neck as she clutched at me. I grasped her firmly around the waist as my feet finally found purchase in the sand. Her legs clung instinctively, encircling my waist as I rose. Holding her in my arms, I waded toward shore.

For a moment we panted in unison, our foreheads pressed together, water streaming off us. When she made to pull away, my arms tightened.

"Joanna," I whispered. "Do not be afraid. I will not hurt you."

"Let me go," she said. "I wish to stand."

I stepped back and released her immediately, holding my hands out, palms up, so she could lean on them for balance if she wished.

"I love you, Joanna," I said, realizing it as I spoke the words.

"I do not know what that means," she said.

She frowned as she regarded me, her face troubled rather than angry. From that I took hope.

"It means that I find you beautiful and strong and courageous. It means that I wish to see you happy above all things. It means I would give my life for you and make any sacrifice to spare you pain."

"Any sacrifice?" She drew the words from the deep well of bitterness within her. "What if I could not offer you physical love? For my body has been used without my consent since I was twelve years old, and I do not know if I could bear for you to touch it in that way."

"Oh, my darling Joanna, I am so sorry." I stepped another pace back, giving her room. "I am sorry that you had to suffer so. I honor your anger and fear. I will do nothing, ever, without your consent. But between two people who care for each other's happiness, the pleasure of physical love can be a joyous experience. I would like a chance to offer that to you."

"I have felt the momentary sensation you speak of," she said. "I know it as humiliation, a trick to make my body betray me. Being enslaved and subjugated did not shame me as long as I held onto my fury. But an instant of what you call pleasure was enough to break me."

My poor darling! My heart ached for her. I thought of Tanama, who had known sorrow when her young husband died but never a moment's unkindness until the very end. I thought of Papa, wise enough to tell me that the act of love was meant for pleasure for both man and woman long before Tanama taught me how.

"I curse those who shamed you so," I said. "But they did not have the right of it. What their joyless intrusions could show you was but a stinking tallow candle compared to the sunlight that is the pleasure of love. If you let their lies rule you now, those who violated you win. You have survived thus far, Joanna, and the world is about to open to you. Do you want them to win?"

"No!" she said fiercely. "I defy them! Take me, then!"

"Hush, my love," I said, "that is not how we will do it. Do not throw yourself at me like a bone to a hungry dog to keep it quiet. I said I would not do anything without your consent. I will amend that. I will not do anything unless you truly wish it."

"How do I know what I wish?" She was trembling, her eyes filled with tears. "You are kind and gentle, Diego, and you are not unpleasing to me. But I told you, I know nothing of this."

"Let me teach you, sweetheart," I said, "slowly, as you taught Babune to swim."

She gave a snort of laughter.

"Babune was a slow learner!"

"See, my darling?" I smiled at her. "You have already learned the first lesson, that laughter has a place in love. I think you will learn this art much faster than Babune learned to swim."

Her body was no longer braced for flight. It was a beginning. Her eyes met mine.

"What must I do?"

"Will you let me put my arms around you?"

"Yes."

I drew her into my arms and simply held her, so that we stood heart to heart.

"Now we will try hugging," I whispered in her ear. "We do it to comfort those we love, not only lovers but parents, brothers and sisters, and children as well."

Awkwardly, she raised her arms and embraced me in return. I could feel her hands, light and hesitant, against my back.

"No one has hugged me since my mother died," she said.

With a sigh, she turned her head and laid her cheek against my shoulder.

"You are warm," she murmured. "I can feel your heart beat. Can you feel mine?"

"Yes, my love," I said. "May I stroke your hair?"

She gave a soft grunt of assent with amusement in it.

"It is wet."

"So is mine, sweetheart. That is no impediment."

I ran my fingers gently up under the tangled locks on her neck and caressed her head. The touch of her shapely skull, her vulnerability, made me tremble. I was afraid that she would pull away. Instead, she nestled closer.

"Are you frightened now, Joanna?"

"No. I feel safe."

"Good," I said. "That is how I would always have you feel. May I kiss your lips?"

"Yes," she breathed. She lifted her face confidingly to mine. "You will be the first to do so, and I am glad."

I brushed her mouth with mine. Her lips parted. I kissed her gently, slowly deepening the caress until she drew a shaky breath, pressed her body more tightly against mine, and started to kiss me back. I sent Ha'shem a silent prayer of thanks.

Joanna murmured, *"Tikkun olam,"* against my mouth and drew me closer.

Yes, I thought, it is love that can heal the world. That is our purpose.

"Do you wish to lie down, beloved," I asked, "so we can kiss and touch more easily?"

In reponse, she drew me down onto the warm sand. Her hands continued to stroke my body and her mouth to explore mine. Her breath began to come more quickly, as did my own. I lay back on the sand, arranging myself so that her body could rest comfortably on mine. I held back until her hips began to move. Then there was no longer any past to trouble us, no more Diego and Joanna, we were one, and at that moment we began to build our future.

Chapter Forty-Eight: Ümīt

It was his wedding day. Indeed, he was already married by the Muslim rite. But Rachel would not feel married until they had stood beneath the *chuppah*, and he wished above all to make Rachel happy. If only Diego had returned before the past year ended! He knew that Baba Efraín and Bibi Elena were worried sick about him, as indeed he himself and Rachel were as well. Nonetheless, they had poured out *matu'm* upon him like water from an overflowing pitcher, treating him in all ways like a beloved son. They had thrown themselves wholeheartedly into the paradoxical roles of parents of both bride and groom in both the Jewish and Islamic traditions.

"He who makes a groom happy," Baba Efraín had quoted Talmud, "is like someone who rebuilds the ruins of Jerusalem."

"Even when the groom is Muslim and not blood kin to you?" Ümīt had said. "Truly, Baba, I pray daily that your seed, the Mendoza line, may not be wiped off the earth."

"As do I, my son," Baba Efraín said. "We must not give up hope. But if Diego's return is not Adonai's will, I could wish for no better continuation of my forefathers' line than grandchildren who are exactly like you and Rachel."

Both the imam and the kadi had been remarkably tolerant too, more so than the rabbis of the Seville congregation.

"They care more about Jewish seed than Jewish happiness," Rachel had said tartly.

The kadi had worked with Akiva to craft two

compatible marriage contracts that, according to Akiva, would satisfy God Himself: the Islamic *nikâh* and the *ketubah*. His new brother-in-law, whom Ümīt had previously considered rigid, a stickler for obedience to the rabbis' rulings, had come out strongly on the side of family. So had Akiva's parents, Cousin Chaim and Cousin Miriam, and Susanna's husband, Nahum. When he had tried to express his gratitude for the abundance of goodwill that had made his unconventional marriage possible, Bibi Elena had said that it was entirely to his and Rachel's credit that so many had been won over.

"Both of you, my dears," she said, "are well loved by all the friends that you have made here."

Since Ümīt had no Muslim relatives and no separate home to which to bring his bride, his friends among the janissaries had insisted on escorting him from the Palace to the Mendoza home on richly caparisoned horses, with a retinue of entertainers from musicians to fire-eaters and servants bearing gifts. They then witnessed the imam's recital and signing of the contract, politely ignoring the fact that this ceremony took place in a room that was not a proper *selamlik*, while the ladies listening from the next room were Jewish and unveiled.

Now he and Rachel stood beneath the *chuppah*. He had not thought Rachel could possibly look more beautiful than at their Muslim wedding, for which the ladies of the Sultan's own harem had made her a gift of the traditional wedding garments, a long red overdress decorated with elaborate gold embroidery over a white silk tunic and *şalvar*, with pearls to thread through her hair and a red veil so fine that her glowing face shone through it like a beacon. Looking at her now, dressed as a Jewish bride in a white gown embroidered with pearls and jasmine in her hair, he felt simultaneously ready to burst with joy and faint with desire.

Ten witnesses, a *minyan*, were required to

witness this wedding. Ümīt had feared they would not be able to find ten Jewish men willing to approve his becoming Rachel's husband. Rachel had been confident they would, and she had been right. Baba Efraín, Cousin Chaim, Nahum, and Kira Chana's son Solomon held the poles of the *chuppah*. It was impossible to look at them without wishing once again that Diego were there to share this moment with them. Akiva, who as officiating rabbi would recite the *sheva brachot*, the seven blessings of marriage, counted as the fifth, and the rest of the *minyan* consisted of Akiva's two brothers, the younger but recently *bar mitzvah*, two printer friends of Nahum's, and a neighbor, Avram, whose children had been taken in Lisbon and who awaited news of Diego's mission almost as eagerly as the Mendozas.

As Akiva read out the provisions of the *ketubah*, Ümīt and Rachel exchanged a private smile. Rachel flashed her palms at him to show him that they were still faintly stained with henna. Since Rachel had no Muslim family, the Sultan's ladies had insisted on holding the bride's traditional visit to the *hammam* in their own bathhouse within the Palace walls and the traditional henna night that followed in the harem. They had even persuaded the Kizlar Agha to allow Rachel's mother and sisters to enter the harem to take part in these rituals along with Kira Chana. For the bathhouse ceremony, they had bestowed on her another elaborate dress and braided her hair into a dozen tresses entwined with jewels and gold coins. They had dressed her painstakingly in this garb and then proceeded to strip her naked for a procession through the bathhouse. After that, they had soaped and scrubbed her and dabbed perfume on her in places that she said Ümīt would discover soon enough.

"Usually," Rachel told him, "this rite takes place in a public bathhouse, no matter how wealthy the bride's family, and even the poorest women are allowed to come and take a look at the bride and the ornaments and gifts the others bestow on her. I knew all the ladies present, of course, but they led me up to each one in turn to be presented and receive yet another gift. I remained naked throughout the proceedings." She laughed. "Since they know me for a modest maiden, I think they expected me to be embarrassed, but I have not been so reminded of my time as a Taino since I left Quisqueya."

That evening, Bülbül Hatun herself, the most imposing of the Sultan's wives, had applied the henna paste to her hands, while the others pressed gold coins into her sticky palms and whispered sly advice and jokes about the wedding night.

"It is really the bride's mother-in-law who is supposed to rub on the henna," Rachel said, "but since my own beloved Mama is my mother-in-law, the *hatuns* said I would not experience the proper feeling of awe if she performed the ritual. If they really wanted to scare me, they should have made Ayşe Hatun do it. But of course they did not know that."

Someone kicked Ümīt's ankle. Coming back to the present with a start, he realized that Nahum, already behaving like a brother, was calling his attention to the fact that Akiva had finished reading the *ketubah*. For the blessings, Baba Efraín, as the bride's father, handed off his *chuppah* pole to one of Nahum's printer friends and stepped forward to envelop both Ümīt and Rachel in a spotless white silk *tallit*. The first blessing was familiar to Ümīt, the blessing of the wine that was always recited on Shabbat.

"Baruch atah Adonai Eloheinu melech ha'olam boray pri hagofen," Akiva intoned.

Someone handed Ümīt a glass. He sipped, barely touching the dark red liquid to his lips, and handed it to Rachel. This was one of the greatest differences between Islamic and Jewish observance. Muslims abhorred wine, while for Jews, it sanctified the occasion. He wondered if this glass was the one that he would have to crush with his foot at the end of the ceremony. A glass still seemed a miracle to him, a piece of magic made from simple sand, and breaking one deliberately a terrible thing.

"It symbolizes the destruction of the Temple in Jerusalem," Baba Efraín had said. "In the centuries since that happened, we have been forced to carry our history with us, so we have rituals to help us remember."

"If that does not seem to you reason enough to break the glass," Rachel suggested, "think of Quisqueya as you do it. Think of the *yucayeque* and the people we loved there and how the soldiers shattered it."

The Jewish people, Ümīt thought now, deem marriage important because it replenishes Jewish seed and keeps the Jews alive as a people. The Muslims go further and consider failure to marry shameful. But in reality, my seed is Taino. Rachel loved the Taino as I did, and when Taino and Jew mingle in our children, they will be keeping my people alive."

Akiva had reached the last blessing. It pleased Ümīt that he could follow the Hebrew. His Judaic studies had not been wasted.

"*Baruch atah Adonai Eloheinu melech ha'olam* . . . who created joy and gladness, groom and bride, mirth, glad song, pleasure, delight, love, brotherhood, peace, and companionship . . . .Blessed art Thou who bestows rejoicing on the groom with his bride."

Now he was supposed to break the glass. They had told him someone would bring it, wrapped in a linen napkin so slivers of glass would not go flying around no matter how hard he stamped. A murmur arose around the room among the assembled guests. Rachel gasped. Ümīt saw an incredulous look of joy upon her face. She was not looking at him, but over his shoulder at something or someone else. As he turned, the *chuppah* dipped and restabilized. Diego, thin, deeply tanned, and heavily bearded, had taken the pole from Nahum's hands. His blinding grin was mirrored in every face in the room, including Ümīt's.

"Go ahead, my brother," Diego said. "Break the glass. We have waited long enough to shout *'Mazel tov'* and celebrate!"

Afterword

In researching this sequel to *Voyage of Strangers*, my previous novel about Diego and Rachel, I found that I had a lot more material to draw on, particularly about the French invasion of Italy in 1494 and the Jews in the Ottoman Empire. In *Voyage*, however, about half of my cast of characters was taken from history, including Christopher Columbus. The basic armature on which I constructed *Voyage* was the timeline of known events between 1493 and 1495. I had to integrate the story of my fictional characters with precisely where Admiral Columbus and the other historical characters were and what they were doing on any given date. In *Journey of Strangers*, most of the characters are fictional, and what happens to them in the course of the novel is entirely the product of my imagination. My challenge was to make their journey fit within the broad sweep of historical events. (See Historical Timeline, below.)

The abduction of the children of São Tomé is fact, but little known and not well documented. It was one of those stranger-than-fiction true stories that the historical novelist is occasionally lucky enough to turn up in the course of research. Like many stories in history, it differs depending on who's telling it, in this case, Portuguese or Jewish sources. The same is true of the other historical threads of *Journey*. The emphasis and even the facts differ, depending on whether the source is Jewish, Christian, or Muslim, European or Ottoman, ancient or modern.

For example, take the contrast between two books about the janissaries, Balkan Christians taken in the *devşirme* as boys and raised as Muslims: Konstantin Mihailović's *Memoirs of a Janissary*, a sixteenth-century bestseller by a supposed janissary who escaped and converted back to Christianity, and Robert Colburn's *The Sultan's Helmsman*, a twenty-first-century novel about janissaries in the Ottoman navy during the reign of Bayezid II. Modern scholars have suggested that if Mihailović really were a janissary who had completed the full course of training in the *enderun* school, he would have been better educated and more loyal to the Sultan; he may have been merely some kind of auxiliary or servant. Colburn is an American who has competed internationally as a member of a Turkish rowing team; his admiration for Turkish culture, Sultan Bayezid II, and the *enderun* school inform his story, along with his detailed knowledge of Ottoman seamanship. Mihailović states repeatedly that the Sultan never had the slightest intention of keeping his treaties with Christians, a point that would have confirmed the opinions of his medieval European audience. Colburn, through his janissary protagonist, insists that it was the Christians, not the Ottomans, who had a habit of breaking treaties.

Considering such discrepancies, I have given myself literary license to pick and choose from the historical record for the sake of telling the story I wanted to tell, while trying to avoid florid inaccuracies and anachronisms. For example, much of the iconic architecture of Istanbul was not built until the reign of Suleiman the Magnificent, Bayezid's grandson, so in my Istanbul, Hagia Sophia has only two towers, not four, and the Blue Mosque does not exist. On the other hand, while the documentation on Jewish *kiras* to the harem begins in the sixteenth century, I have chosen to invent a couple of fictional *kiras* in the late fifteenth century as well.

I have also taken some liberties with the organization of the Ottoman harem. In Bayezid's time, the harem was located in the Old Palace, not the New Palace (not called "Topkapi" until the nineteenth century), which was the Sultan's residence and the seat of government. It is unlikely that any of his women had a sexual relationship with the Sultan once they had borne a son. It is also unlikely that the mothers of sons who had reached manhood, ie over the age of sixteen, would have remained in Istanbul. In Bayezid's time, such sons were appointed governor of provincial capitals, and their mothers accompanied them to these posts. My fictional version exists because while writing *Journey*, I had not yet read Leslie P. Peirce's brilliant book, *The Imperial Harem: Women and Sovereignty in the Ottoman Empire*. In order to correct these details, I would have had to dismantle and rewrite the whole middle third of my novel. As this would have enhanced historical accuracy without necessarily embellishing the story, I chose not to do it.

When I was growing up, most Americans believed the story that in George Washington's boyhood, he confessed to chopping down a cherry tree because he could not tell a lie. I believe that most people know now that the tale is apocryphal. It was invented by Mason L. "Parson" Weems in his biography, *The Life of Washington*, written in1800. I found not one but two stories of this kind as I researched *Journey of Strangers*, ie myths repeated over and over, gathering momentum and credibility over time, until everyone takes them for fact.

Many sources, starting with the helpful but often unreliable Wikipedia and including scholars who should have known better, quote Sultan Bayezid II as publicly criticizing King Ferdinand of Spain for expelling the Jews in these words: "You venture to call Ferdinand a wise ruler, he who has impoverished his own country and enriched mine!" He never said it. The story first appeared in Rabbi Elijah Capsali's 1523 book, *Seder Eliyahu Zuta*. Although the book is considered a primary source, Capsali, a historian and chief rabbi of Candia, Crete, was only nine years old in 1492 and never visited Turkey. Bayezid did welcome the Spanish Jews and send his navy to rescue some of them, but the famous one-liner is fiction.

I had almost completed the first draft of *Journey of Strangers* when I discovered that part of the story of São Tomé (now the independent nation of São Tomé and Principe) that I had drawn on from several sources, including the prestigious *Encyclopedia Britannica* as well as scholarly sources, was a myth. The Angolares are a sub-population on São Tomé who are said to be descended from slaves from Angola who escaped to shore when the slave ship carrying them was wrecked off the island. They are supposed to have built their own community, of which the Portuguese settlement remained unaware for at least twenty years. Amador, the leader of a slave revolt in either 1586 or 1595, depending on the source, was said to be the "King of the Angolares." According to scholar Gerhard Siebert, reviewing a book by Donald Burness, an expert on Lusophone African literature, the shipwreck was a colonial myth "created in the nineteenth century by Portuguese authors based on an oral tradition that appeared in the early eighteenth century." The shipwreck was too good a story to throw away, so I used it. However, I was careful not to use the term "Angolares," since the Portuguese had not yet given the colonial name Angola to that region in Africa.

My treatment of foreign words and names may appear inconsistent, but all spellings and uses of italics were carefully considered. In some cases, I chose to use the form with which modern American readers would be most familiar, eg Hagia Sophia. In others, I used the form that people of that time and place would have used, eg Firenze. I did not italicize words in foreign languages that are used frequently in English, eg harem, seraglio, dervish, janissary, while I did italicize somewhat less familiar words, eg *condottieri, haremlik, selamlik, hammam*. In some cases, I followed forms I found in the course of my research, eg *hatun*, Kizlar Agha. In Hebrew, I used the Sephardic spellings and pronunciations that the Iberian Jews themselves would have used, eg *tallit, brit*. In some cases, I tried to match formats for similar terms; for example, because rabbi, cantor, and priest are in commonly used in English, I did not italicize the perhaps less familiar gabbai, imam, and muezzin. Where I had a choice of forms, I occasionally picked the one I encountered first in my research or felt most comfortable with, eg Bayezid, Mehmet. A note on modern Turkish spelling and pronunciation appears at the beginning of the Glossary.

In Chapter Twenty-Two, my fictional character Moshe Nahman laments the loss of his children in quotations from the Old Testament. Most of these appear in Samuel Usque's *Consolation for the Tribulations of Israel*, a prose poem on the history of the Jews written in 1553 by a Portuguese Jew who lived in Ferrara, Italy, and later in Safed in what is now Israel. Usque quoted these passages from Psalms, Deuteronomy, and Jeremiah specifically with reference to the children of São Tomé. Rather than rely on the available translation of Usque's work from Portuguese to English, I used the King James version of the Bible (1611). It's anachronistic, but you can't beat the beauty and power of the language.

Historical Timeline

1453
Sultan Mehmet of the Ottomans conquers Constantinople, capital of the Byzantine Empire, and renames it Istanbul; Mehmet institutes the *sürgün*, relocating significant numbers of Jews to Istanbul from forty cities in Anatolia and the Balkans
1454
Trade treaty between the Ottoman Empire and the Republic of Venice
1463-1479
First Venetian-Ottoman War
December 1470
Portuguese navigators discover the uninhabited island of São Tomé in the Gulf of Guinea, off the coast of West Africa
January 1479
Treaty of Constantinople: Venice cedes territory to the Ottomans and agrees to pay 10,000 ducats per year for trading privileges in the Black Sea
1481
Sultan Bayezid II ascends the throne of the Ottoman Empire
June 1482
Dispute between Bayezid and his brother Cem for the Sultanate ends when Cem is imprisoned by the Knights of Rhodes
1486
First Portuguese settlement is established on São Tomé
August 1490
Friar Girolamo Savonarola begins preaching in Firenze (Florence), calling for reform of the Church

and accusing Lorenzo di Medici of tyranny
April 1492
Lorenzo di Medici dies; his son Piero becomes de facto ruler of Firenze
August 1492
Columbus's first voyage begins; all Jews are expelled from Spain on pain of death; their possessions are confiscated
1492
As many as 120,000 Spanish Jews take refuge in Portugal; Sultan Bayezid sends Ottoman ships under his admiral Kemal Reis to Cadiz to rescue expelled Spanish Jews and relocate them to the Ottoman Empire
March 1493
Columbus returns to Spain with two ships, the *Niña* and the *Pinta,* having discovered islands in the Caribbean that he believes are part of the Indies
1493
Eight months after allowing the Spanish Jews to enter Portugal, King João expels all except for a limited number of families who must pay an enormous tax; the king orders two thousand Jewish children taken from their families, baptized, and sent as slaves to São Tomé
July 1493
Alvaro de Caminha is named *donatario* of São Tomé, ie is granted the island's governorship
September 1493
Columbus's second voyage begins
Fall 1493
Alvaro de Caminha sails for São Tomé with a band of settlers including *degradados*, men and women culled from the prisons of Lisbon, and the abducted Jewish children
1493
A Hebrew printing press is established in Istanbul, the first printing press in the Ottoman Empire
1494
Duke Ludovico Sforza of Milan invites King Charles

VIII of France to Italy, promising to support his claim to the crown of Naples

February 1494

Columbus sends twelve ships from Hispaniola back to Spain

September 1494

Mutineers take three ships from Hispaniola back to Spain; King Charles VIII of France invades Italy with 30,000 troops

1494

First cases of syphilis appear among the French troops; the disease quickly spreads

October 1494

The French sack Mordano

November 1494

The French enter Firenze; Piero di Medici goes into exile; Firenze declares itself a republic

February 1495

Four caravels leave Hispaniola for Spain with a cargo of Taino slaves; Ottoman prince Cem dies in exile; King Charles VIII of France enters Naples

March 1495

The League of Venice, aka the Holy League, is formed: an alliance between Pope Alexander VI (born Rodrigo Borgia in Aragon), Ferdinand II of Aragon (aka King Ferdinand of Spain and Sicily), Emperor Maximilian I of the Holy Roman Empire, the Republic of Venice, and Duke Ludovico Sforza of Milan, for the purpose of driving the French from Italy; Venice claims its aim in joining is a future crusade against the Turks

May 1495

King Charles leaves Naples, leaving a regent to govern on his behalf

July 1495

Battle of Fornovo; both the French and the League of Venice claim victory

December 1496

King Manoel I of Portugal orders Jews and free Muslims to leave Portugal within ten months, all Jewish children to be baptized, and all Hebrew books to be burned

October 1497

King Manoel submits 20,000 Jews to forced baptism and expels all Jews from Portugal on pain of death or slavery

April 1498

King Charles VIII of France dies after cracking his head on a doorjamb in his château of Amboise

July 1499

Governor Alvaro de Caminha dies in São Tomé; both his will and a letter from the settlers request that his cousin, Pero Alvares de Caminha, be made governor, but the King of Portugal appoints someone else

1499-1503

Second Venetian-Ottoman War; the Turks win

1512

Sultan Bayezid II is forced to abdicate and is succeeded by his son, Selim

Glossary

A note on Turkish pronunciation: The modern Turkish alphabet, which I have used for Turkish names and words, did not exist in Diego's time, when Turkish was written in a variant of Perso-Arabic script. In the modern alphabet, the letter ç is pronounced "ch" as in "chair," the letter ş is pronounced "sh" as in "shop," the letter ı is pronounced "ee" as in "beef," and the letter ü is pronounced like a shortened "ew" as in "yew," with the lips pursed and the tongue against the palate.

Hebrew
bar mitzvah in Judaism, coming of age; literally, son of obligation
Baruch atah Adonai Blessed art Thou, O Lord
Baruch atah Adonai Eloheinu melech ha'olam boray pri hagofen the blessing of the wine: Blessed art Thou, O Lord our God, King of the universe, who has given us the fruit of the vine
Baruch atah Adonai Eloheinu melech ha'olam shelo asani isha Blessed art Thou, O Lord our God, King of the universe, for not making me a woman (sometimes translated as "who did not make me a woman")
Baruch atah Adonai shomei'ah tefilah Blessed art Thou, O Lord, who hears prayer
baruch Ha'shem thank God
Beit Din a Jewish rabbinical court
B'ezrat Ha'shem God's will be done
b'rucha a Hebrew blessing or prayer
brit in Judaism, the rite of circumcision
chas v'shalom God forbid
chuppah in Judaism, the marriage canopy
gabbai the sexton of a synagogue
gerush exiled
im yirtzeh Ha'shem God willing, with God's help
kabbalah Jewish mysticism
Kaddish the Jewish Prayer of Mourning (the prayer is mostly in Aramaic)

ketubah in Judaism, the marriage contract

Mazel tov! Good luck! Congratulations!

mezuzah a small scroll on which prayers are written, placed in a decorative case and fastened to the doorway of a Jewish home as a blessing or protection

mikvah in Judaism, the ritual bath

minyan a quorum: in Judaism, the ten men required for prayer

mitzvah, pl. *mitzvaot* a good deed; literally, obligation

mohel in Judaism, a man who performs the rite of circumcision

Shabbat the Sabbath

shalom aleichem peace be upon you

sheva brachot in Judaism, the seven blessings of marriage

Sh'ma Yisrael, Adonai Eloheinu, Adonai echod
Hear, O Israel, the Lord our God, the Lord is One

tallit a prayer shawl

teba in Sephardic Judaism, the lectern or podium in a synagogue

t'fillin in Judaism, phylacteries bound around the arm for daily prayer

tikkun olam the repair or healing of the world, an important ethical tenet of Judaism

Aramaic
Yit'gadal v'yit'kadash sh'mei raba
May His great Name grow exalted and sanctified
(the first line of Kaddish)

Spanish
Adelante! Onward! said to have been Columbus's exclamation on the voyage of discovery

converso a Jew who converted to Christianity to avoid persecution

doña lady: a title of respect

marrano a Jewish convert to Christianity who continued to practice Judaism in secret; literally, swine

novio boyfriend, betrothed

Portuguese
bolas balls

braço a slave, esp. used as currency; literally, an arm

bruxa witch

degradado, degradada scum, used of criminals taken from Lisbon's prisons and transported to São Tomé

donatario recipient of a land grant

fazenda plantation

fazenda real the royal treasury
fazendeiro plantation owner
feiticeira sorceress, witch-doctor
metiço of mixed blood, halfbreed
Povoação the Settlement

Taino
baba father
batey a ball game similar to soccer
batu the ball used in batey
bibi mother
cacique a Taino tribal chief
cemi the Taino gods
hamaca hammock
matu'm generosity, the cardinal ethical principle of the Taino
matu'n generous
nanichi my love, beloved
nitaino a Taino nobleman or sub-chief
yucayeque a Taino village

Latin
Credo in Deum Patrem omnipotentem
I believe in God the Father Almighty
Creatorem caeli et terrae
Creator of heaven and earth
et in Iesum Christum, Filium Eius unicum, Dominum nostrum . . .
and in Jesus Christ, his only Son, our Lord . . .
remissionem peccatorum, carnis resurrectionem, vitam aeternam
the forgiveness of sins, the resurrection of the body, and life
everlasting
Pater noster qui es in caelis, sanctificetur nomen tuum
Our Father who art in heaven, hallowed be Thy Name

Italian
condottieri captains of mercenary military companies
doge the chief magistrate and de facto ruler of the republic of Genoa or
Venice
signore sir: a title of respect

West African
(precise origin of these words unclear; used by more than one tribal
group and later spread via French colonialism)

foutou a thick paste made of pounded manioc root and water
grigri fetish, charm, amulet, esp. a pouch containing such objects
juju magic, luck
ko ko ko knock, knock

Arabic
Allahu akbar . . . Lā ilāha illā-Allāh
God is the greatest . . . there is no God but God
Asalamu alaykum
God's peace be upon you (Turkish form)
Alaykum asalaam
And upon you also (Turkish form)
imam in Islam, the leader of prayers in a mosque
jaddi Grandpa (Tunisian form)
kadi a judge; in the Ottoman Empire, a judge who applied both Islamic and the Sultan's law
muezzin in Islam, one who calls worshippers to prayer from a minaret
Sufism Muslim mysticism

Turkish
akçe a silver coin, the basic currency of the Ottoman Empire
babouches slippers (from Persian via French)
cereed javelin; in the Ottoman Empire, a game similar to polo, played on horseback with javelins
cizye poll tax the Ottomans levied on the *dhimmi*
dervish a member of any of several Muslim ascetic orders, the equivalent of a monk
devşirme in the Ottoman Empire, the conscription of Christian boys from the Balkans, who were converted to Islam and trained in the Sultan's palace in Istanbul to become janissaries and military and administrative leaders, sometimes achieving high office
dhimmi in the Ottoman Empire, non-Muslims, esp. Jews and Christians
effendi sir: a title of respect
enderun the inner courtyard of the Sultan's palace, which held the Sultan's audience chamber and the school where the boys of the *devşirme* were trained
göbek taşı a giant heated stone, big enough for bathers to lie on, at the center of the hot room of the *hammam*
hammam a Turkish bathhouse
harem the women of the family; sometimes used synonymously with seraglio with reference to the Sultan's wives or concubines and female relatives

haremlik the part of Ottoman residential quarters in which women could socialize with their male relatives

hatun lady: a title of respect

inşallah God willing

janissaries elite corps of foot soldiers, loyal to the Sultan personally

kira a Greek word for lady or dame; in the Ottoman Empire, a non-Muslim woman, usually Jewish, who served the Sultan's harem as a purveyor of goods and services

levrek sea bass

mehr bride-price, paid by the groom's family

nalin clogs or slippers elevated by pegs, used in the *hammam*

nazar an amulet to ward against the evil eye, consisting of a blue and white eye; sometimes referred to as an evil eye

nikâh marriage, Islamic marriage contract

pasha in the Ottoman Empire, a lord or high officithe

peştamal bath sheet used in the *hammam*

şalvar baggy trousers, worn by both men and women

şehzade prince

selamlik the part of Ottoman residential quarters in which men could socialize with their male guests

seraglio the women's quarters in the Sultan's palace

şeriat law the law of Islam

sipahis Ottoman cavalry

sürgün the relocation of populations from provincial cities and towns to Istanbul after the Ottoman conquest

yüksükotu foxglove

Greek

barbounia red mullet

lavraki sea bass

sardeles sardines

Bibliography

Abulafia, David, Ed., *The French Descent into Renaissance Italy 1494-95: Antecedents and Effects.* (1995) Aldershot/Brookfield, VT: Variorum

Benbassa, Esther & Rodrigue, Aron, *Sephardi Jewry: A History of the Judeo-Spanish Community, 14th-20th Centuries.* (2000) Berkeley, CA: University of California: Chronicle Publications

Brummett, Palmira Johnson, *Ottoman Seapower and Levantine Diplomacy in the Age of Discovery.* (1994) Albany: State University of New York Press

Cohn, Paul D., *São Tomé: Journey to the Abyss—Portugal's Stolen Children.* (2006) Bozeman, MT: Burns-Cole

Colburn, Robert, *The Sultan's Helmsman.* (2009) BookSurge

De Sousa, Izequiel Batista, *São Tomé et Principe de 1485 à 1755: Une Société Coloniale du Blanc au Noir.* (2008) Paris: L'Harmattan

Epstein, Mark Alan, *The Ottoman Jewish Communities and Their Role in the Fifteenth and Sixteenth Centuries.* (1980) Freiburg: Klaus Schwarz

Faroqui, Suraiya, *Subjects of the Sultan: Culture and Daily Life in the Ottoman Empire.* (2013) London/New York: I.B. Tauris

Garfield, Robert. *A History of São Tomé Island, 1470-1655: The Key to Guinea.* (1992) San Francisco: Mellen Research University Press

Guilmartin, John F., Jr., *Galleons and Galleys.* (2002) London: Cassell

Kia, Mehrdad, *Daily Life in the Ottoman Empire.* (2011) Santa Barbara, CA: Greenwood

Konstam, Angus, *Renaissance War Galley 1470-*

1590. (2002) Oxford: Osprey

Levy, Avigdor, *The Sephardim in the Ottoman Empire.* (1993) Princeton: Darwin Press

Lewis, Bernard, *The Jews of Islam.* (1984) Princeton: Princeton University Press

Liba, Moshe & Simms, Norman, *Jewish Child Slaves in São Tomé: Papers, Essays, Articles and Original Documents Related to the July 1995 Conference.* (2003) Wellington: New Zealand Jewish Chronicle Publications

Martines, Lauro, *Furies: War in Europe 1450-1700.* (2013) New York: Bloomsbury

Mihailović, Konstantin (b. 1435), *Memoirs of A Janissary.* (2010) Princeton: Markus Wiener

Rozen, Minna, *A History of the Jewish Community in Istanbul: The Formative Years, 1453-1566.* (2002) Leiden: Brill

Shmuelevitz, Aryeh, *The Jews of the Ottoman Empire in the Late Fifteenth and the Sixteenth Centuries: Administrative, Economic, Legal and Social Relations as Reflected in the Responsa.* (1984) Leiden: Brill

Turkish Cultural Foundation, "Ottoman Sailing Ships, from Galleys to Galleons." Available at: www.turkishculture.org/military/naval/ottoman-ships-758.htm

Wheatcroft, Andrew, *The Ottomans: Dissolving Images.* (1993) London: Penguin

Discussion Questions

1. *Tikkun olam*, the repair or healing of the world, is a Jewish concept that is important to the characters in *Journey of Strangers*. In what ways can individuals in our own time repair the world? How important do you think such issues are? What have you done or dreamed of doing to repair the world?

2. After leaving the gods of his people behind, Hutia plans to convert to Judaism so he can marry Rachel but then decides to convert to Islam instead. What do you think of his decision to become a Muslim? For what reasons do people change their religion? How do the motivations of people in our own time who convert from one religion to another differ from those of people in the fifteenth century, including the characters in the book? What do you think of people who make that choice?

3. At different times in *Journey of Strangers*, Diego, Rachel, and Joanna all struggle with their desire to have a sense of purpose. What kinds of changes, both unexpected and predictable, such as stages in the life cycle, can bring up this issue for people in our own time? How important to you is having a sense of purpose? Can you think of anyone whose sense of purpose you particularly admire?

4. Although there are no battle scenes in the book, war plays an important part in *Journey of Strangers*. In what ways does war, past, present, or future, affect the characters' actions and decisions? In what ways does war in the twenty-first century differ from war in the fifteenth century, and in what ways

is it the same?

5. As in *Voyage of Strangers*, the previous book about Diego, an important theme in *Journey of Strangers* is that of being an outsider. In what ways are Diego and Rachel still outsiders even after being reunited with their family? In what ways are Hutia and Joanna outsiders? Do you think they will always be outsiders? What makes a person or a group of people outsiders? Are there people or groups of people whom you perceive as outsiders? In what ways, if any, have you ever been an outsider yourself?

6. The concept of cultural relativism, developed by anthropologist Franz Boas in the early twentieth century, holds that the beliefs, values, and customs of any culture must be understood within the context of that culture, and that therefore all cultures' beliefs, values, and customs are equally valid. To what extent do the main characters in *Journey of Strangers* exemplify cultural relativism? What do you think caused these characters to transcend the absolutism of their era and their various cultures? Do you think it is realistic to portray these fifteenth-century characters as being cultural relativists? What obstacles to maintaining these values do you think they would have encountered? To what extent are you a cultural relativist?

Elizabeth Zelvin is author of a previous historical novel, *Voyage of Strangers*, and is working on *Kingdom of Strangers*, which will complete the trilogy. She is also the author of the Bruce Kohler mystery series. Liz has been writing since age seven and published her first novel at age sixty-four. Her short stories have been nominated three times for the Agatha Award and once for the Derringer Award for Best Short Story. Another story was listed in *Best American Mystery Stories 2014*. A psychotherapist who lives in New York, Liz works online with clients all over the world. Her publications include a book on gender and addictions, two poetry books, and, as Liz Zelvin, an album of original songs, *Outrageous Older Woman*. See http://elizabethzelvin.com, http://facebook.com/elizabeth.zelvin, and Liz's Amazon page, http://tinyurl.com/zelvin-amazon.